REALMS OF REFLECTION
FLIGHT OF THE FALCON

BY HALEY SANBORN

MAP OF THE REALMS

PROLOGUE

The dream begins as it always does. As it has been for the past few weeks. Always the same, plaguing my thoughts like a never-ending nightmare. For it doesn't end, not really. For every night, the dream returns, to the point where I have simply begun to expect it, the fear has long faded away, to be replaced with a growing impatience. So I simply wait. A sea of black emptiness surrounds me, a dark and endless void of nothing, anticipation growing with every second that ticks by. I know what is coming, having had this recurring dream countless times, knowing exactly how it will play out. And sure enough, I remain unsurprised when the darkness begins to push back, curling away like smoke from a flame, to reveal another person standing just out of arm's reach. The silence is almost deafening.

I face the figure standing in front of me, mirroring my position. Her skin is lightly tanned, blonde hair spilling down her shoulders, framing a narrow face. I recognize the face with a now familiar chill; the figure's face is my own. The same delicate features, slim nose, wide eyes framed with long lashes. This figure, whoever she is, smiles, lips curving up at the corners and her eyes shining with something cold and malicious, an expression that I have never worn. I instinctively take a step back, and the girl before me does the same. Her movements are sharp and slow, making the robes she wears sway in a phantom breeze.

I find myself wearing robes as well; long and silky that seem to flow with the slightest movement of my body and billow at my ankles, like water woven into fabric. Why am I wearing such strange clothing? It's one of the many things that confuse me about this dream since I have never seen robes such as these before. But while mine is blindingly silver, marked with strange golden symbols in a language I can't read, the terrifying girl before me wears robes of the darkest night with symbols of blood red. She continues to smile knowingly, tauntingly, and I admit to myself that perhaps my fear of this dream had not yet faded completely.

I swallow, my heart beating unevenly, but I push down that fear and take a step forward, until myself and the girl before me are barely a foot apart. I lift my hand, my every movement being mimicked until our fingertips almost touch. This is how each of my dreams ends; I face the version of myself with a cold and vicious smile, and as I reach out and swallow down my fear, the girl will dissolve into mist. I will wake up.

But nothing happens. My hand strikes something hard and smooth, like some sort of invisible wall between me and the girl. Both of our hands hover in midair, fingertips millimeters away from touching. But I don't wake up. The dream doesn't fade. I notice light glinting off the surface in front of me, like glass. Panic builds in my chest, my palms becoming cold and clammy with fear. Why am I not waking up? This has never happened before. The girl before me just continues to grin, as if she holds some secret over me and is relishing in my uncertainty. I open my mouth to demand some sort of answer, to know who this girl is, despite some tiny part of my mind finding this ridiculous. This is a dream, it isn't real.

But before I can form the words, an ear-piercing screech fills the air, reverberating through the stillness and echoing off of unseen walls. The unnaturally loud sound of flapping wings thunders all around me, beating to the rhythm of my pounding heart, and I throw my hands over my head in blind terror. I feel the prick of something sharp scrape my shoulder, followed by a significant weight and the sound of shuffling wings beside my ear. Compelled by some unknown force, I lift my head from my hands and turn it ever so slightly to the side, and come face to face with a round black eye.

It's a bird's eye, a falcon's, round and completely black with a distinct ring of yellow around it. The bird's hooked beak, only inches from my face, clicks sharply as it smooths its sleek, silvery feathers. At least, I think it's a falcon, but its silvery white feathers speckled with dark gray give it a closer appearance to a snowy owl.

Remembering the strange girl, my head whips back to see her still standing in the same spot, the white bird fluttering its wings indignantly as my hair gets caught in its talons. The girl now has a falcon perched on her shoulder as well, but its feathers are shades of dark gray and black. My head spins, overwhelmed and confused. This girl, mimicking my every move, who looks just like me but *wrong*... It's like looking into some sort of twisted mirror. Wait...

I take a deep breath, repeating to myself *"It's only a dream,"* and instead focus on the wall of glass in front of me. Not a wall of glass... a mirror. I glance, startled, back at the strange girl, my reflection, and the bird on her shoulder. What is this supposed to mean? I hear something beside me, the faintest whisper, and my head whips back towards the silver falcon. Something about it unnerves me. Its eyes, look too... intelligent. And then it begins to speak.

Okay, maybe speaking isn't the right word. It's more like I can hear the words echoing in my head, in a strange and whispery voice. And with every word, my feeling of dread grows.

> *"Falcon brave and bold in flight,*
> *Shall fear the darkness and worship the light.*
> *Shattered glass gleaming white,*
> *And the world's bow down to the Mirror's might."*

There is a pause. My heart beats wildly. There is a feeling of suspense in the air, like this entire dream world is holding its breath, waiting. The glass before me ripples like the surface of a clear pond in a strong breeze, and my reflection disappears. I am alone in the endless darkness, with this strange bird on my shoulder, the only witness to what it says next. This voice is harsher, more urgent.

> *"The time has come to prepare to fight,*
> *And three must become five.*
> *For all of the Realms must forgive and unite,*
> *Or neither world will survive."*

I sit up with a gasp, my eyes flying open and the dream world melting away, replaced by the warmer and more inviting darkness of my bedroom. My hands are clenched tightly in the sheets, my covers were thrown to the side, and cold sweat trickled down my temple. For a long moment, my frantic breathing is the only sound in the otherwise silent night. I swallow back my yelp as I notice movement out of the corner of my eye, whirling toward the other side of my room, sighing relief as I realize it's just the curtains on my window fluttering softly in the breeze.

That dream left me way too jumpy, I absentmindedly run my fingers through my hair, calming my frayed nerves. I shiver slightly as another gust of wind rustles my curtains. Why would I have left the window open in November? It's freezing outside. Climbing out of bed, my bare feet cold against the hardwood floor, I make my way towards the window. And as I go to pull it closed, I could have sworn I saw silvery wings flutter off of the window ledge and dart out of sight.

Flight Of The Falcon

CHAPTER 1

It's early afternoon as I stroll down the sidewalk, enjoying the feeling of the brisk autumn wind on my face. My hair is pulled up in a messy ponytail, several golden blonde strands escaping to hang loosely around my face. My phone is clutched in my hand as I idly trace the looping cursive letters along the back of the case spelling out my name, Emmalina Maren. It is a bit of a mouthful, I know, and I normally prefer to simply be called Lina. I've had this phone case for years now, and the letters, once sparkly, are pretty faded. Maybe I'll buy a new one while I'm out today.

But for now, I just continue my stroll down the busy sidewalk. I live in Amesbury, a town in Massachusetts, and despite the chilly November breeze, the air is surprisingly warm. Wandering around downtown, many people are out and about, walking to and from restaurants and shops along the red brick sidewalks. Amesbury is a gorgeous town, especially the downtown area, with its brick buildings, fountains, old-fashioned lampposts, and outdoor cafes. And the artwork! There are painted crosswalks and electrical boxes, murals on the sides of buildings, and art events. All in all, not a bad place to spend a Thursday afternoon.

I arrive at one of my favorite places in downtown Amesbury, the Mill Yard. Passing under a brick archway decorated with painted murals, I reach the cluster of red cobblestone and scattered outdoor restaurants that make up the space. To my left is a section of concrete ringed by stone steps, forming a sort of small amphitheater, and to the right are the outdoor dining tables roped off with strings of fairy lights. Tall brick buildings encircle the wide space, decorated with flower boxes and trees with leaves in brilliant shades of reds and yellows.

It is about as crowded as I expected it to be on such a warm afternoon, with families dining at the restaurants, couples walking along the paths to view the miniature waterfalls created by the rushing Powow River, and groups of people lounging on the amphitheater steps. A small bird darts overhead, disappearing behind the tall buildings, and startling me out of my pleasant daydreaming, reminding me of the falcon in my dream last night. The words it had spoken have been nagging at me all day, having barely slept at all for the rest of the night, and it's strange how vividly I remember them. I just can't seem to shake the ominous feeling that those words mean something, something I can't quite piece together. I'm no expert, but dreams normally have some sort of meaning to them, don't they? Why not this one?

Maybe I'm overthinking this. I push the thoughts of last night from my mind, making my way to the stone amphitheater. I had texted my friend Cam to meet me here today, hoping for a chance to enjoy the weather and take my mind off other things. I consider confiding in him about my dream, even though I know I'm being stupid. It was just a dream, nothing more to it.

Cameron Adams has been my best friend since middle school. The two of us hang out all of the time, going camping, watching movies, and visiting restaurants downtown. I even convinced him to try learning to surf with me once, which neither of us was any good at. That's when I notice him, his back propped up on the concrete amphitheater wall and his feet kicked up on the lowest step. He isn't looking my way, absentmindedly gazing toward the tops of the brick buildings, lost in thought. His black hair falls in his eyes, and his dark shirt brings out the olive tone of his skin. Sitting beside him is a small blue box tied with a ribbon. He finally notices me when I'm about two feet away.

"Hey Lina," he says, giving me a good-natured grin as he gets to his feet, clutching the little box in his hand.

"Hi," I say, grinning back. "What's that?" I ask curiously, gesturing to the box.

"Oh," he looks down at it as if he momentarily forgot he was holding it. "It's for you," he hands it to me somewhat sheepishly. As he passes it to me, he sits back on the amphitheater steps, tugging me down beside him. I tuck my legs under me, curiously unraveling the ribbon while Cam watches with anticipation. Pulling the top off, I glance inside to see a sparkle of silver. It's a bracelet, I realize, as I lift it from where it's nestled in a tiny bed of velvet, cupping it in my palm. It is simple and beautiful, made of delicate silver links woven into a braid-like pattern, glittering in the midday sun.

"Happy almost birthday," Cam says softly, eyes darting over my face anxiously to gauge my reaction. The bracelet is perfect, and at that moment it was the best thing I could have wished for, simply because it came from him. I throw my arms around his neck, hugging him tightly.

"Thank you," I breathe. "It's perfect," He blushes down to his ears, looking overjoyed and slightly embarrassed.

"But my birthday is tomorrow," I laugh, pulling back enough to slip the bracelet onto my wrist and he helps me clasp it.

"I know. That's why I said almost," he gets to his feet, and I do the same. "I saw it on display in a jewelry store window when I was picking my cousin up at the mall. I don't know why, but it just seemed like the perfect gift. I just couldn't wait to give it to you." We begin making our way back through the Mill Yard, passing back under the brick archway, until we are standing on the wide sidewalk beside the street and storefronts. I'm about to reply when I realize that Cam looks a bit distracted.

His gaze seems focused on something across the street. I look up and realize that he's staring at three people standing on the sidewalk opposite us. Cam looks unsettled, there is something not right. They seem to be around our age, 17 or 18; two girls and one boy. The girl farthest left has long, perfectly straight black hair draping past her shoulders, which starkly contrasts with her fair skin. She is wearing a thin leather jacket over a plain white shirt and jeans, with black studded combat boots. She leans casually against the wall of the small gift shop behind her, her arms crossed. Beside her is the boy, who is tall and broad-shouldered, with straight, messy black hair, wearing just dark jeans and a sweatshirt. His posture is rigid and alert. To his right is the second girl, a bit shorter than me with dark brown hair styled in delicate ringlet curls that brush her shoulders, wearing a thick sweater and heeled boots.

But none of these details are what caused us to pause. What caught our attention is that all three of them are staring directly at us. The teenagers don't break eye contact when we look up, and I make note of their varying expressions. The black-haired girl raises an eyebrow, as though surprised we caught them staring, but doesn't avert her calculating gaze. She looks directly at me, as though she's studying every detail of my face, sending a chill down my spine. The shorter girl on the right stares with open curiosity, her attention directed at me as well, as though I'm some sort of celebrity she's dying to meet but is too afraid to approach. She seems restless, shifting from foot to foot, balancing on the heels of her shoes. But it's the boy's expression that catches me off guard. His eyes are burning with open anger and what looks like distrust, and like the other two, is wholly fixated on me. The force of his furious glare causes my cheeks to flush bright red and I quickly avert my gaze, fixing my eyes on the street ahead. My hand wraps around Cam's, tugging to signal we should leave. Now.

Cam doesn't object. We pick up the pace, not slowing until we've rounded the corner, ducking into a short alleyway that leads onto another street. Neither of us says a word, both on edge, sneaking unnerved glances behind us until we reach a line of cars parked along the sidewalk. Cam fishes in his pockets for his keys, stopping beside his worn blue pickup truck. He leans against the driver's side door.

After a moment of silence, he asks, "Did you know them?" I shake my head, shifting my weight from foot to foot.

"No," I answer honestly. "I'm pretty sure I've never seen them before. Not that I can remember, at least." He frowns, a crease forming between his eyebrows.

"They looked like they knew you," he muses. "And that boy… why did he seem so angry with you?"

"They must have confused me with someone else," I say, without much confidence, doing a poor job of convincing either of us. Cam looks unsure, and I can't blame him.

"They're probably just weirdos looking to pick a fight with somebody," I reason. "That's likely all it is."

We spend the next hour wandering around downtown, until the sun begins to dip lower in the sky, tinging the clouds overhead with the barest hint of pink. Once we get tired of the shops, we decide to visit one of our favorite spots. Cam drives while I lounge in the passenger seat of his truck. Even though we both have our licenses, I hadn't brought my car since I typically prefer to walk. Something about outside just clears my head, like walking downtown or going for a jog around my small neighborhood.

I idly tap my finger against the dashboard to the beat of the song thrumming through the speakers. Some sort of old rock song- Bon Jovi, or something similar, I'm not sure. I'm more of a country music type of person. After several minutes of driving, listening to Cam sing along to the lyrics in an off-key voice until I'm tempted to switch the song, he finally pulls the truck off the road and into a small parking lot beside the street. Through the windshield, I can see a skatepark several yards away, boarded by tall wire fences and a group of 13-year-olds skidding down the ramps on their skateboards and scooters, while too-loud punk rock music blares. But this isn't our intended spot.

As we climb out of the truck and make our way past the skatepark, strolling through the long shadows cast by the scattered trees and soaking my sneakers in the wet dewy grass, we pass by a small baseball field. It's basically just a circle of scuffed dirt separated from the skatepark by chain link fences with protective yellow plastic lining, with only a pitcher's mound and no bases. This isn't our intended spot either.

And just past the skatepark is a playground, Amesbury Park, with an empty splash pad and basketball court, the park itself is a collection of various red, black, and white structures and stone benches sprawling over a stretch of wood chips. A small building for restrooms and a pavilion with picnic tables sit atop a grassy hill, with another parking lot beyond that. Behind the park is a large pond spanned by a wide, wooden bridge, and a stretch of woods beyond that. But the park still isn't our intended spot, we simply need to cross through it.

The park is fairly empty; one couple sits on the stone steps leading to the pavilion watching two young kids attempting to use a four-person see-saw, and a group of younger men stands towards the baseball field playing some game that has to do with throwing flying discs into metal baskets across the open stretch of grass. One of them shouts angrily as his flying disc veers off-course and lands at the far end of the pond, while the other two laugh. Cam and I head for the wooden bridge across the pond, leading into the small stretch of woods. The trees cast large shadows, and with the sun dipping lower in the sky, I'm glad I wore a sweatshirt.

The crunch of woodchips underfoot becomes slick wooden boards, and I brace my hands on the thin railing of the bridge to get a good look at the growing sunset reflecting on the rippling water, and the small toads that croak in the reeds. I laugh, pointing to one sitting on a half-submerged log, its throat puffed out as it croaks loudly.

"He sings better than you do," I snicker, poking Cam in the ribs. He makes a show of looking offended. I lean past the railing, pointing to it. "See, right there," Cam mimes pushing me over the railing. I duck past his arms and bolt for the woods, laughing. Just past the tree line, over the slight incline of trampled leaves and snaking roots, a small stage pavilion becomes visible. It is a somewhat circular-shaped, raised platform made of cobblestones as tall as my shoulders, with several tall, white columns supporting a pointed ceiling. In the shadowy, fading glow of the woods, the pavilion is lit up with colorful lights beaming from the ceiling, bathing the stage in changing hues. This is the spot we're heading for.

Climbing the small set of worn stone steps leading up one side, my feet scuff the painted gray concrete, each step echoing slightly. Closer up, the signs of the pavilion's age are clear; chipped white paint and small bits of graffiti on the columns, and splotches of repainted cement beneath my feet. I'm pretty sure the pavilion was used for outdoor live bands at one point. Cam joins me, the two of us sitting with our legs dangling off of the edge.

"Have you decided what you want to do for your birthday yet?" He asks, fiddling with a small pebble he must have picked up when we entered the woods.

"I've been thinking about it." The truth is I haven't really. Last year, for my 16th birthday, Cam helped me throw a big party at my place, even though neither of us is really the party type of person. It was great, a lot of people from school were there- some that I barely even knew- but I think I'm going to stick to something a lot smaller this year. I just haven't decided what.

I pick at a small thread in my jeans, the silver bracelet on my wrist making a small jingling sound, like a tiny wind chime. Wait, that's odd. A band of metal doesn't jingle on its own. Glancing down, it takes me a moment to notice, but there is something certainly different about my bracelet. A charm now dangles off of the woven strands of silver, glittering like a polished diamond. It has a very distinct shape to it too- it looks kind of like a bird with outstretched wings, almost like...

A falcon.

The charm slips from my fingers, jingling cheerfully, as I sit frozen in place. This must be some sort of mistake, or maybe I'm just hallucinating it. But either way, I am *certain* that charm had not been there before.

"Are you alright?" Cam asks nervously. "You look like you've just seen a ghost." I swallow, my throat suddenly feeling quite dry, unable to hide the slight tremor in my fingers as I lift the charm so he can see it. He looks mildly curious, his face bathed in the blue and green light filtering from the pavilion ceiling, as though I'm looking at him underwater.

"That's odd," he mutters. "I didn't notice that before, I must not have seen it," he ponders for a moment. "What is it?" He lifts the charm, examining the sparkling wings, barely larger than his fingertip. "It's a bird?"

"A falcon," I say softly.

"I'm sure you can have the charm taken off if you don't want it..." Cam reasons, but I interrupt.

"No, no it's beautiful. I was just a little surprised, you know- because I didn't notice it before either," Cam shrugs, dismissing it at that. After all, it's just a bracelet charm to him. A simple piece of silver that went unnoticed, but to me, it means something else. It can't just be a coincidence. Especially because I *know* it hadn't been there before.

Suddenly there's a noise to our right, from deeper in the small stretch of woods. The sound of a branch snapping, and a shout. Then silence. Cam sits straight up, scanning the trees, and I can tell he saw it too; the silhouette of a person dropping from a tree, less than 50 yards away.

"Hello?" I call, a tremor in my voice.

"Lina," Cam says, tugging my wrist gently as he gets to his feet. "We should go." There is another, very faint crackling of branches and leaves from the area where the silhouette disappeared, and without a second thought, Cam and I book it out of those woods, sprinting the short distance to the bridge. We don't look back, and we don't stop running until we reach the truck, slightly winded. Neither of us speaks the whole way home, other than a brief "goodnight" as he drops me off at my house and drives off, rounding the small bend in the road until he's out of sight.

After Cam's truck pulls out of sight, leaving me standing on the sidewalk in front of my house, I stand gazing up at the front door. The house is medium-sized and square, with a pointed roof of dark shingles. It is a pleasant light blue color, with white shutters slightly chipped around the edges and a small set of steps leading to the white-painted door. There are several thin trees, now bare of leaves, sprouting from the small expanse of fenced-in grass, and a miniature flower bed that my mom tends to in the warmer months nestled beside the steps. The driveway is just wide enough to fit my little car and my mom's white Jeep.

A cold wind rustles the treetops, clouds overhead shifting across the rising sliver of the moon. And I can't shake the feeling of being watched. I hurry inside and instinctively lock the door, just in case.

"Lina-"

I jump nearly a foot when I hear my name behind me, spinning to see my mom standing in the kitchen doorway. She raises her eyebrows.

"Is everything okay?" she asks curiously. I nod.

"Yeah, yeah everything's fine," I take a breath to calm my racing heart. "Just a little jumpy today, that's all." My mom doesn't look entirely convinced, her eyes narrowing slightly with concern. My mom, Corrine Maren, is a very beautiful woman, and people always say we look so alike, but I don't quite see it. She has dark brown hair, wavy like mine. But whereas my eyes are a dark gray-blue color, hers are a lighter hazel; a mix of brown flecked with green.

The faint scent of food fills the air, wafting from the kitchen, as the oven timer begins to beep, interrupting my mom from whatever she was going to say next. I follow her through the kitchen doorway, where she continues to work on dinner, lifting a roasted chicken from the oven, and I head for the hallway where the bedrooms are. Small cardboard boxes are stacked along the hall, a few open and spilling empty picture frames and wall hooks. Several framed photos are hanging on the wall, others propped up against it as though they were in the process of being hung.

After tossing my sweatshirt in my room, I come back to inspect the mess in the hall, one large box blocking the guest bedroom. The house has three bedrooms altogether, the largest one is my mom's, and the second largest is mine. But since it's just the two of us, the empty one is the guest bedroom- not that we use it very often. My dad left before I was born, my mom says. She told me he wanted to stay, but he couldn't, for some reason. *Some reason s*eems like a poor excuse to me, however, but she still seems to love him 17 years later, though she doesn't really tell me much about him.

My mom doesn't talk much about her life before she had me at all. As far I as know, she used to live in some tiny town out in Ohio or something but doesn't talk about any other family. She sometimes tells me about an old friend she used to have, named Mirielle, or how she met my dad while hiking near a waterfall. But that's pretty much it.

My mom catches me studying the pictures hung in a pattern on the wall, pulling off her oven mitts to adjust a crooked one on the end.

"I've been working on this for the past few hours," she says, looking pleased. "Do you like it?"

"Yeah, it's great!" I study one of my favorite pictures there; an image of Cam and me when we were nine, at Hampton Beach in New Hampshire, posing for the camera beside a lopsided sandcastle we had built together. Cameron is in the process of sticking a seagull feather into the uppermost tower, basically just a heap of sand, while I grin widely, sand staining the front of my pink bathing suit. Most of the other pictures are of my mom and me, but I just can't help myself from wishing that at least one of them was of my dad. I don't even know what he looks like, just that he's the one I got my blue eyes and blonde hair from. Other than that, nothing.

That night, at dinner, my mom moves to the topic of my birthday.

"So, have you thought at all about what you want to do?" I shake my head.

"Not really," I take a bite of chicken. She pushes around the potatoes on her plate, considering.

"We could go out to that pizza place you like, the one by the Mill Yard," she suggests. That's actually a pretty good idea.

"Cam and I went to the Mill Yard today," I say, taking another bite of my food. "But we saw something weird when we were walking downtown."

"What do you mean?"

"Well, there was this group of teenagers, three of them, standing on the other side of the street and staring at us. At me, particularly. They were really strange." My mom frowns. I can tell I have her attention.

"What do you mean strange? Why were they staring at you?"

"I don't know…" I struggle for words. "There was just something… off about them. Something was not right. Does that make any sense?" I look over at her and find that her entire demeanor has changed. She sits rigidly, her mouth slightly open in a look of shock, which is an odd reaction to hearing about three peculiar teenagers hanging out downtown.

"Where did you get that?" she asks, her voice quivering with what sounds like dread.

"Get... what?" I ask, nervous.

"That bracelet," she points to the hand clutching my fork, the little charm jingling softly.

"Oh," I lift my wrist to show her. "Cam bought it for me, as a birthday gift."

"Oh," she still wore an expression of dread. "That's a beautiful charm. Did he... did he tell you why he chose it?"

Why is she acting so weird? She couldn't possibly know about my dreams... could she?

"No, actually, he said he hadn't noticed it when he bought it. Why?" She looks like I just confirmed her worst fear, but she looks away, avoiding my eyes. She's definitely hiding something- something that has to do with my bracelet.

"It's nothing, I just have one similar, that's all." I can tell she's withholding information, but she abruptly stands, clearing off the table and turning on the sink as she scrubs at the plates. The conversation is over, I guess. I just wish I knew what secret she's trying to hide.

CHAPTER 2

This morning, I woke up more refreshed than I've felt in weeks, and I realize why. My sleep had been peaceful, and most importantly, devoid of dreams. The recurring nightmare that has plagued me for weeks seemingly vanished, and I can't help but feel relieved. Hopefully, the dreams are gone for good.

It was a great start to a so far perfect day. Today is November 17, my birthday.

But since it's a Friday, I still have school. And now, sitting in my last block class, the clock seems to move in slow motion. My teacher, Mrs. Schell, is standing in front of the whiteboard, trying to squeeze in a lesson about formatting essays before the bell rings. Most of the students are either staring at the clock or the doorway, their hands inching toward their phones, others watching Mrs. Schell write with blank, bored expressions, and one or two frantically still trying to take notes. Then the bell rings.

Half of the students are out of their seats and gone before Mrs. Schell can even dismiss them. I give her a wave and wish her a good weekend, slipping out of the door into the throng of people filling the hallways, jostling one another, and shouting. I weave through the crowd, only to slam headfirst into someone. Cam grabs my shoulders to keep me from tumbling backward, laughing.

"Watch where you're going, why don't you," he teases, adjusting his backpack straps and brushing his hair from his eyes.

"Sorry," I regain my footing, grinning slightly upwards at him. He is several inches taller than me, but the slight heels on my boots bring us closer to the same height.

"Are you having a good birthday?" he asks. I nod.

"So far, it's been alright." That's when I have an idea, remembering my mom's suggestion from last night. I should invite Cam to go to that flatbread pizza place by the Mill Yard with us. I know she won't mind- my mom loves Cameron since we had practically grown up together and she's good friends with his parents. I open my mouth to offer, but I'm cut off by a loud *ding* from my phone.

"Sorry, one sec…" Cam waits as I pull my phone from my pocket, the half-faded glitter on the case glinting in the fluorescent hallway lights overhead. It's a text from my mom, that's odd. I silently read what it says-

Lina, I need you to come right home from school. I have a surprise, for your birthday, but I need you home soon.

That's all it says. Weird, I guess maybe I shouldn't invite Cam anywhere just yet, I don't want to mess up whatever she's planning.

"I've got to go, see you later Cam."

"Is everything okay?" he asks curiously.

"Yeah, of course. My mom just wants me home, she says she has some sort of surprise, I'm not really sure."

"Oh, alright then," he gives me a wave. "See you later!"

I turn to leave and freeze in my tracks. There. By the lockers. The crowd had parted just enough for a split second to reveal a familiar girl, small with short brown hair, standing against the wall less than 10 feet away, staring directly at me. Just like before. And just as quickly, a small group passes between her and me, blocking my view for half a second, and...

she's gone.

I search every direction, but the only two nearby classroom doors are closed. She just disappeared into thin air. Panicked, I turn and bolt for the door. When I reach my car, keys in hand, I slide into the driver's seat and quickly lock the door behind me. I take a deep breath. It's fine, everything is fine, I'm just being super paranoid. I start the car, relishing the heat pouring from the vents, warming the interior, and thawing my frozen fingers. It's fine. Everything is fine. I begin the drive home and don't look back.

The sun is blinding in my eyes as I guide my car into the small parking space beside the house, shifting it into park. The first surprising thing I notice is my mom's Jeep, pulled to the edge of the driveway with the back wide open and piled with bags and other assorted random items spilling haphazardly out. My mom was walking out onto the narrow front entryway when she notices my car parked beside hers, waving me inside. Curiously, I follow her.

"How was your day?" She asks, bustling around the kitchen sounding slightly hurried, sweeping piles of canned food into supermarket bags. There are duffel bags scattered around the room, as well as heaps of blankets and a space heater. Our camping gear.

"It was alright," I answer, studying a package of chocolate and marshmallows lying on the counter. "Mom, what's going on? Are we going somewhere?"

"We're going on a weekend trip," she says, sweeping the last of the food into bags, gathering several of them in her hands as I follow her outside.

"A weekend trip?"

"Yes, for your birthday. Surprise! We're going camping." She still sounds as though she's in a hurry, the cheeriness somewhat forced. It's not like I'm complaining- camp is one of my favorite places in the entire world, and we usually don't go so late in the year. But it doesn't mean I'm not curious.

"What brought this on?" I ask, helping her carry the last of the bags to the Jeep.

"Oh, nothing. I've been planning this for weeks," but I can tell that she's lying. She would not have asked me what I wanted to do for my birthday last night if she had been planning for weeks. Why is she trying to hide the truth, why this last-minute decision? Does it have anything to do with our conversation at dinner last night?

Now completely packed, I climb into the passenger seat as she starts the car. I send a quick text to Cam, explaining that my mom and I are leaving for camp for the weekend because we're not going to have cell service where we're going. The drive is about two hours long, and I spend most of it just gazing out of the window as the highway rolls by. At some point I doze off, my head leaning against the window. And as I sleep, I dream.

This dream is, again, different from all of the others. I am once again standing in that dark and empty void, but this time, the silver falcon is already here. My reflection, if that's what she is, is nowhere to be seen. The falcon's talons dig uncomfortably into my shoulder, and it begins to speak in that same strange, detached voice as before, though this time there is a new note of urgency. As though it's trying to warn me of something.

"Falcon brave and bold in flight,
Shall fear the darkness and worship the light
Shattered glass gleaming white,
And the worlds bow down to the Mirror's might.

The falcon tilts its head, gazing at my confused and startled face.

"Your journey will soon begin, the game has been set in motion," the falcon's voice rumbles in my mind. *"Soon. Soon*

you will know, you will understand. Danger is coming, and you must rise to face it."

I somehow manage to find my voice, surprised to learn I actually can speak in this dream world.

"What do you mean?" I demand. "What danger? How do I face it?"

The bird only gazes at me, its strange whispers silent. The entire dreamscape begins to fade, dragging me back to the world of the waking, the falcon disappearing with it. Just before it vanishes into nothing, I hear one last whisper in my head.

"Soon. Danger is coming, and you must rise to face it..."

I awake with a jolt, gasping, my heart racing. The falcon's words ring in my head, a fading echo of its ominous warning.

"You must rise to face it..."

By the time I'm awake, the sun is sinking in the sky, about an hour from sunset. We're about 10- 20 minutes from our destination.

We're in a quaint town nestled in North Conway, in the white mountains of New Hampshire. We pass by many shops and restaurants, many already decorated with strings of Christmas lights and wreaths. My mom looks a lot more relaxed than she did two hours ago, humming along faintly with the quiet country music on the radio. We pull down a winding back road, traveling alongside trees until the ground on the other side of the road drops away and becomes a steep hill towards a gushing river frozen around the edges. Further along, we see cabins dotting the thick expanse of trees mostly bare of leaves, then along a stretch of empty road where I can vaguely make out campers and tents separated from the road by tall oaks and pines. We're almost there.

Then, up ahead, a break in the trees accompanied by a wide sign stuck into a block of cobblestone bricks, half white and half reddish-brown. It reads:

Covered Bridge Campground
White Mountains National Forest

We turn down the wide paved entrance, marked by a wooden bulletin board decorated with notices and maps of the campground, and a fork in the paved road with two paths leading off to different sets of sites. It is far more deserted than it normally is in the warmer months when we usually visit. The tents and campers are squatted in sites few and far between. I have to put my phone on airplane mode so that it won't roam for a signal and drain the battery.

By the time we're settled in our site, ready to pitch the tent and unpack, the sun has begun its descent behind the tall pine trees, and the air is frigid. My mom bundles herself in her sweater, the long sleeves practically pulled over her hands, while I huddle in my jacket. I help her set up the tent, the same tent we've had for years, arranging the sleeping bags, blankets, pillows, and duffel bags inside. She pushes the space heater to the back of the tent, and I go about unfolding the two camping chairs around the small metal circle in the middle of the clearing that acts as the fire pit.

As the evening gets darker, the faint chorus of crickets sings from the underbrush and the far-off hoot of an owl echoes from the treetops.

I sit in one of the camp chairs, a marshmallow on a stick propped over my knee as I slowly roast it over the fire we constructed in the little metal brazier on the ground. My mom sits across from me, curled up in a round-netting camping chair with a book propped in her lap. Tilting my head back, I gaze at the night sky looming above, the moon barely a sliver of light. One of my favorite parts of camping here, in the mountains, is the stars. So many stars, clustered together, peeking behind wisps of clouds, making the night seem so vast and endless and beautiful.

The howl of a wolf pierces the calm night. Curled up in a ball in the camping chair, I glance up from the book I'm reading to see that mom has gone rigid in her seat, staring out into the dark woods where the sound had come from. It's odd- I've never heard a wolf in these mountains before, though I know it isn't unlikely. Luckily it sounded so far off, that it couldn't be anywhere near us.

Several minutes go by, and she still doesn't relax. She's on the edge of her seat, scanning the treeline.

"Mom, is everything okay?" She heaves a large sigh, her shoulders slumping slightly as she seems to resign herself to something.

"Lina, there is something I should probably tell you. Actually, I should have told you a long time ago, and it might not be easy to understand, but…" She goes silent.

"Mom?" I ask.

Her eyes, wide with horror, are fixed on something behind me. Terror freezes me to the spot, my breath hitching. Is it a wolf? Or a bear? Slowly, oh so slowly, I turn my head to see what it is.

It's… a cat? Some sort of wildcat, pale beige colored with black-tufted ears. A bobcat, or a lynx, I think. Its eyes gaze out at me from a scraggly bush, wide and unblinking. Well, that's slightly anticlimactic.

Then we hear the footsteps.

It's very faint at first, just the sound of crackling dead leaves underfoot, coming from a long way off. The two of us are silent, holding our breath, listening. It sounds as though several people are crashing through the woods, heading in our direction. I cast a quick glance across the firepit, barely more than glowing embers now, to where my mother sits. The lynx still watches us from the bushes.

"Emmalina. Get to the car. NOW." My mom stands from the chair. Her hazel eyes are wide, terrified, but her voice remains steady, unnaturally calm, and completely unsurprised, as though this is what she had been dreading all along.

"What?" I ask incredulously. "Why? What's going on? You have to tell me…"

"Just GO!" She roars, waving towards the car parked at the far edge of the clearing, her calmness cracking into urgency. "Please, just go Lina. Get out of here!" she begs.

"What about you? Why aren't you coming?" I plead, lightheaded with panicked confusion. What is happening? But a stubborn determination wells up as she pushes me in the direction of the Jeep.

"I'm not leaving you," I say desperately. I have no idea what's going on, but I can't just take the car and abandon her. The footsteps are louder now, the cracking and snapping of trees more frequent as if whoever it is doesn't care about hiding their approach. As if we couldn't outrun them anyway. I still can't see anybody, however, just the rustling of trees several yards away.

My mother takes my face in her hands, tears streaming down her cheeks, and kisses me on the forehead.

"*Please*, Lina. You have to get out of here. The keys are in the glove box, if you go now you can still make it away," she whispers frantically.

"Make it away from who? And what about you?" my voice cracks with desperation.

"I'm going to slow them down," she answers softly, determination hardening her eyes, blinking back tears.

"But you have to go." She lifts her hands from my face and pulls me into a hug. "I love you," she whispers. At that moment, we hear the soft sound of footsteps at the edge of the clearing, spinning to see three people, two men, and a woman, standing at the tree line. Both are wearing odd clothes, like panels of black leather shaped into some sort of flexible body armor, and have something shiny gripped in their hands. Daggers, as long as my forearm, gleaming and vicious. My heart practically stops.

My mom turns to face them, lifting the right sleeve of her thick sweater slightly, enough to touch a glimmering object on her wrist. A bracelet- made of a thin band of simple gold, with a tiny gold charm of a howling wolf dangling from it. I have never seen this piece of jewelry before, had never seen her wear it, sparkling brightly despite the lack of light.

I can still hear racing footsteps, and now I can see the figures of many people, maybe twenty, emerging from the far side of the clearing. They are all dressed similarly, in plates of dark armor, holding or strapped with various weapons. My mom's bracelet begins to glow slightly like someone had lit a small flame within the metal. She turns back to me briefly, mouthing the word "go."

Suddenly I watch in shock as a massive animal-like silhouette leaps from the woods off to our side, a few feet away from where my mom stands. I barely suppress a scream as I realize what it is-

A wolf. Except it's no ordinary wolf; this thing is roughly the size of a young grizzly bear, with a long, lean body and massive paws digging into the dirt. Its head is huge, with a narrow, sleek snout and thick brown fur. I make a strangled gasp sound as the beast barrels towards my mother, its paws skidding, tearing rivets in the frozen earth. But instead of attacking her, it slows until it's standing at her side, its size making her appear small.

What's even stranger is that my mom doesn't even seem to be afraid of the wolf at all, not even surprised to see it looming beside her. She just turns her head slightly to acknowledge its presence, with the barest hint of a smile on her face as she gazes at it with a sort of familiarity, as though it's a close friend she hasn't seen in a long time. The first three strangers with the daggers launch out of their stalemate, lunging, and the wolf meets them halfway with teeth bared. The rest of the armored mass surge forward, some drawing knives or swords, others with arrows notched in bows. Even the lynx from the bushes snarls, darting forward to join the fray. And as they clash, I tear my eyes away from the horrifying scene, terror stiffening my limbs and blinding my eyes with tears. I stumble as I try to remember how to move my legs, not stopping to think as I pick a direction and dash away on uneven footing.

Several men try to break from the group to pursue me, but they are pushed back by my mom, at sword point. Where did she get a sword?! I feel as though I'm going to pass out from shock, my head spinning and the world swaying beneath my feet. I'm barely even watching where I'm going, just knowing I have to get away. Tears stream down my face as I inwardly beg myself to stop running, to go back for her. For my mother. But I remember her pleading eyes, begging me to go, her determination to protect me. What would I be able to do, besides getting us both killed? I choke back a sob as I think about it. What if she's *killed?*

My feet skid over dead leaves and I tear through the underbrush, trying to follow the winding dirt paths through the campground, trying to find the exit. Where is the street? I'm in a section of the camp that's empty, every campsite vacant. Seemingly endless woods stretch out beyond the nearest site. It should be a straight shot to the road, just through those trees, and it will be faster than doubling back. I need to find someone, I need to get help.

I can no longer hear the sound of fighting or shouting, nor the wolf's low growls, and my steps start to feel heavier as exhaustion weighs me down. Suddenly my feet fly out from under me as my foot hits a root half buried by frozen leaves, and I throw my hands up to protect my face as I tumble to the ground. I lay on the ground for a moment, shivering. I don't think I could make myself run much further anyway. I want to curl up on the forest floor. I want to wake up from whatever nightmare I'm having, yet this just seems too *real.* Is it possible to even outrun whoever is chasing me? I realize with a jolt of despair that I left the Jeep behind in the campsite clearing.

Taking deep, shuddering breaths that build into sobs, I attempt to calm my racing heart, with no success. The panic in my chest builds until I feel as though I could explode. I push myself into a sitting position, leaning against a tree, feeling the rough bark against my face. Should I go back? But… I don't know where I am, or which direction I just came from. I should have stayed, I should have done *something*… Instead, I just ran. I just left her there.

I have to keep going. To the road. Where's the road? It should be right here! Unless I ran in the wrong direction. But it shouldn't be too hard to find; we had only been about a five-minute walk away. The difficult part would come after. I could try to hitchhike. The idea makes me cringe, but it's the middle of the night, and the nearest houses are several miles down the road. I don't even have cell service here. Or a cell phone, since I left it inside the tent. So hitchhiking seems like my only option, since it seems a whole lot safer than running into those strangers with daggers who are apparently hunting for me. Or a giant wolf. I suppress a shudder as I recall the image; the wolf's hulking form, its lips pulled back in a snarl. Perhaps I'm losing my mind.

But if I resign myself to hitchhiking, what do I do when I manage to find a phone? Who would I even call? The police most likely, or maybe even Cam. What would I even say? *"Hi, sorry to bother you in the middle of the night, but I'm stranded in the mountains with a group of dagger-wielding strangers with giant wolves who attacked me and my mom, could you come to pick me up?"* Cam would think I'm insane. I mean, I barely believe it and I just lived it! But it's my only option.

I straighten from where I'm crouched, tugging my sweatshirt free from where it snagged against a half-dead bush. I rub my hands over my face, drying the tears staining my cheeks, and begin the trek uphill in what I hope is the direction of the street. I've walked barely two feet when suddenly I freeze. I don't know why, how, or where, but somehow, I get the feeling that I'm being watched. I peer around the night shrouded tree trunks, turning in circles, and scanning. Waiting. The forest is very quiet.

Unnaturally quiet.

There is a slight crackle of leaves to my left, the shifting of a branch. I turn and bolt. I flat out sprint through the forest, still at a gradual incline, tearing through branches and bushes without caring how many roots I trip over or how many thorn bushes I barrel through. I just have to get away. My breath comes in short gasps, my legs burning from the now steadily uphill run. Very faintly, I can hear the sound of someone giving chase. The quick and close crunching of leaves sounds as though it is right behind me, but every glance over my shoulder reveals no sign of anyone other than the quivering of bushes caused by my strides. If I hadn't been paying attention, the sound is so stealthy I wouldn't have known I was being followed.

The incline abruptly levels out. It's the street. Even at night, there has to be a car or two driving along, or a cabin, or *someone* to help me. In my careless panic, I don't notice the lack of gravel or pavement underfoot, or the break in the trees that doesn't signal a road. Without slowing, I shove past the tangle of bushes, expecting my foot to hit solid asphalt. It doesn't.

Instead, the ground gives way to a very steep decline, dotted with rocks, torn-up roots, and thin trees clinging to the slope. My foot slides on the crumbling dirt, and I'm thrown off balance, my ankle twisting beneath my weight as I tumble forward and my legs give out beneath me. One moment I'm dashing through the woods, and the next I find myself falling, tumbling on my side down the steep hill. I throw my arms over my head to protect my face, praying I don't hit a rock, but I don't make any more noise than a gasp. Fortunately, I make it to the bottom of the slope without colliding with anything. Unfortunately, there is water at the base of the hill. A small, partially iced-over stream.

On the bright side, it is a fairly cushioned landing in the sandy stream bed, better than hard-packed earth. On the other hand, however, mountain streams are freezing in November, and this one is certainly no exception. I am momentarily stunned by the force of the cold water, and as I pull myself out, teeth chattering and breathing heavily, I find my clothes half soaked and water dripping from my hair.

The road must have been in the other direction. Of course.

A quick glance up the slope shows no signs of my pursuer. Maybe I lost them? Gently easing myself onto my feet, leaning my weight against a sturdy oak tree, I test my weight gingerly on my right ankle, the one I twisted on the way down. It is sore, likely sprained, but thankfully not broken. I pause for a moment to wring out my dripping hair, my teeth chattering, but I'm starting to think my unexpected tumble down the hill may have saved me, since there are still no signs of whoever was chasing me. Maybe they don't know where I went, and I feel a slight tinge of relief.

Relieved, that is until I'm grabbed from behind.

CHAPTER 3

Two hands grasp my shoulders tightly and roughly yank me away from the tree I'm leaning on, causing me to stumble and almost eat dirt, but the hands jerk me upright. I twist my head to look over my left shoulder and glimpse a tall figure behind me, his face shrouded and hidden in a black hood. He quickly releases his hold on my shoulders to wrap long, slender fingers covered in thick leather gloves around my wrists and yanks my hands behind my back, the same way a cop would subdue a rowdy criminal. I half expect him to slap handcuffs on me, but instead, he just keeps my wrists locked in his iron grip.

Through my sudden spikes of fear and adrenaline, I can't help but wonder how he managed to get down here so fast, without landing in the stream bed. The slope has no obvious shortcut down…

There is a sudden rustle of bushes from the top of the hill, my head jerking upwards and my heart plummeting further, if that's even possible, as another figure steps from the tangle of leaves. He is shorter than the man behind me but leaner. He's in his forties, perhaps, with a gruff face and close-cropped, ebony black hair. He has a menacing-looking scar running down the left side of his face, stretching from temple to cheek, extending through his left eye and leaving the whole eye clouded and blind.

Well, that answers my question, at least. All this time, I thought I had been outrunning him, but he must have just been herding me, leading me straight into this trap. The slightest bit of anger peeks around my fear. I thought I had hit rock bottom, but instead, I broke through and just kept falling.

The man at the top of the hill smiles coldly, his scar stretching gruesomely, as he makes his way carefully down the slope. He moves with unnatural grace and ease, moving so smoothly it's almost like he's gliding, making it to the edge of the stream in seconds and balancing precariously on the edge of a small stone. His smile seems somewhat amused as if he found my tumble into the stream to be genuinely funny. Jerk.

His hand rests nonchalantly on a small sheath at his side, the dull leather cracked and worn, concealing a dagger similar to the ones the strangers at the campsite wielded.

"Who are you?" I demand. I meant to sound demanding, but instead, my voice came out as a mostly unintelligible squeak. *"Who are you?"* I try again, forcing my voice to remain steady. It only seems to further amuse him, and he raises an eyebrow at my attempt at assertiveness.

"Who we are is not important," the man with the scar says in a gravelly voice, his eyes narrowing slightly. "What matters is who *you* are."

"Who I am? What do you mean?" My voice wavers with confusion.

"Playing dumb won't help you," he says with a smug, matter-of-fact smile. "Drop the act, it will save us all time. Though I must admit, it is a good facade. Almost believable, even." I blink, caught off guard.

"What are you talking about?" I'm desperate now, my voice rising with exasperation. His smug smile wavers.

"You… you really have no idea…?" For some reason, he is now the one that seems confused. He glances at his partner, the cloaked man holding my wrists. "Perhaps you may be more useful than we originally thought…" He is practically talking to himself now, pondering something. His low, rough voice is like nails on a chalkboard. My fear begins to give way to frustration, and as he makes no further attempt to elaborate, my irritation piques.

"What. Are. You. Talking. About." My voice is calm but angry. Yet, he only smiles, as if I'm some child throwing a temper tantrum as if I have no right to know what's going on. With all of the force I can muster, I yank my hands away, twisting to get the hooded man to release his grip, prying at his fingers until I slip free. I have one of his gloves clenched in my fist, having torn it away as he tried to hold on, and I spin to try and shove him away before he can grab me again.

The hooded man lunges, his hands wrapping around my forearms in a vice-like grip, and I twist to pry at his fingers. But as my fingertips brush his bare hand, the one I stole the glove from, he flinches back as if I've burned him. As I try to pull away from the hand still holding my sleeve, he refuses to grab me with his bare hand. For some reason, he doesn't want to touch me without his glove. But why?

The man with the scar- also wearing gloves, I might add- uses his foot to easily sweep my bad leg out from under me, sending me tumbling onto the ground. He puts his boot on my stomach, pinning me there, while I scramble to throw him off. The man with the hood stoops to pick up his glove from where I dropped it in the dirt, and I catch a glimpse of pale skin and an angular face before the shadows hide his features again. I glare up at the scarred man, who sneers, clasping his hands in a "patient teacher" sort of way.

"Now, where did that get you?" he chides mockingly. "We aren't here to hurt you, and you would make this a whole lot easier if you just-"

Suddenly the entire world around me is lit by a strange white glow, my eyes burning as they adjust to the abrupt light. Straining my eyes, blinking, I can see the origin of the glow. It is coming from a strange beam of light protruding above the treetops, maybe about a mile away in the woods. I'm not talking about a flashlight or a searchlight. I'm talking about a cylindrical beam of pure white light, wider than a tree trunk and so bright I can't see through it, spearing from the earth and disappearing into the clouds high above. It lasts for about three heartbeats, and then it's gone.

The two men's faces are turned towards the spot where the light vanished as abruptly as it appeared. I still can't see the taller man's face- it has to be intentional- but the scarred man is tense and baffled. His eyes are wide, his mouth pressed into a firm, confusing line. That's odd. Does he not know what that was either? If it wasn't them, then what was it? Maybe it came from a search party- someone must have heard the sounds of fighting at the campsite and called the police, yes that's it! I gasp, ready to shout as loud as I can, hoping someone hears me, and the man with the scar presses his boot down a bit harder, knocking the breath out of me.

"No, no, no-" He chides. "None of that," he turns to the man with the hooded cloak. "I think it's time to go." The hooded man nods, and as the boot is lifted, he bends to heave me up by my arms. He pins my wrists behind me again, this time holding them tightly enough that I can't snatch his gloves away, and starts guiding me forward, Scarred Man leading the way. I'm walking with a heavy limp, exaggerating it slightly in a desperate attempt to slow us down, though some of it's not really an act. The hooded man grumbles in frustration.

Then he comes to an abrupt stop, the hands gripping my wrists spasming, and to my surprise, releasing me. Then he lets out a strangled shout, the first sound I've heard the hooded man make- a strained cry of pain. Scarred Man whirls on me, his eyes wide.

"What did you-" he sees the hooded man, who's crumpled onto the ground, clawing at the frozen earth. A white-feathered shaft protrudes from his back, buried in his black cloak- the shaft of an arrow. I stand, frozen with shock and horror, unrestrained at the moment. I could try to make a break for it, but I can't look away. He was shot… by who? Where?

That seems to be what the scarred man is trying to figure out. He scans the trees for half a second and slips off a glove. I see what he's about to do half a second before he does it, and I shout as he lunges for where I stand, his ungloved hand grasping my neck. For a split second, when his hand meets my skin, a cold chill shudders throughout my entire body, more frigid than the mountain stream. I freeze, terrified, but he doesn't try to strangle me. Instead, he just disappears. It is the strangest thing- he is no longer there but I can still feel his hand on my throat. It's almost like he's… invisible.

Surprised, I try to pull away, shoving at the solid but invisible mass in front of me, and the hand around my neck tightens slightly in warning, while another grabs and pins my wrists behind my back. But I noticed something even more alarming; when I tried to shove him away, I couldn't see my own hands. I glance down as far as he'll allow my head to move.

My body is gone.

I can still feel everything…the ground beneath my feet, though I see no feet, and the bite of the cold wind in my still-soaked clothes. When I try to move an arm or a leg I can feel them move, but they are not there. I'm invisible too. How… how is this even possible? How is any of this even possible? Is that why whoever shot the first arrow hasn't shot another? Because they can't see us? The hooded man, still on the ground, flickers and disappears, leaving nothing but a tiny trickle of blood on the ground, but I still can see the faintest shimmer where he was.

"It's strange, isn't it?" I hear the scarred man whisper.

Strange doesn't even begin to describe it, the disorienting feeling of moving your body but seeing nothing but the ground beneath you. Is the scarred man doing this, somehow? I feel his hand still pinning my wrists, the first one still resting on my throat, and he begins to tug me away from the stream further into the woods. Now, this is my chance. Maybe whoever shot the arrow can't see me, but they probably can hear me.

"HELP," I scream, as loud as I can. My cry is cut short as the scarred man lifts his hand from my wrists to clap it over my mouth, but the damage is done. I've given the mystery archer our location. I have another idea. I begin to struggle, kicking at the dirt, leaving scuff marks on the frozen ground, even as the hand tightens around my neck to the point where I can barely breathe. The archer can see the scuff marks, where I am, and where the scarred man stands.

An arrow shaft sprouts from his shoulder, and he lets out a furious cry of pain, his form flickering momentarily into view. At that moment, I wrench myself away from him, tumbling to the ground, and as his hand loses contact with my throat, I can see my own body become visible again. The scarred man's form flickers a few more times as he stumbles back towards the safety of the trees, his partner still nowhere to be seen. But the archer isn't finished yet.

More arrows rain down, the man barely managing to dodge them with his strange swiftness, but one finds its mark, sinking into his boot. He cries out again, sounding more like anger than pain. The arrows seem to be coming from a high vantage point. I scan the thick pine boughs, the archer could be hidden in any one of them.

The scarred man draws his dagger- what he's planning on doing with it, I don't know- when suddenly a lithe figure drops from the trees just a few feet from where I lay sprawled on the ground. It's a girl, no more than 17 or 18 years old. Her long, raven black hair is pulled back in a ponytail, her expression one of fierce concentration, her hands gripping a grand bow with a notched arrow pointed right at the scarred man, whose face reddens with fury. I have the vague feeling that I've seen her somewhere before.

I don't have much time to ponder it. I hear a muffled thump behind me, and I turn my head to see the man collapse to the ground as if something *invisible* collided with him. Or someone. Another girl appears; smaller than me about around the same age, her short, wavy brown hair hanging loose around her face as she sneers triumphantly down at the snarling man she pinned to the ground using the element of surprise. My mouth drops open slightly. I was right, she was invisible too. Somehow.

Finally, a third figure appears from the shadows of the trees, a long silvery sword in hand. A *sword*?

The figure, a boy around the same age as the other two, is tall with broad shoulders and built like a football player. His hair is jet black, short, and messy, shockingly good-looking. His head is ducked as he glares down at the snarling man on the ground, who surges upward, twisting with surprising agility as he throws the brown-haired girl off of him. He somehow still has his dagger in hand, its blade gleaming, almost as long as my forearm.

He spins, intercepting a broad swing of the boy's sword, grunting as he deflects it. Moonlight glints like sparks on the silvery sword as it cuts through the air, the force sending the scarred man stumbling back, heels skidding as he fights to keep his balance. The boy is clearly the better fighter; stronger, wielding a sword against a knife. The man, realizing he is far outmatched, frantically searches for his companion, but he's in no condition to help anybody.

The man with the hood stumbles backward, the arrow still protruding from his back near the shoulder blade. I don't know how he's still standing. The archer stalks after him, having slung her bow over her back in exchange for a pair of small, needle-like knives. More subtle than the sword or daggers, but by the way the girl handles them, it's clear she knows how to use them. The taller man in the hooded cloak turns and flees into the woods, and the archer surprisingly lets him run.

Realizing his backup just abandoned him, the man still fighting ducks away from the duel, narrowly avoiding losing his ear as the sword's blade slices through the air where his face had been only seconds before. He turns, lip curling in hatred, before his form flickers and vanishes, his footfalls fading away until I can no longer hear them. The whole encounter, from my fall in the stream to the fight, must have only taken a few moments, but it felt like an eternity.

The four of us stand there for a moment, silent. The three teenagers don't seem to have any interest in pursuing the two men, instead turning their attention to me. The girl with the long black hair flicks her wrists, sliding the two needle-like knives into hidden sheaths on her black uniform. The three of them all wear something similar to the invisible men; black gear that covers everything from the neck down. But unlike the thick, worn leather panels of the two men, these seem thinner, and more flexible. They are also engraved with a silver symbol on the breastplates, two entwined R's.

The shorter girl gives me an odd look, curious and weary at the same time. The black-haired girl's expression is guarded and unreadable. The boy forcefully sheaths his sword with a vicious metallic *shink* sound. He glares in my direction, with no warmth or curiosity or weariness of any kind.

Just complete and utter hate.

Suddenly it hits me. I know where I recognize them from. These were the teenager's Cam and I saw downtown the other day, and again in the hall at school. They've been following me. The archer, the girl with black hair, finally breaks the tense silence.

"I imagine that you have a few questions," she says, slowly taking a few steps towards me, as though I'm some startled animal she's trying not to spook. "I promise, we can explain everything." I speak for what feels like the first time in hours, even though it had realistically only been minutes before.

"Who are you?" I ask, my voice rough, calm. I'm past the point of fear, to the point of barely feeling anything besides an icy stillness, a flickering of grief. Anger. My patience for these vague non-answers wears thin. The shorter girl flinches slightly, looking unsure. The boy's hand drifts towards his sword hilt. But the black-haired girl in front of me extends a hand, a gesture of trust and peace. After a moment's hesitation, I take it, allowing her to help me up. She too is wearing gloves, as are all of them.

"My name is Jane," she says carefully.

"And I'm Alaina," the shorter girl pipes up. Her voice is surprisingly open and friendly. She gives me a small smile, and I find myself relaxing ever so slightly since it seems like I'm not about to be kidnapped for a second time. Not immediately anyway.

"I'm Emmalina," I say in an attempt at politeness, and Jane smiles.

"Oh, we know who you are," Alaina says nonchalantly, weariness seemingly gone. I raise an eyebrow questioningly. How is it that everyone seems to know me, yet I don't have the slightest clue what is going on? Jane turns her head to the boy expectantly. He practically radiates hostility, as if my very existence offends him.

"Reed," he spits out his name as though it's a threat rather than an introduction. I flinch away. Jane shoots him a glare.

"Excuse my brother," she grumbles. "He seems to have forgotten to bring his manners."

Alaina rushes forward to fill in the silence.

"We have to get moving," she says to Jane, who nods. "We can't risk them doubling back with reinforcements." Reed gives a brisk nod, and Alaina's eyes dart in the direction where the two men disappeared. I realize that when she says "we," she means me also. Weighing my options, I have to admit that going with them does seem to be my best choice. They did just potentially save my life, after all.

"Okay, then," I sigh, resigned to the fact that this crazy night is far from over. "Where too?"

I let out a tiny gasp of pain as I try to put weight on my foot. I had almost forgotten about it, too focused on the chaos around me. As the adrenaline wears off, I can feel every ache and pain from my tumble down the slope, as well as the cold wind in my damp clothes. I'm trying to follow Alaina as she leads the way through the trees, but I have to stop every few minutes to brace my arm against a tree, each step sending a white-hot spike through my swollen ankle. Leaning against a thick oak, my palms scraping on the rough bark, trying to take as much weight off of my foot as possible.

Jane wordlessly strides over towards me, extending an arm, allowing me to lean on her for balance. I hesitate, but I give her a small, thankful smile in return.

"Alaina, scout ahead and keep an eye out for any more of Lillian's men," Jane instructs with an air of authority. Lillian? The name doesn't sound familiar, and I file that information away to ask about it again later, one on my growing list of questions.

"And Reed, hang back, make sure we're not being followed." Alaina steps forward, her body shimmering and vanishing as she does. I can't help but stare at the spot where she stood, now empty.

"How did she do that?" I ask, baffled. "Disappear like that, I mean. Is it some sort of illusion?"

"Something like that," Jane and I continue making our way through the thicket of trees, following the stream as it curves around a steep hill. Reed follows several yards behind us, sword gripped in hand, constantly glancing all around us, his face expressionless as stone.

"I promise, we will tell you everything once we get to the safe house," Jane assures me. Behind us, Reed's frown deepens, giving Jane a skeptical look as if to say *"Are you sure that's such a good idea?"* Jane promptly ignores him. What is his problem, anyway? What did I ever do to him?

We have just reached the base of another hill, not quite as tall as the others but still pretty steep. I frown. Normally it wouldn't be a problem, making it up that incline, but how am I supposed to struggle up that hill on my ankle? I certainly can't do it myself. Jane seems to come to the same conclusion.

"Reed," she calls him over from where he had stood, keeping watch. "Help me get her up the hill?" she asks.

I feel my face get warm with embarrassment. Reed doesn't seem thrilled about it either, giving Jane a somewhat resentful look as he sheaths his sword, as though he doesn't appreciate being bossed around. But he steps forward to help nonetheless; Jane taking my right side and Reed taking my left. They throw my arms over their shoulders, almost entirely supporting my weight. It seems like an unwieldy and awkward position, but they heave me up the steep slope with a surprising amount of ease. I brace my good foot against the ground, trying to be helpful. When we reach flat, level ground, I sink to the forest floor with my back against a tree while the three of us catch our breath.

"Thanks," I say softly. Reed raises an eyebrow, as though he's surprised that I would thank him. He nods, the only acknowledgment that he gives me.

A wolf's howl cuts through the air from off in the distance, causing me to shudder, and they look around with concern.

"We better get moving," Jane advises sternly, her brow furrowing. "We don't know how close they-"

"Hey," we hear a voice to the left, right beside us. Reed moves faster than I can blink, drawing his sword with the piercing screech of metal against scabbard. Jane jumps nearly a foot, hands scrambling for her daggers. The voice is accompanied by a small laugh, and a slight sigh of relief passes through me as I glance upwards, finding Alaina sitting in the lower bough of the oak tree I'm leaning against. Having lifted the invisibility, she now perches her small form on the thicker end of the twisted branch, her legs dangling in the open air, humming merrily to herself.

Reed actually cracks a smile, the corners of his lips curving upwards with amusement, sheathing his sword once more. Smiling, with the moonlight filtering through the leaves leaving dappled flecks of silver along his face, I feel something flutter in my chest the way I've never felt before. It's only when his gaze meets mine that I realize I've been staring, and I blush furiously as I tear my eyes away. When I glance back at him, that smile is gone.

Jane, on the other hand, is not smiling at all. She scowls up at the branch where Alaina sits, annoyance written over every feature in her expression as she slides her knives back into their sheaths.

"Sorry," Alaina apologizes, not looking very sorry. "Didn't mean to scare you. I just thought you'd want to know that the coast is all clear. What took you guys so long?"

Jane's eye twitches ever so slightly.

"Alaina," Reed speaks up. "You're *sure* that the coast is all clear?" She rolls her eyes.

"Of course I'm sure, When have I ever not been?" Reed opens his mouth to reply, and she cuts him off. "Don't answer that. The point is, we're all set to go. It's a straight shot to the safe house through these trees."

Jane offers me a hand up, and I thankfully accept her help as Alaina leaps from the tree with a sort of cat-like grace.

"We've already taken longer than we should," Reed muses, checking a strange-looking watch on his wrist. "Marcus won't be happy if we're late. Are you sure we should stop for the explanation?"

"She deserves to know what's going on, Reed," Jane fires back.

"Marcus can wait," Alaina agrees.

"I think I have a right to know at this point," I point out. Reed, outvoted, scowls but falls silent. I file away this new unfamiliar name, Marcus, even though it isn't much. I'm still not convinced that I can trust these strange teenagers, with their weapons, their weird secrecy, and their so-called safe house. But at the moment, I don't really have much of a choice. Even though they aren't physically forcing me to come along with them, I have a nagging feeling that they aren't going to simply let me walk away. I get the sense that I'm still a prisoner of sorts.

But on the other hand, as far as I don't trust them, I like my chances of traveling with them better than being left to wander the woods alone, lost, risking running into those other men from the campsite. Or a giant wolf. The image of that massive beast in the clearing flickers behind my eyelids, and I suppress a shudder.

"We better go now," Jane urges. "It's getting close to dawn, and we don't want to risk being seen. We've probably drawn enough attention to ourselves as it is."

I nearly sob with relief when I see the break in the trees up ahead- an actual road this time- and hear the faintest rushing of the river. Stepping out of the trees, onto solid asphalt, there's nothing but a slightly curving road winding alongside untouched woods on either side. It is still dark, sunrise is about an hour off, and the brisk wind is freezing. I hadn't realized how much time had passed while I wandered through the woods.

We trek alongside the pavement, close enough to the trees that, if we spot approaching headlights, we could duck into the safety of the bushes. What they don't know is the moment that I glimpse signs of other people, I am making a break for it. These strangers may have saved my life, possibly, but I can tell they did it for other reasons besides the kindness of their hearts. There is more to this than I can even understand, and I have no interest whatsoever in waiting around to find out what those reasons are. But unfortunately, no cars come along, there are no houses along this winding back road.

I believe I know where I am, and it is confirmed as we finally spot several cabins nestled in the woods up ahead. Behind us, the way we just came, is the entrance to the campground, and further along, is where the river meets the edge of the road leading to a covered bridge. Ahead of us begins the seasonal camping sites, not part of the Covered Bridge Campground, and eventually the road back to town. As we pass by the cabins, my hope plummets a bit more as I see that there are no cars parked in the driveways, no lights on in the windows, or furniture set outside them. Empty. Their owners home for the winter, leaving the cabins cold and dark.

One driveway, wider than the others and paved with gravel and dirt, branches off from the road and slopes downward, flanked by cabins forming a small development of seasonal sites. Jane, Reed, and Alaina venture down this driveway, with me in tow, turning right where the path splits. Finally, we stop in front of an old structure, another cabin, small and wooden. Its unpainted brown walls and sagging roof display its age, protected by a barrier of trees that further conceal its appearance, making it seem quite unnoticeable. As we get a little closer, Jane still helping me along a worn narrow path through the trees, I can see an old porch with rickety rocking chairs and tiny wind chimes dangling in front of the windows. To anyone else, this place surely would have appeared to be a snug little summer retreat owned by an elderly couple who liked their privacy. At first glance, many would not notice the miniature hidden cameras dotting the property, or the apparent lack of use. The rocking chairs seem to be mere props in the cabin charade, looking as though they would collapse if someone were to actually sit in one.

We hang back as Alaina, invisible again, inspects the structure and the area around it. She reappears at the door, working on the lock. Taking this as an all-clear, Jane and Reed rise from the spot where we're crouched, helping me along. My ankle is still really sore, but I'm finding that I can put a bit more weight on it than before. Perhaps it was not quite as sprained as I thought. Nearing the porch, I can see little solar panels, the only things that look well kept, fitted to the warped shingles of the roof. They must be what powers the little security cameras since electricity is practically nonexistent so far from the towns. Alaina unlocks the door with a strange mechanical click, and the three of us follow her inside. I limp over to one of the wooden chairs at the tiny table near the corner, now able to move a little more freely on my own, and I take a look at the cabin's interior. It is practically bare, just the table and chairs I'm seated at, a dusty and antique-looking cloth couch pushed out of the way, a ratty rug in front of the couch, and thick dark curtains. Jane strides for the curtains, tugging them closed, blocking out whatever little light filters through.

Alaina lifts a small handheld lighter from the table, lighting the wick of a candle, and bathing the room in a faint warm glow. It is one of those weird, old-fashioned candles, tall and made of dripping white wax. My palms become sweaty, and I fold my hands against my sides in an effort to stop the shaking, whether it's from the cold or my frayed nerves. I shouldn't be here, this isn't right.

Reed nudges aside the edge of the matted carpet with the toe of his boot, exposing the slightly warped wooden boards beneath. He kneels, staining the black leather on his knees with layers of dust, but he doesn't seem to care much, his gloved fingers hovering over one particular board. It is unimpressive, warped like the others from years of water damage, the only thing marking it as different being a little knot in the wood. Reed peels his glove off, placing the tip of his forefinger in the little grooved knot on the floor.

Something clicks, sharp and metallic from beneath the wooden boards, and then there is a sound of whirring, clicking, and the shifting screech of metal. I watch in awe as a square-shaped panel of wooden floor retracts, leaving a gaping hole beside Reed's knees. Some kind of trapdoor. Reaching inside, shaking away a stray cobweb, he lifts something small and oblong in his hand. I lean forward slightly, reluctantly curious, trying to get a better view of what it could be. A weapon? Some kind of gadget? Maybe the trapdoor is a sort of secret entrance, and that object is some kind of key? Reed strides towards the table where I sit, and where Jane and Alaina have settled themselves in the chairs beside me, turning the object in his hand. It is… a mirror?

It's a small, handheld mirror no bigger than my palm, oval-shaped with an intricate golden frame and curving handle. I have to admit, I was expecting something a little more… impressive. But as Reed sets it face up on the rickety table, sliding into the only vacant seat, the one across from me, the mirror's glass catches my attention.

It is polished, silvery, and flawless, with not a speck of dust or cobwebs despite being in that secret compartment inside the floor. It is as clear and smooth as liquid, and I almost expect it to ripple as Reed's fingertip brushes its edge, not leaving a single smudge or fingerprint. I can see his face reflected in the mirror, the emerald-tinged green of his eyes meeting mine for a brief moment. Gently, he draws his fingers across the glass surface, and the image of his figure wavers and shimmers, as if it is barely a trick of the light. Alaina smiles with amusement as my eyes grow wider.

"Why does it do that?" I ask, reaching out a hand curiously. The glass is startlingly cold and smooth as silk as the image again ripples under my touch as if it truly is liquid. Reed lifts his head, the reflection of his green eyes disappearing from view. Jane reaches over, cupping the little mirror in her palm, her face now appearing on its surface. Her eyes are the same color as Reed's- emerald green fringed with dark lashes.

Their eyes aren't the only thing they have in common. They have the same raven black hair; Jane's completely straight hanging down her back in a ponytail, while Reed's short, messy hair has a slightly wavy look to it. There are also similarities in their angular faces, and the small furrow they both have between their eyebrows when they're frowning. Jane had said he was her brother- they could even be twins.

Then there was Alaina, I had thought her eyes were blue before, or maybe even a bit gray. But in the candlelight, I now see that they're a peculiar turquoise color, not quite blue and not quite green. Alaina doesn't appear to be related to Jane and Reed; she is several inches shorter than me, with dark brown hair cropped to her shoulders styled in elegant curls, and paler skin.

Reed slumps back in his seat, again checking that strange little watch on his wrist. It seems to have little symbols, similar to roman numerals, instead of numbers.

"Jane, if we're doing this whole explanation thing, we might want to speed it up a bit. We're already running late as it is," Reed says impatiently, sneaking glances at the tiny sliver of sky visible through the curtains. Alaina gives him a dirty look, while Jane simply looks at him quizzically.

"Where to begin," Jane muses, as Alaina drums her fingers on the tabletop. Strangely enough, Jane, Reed, and even the two men in the woods all wear regular gloves, while Alaina's are fingerless.

"I think it's time to start from the beginning," Jane decides, carefully laying the mirror face down. "What is this?"

"A… mirror?" I answer slowly, unsure what this has to do with anything.

"Yes, and what does it show you?" she prods.

"It shows… my reflection?" I'm still confused about what she's getting at, but Jane only nods.

"And what exactly is a reflection?" she asks.

I'm not even sure how to answer that question, but she speaks before I have much time to think it over. I still don't see how any of this is relevant.

"A mirror, to most people, is just a piece of glass. An ornament to hang on a wall, or carry in a purse to admire oneself. They think that a reflection is simply light reflecting an image on a sheet of glass. That's how they have explained this object, without realizing that their theories are far from correct."

"Okay…" I say, waiting for her to get to the point. Is this some kind of metaphor?

"Mirrors are not simply reflective surfaces, they are windows. Windows to another world."

"Another… world?" I ask. "And what exactly does that stand for? Listen, I really don't want to hear your cryptic words and vague metaphors, I just want a straight answer-"

"It's not a metaphor," Reed says snarkily. "If you would just listen for a moment-" Jane cuts him off with a sharp look, and he has the decency to fall silent. Reed and this attitude of his are really starting to get on my nerves.

"Reed's right, it isn't a metaphor," Jane says in a much softer tone. "There are two worlds that exist, side by side. One of them is familiar to you, Earth. The other is Allrhea, basically Earth's twin. Both are identical to one another."

She absentmindedly strokes the gold frame of the mirror with a gloved finger, as she continues with her story.

"And what binds the two together is magic."

Magic? Other worlds? They must be crazy. Are they trying to mess with me, or do they actually believe this? One glance at Alaina and Reed shows them listening patiently, Reed scowling ever so slightly, but neither of them looks confused by what Jane is saying.

"Let me guess," I say, my voice now heavy with sarcasm. "You three are from this other world?" Jane shakes her head.

"No, we're not," she gives no sign she even heard my sarcasm. "The magic that binds Earth and Allrhea together comes from the Realms, which exists between them."

There's that word again, magic.

"So, there are three worlds?" I ask, playing along.

"Not exactly," Alaina interjects. "Earth and Allrhea are planets, existing each in their own physical universes in what you would call *other dimensions*. They are separated by space and time, and the only bridge between them is the Realms, a different dimension of its own."

I laugh out loud. None of what she's saying makes any sense, the three of them must be delusional. Or maybe this is some sort of game show. Maybe this whole thing was just some massive prank, and someone's about to walk in here with a video camera laughing at how dumb I am to believe any of this.

"If this was all a joke," Jane says slowly, "Then how would you explain the invisibility? Or this?" She lifts a hand, pausing for a few moments before a strange glow begins to emit from her fingertips, and tiny flecks of light like miniature stars begin to wink into existence over the tabletop. As I watch, transfixed, the light begins to gather together until I can make out the form of a little animal- a wolf. The wolf, barely bigger than my hand seems to be made of starlight, and it paces back and forth in the air, ears pricked, as though it's alive. And from in the sheaths at her waist, the two daggers Jane used earlier also begin to glow softly, as if in response.

Finally, the wolf begins to dissipate, dissolving into mist as the light dies away and the daggers' glow dulls. Jane lowers her hand, her face a shade paler, meeting my eyes which are wide with awe.

"Magic does exist, and so do other worlds. Now, are you willing to listen?"

CHAPTER 4

"The Realms act as the gateway between the worlds," Jane continues, as I now listen silently. What if what she's saying… is true?

"Allrhea is identical to Earth, everyone born on Earth has an exact counterpart born on Allrhea. Meaning when someone from Earth looks in a mirror, they are really looking through a window at their counterpart in Allrhea, and vice versa. If you can find the right mirror and can wield the right magic, you can use the mirror as a doorway into the Realms. From there, you can travel between the two worlds."

"So, let me get this straight," I interrupt, my head spinning with questions and doubt. "When I look in a mirror, what I'm really seeing is Allrhea? Another world? But if I were to travel *through* a mirror I would end up between them?" This is nonsense.

Jane, however, nods, as if this is all supposed to make perfect sense.

"How do you even travel through a mirror anyway?" I ask, exasperated.

"Ahh, that's the tricky part to understand," Alaina says, casually studying her nails, which are short but painted a rosy pink color.

"*This* is the tricky part?" I groan. "Then what was everything else, a casual chat about the weather?" I notice the corner of Reed's mouth twitch upward in an amused smile.

Jane holds up the mirror, the golden frame glinting in the dim candlelight, before resting it back on the table.

"Not just anyone can do it," she begins. "You need to possess magic to open a gateway and only certain mirrors are even powerful enough to open one. Most are just windows."

"Basically, if you possess both magic and a gateway mirror, then you can open a portal to the Realms," Reed adds, summing it up.

"So, you three can open portals?" I ask, rubbing my temples. This is all too weird. "How do you even know about this? I mean, like, who even are you?"

Jane pauses.

"We live in the Realms," Alaina explains. I raise an eyebrow.

"But why are you here? Does this have something to do with those men at the campsite…? And why are they after my mom and me?"

Jane's eyes soften, her expression one of sympathy.

"I'm so sorry to hear about your mom, Emmalina, I truly am. Those men in the clearing weren't after her, she was just the only thing that stood between them and you."

"Me?" I ask softly. "What do they want with me?"

"Because you also possess magic, Emmalina. Very powerful magic, if our suspicions are correct."

I snort bitterly.

"I don't have magic," I say. "You've got the wrong person."

"I don't think we do," Reed says bluntly, but after I mentioned my mother, the edge in his voice seems to have softened slightly. He gestures to my wrist, where the charm of my bracelet peeks out from beneath the still-damp sleeves of my sweatshirt.

"That right there, the charm on your bracelet, is a mark of your powers," he says matter-of-factly. "There are three types of magic, categories of sorts, that a person with magical gifts falls into depending on their abilities. They are Wolf Soldiers, Lynx Assassins, and Falcon Warriors. You possess the abilities of a falcon."

I shake my head. "I don't know what any of that means," I protest.

"It's a bit of a lengthy explanation," Jane says. "And Reed was right before, we've already spent as much time here as we can. We have to go."

"Go where?"

"To the Realms," Alaina answers with a spark in her eyes. I abruptly stand from the table, bracing my hands on the top, surprised to find that my foot holds my weight fairly decently.

"Okay, well you three have fun with that," I say. Magic or not, I'm not going to *another dimension*, if that really exists, not with these strangers I barely know. I have more pressing matters, like finding my mother.

Suddenly there is a noise outside. The sound of tires rolling along the gravel along the hill. The four of us are tense, waiting, and Jane slowly inches her way towards the window. She flicks the curtain back ever so slightly, peering out of the little crack into the early dawn outside. The sky has lightened a fraction, the sun still about a half hour off, but it provides just enough light for a clear view of the vehicle rumbling down the dirt roads along the seasonal sites. Heading in our direction.

It's a massive black armored truck, like what I imagine the military would use- the thing is practically a tank. Its giant tires leave rivets in the frozen ground, and I watch as two men dressed like the ones from the campsite jump out of the back.

"Alaina," Jane says, her voice steady but urgent.

"I've got it," she replies, lunging for the little mirror, scooping it into her small hands. The truck rumbles closer. The men spread out, peering into the windows of each of the abandoned cabins, searching. Searching for us.

Reed quickly blows out the candle and draws the curtains shut tight once more, while Jane moves for the trapdoor. I hear the little mechanical click as the hatch in the floor closes, and Jane rolls the matted rug back over to conceal it. Meanwhile, Alaina stands hunched over the mirror cupped in her palms, silent, concentrating, her eyebrows furrowed. Then the glass of the mirror begins to glow, softly at first, growing brighter with each passing second, until it's practically blinding, and a wall of pure white light almost eight feet tall forms in the air beside her. A portal. Shouts from outside indicate that the men in the truck have noticed the light leaking from the windows, leaving us maybe seconds before they're at the doorstep.

"Alright," Alaina breathes. "It's ready, we have to go!" She holds out the mirror in front of her, eyebrows still scrunched slightly in concentration. Jane goes first, glancing over her shoulder only once before stepping into the wall of light, and disappearing without a trace. Okay, I've seen enough, no way am I doing this. I've reached my limit of crazy for one night.

I try to back away, shaking my head, but Reed grabs my arm.

"What are you doing?" he asks, his voice urgent.

"I- I can't…"

"You have to," he insists, tugging me forward, but I dig my heels in. I can't, I won't.

"What, would you rather stay here?" he asks, his question accentuated by the sound of splintering wood as the men outside attempt to kick down the door. The lock is holding steady, but the wood is gradually giving way, and I can hear shouts from outside. I don't know what to do.

"Reed…!" Alaina shouts a bead of sweat on her forehead. He yanks me towards the portal, holding firm as I try to shove him away. The two of us step into the portal, submerged in light, just as the door caves in, leaving the metal lock mechanism clinging to the doorframe. Then the world is engulfed in white.

At first, I feel as though I'd gone blind. Everywhere is nothing but vast and empty light, like a peculiar opposite to the dark void from my dream. I feel weightless and immensely heavy at the same time, the light is warm to the touch but leaves a chill in my bones. The light begins to dance with oranges, reds, and a pale yellow, as though I've stepped into an inferno, as if the world around me is on fire. I close my eyes tight until I feel solid weight beneath my feet again.

I blink, my eyes adjusting to the brightness of the room, and my blind panic is joined with awe. I'm standing in a room made of glass, several hundred feet above the ground, the magnificent sunrise far off in the distance causing the room to sparkle in shades of reds and oranges. Thankfully, the colors are not an inferno, the room is not on fire. But the issue is the *hundreds of feet in the air* part, the glass floor allowing for a straight view to the ground.

I've never been quite afraid of heights before, but this is terrifying. Only when Reed tugs on my arm do I realize that I've been standing frozen, unable to look away from the immense distance below my feet, unable to move for fear that the floor will shatter and fall way from beneath me. Reed tugs again, pulling me several feet to the right, away from the wall of light still behind me. My breathing is rapid, my heart beating so fast it feels as though it's barely beating at all, strangely enough. Reed releases his grip on my arm just as Alaina tumbles from the portal, mirror clutched tightly in hand, and the portal dissipates as quickly as it appeared.

Alaina is breathing harder than I am as if it were a physical effort to keep the portal open for so long and allow several people through. I realize that I'm standing in between Jane and Reed, as Alaina moves to stand on Reed's right. As I'm watching, Reed bows his head, Jane and Alaina following suit, and I turn to see who they're bowing to. I'm completely surprised to find that we are not alone in this room.

The room is fairly large, the entire back space dominated by a wide dais, where atop sits a man seated on a grand throne. My eyes grow wide with astonishment. The throne is magnificent, made of what appears to be polished blue-tinged crystal, with a high back carved with swirling engravings and markings that I can't read. The man upon the throne is tall and regal, wearing a dark plated leather jacket lined with gleaming brass buttons, a thick silvery cloak draped over his shoulders which flows to the floor to pool around his feet. The cloak is embroidered with golden thread, the same strange markings as the throne. For some reason, the cloak looks so familiar.

The man has sandy blond hair, cropped short and neat, and piercingly dark brown eyes studying me with a contemplative expression. Nestled atop his head is a crown- a spiked band seemingly made out of the same crystal as the throne. He looks like some sort of prince or king, like the kind you would see in a fantasy movie on TV. He has a certain aura of power, of royalty.

The man on the throne waves his hand in acknowledgment, and Jane, Reed, and Alaina take that as their cue to stand from their bows. Who *is* this guy?

Someone clears their throat, the man on the throne turning his head slightly to face a second figure who strides forward from where he had been standing, unnoticed, in the corner. This man, in his late 30's, or 40's perhaps, is about average height, with close-cropped black hair. He wears a neat black tunic and pants, a scabbard for a sword strapped to his belt, and large boots. He is wearing a stern and unreadable expression, holding himself with an air of authority.

As he steps forward, I see Jane incline her head respectfully, and he raises an eyebrow. The man on the throne simply watches, his gaze unreadable.

"Miss Windervale," the second man addresses Jane. "We were told to expect your arrival over twenty minutes ago," he sounds deeply annoyed.

"It's my fault we're late, Your Majesty," Jane confesses, addressing the man upon the throne, who listens wordlessly. *Your Majesty?* Is this guy actually royalty? I guess that would explain the throne, the crown, and the strange outfit.

"We were just explaining a few things to Emmalina, before we brought her to you," Jane explains. He nods.

"That is quite understandable," he smiles softly, the first show of emotion I've seen him give. I cower slightly as he turns his attention to me.

"I imagine this is confusing for you," he begins, his voice a deep rumble. "Nonetheless, welcome to the Realms, Emmalina Maren."

"Please, Lina is fine. Your Majesty," I stumble over the words, unsure what else to say.

"Of course. Welcome, Lina. I am King Orlon, of the Mirror Realm," he pauses for a moment, spreading his hands in a grand gesture, but upon finding no reaction on my part, looks slightly confused.

"You... you have been informed of the Realms, yes?" he questions.

"Kind of- only that there are worlds... and other dimensions... and magic." He seems to be able to tell that I don't have much idea of whats going on.

"Ah, I see. Well, allow me to fill you in on a few important details," he says kindly.

"The Realms are a collection of three kingdoms, tasked with the job to defend the two worlds against any sort of magical interference."

"What do you mean?" I ask. "What sort of *magical interference* do you protect against?"

He shakes his head. "That may be a story for another time," he advises. "There is always evil in the world, in some form or another, that uses magic for its own end. It is the job of the Realms to prevent the two worlds from being harmed or the balance from being broken."

"But what do I have to do with any of this?" I protest. "I just want my mom back, I want to go home." I pause, aware that I just spoke to a king that way. Could he have me beheaded or something for being so disrespectful? The second man standing off to the side sure looks like he wants to, from the way he glares in my direction, my rudeness not going unnoticed. Alaina flinches and Jane's mouth tugs into a disapproving frown.

But the king doesn't look offended, but rather sad. Sympathetic.

"Lina, I am truly sorry," he says, clasping his hands in front of him. No, no I don't want to hear this. She isn't dead, she can't be.

"I knew your mother, a long time ago. She resided here, in this very palace."

"No," I protest, cutting in. "She couldn't have been, it's not true. She grew up in Ohio…"

"Lina, what has your mom ever told you about her life growing up? Any family or old friends come by to visit? Did she ever even tell you what town in Ohio she grew up in? What school she went to?" The king questions, his voice gentle. My mind spirals, coming up blank. No. She never told me anything, only about an old friend she used to have, who I'd never met. She never even told me about my dad. King Orlon can read the answer in my eyes.

"Your mom was a guard, a Wolf Soldier. In fact, she used to be my Second-in-Command," the king explains, and the second man's scowl deepens. Wolf Soldier? Like the three types of magic Jane explained. Could that have anything to do with the massive wolf at the campsite, the one that seemed to be defending my mom?

"Please, my mom was attacked, I need to help her," I beg. "If you're a king, that means you have an army, right? I was saved, why can't we send someone to rescue her?" The king's eyes soften sadly, making him look older. Strangely, he seems quite young for a king, maybe 30 at the oldest, his face a tanned golden brown, clean-shaven. He vaguely reminds me of a movie star that I had seen once or twice on TV.

"I'm afraid that the person who came after you in the woods- Lillian- is not one to be taken lightly," he says carefully.

There's that name again, Lillian.

"She is very powerful, she commands a great army of her own. They don't tend to take prisoners," he pauses as if allowing that to sink in. "I'm afraid Lina, there is nothing that can be done for your mother." I shake my head.

"No, no I refuse to believe that," I say, my vision blurring, but I refuse to cry. Not here, not in front of these strangers. Surprisingly, Reed speaks up, the last person I would have expected to defend me.

"There's a chance they could have kept her alive, to use as bait," he suggests, that strange sympathy in his eyes again.

"They could have taken her back to the Realms, that beam of light in the woods must have been some sort of portal."

"What beam of light in the woods?" the second man demands skeptically. Jane nods as if remembering what Reed's talking about.

"There was a spear of light, taller than the treetops," she recalls thoughtfully. "I've never seen a portal do something like that before, but that's what it must have been."

The king now looks intrigued, if not fearful.

"Can you describe it in more detail?" he presses.

"Well, it was tall enough to reach the clouds," Reed muses. "White light, thicker than a tree trunk, and disappeared after only a few moments." The king still looks troubled, wearing an expression of deep concentration lined with doubt.

"I'll look into this," he says, at last, not seeming inclined to elaborate.

"And my mom?" I ask hopefully. He gives a heavy sigh.

"It is unlikely that your mother is still alive," he repeats, his voice gentle. "That description of the beam of light doesn't sound like any sort of portal I've ever heard of, it would be better to put it behind you."

Put it behind me? How could he even say that? It feels as though the floor is crumbling beneath my feet, the last bit of hope I clung to now destroyed. She can't just be *gone*. I refuse to believe it.

"I'm tired," is all I say, my voice quiet. "I would like to go home."

"I'm afraid I cannot allow that, at this time," the king says apologetically. "It certainly isn't safe. Lillian will not have let you go so easily. She will still be after you."

"But why me?" I ask. That's the question above all that's been weighing on me. Why me? Why did this have to happen to me?

"It will all make sense, eventually," the king says, meaning it to sound reassuring. "But for now, you should rest. It's been a long night. Jane, will you show Lina to her room?" Jane nods stepping forward.

"And Lina," the king says, lifting himself gracefully from his throne, grasping a staff at his side that I hadn't noticed before.

"I'm sorry that you had to find out about the Realms in this way, but this is happening for a reason. We have been waiting a long time for you to learn to use your powers. For better or worse, that time has come."

CHAPTER 5

I wake from a dreamless sleep, blinking my eyes at the too-bright light filtering into the room, and I roll reluctantly onto my side. Half asleep, I push myself into a sitting position, prepared to fumble for the curtains I must have left open last night, but as my feet slide onto the ground I am startled by the feel of cold hardwood instead of the soft carpet of my bedroom floor.

It's because it's not my bedroom.

The events of last night come rushing back like a crashing tidal wave, and my eyes snap open, taking in my new surroundings. I'm in a palace, they had said, in the Realms. I am no longer on Earth.

I slide off the bed, which is bigger than my bed at home, the silver sheets are silky against my skin. To my amazement, the light in the room is filtering in, not from a window, but from the entire left wall, which is entirely made of glass just as the floor of that throne room had been. Luckily these floors are regular wood, and I can look down at my feet without the feeling that I'm floating hundreds of feet in the air. The view from the wall is just as astonishing. From this height, I can see for miles, past a large expanse of thick forests, to the base of a majestic mountain range in the distance, where the silhouette of a town nestles in the mountains' shadow.

The room around me is quite big but mostly empty and unadorned. Other than the bed, an armchair is nestled in the left corner, and a thick silver carpet is draped across the floor. There are two white-painted doors, one on the far wall and one to my right. Everything in this place seems to be varying shades of white and silver. I mean seriously, what do these people have against color? The size and the simpleness, as well as the lack of color or decoration, show that this room is empty and unlived in, reminding me of a fancy hotel room.

I see something gleaming on the small bedside table, my bracelet. I had forgotten I left it there last night before I passed out. I slept surprisingly well, despite everything that had happened only hours before. As I slip the bracelet on, I notice the small digital clock sitting on the edge of the table as well, reading 1:43 p.m., which catches me by surprise. The Realms, or what little I had seen of them anyway, didn't strike me as a technologically-reliant type of place. I don't know what I expected- maybe something more old-fashioned like a fantasy world in the books I have read, with horse-drawn carriages and magic wizards with wands, or something like that. Not digital alarm clocks, and lightbulbs in tiny chandeliers like the one dangling above my head. I guess digital alarm clocks and electricity are certainly convenient, even for a magical king. The thought makes me laugh quietly to myself. I wonder if the Realms also have smartphones or McDonald's.

As I take a few steps across the floor, I notice the silvery nightgown I'm wearing brushing against my heels. I was barely awake last night when Jane handed me something to wear, to replace my dirty, river-soaked clothing. I had barely registered her directing me to a bathroom through one of the two doors in the room, though I can't remember which it was, and I had swapped my clothes for the nightgown.

I venture in the direction of the doors, trying to remember which was the door to the bathroom. Going for the one on the wall across from the bed and opening it wide, my first thought is that I guessed correctly. My second thought is *wow*, my mouth hanging open slightly.

The bathroom is big, almost as big as the bedroom, with glittering marble floors, a walk-in shower with glass doors, an ornate sink and toilet in the far corner, and a massive bathtub. The ceiling accommodates a circular skylight, allowing light to spill into the room. All of this I had been too tired to register before, my clothes lying in a heap on the ground exactly where I had tossed them. I absentmindedly scoop them into a woven hamper beside the sink, since they are too filthy to put back on, but I can't just strut around the palace in a nightgown. I try the set of double doors across from the shower, which as I guessed, is a closet. The closet is spacious, lined with clothing racks, shelves, and ironically, mirrors. I stand in front of the closest one, studying my reflection more closely than I ever have before. My hair is a mess, my eyes wide, the flowy nightgown clinging to my body. I can't help but marvel disbelievingly at my reflection. It doesn't look like the reflection from my dreams, thankfully, but rather ordinary. Just a reflection in the glass.

I look away from the mirror to study the racks of clothes. Despite its size, the closet is pretty empty. But at least all of the clothes aren't silver and white. I finally decide on a simple blue, long-sleeved shirt and dark jeans, with a pair of plain sneakers. Everything fits perfectly, down to the size of my shoes. How did they get my shoe size? I find a hairbrush, as well as a toothbrush and toothpaste, on the sink. Once I clean myself up, emerging back into my room, I am suddenly a bit nervous. I have no idea what to expect.

Opening the second door in my bedroom, I step into a long hallway. It has a fancy arched ceiling, tall floor-to-ceiling windows, and white walls (what a surprise). The hallway stretches a long way, my light footsteps echoing slightly on the marble underfoot. I pass a few other doors leading to other rooms, all closed, and I can see a sort of garden outside through the windows. I appear to be walking in a very large circle around the garden, but there seems to be no one around. This place is a labyrinth.

"Hey," I hear a voice from behind me, and I spin with a momentary burst of surprise.

It's a boy, around my age, his hands held up in mock surrender.

"Sorry-" he says, his mouth curving into a joking smile. "I didn't think I was that scary." My face warms with embarrassment.

"And, by the way, why did you have to wander off like that?" the boy chides. "I mean, you could have picked any other moment to venture out of that room of yours, and you choose the one moment that I left my guard post," he rambles, sighing in frustration as I listen, bewildered.

"What?"

"I was supposed to be standing guard outside your room," he confesses bluntly. "In case you woke up, so you wouldn't be wandering around the palace like a lost puppy," he gestures his hand around as if indicating that's exactly what I'm doing.

"Just standing there, for three hours, doing nothing… well, I thought I might step away for a moment to grab a doughnut- this place has fabulous doughnuts by the way- and of course, you had to wake up and wander off in the mere five minutes I was gone." He pauses his rambling. "Well, okay, maybe it was more like 10 minutes…and three doughnuts, but that's not the point."

"I'm sorry," I cut him off, pinching the bridge of my nose. "Who are you again and what exactly are you talking about?"

He looks baffled at my question. "You don't have doughnuts on Earth?" he asks, looking scandalized. "You poor thing. Well, you see, they're this kind of sugary, doughy circle…"

"No," I interrupt again, torn between amusement and annoyance. "I know what a doughnut is. I meant about the *standing guard outside my room* thing. What is that all about?" He isn't dressed like a guard… or at least, he isn't wearing those black suits that Reed, Jane, and Alaina wore last night. Just jeans, and a buttoned-up jacket. He's a lot taller than me, with warm brown skin and dark, curly hair that he brushes out of his eyes.

"Ah, I see," he says, leaning casually against the wall as if this were just a normal conversation. He is taller than me, even when leaning, but he ignores my question.

"You're Emmalina, right?" he asks, though it doesn't seem like so much of a question, but rather a confirmation, but I nod anyway.

"Yeah, but you can call me Lina if you want."

"Cool. I'm Nate, and as for the *guarding your door* part, Jane told me to."

"Jane?"

"Yeah, the one you met last night, that Jane."

"Where is she? And Reed, and Alaina?"

"They're training right now. I could take you to them if you want."

I nod."Yes, please."

"Sure thing," he stands, waving to indicate that I should follow him, and doesn't so much as turn back to see if I do as he saunters forward.

"Also, maybe when we get there, don't mention to Jane anything about the, uh, doughnuts?"

I turn my laugh into a cough. "It'll be our secret," I promise.

We stop at a set of plain, unadorned double doors made of heavy wood set on thick metal hinges. I can hear the sound of voices, and the distinct, muffled clanging of steel.

"Here we are," Nate says, crossing his arms.

"And where is here?"

"A training room," he answers.

"Training for what?" I question.

"Stuff," he says, tapping his foot irritatingly. I sigh, exasperated, and reach for the door handle to find out for myself.

The door is kind of heavy, the brass handle twisting with an echoing click, swinging wide to reveal a peculiar room. It is very large and spacious, lined with what resembles wrestling mats, the far wall hung with wooden sticks of different widths and lengths. In this so-called training room, I first spot Reed. He has one of the longer wooden staffs in his hand, spinning and jabbing it, and adjusting his hands on the leather-wrapped end as he gives pointers to a group of people gathered at his feet, watching.

They're kids, I realize, no more than 11 or 12 years old, seated cross-legged on the mat-lined floor while Reed gives some sort of demonstration, using the wooden staff to block imaginary attacks. Are they training kids to *fight*, like the three of them fought in the woods?

Alaina doesn't seem to be here, but I spot Jane leaning against a wall, watching Reed speak. He barely glances my way as the door opens, continuing his lesson as if I weren't here, but he has clearly lost the group's attention.

All of the kids turn towards me, maybe 20 of them altogether, Reed grudgingly pausing his lesson as he lowers the staff to his side and brushes his hair from his eyes. Jane looks up curiously, pursing her lips together.

"Uh, hi…" I say, wringing my hands as I awkwardly linger in the doorway. "I didn't mean to interrupt." The kids watch me with wide-eyed curiosity. They almost look… afraid.

"Ah, you're too polite," Nate grumbles, pushing past me as he strides into the room. "You're not even interrupting anything." He plops himself down on the floor, leaning back against the wall and crossing his arms behind his head.

"Well, actually," Reed speaks up, his brow creasing in annoyance. "We were kind of in the middle of an important lesson."

"Oh, of course," Nate interrupts, propping one leg up over the other, shifting into a more comfortable position. "My bad, carry on with your *incredibly important* lesson. Don't mess up."

Reed's eyes narrow, and Jane rubs at her temples as though Nate is giving her a headache.

"Why exactly are you here?" she questions.

"I asked him to bring me here," I pipe in. "I was looking for you and Reed."

"Of course you did," she sighs. "Well, that's Nate, Alaina's boyfriend. And Nate, this is-"

"We've already done the introductions," Nate says. "I beat you to it."

One kid, a young boy sitting in the center of the group, raises his hand, his eyes wide and round as he stares in my direction. As I turn to him, he blurts out.

"Are you Lillian?" three other kids gasp, and Reed's eyes widen at the question. Lillian… that's the person the king mentioned, the one who was after my mom and I. The brief thought of my mom is like a punch to my gut, but I force my attention back to the kids at my feet.

"No, she is not Lillian," Jane speaks up, casting a glance at me.

"But she looks just like her," the kid protests, eyeing me distrustfully.

"She's not Lillian," Reed says firmly.

"But-"

"Connor, that's enough," Jane commands. "You know what, I think we should end this lesson early." There was a collection of muttering, some happy and some disappointed, as the kids scrambled to their feet and began to collect their things. The young boy, Connor, remained seated, staring in my direction.

"Connor," Reed says warningly, and the boy gives in with a grumble. It only takes a minute or two before all of the kids are packed up and filed out of the room, some carrying backpacks and notebooks in their arms, many casting questioning looks in my direction as they leave. Once we have the room to ourselves, I speak up.

"What was that all about?" I ask.

"Nothing," Reed answers briskly, gathering staffs and random wooden swords that lay scattered throughout the room and hanging them back in the display on the wall. What kind of place trains children to fight?

"What did he mean, when he said I look like Lillian?" I press, refusing to drop the matter. "Did he mean Lillian, as in the lady with the army? The one who was hunting me in the woods?"

"Yes," Jane says gently. "They were just a little confused since most people have just been really on edge since… well, since the war…" She seems to be grasping for excuses.

"What war?" I question. Jane looking at a loss for words. "What does it have to do with me? What does any of this have to do with me?"

"Well," Nate chimes in, "Let's just say you two share a certain resemblance."

"It's nothing you need to worry about right now," Reed says, as he puts away the last of the weaponry. Jane nods.

"Well, if you're not going to explain that, then, why don't you explain why I was brought here."

"We brought you here to protect you," Jane says. "Lillian was after you, for reasons you don't understand, and we saved your life by bringing you here."

"You're right, I don't understand," I say, frustrated. "So explain it to me then. Why is Lillian after me? What did I ever do to her? I don't even know who she is."

"She's a psychopath," Reed interjects, his voice cold. "A crazy person with magic stronger and deadlier than anyone in the Realms has ever encountered, stronger than the king himself. About two years ago she snapped and went on a complete rampage, with the singular goal of bringing the Realms and everyone in it to their knees. The Realms have been fighting back with all we've got, and it isn't enough. As for why she's after you…"

"That's enough, Reed," Jane hisses.

"No," I say, my voice quivering. "Tell me. I believe I deserve to know, at least."

"You remember what we told you, about everyone born in one of the worlds having a counterpart, a doppelganger of sorts, in the other world, which is what you actually see when you look in a mirror?" I nodded, vaguely remembering something like that from the lengthy explanation in the cabin.

"Well, Lillian is your counterpart. She looks exactly like you, talks like you, she basically *is* you."

My mind is having trouble comprehending what Reed is saying. I laugh, dry and humorless.

"But wouldn't that make Lillian just a 17-year-old girl?" I question. "I am probably the least threatening person you will ever meet, so how could my doppelganger-person-thing-"

"Counterpart. Or reflection," Reed corrects snarkily. I scowl at him.

"Fine. How could my *counterpart* be Lillian? What magic could she possibly have that a whole world of magical warriors can't defeat her?" I demand.

"Her magic is death," Nate pipes in, serious for the first time since I've met him.

"But what about it makes her so deadly? I'm guessing it isn't invisibility," I say, unable to keep the sarcasm from my voice. "What, can she shoot fireballs from her hands or something?"

"No, her magic is *literally* death," Reed answers. His face was as expressionless and cold as ice.

"Though fireballs would be pretty cool," Nate says, pondering.

"Not the time, Nate," Jane mutters, and he has the decency to look apologetic.

"Lillian's magic is centered in her hands," Reed explains. "If her hand directly touches someone, her skin to theirs, she can kill them if she wishes to."

I blink in surprise. "What do you mean...?"

"Her touch is like poison," Jane explains softly. "She can choose to channel her magic into whoever her hand touches, and no living thing can survive it. Her magic is quite literally the power to kill someone within seconds." I gape at her, at a loss for words, but she continues.

"Since she is your counterpart, you both share everything. Same looks, same voice, same way of thinking. Same abilities."

I can feel the blood drain from my face, a sense of dread settling over me like a dark and heavy cloud. No. No, she can't mean what I think she means, but I can read the confirmation in her eyes. I remember how the men in the clearing had refused to touch my hands without their gloves, one of the men resorting to grabbing my neck to turn me invisible. How the taller one had flinched away when I tore off his glove. How Reed, Jane, and Alaina had all been wearing gloves as well. Likely not to protect against the cold, but to protect against *me*. Against what I could do. Jane seems to read the understanding in my face, sympathy was written across hers. Reed's expression remains unreadable.

"I'm sorry, Lina, but we have every reason to believe that you and Lillian possess the same magical abilities. That you possess the power of death."

The power of death.

The thought still rings in my head, even several hours later. It can't be true... can it? And what they said, about also sharing the same way of thinking... Lillian is a sociopathic crazy person who commands an army and seems to want me dead. These people don't even know me, and if they did, they would know that I'm nothing like that, I wouldn't ever hurt anyone. If they're wrong about that, then they could be wrong about my abilities too.

But what if they're not?

What if somewhere inside me, I have the power to kill someone with a single touch. What if I'm a monster, like her?

It can't be true.

The next several hours pass in a daze. Jane had decided it would be a good idea to give me a tour, perhaps to distract me from the alarming truth she had struck. I can tell her heart isn't in it, and neither is mine, nor Reed's. The only person that seems to be getting a kick out of showing me around is Nate.

"-And those are the gardens," he continues, gesturing outside the windows. From what I can see, it looks like the castle is built in a circular shape, the crystalline building wrapping around a towering glass dome at the very center. It's massive, taller than the lower towers, constructed of interconnected glass panels forming a dome shape. The glass is foggy and blurred, obscuring the view of what's inside. Wrapping around the outskirts of the dome are the gardens, a sprawling tangle of plants dotted with gushing fountains of water. Most of the plants are leafless, scraggly, and bare from the touch of winter, but the carved stone benches beside the fountains are still polished, the worn paths lined with twinkle lights, providing a warm and welcoming glow.

Reed notices me admiring the gardens, and the glass dome nestled at the center. It's the first thing I've really admired all day.

"That is what we call the Centerdome," Reed says, following my gaze.

"What's inside?" I ask, curiosity beginning to bubble tentatively to the surface. Reed actually cracks a rare smile.

"Why don't we show you?"

Reed leads our small tour group back through the winding hallways, and down several flights of stairs, until there are no more windows and the halls are entirely lit by miniature chandeliers dangling at intervals in the ceiling. I think we're below ground level now.

We finally come to a halt at a set of doors, but unlike the other doors of the palace which were ornate and decorative, these were clearly meant to keep people out. I shiver, the air slightly colder down here, the dimmer lighting slightly ominous.

The doors are made of thick metal- iron or steel. No carvings, no decorative markings, doorknobs, or fancy locks. Just a metal square fitted on the wall beside them, with a single slot through the middle. Before I could ask how we're supposed to get inside, Reed grasps a laminated card dangling off of a thin lanyard around his neck, swiping it swiftly through the slot in the metal square. A little light blinks green, and with a satisfying click and a mechanical hiss, the metal doors begin to slide open and retract into the wall. All I could think was, cool!

The hallway beyond them, however, is not nearly as cool. It is just another hall identical to the one we just came through. As we go, we have to pass through two more sets of doors just like the ones we came through. Why the intense security? Each door slides shut as we enter, locking us in as we travel deeper.

When we reach the last hallway... a dead end.

There's nothing, not even a doorway. This doesn't deter Reed though, as he strides to the wall, and presses the card against it. I watch curiously as blue light, emitting from the wall itself, slides over the card face as if the wall were one big scanner. I jump as the ceiling begins to open up, Jane tugging me forward as the floor we're standing on begins to rise so that I don't topple off. I gaze in wide-eyed amazement as the floor lifts us higher, into a new room, and I take in the space around me.

It's circular shaped and about as wide as a football field, the walls and ceiling towering above us to form a dome of glass panels. While the glass had looked blurred from the outside, preventing me from clearly seeing in, the view from the inside is clear as day. I watch a cluster of birds circling, many stories above.

"This is…" I begin to say, struggling to find the words.

"Amazing?" Nate suggests, grinning. I nod.

It appears to be a training room of some sort. The lower walls and floor are lined with mats in certain spots, other sections roped off like wrestling rings. The upper half of the room is divided from the floor by a wide, tightly woven net suspended in the air, connected and spanned by metal catwalks. It hangs just below what appears to be an obstacle course.

The course looks like something straight out of those Ninja Warrior TV shows, where the contestants pull off crazy stunts on complicated obstacles. In other words, it is awesome.

"Impressive, isn't it?" Jane asks, surveying the course above our heads. She frowns, glancing back towards the ground where several wooden swords lay scattered on the mats.

"The trainees," she explains, nudging one with a toe. "They never clean up after themselves."

"This is a training room?" I ask incredulously. "For children? Isn't that a little dangerous?" I picture the 11 and 12-year-olds Jane and Reed had been instructing. Jane laughs.

"Yes, the trainees practice here, but the obstacle course is more geared for 17 and 18-year-olds to train."

"Wait, you three are trainees too?" I ask.

"Kind of," Reed answers. "We aren't full guards yet- you only become a full guard at age 19. We still train, but we can be trusted with important missions and teaching the younger trainees. It's kind of like a part-time job. 17 and 18-year-olds get assigned to a small group, a legion, where you finish your guard training."

"Booringggg," Nate interrupts in a singsong voice. "Can we get on to the fun stuff please?" he asks, impatiently crossing his arms.

"Nate, you're such a child," Jane says, rolling her eyes, but Reed's eyes glint with excitement.

"If you think this is impressive," he says, "Wait until you see what it can do."

Reed opens a massive panel attached to one of the walls, looking like a giant electrical box. It holds a control board filled with wires and tiny computer monitors. He seems to have dropped his usual gruff dislike for me for a moment, too eager to show off the training room gadgets.

Before I can wonder what might happen, Reed flips a small switch, and the mats on the floor begin to fold back. The floor beneath is made of thick metal panels arranged in a spiral, which slowly begin to retract, creating a massive hole in the floor. It's circular, like the room, and very deep. Lights flicker on, illuminating rows of seating around a wide-open floor, like an old-fashioned gladiator arena.

"The Centerdome is equipped with a fighting ring and the obstacle course," Reed explains, gesturing to the arena below us and the obstacles suspended above our heads.

"It also has a swimming pool for water training, a running track, a rock wall, a war council room, and a basketball court," he pauses, frowning in thought. "Don't ask me why there's a basketball court, because I don't really know why."

He presses a few more buttons, flipping a few more switches, and the floor of the arena retracts to reveal a swimming pool even farther below, which rises until it's level with the floor we're standing on. Panels on the walls slide outward, revealing a rock wall that towers over our heads and basketball hoops protrude from the lower levels. Finally, a disco ball emerges from one of the catwalks above us, casting the room in swirling colors that reflect off of the glass and playing old-fashioned disco music.

Jane arches an eyebrow at Reed, who glances at the disco ball in confusion.

"That's new," he mutters, and Nate begins to laugh until he's doubled over, wheezing. Reed, his face flushing red, tries to find the button to retract the disco ball, but only succeeds in making it spin faster, like a top. The swirling colors make me dizzy. Nate cannot control his laughter, gasping for breath as he suggests, "Play some rock and roll!"

Frustrated, Reed scrambles to press another button, and the disco ball begins to blare rock music and flash red and blue, not slowing in the slightest, while Nate howls with glee.

Giving up, Reed slams a big red button, causing the disco ball to successfully retract, as well as the pool, rock wall, and basketball hoops until the room looks like it was before. Jane suppresses a smile, Nate steadying himself against the wall Reed gives an apologetic smile.

"Ta-da!" he says, his voice strained by the chaos he just caused.

Jane gives a slow and sarcastic clap.

"That was incredible!" I say, my eyes wide and grinning like a crazy person. "A bit strange, but incredible!" Reed surprisingly grins back, and for a moment there is no hostility or detachment. Then he seems to remember that he doesn't actually like me, because he quickly turns away, and I feel a strange twinge of disappointment…and anger. Why is he so determined to hate me? For a moment, just a moment, I got a glimpse of who he is behind that mask he wears. Why is he so determined to hide behind it?

"Well, now that the show's over," Jane begins, crossing her arms. "Would you like to see more of the palace?" I nod enthusiastically, my newfound admiration of this tour renewed. I wonder if any other parts of the palace have swimming pools or disco balls.

"Lead the way," I say.

CHAPTER 6

Sadly, the rest of the tour doesn't involve any more chaotic disco music. But on the bright side, there's food. The tour leads past the kitchens, and I can smell the scent of food wafting from several halls away. My stomach grumbles, reminding me that I haven't eaten since yesterday, and it's already getting late. Jane promised that we will stop by the dining hall for dinner.

"So, your ankle must be feeling better," Jane says after we've walked in silence for several minutes.

"Hmm?" I ask, jolted out of my thoughts, which were mostly about food.

"Your ankle?" she repeats quizzically. Right. That's strange. Yesterday I could barely walk, and today I've been trekking around the castle without so much as a twinge of pain. I also realize that all of my other bruises and scrapes from the night before have miraculously disappeared. Weird.

"That's odd," I say out loud. I test my weight harder against it, going as far as to hop up and down on my foot, but there's nothing. "I guess it must not have been so bad."

At that moment, we're interrupted by a voice to the left.

"I absolutely loved the light show, Reed," we hear, as I turn to see a familiar face materialize out of thin air. Alaina.

"It was a spectacular display of how *not* to use a disco ball," she chides, leaning against the wall she appeared in front of. Her eyes, a startling turquoise color, fix on me and she smiles welcomingly.

We hear footsteps moments before another figure rounds the corner of the hall, coming to a stop a few feet away. It's a boy, also around my age, several inches taller than me with blonde hair a few shades lighter than mine, and a friendly smile. He waves at the group, but his eyes catch on me.

"Stefan," Reed says, surprised. "I thought you two were working in the Com's room. What are you doing outside of the Centerdome?"

"It's almost dinnertime, silly," Alaina corrects him. "Our shifts just ended. As for why we're here, we were curious as to why the Centerdome had suddenly become the Realm's largest strobe light," Reed's face flushes with embarrassment. Taking that as a sign of confirmation, Alaina laughs.

"See!" she says, whipping towards the boy named Stefan with a victorious grin on her face. He sighs and passes her what looks like a five-dollar bill, and she pockets it gleefully.

"You two bet on this?" Jane questions, glancing between the two of them.

"Well," Alaina confesses, "Stefan bet me five bucks that it was Nate who set off the light show, while I was positive it couldn't be him because Reed would never allow Nate to touch his precious control panel, so I bet that it was Reed." She grins.

"Hey, it was so not my fault," Reed protests, "Aravian needs to put labels on the things he adds."

"Aravian?" I ask curiously, "Who's that?"

Alaina rolls her eyes dramatically.

"Ugh, Aravian," she says, her tone implying that he is not very well-liked. "He's the king's architect and strategist."

"And a total jerk," Nate snorts.

"No one likes him," Reed chimes in, "But he is one of the best architects the Realms have seen in years. He redesigned the Centerdome."

"Really?" I ask, wondering how one person could have designed something so spectacular. "What do you mean re-designed? What did it look like before?"

"I don't know," Reed says, shrugging. "I was only like, eight years old when the original Centerdome was destroyed. I'm told that Aravian didn't change much from the first design, only added on features."

"Like the disco ball," Alaina snickers at Reed's answering scowl.

"Wait," I say, "How was the Centerdome destroyed? Did Lillian do it?" I ask, genuinely curious.

"No," Jane snorts. "Lillian, and you, would have been only seven years old at the time. No, the Centerdome was destroyed in another war, when its original creator, Malcolm, promised everyone that it was foolproof, impenetrable. It was used to house something very valuable that the king didn't want the other side to steal, and when its mechanisms failed, the object was lost as the Centerdome went up in flames. We later found out Malcolm rigged the whole thing, turned traitor, and stole the object, before fleeing into the night."

"Are we seriously giving a history lesson right now?" Nate sighs dramatically, crossing his arms. "We're going to be late for dinner." As if on cue, my stomach grumbles in agreement.

Jane gives Nate another of her trademark annoyed looks. "Lead the way," I say.

The walk to the dining hall is brief, and I find myself strolling side by side with the golden-haired boy. Alaina and Nate, leading our group, are talking and laughing with each other, and Alaina casually winds her fingers through his. Behind them, Jane and Reed are quietly discussing something, while Reed fiddles absentmindedly with the watch on his wrist- the one with the weird symbols instead of numbers.

"I don't think I ever got to introduce myself," the boy beside me says. "I'm Stefan. And you're Emmalina, right?"

"It's just Lina," I answer, feeling strangely shy, and he smiles.

"How are you liking the Realms so far, Lina?" Stefan asks idly.

"It's… weird," I say, struggling to find the words to describe it. "Everything here is so bizarre- I'm still having trouble wrapping my head around the idea of magic," I laugh a bit humorlessly. "It's even strange to say the words out loud."

He laughs. "You'll get used to it." His eyes catch on the bracelet hanging around my wrist, the glinting silver charm. Gently, slowly, he lifts my hand in his to study the bracelet, amazed.

He asks, "Are you excited to know that magic is real? That you can do things that you never knew were possible?" He smiles knowingly. That's when I realize, he's touching my hand, holding it in his. He must be aware of what I can potentially do, but unlike the others, there is no fear.

Then Reed clears his throat. His head is turned, glaring at Stefan and me, at my hand resting in his. I quickly pull away. Jane also glances over her shoulder, looking worried.

As for his question, as amazing as this all might be, I can't say that I'm excited for this to be happening to me. Losing my mom, being practically kidnapped from my home by strangers, and getting told I'm a monster are nowhere near what I'd call *exciting*. More like some twisted bad dream.

But I don't say any of those things. Stefan and I walk in silence the rest of the way, until we reach a wide entryway, leading to what must be the dining hall. The room is massive and open, with rows of tables facing a raised platform. Atop the platform is another table, smaller, with only five seats. In the middle, perched in a chair that almost resembles a throne carved

of wood, is King Orlon himself. The king sits in a casual
position, talking and laughing with those seated at the head
table, drinking from a wine glass.

In the seat to his left is the man I had seen before in the
throne room when we first came through the portal. He sits
straight-backed, a platter of food barely touched before him. He
is likely in his early forties, with dark hair and a graying goatee.
His face is pinched into a scowl, just as it was when we arrived,
as though that's the only expression he knows how to make.

Sitting beside him, the farthest to the left is another man.
He is very tall, even sitting down, with a long and lanky form.
He is younger, maybe in his thirties, with a narrow face and
reddish-colored hair. He is smiling, but in a smug and self-
satisfied way, his eyes too small and beady looking, like a rat's.

On the king's other side sits a man and woman. The
woman is young and pretty, likely in her twenties, and easily the
youngest at the table. Her skin is a rich, dark color, with curly
brown hair hanging loose around her face and a brilliant smile.
The man beside her is old, his face wrinkled and worn. He also
seems to be very short, his feet barely able to touch the floor,
and wearing full body armor as if he's planning to go to war
with his dinner.

"That is the king's court and council," Stefan says under
his breath, following my gaze. "The man there beside Orlon, the
one who looks like he just swallowed a lemon, that's Marcus.
He's the king's second-in-command. The walking scarecrow on

the left is Aravian, Royal Architect and Strategist. Also a Royal Jerk," Stefan mutters.

"The woman, that's Ivory, one of the three Captains of the Guard. And the old guy, that's General Vaan, who leads the armies."

I just know I'm never going to remember all of their names.

Jane ushers us all to one of the tables, which is practically overflowing with people of all ages. One table is teeming with kids, all around 12 to 15 years old. They must be the trainees. Another table is designated for the older trainees, 17 or 18, which is where Jane leads us. The other tables are filled with adults, some dressed in armor. The guards.

Waiters and waitresses wander around the hall with platters filled with food- plates of roast chicken, steaks, turkey, and other cuts of meat. Others have plates filled with kinds of pasta, salads, tofu, roasted vegetables, and bowls of soups. One waitress places glasses in front of each of us, filling them to the brim with drinks of our choice.

I'm squeezed onto a spot on the bench between Stefan and Alaina, with Reed, Jane, and Nate sitting across from us. Nate immediately begins shoveling food into his mouth, digging into the spread before us, while both Jane and Alaina give him judgmental looks.

The food smells heavenly and tastes even better, but I still can't find it in me to enjoy it. The clatter of silverware and chatter of hundreds of voices echo throughout the hall, off the towering ceiling. Massive windows along the walls offer a brilliant view of rolling mountains and the far-off town. The noise heightens with excitement as flurries of snow begin to drift through the air, stark against the fading colors of the setting sun.

"It's beautiful, isn't it?" I hear Stefan beside me say, staring out of the window closest to us. I nod, my fork pausing over my plate as I watch the snow.

"The Mirror Palace has some great views," Alaina agrees, moving from her meal to dessert as she picks apart a raspberry tart. "But if you think this is amazing, you should see the views from the Soul Realm towers," she sighs. I perk up a bit at that.

"When do you think I'll be able to see the other Realms?" I ask. "The Soul Realm and the Shadow Realm?" Jane frowns slightly as Reed speaks up.

"Well, that's kind of the issue," he explains. "Trainees have a summer break and a winter break, to go home. Then you can do whatever you want, go wherever you want. Unfortunately while training, we're not allowed to leave unless we're specifically sent on a mission by someone in the king's Court," he gestures to the head table. "Or you get permission from the king or Marcus for a different reason. Leaving without their permission is forbidden by law."

"So we're not allowed to leave?" I ask. Jane shakes her head.

"Not until winter break, in December."

"But how else will I find my mom?"

Jane looks up from her food with surprise, "What?"

"Lillian has to have brought her somewhere, one of the other Realms maybe, somewhere we can send a search party to get her back."

"Lina, I'm sorry to say this," Jane says, her voice softer than I would expect, "but your mom probably isn't even alive. Lillian doesn't take prisoners unless she has a specific need for them, and she was after you, not her."

"Exactly, she was after me," I protest, refusing to take that as an answer. "So wouldn't she keep her alive to get to me? Someone should at least try."

"Even if she did, you're not going anywhere near her," Reed says sharply. "You're not trained, you're not a guard. She wants you for a reason, so there is no way we're just going to hand you over. And besides, we don't even know where Lillian's stronghold is- if we knew that, things might be different."

"But I'm not just going to stay here as your prisoner."

Reed fixes me with a look, and I grudgingly drop the matter, for now at least. I sit there, fuming for a moment, until Stefan says, "You're not a prisoner." He fixes me with a gentle look. "We're just keeping you here for your safety, and to prevent Lillian from getting what she wants. Besides, we're allowed free roam of the Mirror Realm, and guards are allowed to go home for a Winter Break."

"Home? So you don't live in the palace?" I ask.

"Stefan and Nate don't live here, we just stay here while training. The Mirror Palace sort of acts as a boarding school, for trainees."

"Then do you live in the other Realms?"

Stefan chimes in, "I'm from the Shadow Realm."

"I live in the Soul Realm," Nate adds, his mouth full of cheesecake, "With my dad." He adds in that last part almost like an afterthought, his tone sounding a bit bitter.

"Jane and I used to live here in the Mirror Realm," Reed says, gesturing out the window at the town in the distance, shrouded by the growing snowstorm. "Right over there in Penrith." His voice has a strange tone to it, almost mournful. Jane's eyes are downcast as she gazes out of the glass pane crusted with ice.

"Used to?" I ask, and immediately wish I didn't. Reed's eyes take on that distant coldness again.

"Yeah, used to. Now our home is here, at the palace," he offers no other explanation, and I don't push for one. His eyes flash with anger, anger directed my way, as though he somehow blames me for whatever caused him to leave his home in Penrith. It doesn't make any sense. But quickly, Alaina breaks the lingering silence.

"I live here too," she pipes up. "I've been in this palace my whole life."

"Are you royalty?" I question, my eyes a bit wide, but she only laughs.

"No, I wish," she says. "That would be cool. But no, I live here because.. well… it's kind of complicated," she seems to struggle to find an explanation. Nate chuckles.

"I think that kind of sums up everything," he says, again with that strange bitterness. "It's complicated."

I open my mouth to ask another question, but all at once, the entire room goes silent. The talking fades to whispering, then absolute silence. Even the clinking of silverware and dinner plates was quiet. Everyone seems to have turned towards the front of the room, towards the head table. As I look over my shoulder behind me, I see why.

King Orlon has stood, his cape fanning out behind him like the wings of a silver falcon. The analogy is almost ironic. His face is composed and regal, his crown sparkling atop his brow. It feels surreal, to see him standing there like this is a dream or a movie I'm watching from afar. Like a play, thrust into this made-up world with these unreal people, and I can't seem to remember what my role is here.

"I have an exciting announcement to make," the king declares, his smile warm, "As you all know, an expedition was sent out a week ago, tasked with an important mission. And as many of you may have realized, they have been successful."

His words were met with muttering, some excited and some nervous. The people closest to us looked up, right at me. Seeing the directions of others' gazes, the majority of the room began to turn in my direction, mouths agape with awe and surprise. No. No, this can't be happening. Don't say it, don't let this "exciting announcement" be about me. I shrink back under the gaze of so many, but Orlon continues his speech.

"I want to welcome our guest, Emmalina Maren," his eyes meet mine across the room, still smiling warmly and welcomingly. The man sitting beside him, however, the man named Marcus, only fixes me with a cold and distasteful glare. The other court members were also gazing my way- the tall, thin man with a look of shrewd curiosity, the woman with a smile as friendly as Orlon's, and the short man in the armor with narrowed eyes.

I shrink further in my seat.

There's a girl, sitting at the table across from us, glaring in my direction. Her hair is a silvery blonde, and her eyes… one is a light golden brown, the other is jade green, both glinting with disdain.

First Reed, and now this girl? What did I do to offend these people? Could it be my likeness to Lillian?

"Ignore her," Stefan mutters, catching who I'm looking at. "That's Eliza. Don't take the bad attitude personally- she's like that with everybody, and I mean *everybody*. Best to just stay out of her way, it's what I do."

I sneak another glance back, relieved to see that she's turned away, but plenty more people are still staring.

"I think I'm finished," I say quietly, pushing away my empty plate, the food roiling in my stomach from grief and embarrassment.

"Of course," Stefan says, understanding in his eyes. "Dinner will be finished in a few minutes, and I can show you back to your room if you're tired."

"No," I say. "Before I go, I need to talk with King Orlon."

"About what?" Jane asks, poking her food with her fork.

"I need to convince him to let me find my mom."

None of them thought that this was a good idea, but finally gave in when it became clear I wasn't dropping the matter again. They probably just think Orlon will shoot down the idea, and that will be that, but I'm not going to just sit in this palace and do nothing when there's still a chance I can save her. I'm not taking no for an answer.

Jane walked me up to the head table. Orlon and the members of his court waited patiently while I again asked them for a search party to find my mom. The response was pretty much exactly what I expected, and what my friends had said would happen.

There was a mix of expressions from pity to suspicion, the man named Aravian fixing me with an assessing glare. Orlon only says, "I'm afraid we do not know where Lillian could be keeping her, or even if she is still alive. We're doing all we can, but I'm afraid that there is nothing we can do, at least at the moment."

"Then let me try to find her. I'll go back to the campsite, maybe find a clue as to what Lillian did with her," I begin to beg, but Orlon cuts me off with a dismissive wave of his hand.

"I can't let you do that. You are not a Realm Guard, you have no chance against Lillian without training."

"Then train me," I say, taking a deep breath. "Train me to be a guard, or whatever it's called, and then I can search for her."

The dark-haired man with the scowl, Marcus I think, gives a harsh laugh.

"It isn't that simple, girl. Being a guard isn't something that you can just do. It requires years of training before you even become a trainee. I doubt you've ever even held more than a dull kitchen knife, never mind fought with a sword, or magic. You would probably turn tail and flee the moment you came across an actual challenge, barely more than a Worlder. You've never even seen real magic since before last night, and now you want to just *become* a guard?"

I wince at the verbal onslaught, but I stand my ground.

"I can't wait *years*," I beg, "I know I can't just become a guard, but what if I can prove myself? I can train, learn to fight if you just give me a chance…I can handle it. It's my mother's life on the line, I'm not going to run away. If I have to stand up against Lillian herself, I'll do it, just, please. Give me a chance."

Orlon seems to think long and hard about my offer.

"Becoming a guard is complicated for many reasons, not just the training you would have to face. Being a Realm Guard means swearing to protect the Realms, not just for your own personal gain. If I were to allow you to join our ranks, once you take the oath, you would be sworn to me and the Realms by magic. Are you willing to hand over your future for this?"

Jane looks like she's about to object, but changes her mind. Orlon's council and court watch me closely, my first real test. Not that there's any question in my mind.

"Of course. To save her, I'll do it. I'll become a Realm Guard, I'll even help you fight against Lillian. I just need to save my mom."

Orlon nods, as if that was the answer he wanted to hear.

"Alright then. I can't simply make you a Realm Guard, you still need to be a trainee first. But I'll make a deal with you, you have a week to train, and after that, you must prove you have what it takes to become a trainee. If you can prove that to me, then you will be placed in Miss Windervale's legion," he gestures to Jane standing behind me. "Then we'll talk further about letting you save your mother."

I nod, "But how will I prove myself?" I ask tentatively.

"I'm afraid I can't give it away, not entirely," he says, with a twinkle in his eyes, "But I have faith that you'll be up for the challenge."

CHAPTER 7

I wake once again to bright, glaring sunlight filling the room, pouring in from the glass wall. Normally I would have been annoyed by it, but I've begun to welcome the early start. I have work to do.

It's been three days since I arrived in the Mirror Realm and my old life was scattered to the wind. Orlon had given me only a week to prepare for whatever challenge he has in mind, to prove myself able to handle becoming a trainee, and only then will I be able to begin finding out how to rescue my mom. If I fail, it will be years before Orlon deems me ready to help find her, and by then it will be far too late.

I'm determined to get this right.

I've spent the past days training, my newfound friends agreeing to help, and Orlon granting them time off from their usual duties. First, Jane gave me a basic rundown of fighting like a guard- how to handle a dagger, a sword, and armor. It became clear very quickly that I'm useless with a bow, and can't possibly learn that skill in a week. Alaina has helped me out with agility training and exercises in the lower levels of the

Centerdome, and that at least felt a little more familiar, no more than training for a sport, though Alaina was quite the drill sergeant about it.

Today, Stefan volunteered to teach me specifically about self-defense, both with and without a weapon.

I can't believe I'm doing this. What have I agreed to? But I signed up for this boot camp of ridiculousness, and for my mom, I'm going through with it.

That's what I try to tell myself each time I end up on my butt, in the dirt of the small forest clearing outside the palace that we are using as a sparring ground. Stefan smirks, helping haul me back to my feet.

"You have to work on your balance," he corrects, "When sparring, you don't need a whole bunch of fancy footwork, you just need to keep moving, and keep yourself grounded. Try it again."

I settle into the stance Stefan demonstrates, trying to anticipate which way he'll go… I hesitate too long, and he leaps forward. I move as he told me to - trying to dodge and block each swing of his sword, the edges thankfully dulled and mostly harmless, but he's moving too fast. I throw my sword up to block a swing, metal grinding on metal, and my legs are swept out from under me. The world spins sideways, and I land on my face, spitting out dirt.

"Hey, that was totally cheating," I protest, "You kicked my ankles."

"You could say *I swept you off your feet*," he says, with a slight wink.

I cross my arms, still sitting on the ground. "The least you could do is catch me, like a gentleman."

"You're right, my bad, *my lady*. Now, work on that balance."

"This is impossible," I sigh. "How am I supposed to keep moving my feet, keep my balance, and block your attacks?"

"That's the thing," he says, twirling a dulled practice sword in his nimble hands. "The key to any self-defense, whether it's in a fistfight, or swordplay, or sparring with a dagger, isn't blocking and dodging your opponent's attacks. It's the offense. You need to attack, force me into blocking and dodging, and gain the upper hand. Now, try it again."

So that's how the entire morning is spent. Working, and practicing until the sun is high overhead, the mostly bare tree branches are casting jagged shadows onto the dusty forest floor. The forest floor that I'm now sitting on, my back against a tree, taking a long drink of water out of a canteen.

"Stefan," I say with a defeated sigh. "I don't think I can do this. I'm not cut out for this- I don't even have any clue what I've gotten myself into. And if I fail, if I can't prove myself to Orlon…"

"Lina," he slumps to the ground beside me, back braced against a tree of his own, his golden hair gleaming with sweat. "You've got a warrior's spirit, a fighting spirit. I mean, who else, upon finding themselves trapped in this impossible situation, could handle it as well as you have? What you did, what you agreed to, was crazy, I'll admit that."

My head ducks, but he moves closer, tilting my chin up until my eyes meet his.

"But it was also brave and the noblest thing I've ever seen anyone do." He pauses for a moment, considering.

"But what if I can't back it up?" I say. "I'm not good at fighting like a guard should be, and I can't learn in one week."

"Then don't focus on what a Realm Guard should be," he says, getting back to his feet. "Focus on who you already are. If you aren't good at swordplay yet, don't just fight with a sword. Fight with your wits, find what works for you. A guard doesn't mean just being a good warrior, it means being able to think under pressure, being able to make a plan, and being crafty and brave enough to carry out that plan."

I nod. Maybe what he says could work.

An idea pops into my head. I remember watching an old movie once, with Cam, and it had a ridiculously over-exaggerated fight scene involving swords. There was one character who managed to disarm the other by using the flat of his blade and twisting the other guy's wrist. Cam and I had declared there was no way that would actually work, but practicing it with cheap plastic swords taken from pirate Halloween costumes, we had tried it out, and I had sent his flying from his hand with that exact move.

Now, I realize that cheap Halloween costume swords are far from the real thing, and Cam was far from a trained fighter, but Stefan won't be expecting something like that. It's worth a shot.

"Are you ready to give it another go?" he asks, getting back to his feet.

I flex a bit of the growing soreness from my shoulder, getting back into that stance he had worked so hard to drill into my mind. As we begin to circle each other for what feels like the millionth time today, I keep back, seemingly hesitating, specifically as he told me not to. Letting him come to me. He looks slightly disappointed, but I move, as he told me to, lunging for his sword and twisting it against my blade. The surprise, and pride, on his face as his sword clatters to the ground is the best reward I could have gotten.

I take advantage of that surprise, shoving him to the ground, and stand over him with my sword pointed down as I laugh in triumph.

"Watch your balance, Stefan."

His answering grin makes my heart soar.

"See, I knew you had it in you."

Sparring with Stefan put a new spring of much-needed confidence in my step. Not only my singular victory but the pep talk he had given me out there in the woods.

I can be brave, I can be clever, and I can beat the king's challenge in my way. I can become a guard the likes of which nobody has seen before. I can save my mother.

Stefan and I return to the palace at half past noon and are greeted by the others before we even make it through the doors. I mean all of the others. Reed, Jane, Alaina, and Nate all stand, chatting with the guards on duty, and Alaina waves us over when she spots us appearing over the hill.

"What are you all doing out here?" Stefan asks.

"Waiting for you two, actually," Jane answers, crossing her arms over a leather jacket with too many zippers. They are all dressed in casual clothes, no training gear to be seen.

"Why?"

"We're going out for the afternoon, that's why," Alaina chimes in, snuggling deeper into a cream-colored fur-lined coat. "And you two are coming. Today Lina gets to see more of the Mirror Realm. Penrith, in particular."

"But Stefan and I haven't finished training."

"You are going to train yourself to death if you keep at it like this," Nate says, rolling his eyes, his arm over Alaina's shoulder. "You need to take a break sometime."

"I'll rest after I've passed Orlon's test," I insist, "After my mom is safe."

"Lina, I know you want to get your mom back, but wearing yourself to the ground isn't going to help anyone."

"You know, she does have a point," Stefan says.

"Traitor," I answer, smacking him with the flat of my practice blade. Then I hit him again for good measure.

"Quit it, I'm not a piñata," he swats at me with his sword.

"Fine," I say, giving in. "One afternoon of sightseeing. Then it's back to work."

"If you say so," Alaina says. "Now go get cleaned up and meet us out here."

"My room's over there," Stefan gestures to the shape of another building, separate from the palace, looming across the grounds.

"Oh, right. Lina, I'll take you back to your room, if you don't remember the way," Alaina offers.

"I think I remember how to get there, but thanks," I reply. After a few days of being here, I still certainly do not have any familiarity with this maze of a castle, but I've walked the path from my room and back to have a fairly solid idea of where I'm going...or so I thought.

I eventually do find my room, after not one, but two wrong turns, and freshen myself up. They said we're headed to Penrith, and if I remember correctly, it's the nearby town that I can catch a glimpse of from my room, nestled at the base of the mountains.

The mountains. They look so similar to the White Mountains in New Hampshire, North Conway, where my mom and I have been camping at that same campground since before I could walk. I wonder if the mountains will ever be the same for me- I wonder if I could even stomach camping again after what happened, especially if I never get her back.

No, I can't think like that. I will get my mom back, and we'll visit the mountains again. I have to believe that.

Stefan beat me back to the group, training gear swapped for jeans and a jacket. I pull my own thick sweater tighter around my arms.

The trip to the town is brief. We borrow a car, one of the many the king owns, all of which are sleek, uniform silver in varying sizes from fancier sport car-like vehicles under strict surveillance, to sedans and minivans for guard use. According to Reed, instead of running on gas like Worlder vehicles, these cars run on a certain magic-infused mineral found only in the Realms that acts as an endless battery, so each vehicle is made eco-friendly and made to last, no refueling required.

"If a car is wrecked, say, in an accident," Reed continues with his explanation, "We reuse the mineral, so we don't have to mine so much of it to make new cars."

"How do you know so much about this?" Nate asks, rolling his eyes as he fiddles with what looks like a yo-yo in his hand. Where did he even get that from?

"My parents were friends with Varrow, Penrith's head mechanic. He taught me a thing or two when I was younger."

The town comes into view outside the windows of the car, driven by Jane. We pass by clusters of small houses, rolling hills of farmland in the distance, and several vendor stalls and shops lining the streets. The town is small and rural, the tallest buildings seeming to be only a few stories high. It's very quaint.

Jane parks the car alongside a busier street, leading to a hub of activity towards the center of Penrith.

"The markets," Reed says, gesturing to the crowded square. "The Mirror Realm, despite being the largest, most powerful, and most influential of the Realms, isn't known for big, impressive cities like the other two. We're known instead for our guard training program and our markets. Whatever you're looking for, you can buy it here."

We move on foot from here, along the sidewalks by the markets, and I take the time to observe the stalls and shops. One is advertising milk, rare cheeses, butter, coffee cream, and various other dairy products. Another displays spices and herbs, everything from cinnamon, to lemongrass, to saffron. Yet another has silks, there's one showing polished and decorative swords, one advertising paints. The markets seem to make up the entire heart of Penrith.

We pass a bakery, a heavy and rich aroma drifting from the propped open doors. Across the street, another sight catches my eye.

It's a bookstore- a tiny building smooshed between two larger ones, with a slanted roof and vines creeping decoratively around the windows, lit by a soft glow from within. A tiny, old-fashioned sign swings above a red painted door reading *Tales Beyond Time Bookstore*.

I turn to Stefan walking close beside me, tugging on the sleeve of his jacket.

"That place looks nice," I say, gesturing across the street.

"The machine shop?" Stefan says, raising a questioning eyebrow.

"What? No, the… wait for a second," I turn back to the bookstore, where it had sat between the machine shop and an unidentified office building. It's gone. I blink.

"There… there was a bookstore…" I try to say, gesturing to the other two buildings sitting side by side, with an alleyway barely big enough to squeeze a fence between them. Nothing else.

"A bookstore?" Alaina says, pausing to raise an eyebrow. "The only place that sells books around here is the old lady at the south end of the markets. Nowhere near here."

"But-" I realize I've stopped at the edge of the sidewalk, staring almost directly into the machine shop where I could have sworn *Tales Beyond Time* stood just moments before. It was way too real to have been made up in my mind.

"It was there," I protest. "I saw it, but now it's gone!"

The burly man in the machine shop has taken notice of my staring and looks a bit surprised as if he recognizes me from somewhere. Oh, right, the resemblance to Lillian. I assume the king has told his subjects by now, but I doubt it makes it any less shocking to find the lookalike of your world's most feared villainess just staring into your shop like a creep.

Reed steps in front of me, casting a friendly wave and a too-forced smile in the direction of the mechanic, calling, "Good afternoon, Varrow."

Oh, Varrow. The one he said his parents had been friends with. The mechanic gives a wave of greeting in return, and Stefan quickly steers me, and the rest of the group, away.

"Quit causing a scene," Reed says, rolling his eyes. "There's no bookstore there. Unless Varrow's become a librarian in the past year, which I highly doubt."

"Besides, books are boring anyway," Nate says, getting bored with his yo-yo and sliding it into his pocket. He pulls out a deck of cards instead and begins shuffling them in his hands with amazing skill.

"When was the last time you tried a good book?" Jane says.

"Pfft, Nate doesn't know how to read," Alaina says, nudging him with her shoulder, and he narrows his eyes at the joke.

"The two continue to bicker as we stroll down the sidewalk, away from the markets. I can't help but glance back one last time, to the spot where I know that bookstore had been. It leaves me with too many questions, the biggest of which being, how had I seen it when no one else had, how did it disappear into thin air…and why?

My friends lead me all the way to the town's edge, right up to the woods behind the last of the houses.

"Where are we going?" I ask. "There's nothing here."

"To most people, yes," Reed says, heading for the trees, "But for a few of us who grew up in Penrith, we know its secrets. The best beauty lies beyond the town lines."

He shoves aside a few overgrown willow branches, revealing a thin dirt path leading into the woods.

"Stay on the path," Stefan warns, golden eyes stormy. "Woods can be dangerous around here if you stray away from the known."

"Wow, Stefan. That was very cryptic," Alaina says with a disapproving frown. "You're going to give us all the creeps."

He only shrugs, "It's good advice."

Alaina was right, that was a terrifying way to put it. Every noise in the sunlit, frost-coated woods sets me on edge, wondering what kind of danger Stefan could have been talking about.

We stick to the path, trampling down the weeds and climbing fallen logs that indicate that this trail hasn't been used in a while. I'm about to get impatient, wondering what could possibly be at the end of this hike, when I begin to hear something. A very faint roaring. My muscles freeze up, but Nate only nudges me forward.

"Relax. It's just rushing water."

As soon as he says it, I can recognize the sound, so similar to the river running by the campground back home.

Home. Every time I stumble into those memories, it's like a spike of grief to the gut.

"Come on, it's just up ahead," Alaina says, as the roar of rushing water grows louder, more forceful than ordinary river rapids. What could it be?

I shove a branch out of my face, catching the gleam of late afternoon sunlight on water, the air ahead of us slightly clouded, with fog or…

Mist. Mist caused by the spray of water from a massive waterfall, flowing from jutting cliffs high overhead, thundering down into the churning whitewater of a lagoon at the base, with a riverbed that seems to be glowing.

No, not glowing. The "glow" is actually the reflection of the sunlight on the thousands upon thousands of tiny, diamond-like rocks beneath the lagoon, like a riverbed of crystal.

"What-" I begin to ask, breathless with awe, stooping over to scoop a handful of the tiny diamonds from the riverbed, chunks of it mixed with sand and pebbles. "What is this?"

"Crystalfire Falls," Jane breathes, gazing out over the magnificent display. "These tiny crystals are the minerals that power the cars when infused with magic. It's also what makes up part of the castle. Stronger than even diamond and just as pretty, though not nearly as rare or expensive."

"It's called Crystalfire Falls, because the material is so reflective, that at sunrise and sunset, the color of the sky catches in the crystals and makes the whole waterfall appear to be on fire," Alaina explains.

I nod, remembering that morning I arrived in the Realms, how the entire throne room, made of that crystal, looked like an inferno due to the rising sun.

Alaina leads us to a steep path up the side of the falls, climbing atop water-slick rocks from the spray of the falls in what looks like… are those heels? Who wears heels on a hike up a waterfall? Is she crazy?

I follow behind Reed, the drop below a little too far and cluttered with rocks for comfort. We all arrive safely at the top, if not a little damp from practically walking through the water spray, and the view is incredible. I can see the tops of trees, the glittering lagoon below, and the cascading water casting a pleasant white noise as the backdrop to it all.

I take off my shoes, dipping my feet in the shallows at the top of the falls, perched on a rock. The water is so cold it almost burns, likely flowing straight from the nearby mountains. I used to go tubing down rivers like these with Cam, minus the waterfall obviously. I wonder if I'll ever get the chance to again.

So much is riding on passing whatever challenge the king has in mind, becoming a trainee. If I have to embrace the strangeness of this life to get back to the normalcy of my old one, so be it. But if I'm going to embrace it, I might as well take the time to appreciate the wonder of it all, like a beautiful waterfall lined with crystals.

Alaina moves from one rock to another, making her way out across the river and closer to the steep drop. There's a narrow, flat rock protruding directly over the edge of the falls, which she perches herself atop, letting her legs swing idly over the spray of the water far below her.

I guessed right before- she is crazy. But at least she's barefoot now, heels discarded at the river's edge.

"Alaina," Jane says with a frown.

"Oh come on," she says, strands of her short hair rippling around her shoulders in the breeze. "It's perfectly safe, I've done this a million times before."

"You've only ever been here, what, twice?" Nate snorts. A comment that she ignores.

"So not many people know about this place?" I ask, hugging my knees as I watch the sun dip lower in the sky.

"No," Reed answers, from where he sits, skipping flat stones across the water. "People who live in Penrith typically know about it, but it's never really advertised as a tourist attraction. If too many people knew about it, it would always be crowded, or they would mine it for its crystals, or something along those lines. Some things are just better kept secret."

"You know, Lina, your mom grew up in Penrith," Jane says, her eyes staring off over the trees in the distance.

"Really?"

I turn to look at her as she says, "Yeah. Our parents were friends, you know. They would visit this place too, as kids."

I don't even know what to think about that. It just doesn't feel real, that she grew up here and never told me about this whole other life she had lived. She probably sat at the top of this waterfall once, maybe even exactly where I'm sitting right now, staring at the same view. It's comforting in a way, but also makes me wonder how well I had known my mother.

Stefan moves to sit beside me, a comforting presence to remind me that while my old life, the only family I've ever known, feels so far away, I'm not alone.

The fact that all five of them, even Reed, are here with me means more to me than I can say. These strangers who have become friends, who have welcomed me into their group, who are giving their time to train me and teach me about the Realms, all to make me feel like I can belong.

We stay by the falls, talking and laughing with one another until the setting sun is a blaze of light on the horizon, and the most magnificent thing begins to happen. The deep oranges and reds and golds of the sunset streak across the water, and every crystal in the riverbed seems to come alive, like tiny fires burning beneath the ripples until the whole waterfall glows as though it's been lit ablaze.

And by the reflected light of the river of fire, sitting with the five of them, my newfound friends, I suddenly don't feel so alone.

Several days later, the clock ticks towards the end of my eighth day here in the Realms. The end of Orlon's deadline. My week of preparation and training is up. It's time to find out what challenge I'll have to face, to prove myself worthy of becoming a Realm Guard. No pressure.

Each day, I've worked myself harder than the last. I'm learning to fight and defend myself, how to be stealthy. I'm also becoming quicker and more agile. But a week can only do so much, no matter how much dedication I put into it. I'll just have to hope it is enough.

"Lina, you'll be fine," Stefan says, grasping my wrist to stop me from pacing back and forth in front of my bedroom door.

"But what if I'm not ready?" I ask, wiping my sweaty palms on my pants, glancing desperately back at him. "What if the challenge is something we haven't considered? Or worse, what if I need to use magic to complete it?"

The one thing I hadn't been able to make any progress on was magic. I had tried everything, but nothing had happened, not even a stirring of power. If Orlon's test requires me to use magic in some way, I'm done for.

And my friends know it too but are trying to act like they don't. Hence Stefan's pale face, despite saying I shouldn't worry. Hypocrite.

"Come on," he says. "Dinner will be starting soon. You can't put it off forever."

The rest of our friends are meeting us at the dining hall, where I'll be confronting Orlon about our deal, and where he'll most likely assign me my test, whatever it may be. The suspense is killing me.

Stefan grips my hand tightly as we make our way to the dining hall giving it a reassuring squeeze before we enter, but Orlon isn't here. His spot at the head table lies empty even though the rest of his court and council are present. The man named Marcus fixes me with a sour expression of distaste.

I have no choice but to take my seat at the table with the others and wonder why he might be missing. In the week that I've been here, Orlon has never been late or absent from dinner. It must be because of the challenge somehow, or maybe he doesn't want me seeking him out ahead of time. Whatever the reason, it does nothing to calm my nerves.

It isn't until halfway through dinner that Orlon finally makes an appearance, striding through the doors. His absence hadn't gone unnoticed by the guards either, and the room immediately falls silent as he enters, waiting.

He moves slowly, standing before his chair at the head table, but not taking a seat. He thumps his staff against the ground for everyone's attention, not that he needed to. The attention of every single person in this room, even his court, and council are fixed on the king. He runs his hand over the crystalline orb atop his staff, as if letting the silence linger for the suspense, before speaking.

"I have an announcement to make. One that I believe you will all find very exciting."

Is he really going to make a spectacle out of this? Will I have to face the challenge in front of everyone?

"The time has come… for the Winter Tournament of the Guards."

There is a beat of shocked silence before the entire room erupts in cheering and clapping, Nate giving a loud cheer of his own. Jane and Reed share surprised elated grins. The king raises his hands for silence, and the room dutifully quiets to whispers and murmurs of excited conversation.

"What is the Winter Tournament of the Guards?" I whisper to Stefan beside me.

He opens his mouth to respond, understanding dawning in his eyes, but the king continues speaking, and we fall silent to listen.

"Due to a recent attack on the Shadow Realm's arena, King Umbra is unable to host this year's Tournament." The hall falls dead silent. Looks of shock and disappointment ripple around the room, followed then by protests among the guards and trainees alike. The king has to shout to be heard above the roar.

"The Shadow Realm is unable to accommodate the Tournament," he says. "The Soul Realm's arenas are booked for sporting events. So the Tournament will be held here, at the Mirror Palace."

The protests stop. As the king's words sink in, the room slowly begins its excited murmurs once more. Everyone seems confused - the mood of the room having swung back and forth like a pendulum, from excitement to disappointment and back, so fast it seems to have given everyone emotional whiplash.

The man named Marcus, the king's second-in-command, turns to the king, his eyebrows raising, his mouth twisting into a deeper frown of confusion.

"But my king," I hear him hiss, not attempting to quiet his voice. "We do not possess an arena with the capacity for-"

The king waves his hand dismissively. "While it is true we may not possess an arena fit for the Tournament, I think you may find that the Elder Woods will be more than suited for the games," he reasons. At this Marcus's face twists into a displeased sneer, and even the others at the head table and around the room shift uncertainly.

Across from me, Jane leans forward on her elbows, her eyebrows scrunched in thought as she considers Orlon's words. I have no idea what this Tournament even is, what the Elder Woods are, or why everyone seems so confused. Does this Tournament have something to do with how I'll prove myself?

"The Elder Woods? For the Tournament?" Stefan mutters as he fiddles with his fingers. "That can't be safe."

Nate laughs, he and Reed sharing growing, adrenaline-fueled grins.

"Since when is it ever safe?" he chides.

"The woods have been prepared," the king continues. "The games will be held tomorrow evening, at sundown." The room erupts with a newly refreshed vigor, cheers and shouts echoing across the vaulted ceiling of the dining hall.

"So rest up, be prepared," Orlon finishes. "For tomorrow, the games shall begin."

CHAPTER 8

The Winter Tournament of the Guards is about to begin, and I could not be more terrified.

Last night, King Orlon gave his speech, announcing the event that begins at sundown. In one hour.

My new friends had pulled me aside, answering my questions almost as fast as I could ask them. Apparently, this Tournament is one of the biggest Realm-wide events of the year. It's a competition, with three rounds, one for each level of guard, with a whole set of complicated rules and regulations. Each round is basically a giant battle between three teams, each competing to be the winner, using actual weapons with traps layered throughout the Elder Woods (the stretch of pine forest beyond the palace grounds). The way they described it, it sounds like an Olympics-level game of three-way capture-the-flag, but in the dark with deadly weaponry wielded by trained warriors. As if that wasn't worrying enough, the competitors have an audience, those who don't wish to participate. People from all three Realms come to watch the games, making a sport out of it.

And the terrifying part is that I have to participate.

Orlon pulled me aside during the exciting aftermath of the news, informing me that my challenge, the task I must perform to prove myself worthy of being a guard, is to participate in the Tournament. To succeed, my team needs to win.

Yes, I know, it's absolutely insane. The only requirement to sign up for the trainee round is that you must be 16-18, so *technically* I'm eligible. I only have one week of training under my belt, going up against every seasoned trainee in the Mirror Realm. It had been a debate among my friends- Jane and Stefan had been adamant that I should call off the deal, claiming that the Tournament was more than I signed up for. Alaina was hesitant, but thought I can handle it, while Nate was all for it, claiming it would be "fun." Reed didn't give much of an opinion, but he seemed to side with Alaina and Nate, claiming that if I were to become a real guard, I needed to experience what I'd be getting into firsthand.

As terrifying as this challenge is, there is no way I'm backing down. Something deep inside of me began to stir- maybe my magic rising within me- but whether it was pride or some long-dormant guard instinct, I know I can handle this. I have to try, for my mom's sake.

Whatever confidence I had completely faded when I saw the crowds. Also when I donned the strange, leathery black armor that I remember Jane, Reed, and Alaina wearing when I first met them. When I saw the gigantic beacon of light spearing from the sprawling woods my heart began to beat in a terrified rhythm. It matched the beat of the drums echoing from the direction of that light beacon, reverberating in my bones.

I now find myself walking close behind Reed, following the group of about 20 trainees all around 17 or 18, all in that same strange clothing. The armor is perfectly fitted to each person's body. It is leathery, but flexible to allow for a full range of movement, and is fitted with bulletproof plates over areas such as the chest, shoulders, forearms, and parts of the legs. It's also colored all black and dark gray, perfectly designed to blend in with the woods around us, now shrouded in shadow as the sun slowly disappears behind the horizon.

The group follows the worn, wide dirt path winding through the Elder Woods, the tallest spires of the palace, and the glass slope of the Centerdome peaking above the tree line, gleaming with the last colors of sunset behind us. The shadows of the forest seemed to grow with every step.

Soon another light becomes visible in front of the group, brighter than the setting sun at our backs. My eyes widen, trying to take in the structure in front of me, the source of the beam of light cutting through the oncoming night. It is almost an exact copy of the Centerdome- a gargantuan dome made of glass, or probably crystal, stronger and thicker than the castle walls, spider-webbed with crisscrossing steel beams across the outside of each glass pane starting about 10 feet up. Craning my neck, the group gathering around at the base of this dome, I take in its sheer size. Having entered the Centerdome from a branching hallway, I had trained inside of it, but I hadn't got the chance to witness what the outside looks like close up.

Most of the trainees seem unfazed by the structure before us- with its size, the pounding of drums that are almost deafening now, the blurred glass obscuring the scene inside, and the light streaming from within like a beacon in the dark. Stefan notices my marveling.

"We call this the Outerdome," he whispers to me under his breath.

"Are you excited?" Alaina asks, her voice barely lowered as she bounces back and forth on her feet. All I can manage is a nod, though dread, rather than excitement is threatening to buckle my knees, and I fold my hands over my arms to hide their slight shaking. Stefan notices this too.

"Hey," he says, lowering his voice even further, his tone calm and reassuring. "You're going to do fine. Trust me, this might actually end up being fun," he smiles, his gold-tinted eyes glinting with warmth. And I believe him. I let myself take a deep breath, forcing myself to relax my rigid stance. Everything will be fine.

Then a horn sounds, low and deep, from inside the Outerdome. The group takes that as the cue to push forward, a wide panel sliding open in the glass to reveal an entranceway wide enough for an elephant to comfortably fit through. Herded along in the group of trainees, I'm ushered through the entranceway.

We're greeted by the roar of the crowds. There are hundreds of thousands of people filling the stands of the Outerdome like a football stadium. Along with the rhythmic beating of the drums and the chatter of guards and trainees alike, gathered before the raised podium in the center of the room, atop which stands the king with Marcus at his side.

The king turns to our group gathered together at the base of the dais, his elegant silver robes swishing with the movement, surveying the two other groups already gathered that appear to be made up of full-fledged guards.

"Welcome," the king shouts, a microphone clutched in hand to be heard over the noise of the crowds, which grudgingly begin to quiet. "...to the Winter Tournament of the Guards." His words are followed by a new eruption of cheering.

"I speak on behalf of the Mirror Realm when I say it is my utmost pleasure, and greatest honor, to host this year's Winter Tournament here at the Mirror Palace, for the first time." The king again waits for the applause to die down, before giving a nod to the highest and most decorated section of the stands, where two regal figures rise to their feet.

"And it is also my greatest pleasure to welcome King Umbra, of the Shadow Realm, and Queen Anima, of the Soul Realm. And all of those here tonight who have made the journey to the Mirror Realm, welcome."

King Umbra, a tall, thin man with lovely dark skin, rich purple robes, and a warm smile bows ever so slightly before taking a seat. Queen Anima beside him, a gorgeous woman with honey golden hair and a flowing rose-colored gown, inclines her head as well and follows his lead.

This is crazy, and not just a little crazy, but like, full-on Game of Thrones type stuff. They are actual royalty, like something straight out of a fantasy novel. How is this even real?

"Now, for the reason you've all come today," Orlon continues, "The Tournament. Before we begin, there are a few procedures everyone must abide by, as well as alterations made along with the change in the arena. As many of you know, there are three rounds, beginning with the trainees, then the newly appointed guards, and finally the senior guards. To begin- the trainees will be split into their three legions, and will compete to capture both flags of the opposing teams while holding on to their own." The king holds up three scraps of different colored fabric, one white, one silver, and one gold.

"To win, your team must obtain all three flags, and return them to your team's base. These drones," the king gestures above his head as a small mechanical object, a drone, drifts to hover a few feet above him. Giant screens descend from the ceiling, five of them in total, each displaying a different angled view of the king's face, likely from more hidden drones. "...they will monitor the games and broadcast them here, for the audience to watch. Now, Marcus, the rules if you would."

Marcus, that ever-remaining scowl across his face, pulls out a scroll and begins to read aloud.

"During the games, every participant will be on a team according to a legion. There will be no switching teams or

turning on your teammates. You will remain within the bounds
of the arena, that is the Elder Woods. You may not enter the
Outerdome once the games begin. There will be no killing or
inflicting of potentially permanent injuries, no taking hostages,
no use of fire, and halt all battle once the end of the game is
announced by the sound of the horn."

What? He has to be kidding. This is a joke, right? What
kind of game needs to list *no killing, taking hostages, or
permanently harming* in the rules? Has this actually been an
issue before? Oh, I don't know what I've gotten myself into this
time.

"Vitalums are allowed," Marcus rambles on, "But the
same rules apply to them as well."

He pauses, his head swiveling to glare at the gathered
crowd of trainees, as though referencing some past incident.
What is a *vitalum* anyway? I open my mouth to ask Stefan for
some sort of clarification as to what Marcus is talking about, but
he continues with his speech before I can utter a word.

"Any spectators must remain inside the Outerdome, in
their seats. Failure to follow any of these rules will result in
expulsion from the games, and prevention from participation in
any future games. *Am I clear?*"

The trainees and guards nod.

"Well then," the king beams, with a glance in my
direction, "Let the Tournament begin!"

After the horn sounded, there was a mad rush of trainees, a flurry of excitement. Full-fledged guards take their seats in the stands, awaiting their turn, while the trainees begin to divide into three separate groups. Stefan, catching my bewildered look, grasps my wrist and tugs me forward out of the fray to where my friends stand.

"Are we one team?" I ask, glancing between Reed, Jane, Stefan, Alaina, and Nate.

"Oh yeah," Nate says, spinning his sword around, making motions in the air like he's jabbing at an opponent. Alaina, quick as a viper, unsheathes her sword from her belt, swiping it at his and blocking his swing with a clash of metal. My dagger, strapped to my waist, feels heavier. I don't know what I was thinking. My hands are shaking so badly that I'm not sure I could even get my dagger out of the scabbard without slicing my fingers off.

"Hey, knock it off," Stefan chides the two of them, catching the annoyed glance thrown their way by Marcus.

"Yeah," Nate smirks. "No turning on your own teammates, remember?"

Jane rolls her eyes. "Come on," she says, gesturing towards a new doorway opened in the glass wall. "The other teams are already moving, and if we want to beat Eliza's legion for once, we have to be quick."

"Eliza?" I ask, grasping for my curiosity to distract me from my fear, recognizing the name.

"Yeah. That girl from the dining hall, the one I warned you about," Stefan explains.

"She's quite the jerk."

"A jerk she may be," Reed snorts, "But that doesn't stop her team from winning the Tournament every year."

"Let's go," Alaina presses, already heading for the door. "The other teams are beating us to it."

The first thing we had to accomplish was getting to our base. Three giant towers had been hastily constructed among the woods, towering over the trees, equally spaced from the dome to form a sort of triangle. That made the arena space roughly 3 acres. No wonder they were having trouble finding someplace with enough space to host this event.

We aim for the tower glowing with silvery light - matching the silver flag clutched in Reed's hand, given to him by Marcus. In the distance, I can see the other two towers lit up in white and gold, but no sign so far from the other teams.

Now, this odd armor makes a bit more sense, the leathery bodysuit, and minimal metal coverings make it easier to move stealthily. Each person had been given a breastplate engraved with a different colored symbol, entwining R's- white, silver, or gold- to signify a person's team. In the growing shadows, the marks become hard to discern, and every shadow and sound in the woods sets me on edge. Stefan sticks close by my side.

Finally, we reach the base of the tower, gazing up at the top. It's pretty high, completely made of iron posts and a winding staircase to a singular open-air room at the top where the silvery light glows. My knees begin to quake, my palms sweaty under the gloves.

"So," Jane says, taking charge. "We need offense, defense on the ground, and defense in the tower. We should split into three groups of two."

"Obviously Stefan and Alaina should take offense," Reed points out.

Right, because of the invisibility. Something in my heart shrinks in fear at the implication that Stefan won't be beside me, but they would have the best chance at retrieving the flags without being seen.

Everyone else nods in agreement.

"Nate and I should take ground defense," Reed adds. "Jane, you would be better in the tower, since you have the long-range and short-range weapons," he nods to her bow slung over her back, and the sword at her waist. She nods.

"And Lina, you'll be with me," she finishes. "The tower tends to be a bit safer than on the ground, easier to defend." I nod, feeling grateful.

"And don't worry," Nate says, throwing an arm over my shoulder, "Reed and I have it covered anyway," he says smugly.

Stefan looks towards me with concern, then towards the other towers in the distance.

"We really need to get moving," he says to Alaina. "You take the white base, I'll take the gold one?"

"Ooh, splitting up," Alaina muses. "Risky, but bold. I'm in." With a nod, Stefan flickers out of existence, followed closely by Alaina.

Jane angles her head towards the tower, indicating that I should follow her up the winding, iron steps. I'm stopped by a firm hand on my shoulder, and I turn my head to see Reed.

"I just wanted to say good luck…and don't worry," he says, his voice strangely gentle. "You'll be fine, Nate and I have your back." Nate gives me an enthusiastic thumbs up for emphasis.

"Thanks," is all I can say, as I turn to follow Jane back up the steps, forcing myself to look straight ahead, while some part of me oddly wants to look back.

Reaching the top of the steep climb, we enter the small space at the top, large enough for maybe five people to stand comfortably, open almost completely to the air with an iron railing running along the edge and a roof over our heads. Jane hangs the fabric from a small set of three hooks dangling from the ceiling, the other two empty and waiting for the rest of the flags.

At first, everything is quiet. Jane leans against one of the railings, her bow in hand with an arrow loosely notched, running her fingers absentmindedly over the feathered shaft. I find myself pacing, wringing my hands nervously.

"I'm judging, from your nervousness, that the worlds don't have games like this?" Jane speaks up curiously. I look up, thrown off by the question.

"Um, well, not exactly," I answer. "We do have games, like sports events and things like that. We also have a game called capture-the-flag which is a lot like this, but it's usually a thing played in a gym class at school rather than a big event with crowds. And there's no, you know, fighting."

"So fighting isn't a thing done for sport then?" she asks.

"Uh, well I guess there are martial arts... and wrestling... and there's fencing..." I trail off. She just looks confused, so I try to explain.

"Well, it isn't really-" But my voice is cut off by the sounds of a skirmish from down below, on the ground. The harsh clash of metal, and a shout. A warning. Instantly Jane is upright with her arrow fully notched, aiming at some target on the ground.

Nervously I peer over the railing, watching the scene unfold.

It was an ambush, but an unplanned one it seems. It appears that, by some stroke of bad luck, both of the other teams had come here first. Two warriors bearing a gold mark, and three with a white mark. Reed and Nate fight to hold back the five of them, all trying to get to the tower first. I watch as one gold-marked warrior and one white-marked push back Nate together, only to turn on one another in their haste to get to the iron staircase.

Jane's arrows fly, one after another, their dulled tips striking their marks and knocking them to the ground. One makes it to the stairs, his footsteps echoing against the metal as he dashes upward. Jane reaches for another arrow, only for her hand to fall on an empty quiver. With a hiss, she unsheathes a dulled knife. I copy her, my hand shaking. I hear Reed shout again in warning, but both he and Nate are occupied with holding back the other three. Wait. Three? Three on the ground and one on the tower - wasn't there five before? Where is the other warrior?

"Jane," I shout, preparing to warn her, but she's busy holding the other trainee at bay. Spinning around, I spot him. Heaving himself over the railing, into the tower.

Grabbing our flag in his fist.

As he turns to leap back over the tower edge, to retreat the way he came, I do the first thing that comes to mind. I jump for him, knocking him off balance, trying to grab for the flag, only succeeding in causing him to slip off the railing.

He twists, wrapping his other hand around the rail, dangling off the edge, flipping me over the edge with him. The world spins in a blur, my breath catching in my throat, and I grab onto the first thing I find- a metal rung- as my body swings and slams into the side of the tower. My fingers spasm, but I manage to keep my grip, dangling slightly lower than the warrior I'd attacked. The ground looms below me- not a drop that would kill me, hopefully, but enough to hurt.

The warrior glares down at me, his dark hair in his eyes and a mocking laugh on his lips as he begins to hoist himself upward with impossible strength. I grab his foot with one hand, pulling my weight onto him, and he grunts as his hands almost slip.

Then I watch as the trainee who'd been climbing the stairs, a girl with dirty blonde hair pulled back in a bandana and a gold mark on her breastplate goes tumbling and hits the ground with a thud. I hear Jane's victorious cheer of triumph, which becomes a strangled noise as she spots the other trainee and me dangling from the edge of the tower, as she spots the flag clutched in his hand.

She lunges as I release his foot, slamming the butt of her dagger into his head, and he loses his grip with a shout and plummets to the forest floor, but my grip isn't going to last.

Jane reaches for me, her fingers outstretched, her body leaning almost dangerously far over the rail. She manages to grab my hand, straining to heave me up with a strength that should not have been possible- until the gloves side off.

And I find myself falling.

I hit the ground with an impact that makes the world go black.

CHAPTER 9

I didn't pass out. My vision blurs, my whole body aches and I can't breathe.

I struggle to take a breath, feeling paralyzed, panic building in my chest. I can see again, but I can't make out what I'm hearing. Jane is shouting something, and I can see her atop the tower, and the other warrior beside me where he fell.

The feeling gradually begins to pass, and I gasp as I take a shaky breath, then another. Within seconds the paralyzing feeling eases, and even the aches begin to fade until I can struggle into a sitting position.

I seem to be fine, nothing so much as sprained. Even the ache of the impact has dulled. I had only gotten the wind knocked out of me, and even that has faded so quickly. The other guy hadn't been as lucky. I scramble over to him, where he lies unconscious. Checking his pulse, he appears to be alright.

The flag…the little scrap of silver fabric glimmers beside his hand. Feeling a bit guilty, I snatch it and duck into the bushes to avoid being found by the others still fighting by the stairs of the tower.

Turning, I come face to face with a snarling wolf.

My heart nearly stops dead in my chest. The beast is larger than a bear, with a dark mottled gray coat of fur, and piercing yellow eyes that hold a sort of intelligence. Those eyes fix on the flag in my hand.

It growls, inching forward, as though it too wants the flag. Suddenly I'm thrust back into that clearing with my mother, what feels like a lifetime ago, watching the massive wolf leap from the woods, the terror that had filled me completely.

Had my friends mentioned anything about the wolves? Reed, Jane, and Nate had called themselves Wolf Soldiers- did that have anything to do with it? It lunges, jaws snapping for the scrap of fabric, and I bolt out of the way as fast as I can move.

I take off, dashing through the woods in a blind panic. I can't outrun a wolf, what am I thinking? Glancing back over my shoulder, I nearly get my ear bitten off by snapping teeth, and I hear not one but two sets of paws pounding on the ground, giving chase. Two wolves. They aren't outright attacking me- if they wanted to, they would have done it already- but rather they seem to be herding me around the Outerdome towards the other towers. Towards the gold team's base.

I can hear a loud roaring from up ahead, and see the light of the dome. The Outerdome is so close. Once I'm past it, I'll be in gold team territory, and the flag will be as good as theirs. I can't let that happen.

I look slightly upwards, spotting a lower-hanging tree bough. If I can pull myself onto that branch, I can climb the tree. Wolves can't climb trees, right? Yes, I need higher ground.

So I loop the flag through my now empty dagger sheath, my legs beginning to tire and ache from running, but I brace myself until I'm almost beneath the branch, pushing off with all of my strength. My hands scrape tree bark, but I hold on, tucking my legs up beneath me. I am basically letting my instincts guide me at this point, with no reasoning, only adrenaline pumping through my veins. The wolves skid in the dirt as they try to stop, their paws digging rivets in the frozen earth, and my feet barely skim their fur as they pass under my tucked legs.

I have to move fast. They can easily reach me from this branch, I need to get higher. I pull myself upwards, arms burning, suddenly very grateful for the light armor. I hear baying and growling of frustration from below me, but I don't look down, climbing higher until I'm at a height almost as tall as the tower had been. Now what?

No team can win the game without this flag, they will come looking for me soon enough. They will be able to climb trees and besides, my team can't win either without this flag. I need to get it back to my own base, preferably without being eaten by giant wolves, or I will have failed the challenge.

I shift through the spindly branches, poking my head above them, towards the light of the dome now directly beside the tree I'm perched in. I can see shapes and colors moving inside, along with cheering loud enough to be heard out here, but I can't make out anything distinct through the glass and crisscrossing steel beams.

Wait. The steel beams, like window frames, provide a sort of metal skeleton for the Outerdome. Lying on the *outside* of the glass, like handholds. An idea- a crazy, foolish idea- begins to take form.

Before I can talk myself out of it, I'm moving, scaling my way along the farthest outstretched branch of the tree. It's thick and sturdy, hopefully enough to hold my weight. I swallow hard, judging the distance. I really don't feel like taking a swan dive down to the ground again, I've had enough of that.

Bracing myself as far as I can go, the thinner end of the bough bobbing beneath me, I take a deep breath and leap. The branch, which I used as a springboard, gives a mighty *crack* and breaks off of the trunk. For a split second, there is nothing beneath my feet but empty space, my body in a free fall. I spot the wolves below me as if in slow motion, watching me with their baleful eyes. Then I hit the dome surface, grasping for a hold, my fingers catching on a steel beam no wider than my palm.

I wince as I feel a few of my nails break. Burning pain races through my fingertips as I hold on for dear life, scrambling for a foothold. My boot catches another beam, and I crouch on the sloped surface of the dome, breathing heavily. My heart pounds with delayed terror and adrenaline. For a moment, all I do is crouch there, clinging to the side of the Outerdome.

I just jumped out of a tree, like some sort of daredevil. I grin to myself, a small excited smile. I pat my sheath, where the flag remains tied, but my excitement is short-lived.

I hear voices, shouting, from below and I look down to find two trainees from the gold team standing at the base of the dome, the wolves standing docilely beside them. They are glaring up at me, in surprise and indignation. The crowd inside has also died down, and I realize why. A little drone hovers three feet away from me, tiny cameras trained on my face, and beneath me, the shapes of the crowd are looking upward, able to see me through the glass above them. The attention is now focused on me.

I make out what one of the trainees below is saying, "Is she allowed to do that?" The other shrugs. One attempts to scale the tree, as I did, but the branch I jumped from has broken off. The gap is suddenly much wider, practically impossible for anyone else to make the leap. Quickly I begin to move, realizing that I make an easy target for archers waiting on the ground. I go higher, aiming for the top, where even the arrows wouldn't be able to reach.

More people have begun to notice, a few attempting to follow, but the steel rungs don't go all the way to the base of the dome, leaving about 10 feet of space between the trainees and the first handhold. So I keep climbing before one of them gets smart and decides to shoot at me. Higher and higher, my whole body trembling with fear, adrenaline, and exhaustion. Until I'm three times as high as any metal tower, far out of range of the archers' arrows that have begun to splinter against the dome's glass below. I have to be extra careful- no one could survive a fall from this height.

But, what now? What was my grand plan here? Sure, the other teams can't reach the flag, but neither can my team. I spot Jane staring at me from her position in the tower, eyes wide. I hear a faint whoop of excitement from the ground, the figure so small it's hard to make out. Nate. Cheering me on.

I also notice something else. My team's tower seems to be surrounded by almost every trainee in the game. I see why, Stefan and Alaina are visible at the base of the tower, defending the two flags gleaming at the top. White and gold.

I study the flag tied at my waist, the last one. If I can get this back to the tower, we will win, as long as they manage to hold onto the other two until I do.

But how?

A drone buzzes nearby, watching my every move. I just need some way to get the flag to the tower. Some stroke of luck, of magic, a miracle. I did not come all this way to fail now. My desperation seems to unlock something deep within me, some silvery thread of my soul, calling for me to take it. To reach for it.

Magic.

And I do. I tug at that thread of magic, something alien and strange and wild, and I distantly feel my bracelet grow warm against my skin. The bracelet with the falcon charm. There is a shimmer of light and a wisp of a shape begins to form, spiraling from the bracelet itself. It is translucent at first, no more than a ghost of wings, that begins to solidify. Perched before me, talons curled around a steel rung is a beautiful silver falcon.

The bird from my dream.

I stare open-mouthed at the bird, its feathers ruffling against the November chill in the air. Silvery feathers speckled with black, so unlike the usual brown and black of a regular peregrine. I swallow, once, twice, trying to find my voice.

"Hello...?" I say tentatively. The falcon fixes a yellow-ringed eye on me, and I swear I can sense a sort of intelligence. As if it is pausing to listen. Did I...did I summon it? But how?

I slowly unknot the flag from my sheath, keeping one hand firmly braced on a metal rung for balance, glancing between it and the strange bird. Then at the silver tower, where I can make out Jane staring with straight shock written over her features.

If I could somehow get the bird to take the flag, to fly it to the tower...but I have to hurry. The other teams are breaking against the tower like a tidal wave, and my friends can only hold their own for so long. So I ever so gently extend the hand loosely holding the flag, praying that the bird won't peck my fingers off.

"Would you-" I pause, fully aware that I'm about to ask a favor from a bird. "Would you take this, and fly it over to that tower? To the girl with the black hair-" I barely finish Jane's description, before the falcon pushes itself into the sky with a mighty flap of its wings, snatching the fabric from my fingers with its talons. I hope this wasn't a mistake- I mean, can the bird even understand me? But I watch in awe as the falcon glides on the wind, narrow wings pulled in as it dives for the tower with incredible speed. It banks sharply, catching the air beneath its wings as it aims for the tower opening.

Jane lunges, shoving past another trainee, who fights back viciously. The other trainee, a girl with hair so blonde it's almost white, Eliza, matches Jane blow for blow, not yielding an inch. The silver falcon circles overhead, unable to deliver the flag with the blonde-haired girl in the way. Reed, who has now made it to the tower, reaches out his hand towards the bird, having a clear shot for the flag hooks. The falcon looks my way, still circling as if looking for confirmation.

"Yes," I try to yell over the distance, "Give it to Reed!" There is no way I could have been heard by a person, not with the noise of the fighting and the distance, but somehow the falcon heard me. Understood me. Maybe birds have better hearing than people, or perhaps it's some sort of magical connection, I don't really know how this stuff works. Nonetheless, it tucks its wings and dives for Reed, releasing the flag to flutter into his outstretched hands.

He lunges for the flag hooks, swinging his sword in a wide arc to deflect against the blonde-haired girl, who tries to break away from Jane and attack him. Within three strides he makes it, hooking the flag beside the others with enough force to nearly tear it. Eliza cries outraged.

Almost immediately, a horn rings in the air signaling the end of the games. We won. The Tournament is over.

A cheer goes up from my team, drowned out by the thunderous applause of the crowd from within the dome. I sigh with relief, not daring to relax my grip on the steel rungs. Down below on the ground, I can see Alaina hug Nate with excitement. Reed and Jane are cheering with triumph, Reed pumping his fist in the air. I also catch the look of complete resentment Eliza aims first at my friends, and then towards me.

The falcon circles around the tower, silver wings standing out starkly against the night, before gliding back in my direction. I could have sworn it looked almost…proud. Coming to a graceful landing beside my hand, it puffs out its feathers. It seems to regard me in the same way I'm regarding it.

"Good boy," I say hesitantly, followed by an indignant and angry squawk, "I mean girl. Good girl," I correct. Then I pause, still very keenly aware I'm talking to a bird. "Thank you," I say finally, completely genuine. With that, the falcon slowly begins to fade, becoming nothing but silver light, my bracelet growing warm for a slight moment before the bird is gone.

After the falcon disappeared, came the next issue- how to get down from the top of the Outerdome?

It really only took less than 10 minutes. The way that the doorways had been opened and closed in different places in the Outerdome walls apparently applied to the whole dome. The glass panels could be controlled individually via the control panel Reed had shown me before. So Aravian, the guy who had designed the dome, one of the people from the king's council, could use the control panel to raise the safety net used for the obstacle course that typically resides at the top of the dome, and position it 5 feet beneath where I was crouching. He then created an opening in the glass panels that I could slide through, and land safely on the net.

Then came the slow descent, as the net lowered to the floor of the dome, all the while the crowd gathered in the stands applauded, cheered, and shouted. I spotted King Orlon and Marcus still standing atop the dais, the king watching with an amused glint in his eyes, and Marcus stone-faced as always. Aravian wasn't so happy.

Now, standing among the other trainees once again gathered before the dais, I try not to look at the king's Architect and Strategist, who is glaring in my direction as he has been since I climbed off the net. Many people are looking my way, some with amusement, some amazed, and a few with disapproval.

"I want to congratulate the silver legion," King Orlon begins, "On their extraordinary victory. You all showed great skill, bravery, and intellect..."

"Your Majesty," Aravian interrupts, his voice oily and whiny, to match his sneer that he aims at me. The king balks at the interruption, the whole crowd shifting with surprise, but Aravian continues.

"That stunt the girl pulled, there is no way such a thing could be allowed. Using the dome itself to her advantage, it's specifically off-limits-"

"No it isn't," Reed speaks up, interrupting him right back. "The only off-limits areas were outside the woods, or *inside* the dome. Climbing it was certainly legal…and impressive," he adds grudgingly. Aravian's sneer turns more into a grimace, his features twisting in anger.

"Now listen here-"

"No," The king says. "Reed is correct. Climbing the dome, while never been seen before, was not technically against the rules."

"Well, what about the bird?" Aravian asks, trying to keep his voice polite speaking to Orlon. "The use of that flying silver chicken certainly was an unfair advantage-"

I could have sworn I felt my bracelet warm slightly at the insult, but then the last person I expected to defend me spoke up.

"Unfortunately, Aravian," Marcus drawls, disappointment written on his face, as if he didn't truly agree with what he was about to say, "As stated in the rules, the use of vitalums is allowed."

"But-"

"That's enough," the king says.

Nate leans over, and loudly whispers to me, "Don't worry, Aravian's only mad because you left footprints on his precious Outerdome," with enough volume for everyone to hear. I wince. I did leave footprints, large smears of dirt, and smudges on the pristine glass from the dirt all over my boots and hands, from running through the forest and climbing trees. Aravian's face almost turns purple with fury.

Alaina smacks Nate's arm. "Not the time," she mutters, though her mouth twitches upward with amusement.

"This concludes the first round of the Winter Tournament of the Guards," the king says quickly before things can escalate. "Next, we have the round for the newly appointed guards- those who have been full-fledged guards for three years or less."

There is excited murmuring from the large section of young armored men and women gathered in the front rows.

"Trainees, you may use the changing rooms to change into clean clothes provided for you, and for those that require medical attention, there is a medics station through that door," the king motions to the dressing room and medic doors at one side of the dome.

I head for the dressing rooms, assessing my injuries. My back still aches somewhat from my tumble from the tower, but not badly. What's startling is my lack of minor scrapes or bruises. I had torn through a forest running from wolves, yet I have not a scratch on me. Even my hands aren't as badly scraped up as I thought they had been.

Looking around at the others, those who had been in combat were worse off than me. Reed has a large bruise already forming on his temple, and his arm has a shallow cut that had torn through the sleeve. Jane is nursing a bleeding shoulder and Nate's face is covered with minor scratches. Stefan and Alaina seem alright, nothing major. I guess it's hard to fight someone when they're invisible. The other trainee, the one who had fallen off the tower with me and been knocked unconscious, is up and walking around, to my infinite relief.

We get changed, clothes for each of us laid out in the changing rooms, a clean pair of comfortable pants, and a cotton t-shirt. The shirt is spotless white, with golden letters printed across the front reading *Winter Tournament of the Guards,* embellished with the same entwining R's that are engraved on the breastplates. I wonder what they stand for.

When I leave the changing room, I head for the medic's station, spotting Alaina already there, already dressed in the same pants and cotton t-shirt. A medic is inspecting an awful bruise on her back, right below the shoulder blade. Alaina gives me a trademark welcoming smile as I come to sit beside her on a vacant stool.

"How did that happen?" I ask, inwardly wincing at the sight. "Did you fall out of a tower too?"

Alaina snorts. "No, I took a blunted arrow to the back," she says, cringing.

Oh - I remember Jane firing those blunted arrows, knocking over trainees when they met their mark.

"I think I would rather fall out of the tower again," I admit. Alaina laughs slightly.

"I did hear about that," she says. "I had just made it to the enemy tower base, and I heard Jane shout your name. When I finally got back with the flag, you were gone, and no one knew where you disappeared after falling out of the tower."

"You scared the life out of all of us," Nate chimes in, plopping himself on the stool beside me, with Jane, Reed, and Stefan following at his heels. "We could all hear Reed yelling at Jane," Nate raises his voice in a poor imitation of Reed, "*You dropped her off a tower?!* And then Jane was like *I didn't drop her...* and then I was like *Uh guys, if Jane dropped her off a tower then where'd she go?* Cause you weren't there anymore you see-"

"Okay Nate," Alaina says, rubbing at her temples as if Nate's begun to give her a headache. "We don't need the play-by-play."

"Also, I didn't drop her off the tower," Jane grumbles.

"But Nate was right, you were just gone," Stefan says. "No one knew where you went. Then Reed was like *What the...?* And you were climbing the Outerdome, of all things."

Jane laughs. "Then Eliza led a full-on attack on our base," she adds. "We thought she was going to get the flags, but then that bird..."

"Yeah, where did that come from?" Nate asks, folding his hands on his lap. "How did you suddenly just summon your vitalum like that?"

"My vitalum?" I ask. "Is that what the falcon is called?" Stefan nods. I shrug.

"I have no idea," I say honestly. "I just knew I needed to get the flag to you all, and it just… happened."

"That's good," Stefan says. "That's just proof that you do have magic." His eyes glint with excitement.

The medic, having finished with Alaina, moves to me, spotting the scrapes on my hand instantly. Frowning she inspects them. She seems confused, and I feel the sting of disinfectant as she rubs an ointment into my palms.

"I don't quite know how," she says, her voice with a slightly heavier version of the accent I've begun to associate with the Realms, "But your hands aren't nearly as bad as I thought they would be. That jump you did…" she inspects a broken nail, nowhere near the nail bed, even though I could have sworn it had been bleeding before. "Well, let's just say you have a lot of luck!" She raises an eyebrow but moves on to the cut on Reed's arm. Another medic wanders over to work on Jane's shoulder.

"Could you do it again, if you wanted to?" Stefan asks, continuing our conversation. I shake my head.

"I- I don't even know how I did it in the first place," I say, wringing my hands.

"We can keep training you," Jane offers, with a smile. "Now that you're officially a trainee and all. With a little hard work, using your magic will be almost as natural as breathing."

There's a pause of silence, and Reed frowns deeply. I can tell why, what everyone is thinking- is it really a good thing for me to learn to use my powers? I mean, if they seriously are so dark, so potentially dangerous, maybe they're best left dormant. Alaina seems to read the uncertainty in my eyes, in everyone's eyes.

"Lina," she says, her voice firm, reassuring, "Your powers are a part of you, and you shouldn't be afraid of them. The more you try to ignore them, the worse it will eventually be. You can't shove them aside and pretend your abilities don't exist, it isn't healthy. Besides, no magic is inherently good or bad, it's how you chose to use it that matters. And If you don't want to use it, you should at least learn to control it, to master it, to embrace it without fear."

Jane nods in agreement. "Alaina's right," she says. "Fear of your powers is a magic wielder's worst enemy- if you don't learn to become comfortable with that part of you, it will become restless and unmastered. It can be dangerous."

"Besides," Nate says, "There is more to your abilities than the death magic or even your falcon. There's also this…" Nate lifts a hand, and the air ripples, before his eyes shift from deep bronze to bright green. The image wavers slightly, and his eyes slowly fade back to their usual brown hue.

"Wait, how does that work?" I ask.

"Illusions," Alaina says with a Cheshire cat smile, her own eyes shifting to match the blue of mine, her hair taking on a golden color, but only for a moment. "Everyone in the Realms possesses raw magic, to a degree. The ability to manipulate appearances, kind of a smaller scale of the magic used to craft reflections."

"So you can shape-shift?" I ask, my eyes wide. Reed snorts.

"Hardly," he answers. "No one has enough raw magic to appear as another person, to change their appearance that drastically, except for maybe Orlon, and he would only be able to do it for a few seconds at most."

"Color is the easiest to alter, and it disappears as soon as concentration is lost. It takes a lot of effort to use raw magic - illusions, or opening mirror portals," Jane supplies.

"Jane and Alaina are our best illusionists," Reed says. "I'm not too bad myself," he smirks.

"Alright," the medic interrupts, tying off the bandage on Reed's arm, the other medic having already finished checking in on Jane, Nate, and Stefan. "Run along," the woman shoos us away from the medic center, clearing up space for more trainees. Stefan leads the group to a section higher in the stands, where we make ourselves comfortable just as the horn blows to signal the beginning of the next Tournament round.

Gazing up at the wide screens, watching the games begin to unfold, I smile. Slowly, I feel a hand loop through mine, glancing over to see Stefan, still gazing towards the screens with a smile playing across his lips.

I did it. I actually did it. I'm going to be a trainee. They're going to show me how to master my magic and hone my fighting skills until I can stand up to Lillian and stand a chance. And then I'll get my mom back.

CHAPTER 10

My feet trudge along a winding dirt path, my eyes heavy with sleeplessness, my feet already sore from walking in these boots.

Almost a week after the Winter Tournament, the victory my team has been basking in has begun to fade, the excitement and celebrations officially at an end. Some parties lasted for three days and all the nearby hotels filled to bursting with people from all three Realms staying for the festivities. Feasts, dancing in the streets, and celebratory parades through the city.

Well, I say city, but realistically it's more of a village than anything. The capital of the Mirror Realm, Penrith, is shockingly small, but lively and full of wonderful cafes, restaurants, and parks, all having gone out to host their first Winter Tournament celebrations. Some people treated me and my team like victors, with cheering and congratulations. Others, mostly those who had watched the Tournament, claimed we were cheaters because of that stunt I pulled with the dome and the falcon. Most were just amazed to see me, some afraid, and I got many requests to summon my vitalum. The only issue is that I can't.

That brings us back here, right now, to my aching feet as Reed leads Alaina and me along a path through the Elder Woods, skirting around the Outerdome to another spot entirely.

"Are we there yet?" I whine, only half joking, an unwieldy sword at my side weighing me down.

"If you ask that again," Reed growls, "I'm going to lead us in a circle just out of spite."

"We haven't been going in a circle already?" I ask, feigning surprise. "I thought maybe you were just lost at this point."

"Guys, just stop bickering already," Alaina grumbles.

I sigh. If Reed hasn't dropped his attitude in the time that I've known him now, I don't see why I have to keep being pleasant about it. He still refuses to explain what his problem is, even though he doesn't act like such a jerk around anyone else. Well, if he's determined to hate me, then I don't see why I have to put up with it.

I fall into step beside Alaina, allowing Reed to go ahead. She frowns toward him as if trying to figure it out as well, but she says nothing.

And finally, after what feels like ages of trekking through the woods at 8:00 in the morning, we stop at a wide clearing off the path. It is clearly meant to be used for training- lined with log benches and a rack bolted into the earth, meant for holding weapons- which is exactly why we're here. Exactly why we've been coming here at 8:00 in the morning for the past two days.

Today is day three of trying to summon my vitalum…and failing.

I hoist the sword I'm carrying onto the rack at the edge of the cleared, packed dirt. I won't need that until later. Magic training comes first- not that I've accomplished anything yet. Whatever stroke of luck I'd had during the Tournament seems to have vanished on the wings of that silver falcon.

Taking up position in the center of the packed earth, I close my eyes and concentrate.

After several days of trying, with no luck, I would usually be discouraged. Maybe dismiss it as a fluke. But I can feel my magic, tightly coiled into itself, dormant. I had never noticed it before- when I'm not concentrating, its tiny flicker of warmth and subtle inner glow is practically nonexistent, dimmed, but still there.

I try to unravel it, try to coax it out of hiding, but it seems to be resisting me. Pulling away when I reach for it, slipping out of my mental grasp. My hands clench with frustration.

"You're not even trying," Reed drawls. A bead of sweat slips down my forehead, my whole body warm despite the chill in the air. I ignore him, gritting my teeth. He sighs.

"Summoning your vitalum shouldn't be so hard, especially after you've already done it once. It should be as natural as breathing, without barely a thought."

A roaring fills my ears, anger and annoyance bubbling up inside me. At Reed, at his drawling voice, at my magic.

"Just *concentrate*," he hisses.

"I am," I snap back.

"You're not."

"Just shut up, Reed," Alaina fires. My eyes fly open, the only thing I've accomplished is making my hands sweat, my nails biting into my palms. I was so close, I can tell. I can sense the tendril of magic inside of me, which seems to shy away from every attempt to harness it. I glare at Reed.

"How did you get stuck with training duty anyway?" I snap, needing somewhere to vent my frustration. "You clearly don't want to be here."

Reed scowls but doesn't answer my question.

"I need a break," I say, turning for the clearing.

"But we've only been at it for two minutes," Alaina protests, perched on a log bench, her fingers drumming on her knee.

"I just need to clear my head," I say. "I need to concentrate. I only need a minute." A minute alone, without being watched and mocked. Alaina looks at me with concern.

"The reason I'm here," Reed says coldly, "Is that the woods are dangerous. It's always better to stay here in larger groups. Meaning wandering off is out of the question."

"I'm not wandering off-" I begin to shoot back, but Alaina gently interrupts.

"He does have a point, Lina."

I raise an eyebrow. "About the woods being dangerous? But the Tournament was here, and the only dangerous thing I came across was other trainees and falling out of towers."

Alaina just shrugs.

"The Elder Woods themselves aren't that dangerous. It's the woods right beyond their borders that are trouble. I guess as long as you stick to the paths, you should be fine."

I give her a small smile, before making to turn and leave the clearing.

"But Lina," Alaina says, her voice strangely serious. "The woods aren't warded like they were during the Tournament. Whatever you do, *stay on the path*."

I nod, feeling strangely spooked, but I briskly walk until I'm hidden by the trees.

The Elder Woods are beautiful. No longer shrouded in night, sunlight dapples the ground, glimmering on the frost that clings to the bare branches of trees towering overhead. The dirt path winds, further along, doubling back around towards the dome, the arch of which is visible through the leafless boughs. The sky is a pale and watery blue, and I can see thick clouds gathering far off on the horizon.

My new and barely broken-in training boots scuff the frozen leaves and my breath clouds the air in front of me. I'll be grateful to get to the physical part of training today, sparring with a sword, because it will at least be warmer.

I take a deep breath, calming myself, trying to delve into the hint of power I can still sense sleeping within. It doesn't feel the way I would imagine such dark and deadly magic would feel- light and airy, warm as a summer breeze concealing, an icy cool core. Again it coils away, out of reach.

Coming back to my physical surroundings, I look around, and I come to a stop. I've gone a lot further than I thought, the path doubling back around towards the Outerdome. I've been gone for maybe 10 minutes, probably a good time to pick up the pace and get back before anyone starts wondering where I am.

I turn on my heel, walking at a brisker pace when I hear something. A voice, shouting. At first, I don't think much of it, other training sessions have been meeting out here as well, so it's likely another trainee. Listening closely, I hear it again. It sounds almost like...

It's her. My mom.

"Lina!" her voice echoes again, louder and panicked. "Emmalina, are you out here?"

It's her. Somehow, some way, she made it here. She looking for me. She's okay! I take off in the direction of her voice, veering through the trees and underbrush, my feet flying. I spin, certain it had come from this direction. But as I pause, some small part of my brain whispers that I've forgotten something. Ignoring it, I make my way deeper into the woods, frantic.

"Mom?" I call out, my heart bursting with hope.

That part of my brain whispers again, there's something I'm forgetting. But she's so close, she's alive!

"Mom?" I call again, doubt creeping into my voice. Why isn't she answering? I take a breath to call again, and a hand clamps over my mouth from behind.

My scream is muffled, and I've spun around with violent force until I'm facing- a girl?

Her eyes are what I notice first. The left one is a light golden brown, the right being a pale sky blue. Both are livid with anger.

Eliza.

I yelp, scrambling backward, and she doesn't even try to hold on as I shove her away.

"What in the name of the Realms are you doing out here?" she hisses.

"I…"

"Are you trying to get yourself killed?" she demands, keeping her voice low, and quiet, those strange eyes narrowing.

"I… but I heard… she's out here somewhere. My mom," I struggle to explain. The more I think about it, some sort of fog that had clouded my brain begins to dissipate, allowing me to think clearly. Why and how would my mom be out here? Suddenly I can remember what I've been forgetting, Alaina's warning. *Whatever you do, stay on the path.*

My eyes widen, and I look around me, at the half-dead underbrush and trees, and no path to be seen.

Eliza scoffs.

"How can you even be so gullible? That wasn't your mother, and we better get out of here before it finds us." A chill shivers through my bones.

"Before what finds us?"

But as the words escape my lips, Eliza's face turns a shade paler, and she cranes her neck to look at something behind me. I hear a noise like sandpaper being rubbed together, and I freeze. Eliza moves quickly, shoving me over as something huge strikes the ground where I had been standing seconds before.

"You idiot!" she shouts. "Don't just stand there, *move!*"

I scramble to my feet, spinning to see the terrible creature towering behind us.

It's a snake. A very, *very* big snake, its body thicker around than the young oak tree it coils in, likely longer than a bus. Its head is diamond-shaped, spines are along its crown, and piercing yellow eyes with slit pupils are fixed on us.

It shakes its head, spitting out the mouthful of frozen dirt carved from the spot where I had been standing. It hisses, the sandpapery sound harsher than any noise I've ever heard. It moves to strike again, faster than lightning, but Eliza leaps in front of it with her sword swinging in a wide arc. There is no fear in her eyes, just cold determination.

The snake whips its tail- or should I say tails? Its tail is forked, both tips lashing for her feet. I take a breath to warn her, but she's already leaping, swinging her sword for the creature's head. It dodges, jaws snapping for the blade. Its fangs are as long as my forearm.

Hands shaking, I reach for my sword... that isn't there. I left it in the clearing. Eliza, glancing over her shoulder, rolls her eyes as she comes to the same conclusion. She tosses her sword, clattering to the dirt at my feet. I look up, my eyes wide.

"But..." I start to protest, but she unsheathes a dagger from the belt around her waist. She juts her chin in the direction of the blade on the ground.

"What are you waiting for? Make yourself useful and distract it."

My hands fumble on the hilt, the metal of the sword flashing in the watery sunlight. The girl leaps for a low-hanging branch of a tree- she's stealing my move- but the snake simply raises its head to her level, hissing.

Not bothering to think it through, I act on impulse. I dash forward, angling my sword for the creature's exposed underbelly. But it's not stupid- it sees me coming. Losing interest in Eliza, it lunges for me. I fall to the ground, sliding home run style under the snake's bared fangs. The tip of one grazes my jacket, tearing the fabric, but I barely notice the sting as I manage to barely avoid being impaled. It moves to lunge again, and Eliza leaps from the tree to land on its back. Oh, now she is definitely stealing my moves.

She clings to it as it thrashes, riding it like a bull at a rodeo, gripping the spines on the back of its head and trying to jab her dagger into its eye. But it bucks, throwing her off, and Eliza hits the ground hard. It spins back to me, standing frozen in shock.

It makes a horrible sound, a mix of a roar and a hiss, as a dagger appears lodged in its side. Alaina materializes next to it, releasing the hilt, and leaving the dagger behind. Reed stalks out of the trees seconds later, slashing with his training sword. Energized, I lunge forward with my blade as well. Eliza, battered but still very much angry, palms her dagger once more, and together the four of us advance on the snake. Being the intelligent reptile it is, it takes one look at the four armed warriors, gives one last frustrated hiss, and slithers back into the underbrush. Within seconds, its forked tail disappears into a bush, and the woods fall silent.

Reed turns to me, breathing heavily. Alaina frowns.

"Well, there goes my favorite dagger," she sighs. "It had sapphires on it," she pouts.

Eliza snorts. "Of course, you would be concerned about your bejeweled dagger," she scoffs. "Though of course, only you would own such a ridiculous thing anyway."

Alaina bristles at her tone, but Reed steps in.

"Eliza," he says. "What are you doing here?"

"Saving this imbecile's life," she says scornfully, temper flaring brighter than a flame in her mismatched eyes. She flips her hair over her shoulder. "I was expecting more of a thank you."

"Thank you," I say genuinely. But she only fixes me with a baleful look.

"What happened here?" Reed questions, but he doesn't look as angry as I thought he would.

"I was training with my legion," Eliza explains. "I heard the serpent's call. Obviously, I ignored it, as any sane person should do, but then I heard *her* crashing through the woods and shouting after it."

Alaina sighs.

"Lina, I told you not to leave the path."

"But... I thought I heard my mom," I said softly, embarrassed. I'm such a fool. Surprisingly, Reed's eyes soften ever so slightly. As if he actually feels sympathy.

"That's called a mimic serpent," he supplies. "They have a certain call that they use to lure prey. Anyone around will hear whatever they most want to hear, whatever is most likely to draw them in. Usually, it's a friend or a loved one. It even impairs your ability to think clearly. Most people learn to recognize it, and know not to follow voices calling out to them in the woods."

"We should get back to the path," Alaina suggests.

The four of us head back the way I came. Reed leads the way, Eliza lingering towards the back as if she doesn't have any interest in talking to any of us.

"Thank you," I say once we reach the path when she moves to break away from our group and head in the other direction. "Thank you for saving my life."

She only snorts, not looking back as she strides away. Once she disappears through the trees, Reed lets out a breath.

"Such a lovely attitude that one has," Alaina's voice is layered with sarcasm.

"Anyway," Reed says, rolling his eyes. "That was a good warm-up."

"A warm-up?" I groan. "You mean we're still going to train?"

"Of course," Reed answers. "We can give the magic training a rest for today, but that doesn't mean you're off the hook completely."

I scowl at him, but he just turns and begins walking back towards the clearing. Alaina follows, whistling a cheery tune as if we hadn't just fought a monster in the woods. I sigh, I guess I'm just going to have to get used to this.

The rest of the morning is rough. Reed pushes me hard, practicing against both Alaina and himself.

"So I know Alaina has the invisibility, because she's a lynx," I say, as we sit on a log bench taking a break. Reed takes a swig from his water bottle.

"Also speed, agility, and flexibility," Alaina brags. "Perfect for spies, assassins, and scouts."

I nod. "That too. But what about Wolves? What can you, Jane, and Nate do?" I ask Reed.

"Strength and endurance, mostly," he answers. "Wolf Soldiers are physically stronger than an average person. We also have a talent for picking up skills quickly. It gives us a good advantage, being able to master many things."

"Also, Wolf Soldiers are naturally right *and* left-handed," Alaina pipes up. I raise my eyebrows.

"That's pretty cool," I say. Reed nods.

"Watch this!" He stands, gripping a throwing dagger in each hand. Aiming for a tree at the far end of the clearing where a battered target had been hung, he throws a dagger with his right hand. I watch it fly, striking close to the innermost ring of the target. He then throws the other with his left hand, striking just below his last shot. He turns, sketching a bow.

"Impressive," Alaina says with an approving nod. I take another long drink of water. My mouth feels too dry, my arms are heavy. My whole body feels exhausted, and it's barely past noon. My eyelids even begin to droop.

"Are you tired already?" Reed taunts, raising an eyebrow. Alaina crosses her arms.

"We've been at it for over 3 hours," she grumbles. Three hours, and no progress with my magic. Just aching muscles and a headache from exhaustion. Finally, Reed yields, re-sheathing his sword.

"Alright. How about we meet Jane, Nate, and Stefan for lunch then?" he suggests. Alaina nods fervently.

"I like this plan."

Together, we pack up our supplies, and I grab my sword. I swear it's gotten heavier. The trek back to the castle feels longer. There's a throbbing pain in my shoulder, my legs feel like lead and my head is spinning slightly. I don't remember my endurance ever being so bad. I've never been the most athletic, but I had been on a volleyball team and tried track. I was used to physical activity. It must be the magic practice, hadn't Alaina once mentioned that it took a lot out of the wielder? Does attempting to use it still apply in the same way?

As we enter the castle hall, I turn to Reed and Alaina. "I don't think I'm going to meet you guys for lunch," I say, my vision wobbling. "I think I need a nap."

"Maybe we tried pushing your magic too hard," Alaina says, looking me over with concern.

"We all need to freshen up anyway, we'll head back to our rooms," Reed suggests, gesturing to the torn and dirty clothing we're still wearing from our morning in the woods. "I can bring you some food later. A magical burnout usually only takes a bit of sleep and something to eat, and you'll be fine." I nod, the idea of sleep relieving.

When I get to my room, I barely have the will to change into fresh clothes, tossing my filthy ones onto the floor by the doorway. I'm asleep the moment my head hits the pillow.

My dreams are strange and fuzzy as if I'm looking at them through smudged and cloudy glass or fog. It's a lot of white light, and I catch the sight of falcon wings. Then I hear the words I had almost forgotten, echoing in that ethereal voice in my head.

Falcon brave and bold in flight.
Shall turn from darkness and worship the light,

Shattered glass gleaming white,
And the worlds bow down to the Mirror's might.

I wake once more in a cold sweat, to the sound of someone at the door. Knocking.

"Come in," I say, sitting up and shoving off the blankets. Thankfully, by some miracle, my head has cleared. The headache and crushing exhaustion are gone.

Reed pokes his head in the doorway, a plate piled with food clutched in his hands.

"Hey," he says, "You're awake." He nearly trips over the pile of training clothes I left in the doorway. I wince.

"Sorry about that," I move to climb out of bed to clean it up, but he raises a hand to stop me.

"It's fine, I've got it," he says with an amused smirk. He sets the plate of food on the nightstand, and my stomach rumbles. It's roast chicken, with vegetables, and drizzled with a lemony scented sauce. That doesn't look like lunch, that looks like dinner, but I couldn't have slept that long. My head whips towards the clock beside the bed.

9:46 p.m.

I blink, the numbers taking a second to process in my mind. 9:46? It was barely noon when I came here to take a quick nap. I had slept almost 10 hours!

Reed notices my surprise as he stoops to scoop up the pile of clothes.

"Yeah, you slept for a long while," he says. "We were starting to get worried."

I shake my head, reaching for the plate and digging in. But when Reed falls silent, I look up, my mouth stuffed with chicken. He's staring at my discarded jacket, at the jagged tear in the sleeve, with narrowed eyes.

"What?" I mumble, swallowing the mouthful of food.

"How did this happen?" he asks, indicating the tear, the bit of dried blood around the edges. I cock my head, trying to remember.

"Oh," I say. "That was from that awful snake-thing, in the woods. You should have seen it, it was coming at me and I did this cool slide underneath it, and its stupid fang caught my shoulder."

Reed stiffens, his eyes going wide as if an electrical shock went through his body.

"You got *bitten* by the Mimic Serpent?" he says, the look on his face nothing short of horror. I frown.

"Uh, not exactly. It was more of a scrape I guess."

Within seconds, he's at my side, rolling up the sleeve of my shirt to expose the slash in my upper arm. It's a lot better than I would have expected, no longer even bleeding, not as deep as it had felt before. But Reed's face is white as paper, bloodless with what looks like dread and shock.

"What's wrong," I ask hesitantly. "Reed, seriously. You're freaking me out."

"The Mimic Serpent's fangs," Reed says slowly, "Are deadly venomous. One prick, without immediate medical attention, and the victim is dead within two or three hours." I frown, looking again at the cut.

"Well obviously it can't be that bad," I say. "I'm fine."

"No," he says, grabbing my wrist and hauling me to my feet before I can react.

"We need to get you to a medic, right now." I pull away.

"Reed, this has to be an overreaction," I protest. "It's been way longer than three hours, and I'm not dead."

"Emmalina, you don't understand," he growls. "*No one survives Mimic Serpent venom. It must have been why you were unconscious for so long, you need to see a medic.*"

I stop protesting, mostly because Reed has to know more about this than I do, and I don't feel like dying. So I let him drag me to the castle infirmary, down a flight of steps and through several hallways, before finally passing beneath a beautiful cobbled archway with no door that leads into what looks like a waiting room. A few people in white scrubs, hair nets, and surgical masks bustle in and out of a swinging door in the far wall, past the desk in the front, and comfy-looking chairs placed along the walls.

After informing the receptionist that I had been bitten by a Mimic Serpent, there was a mad rush of nurses and medics, despite my protests that I was fine. They ushered me to a room in the back, where the medics inspected the cut on my arm. Reed explained everything, from the fight in the woods, to my tiredness afterward, to how long it had been since I was bitten.

The lead medic in charge took a look at the scratch left by the serpent's fang as he applies a salve and bandages it.

"I don't understand," Reed says. "How is she still alive?"

"I don't know," the medic answers, his brows furrowed. "Normally a person needs to take the antidote within a half hour of being bitten to have a good chance at getting the venom out of their system. My guess would be maybe you remembered wrong, and it wasn't actually the fang that caught your shoulder." I bristle at the implication.

"Upon further examination and testing of the wound, there definitely was Mimic Serpent venom in your system. Keyword *was*- it still lingers but has been neutralized somehow. As if you had already taken the antidote, or your body somehow fought it off on its own."

"I thought that wasn't possible," Reed says. The medic shakes his head.

"It isn't. This must be some kind of miracle, or perhaps," he studies my face as if realizing who I resemble for the first time. "Perhaps this has something to do with your magic."

"My magic?"

"Yes, it would make sense, in a way. If you truly do share Lillian's powers of darkness," I flinch at the blunt wording, but the medic forges on nonetheless. "Then perhaps a side effect of wielding death makes you harder to kill."

Reed frowns at the outrageous claim.

"Lillian never showed any signs of something like that."

"When was Lillian ever bitten by a Mimic Serpent?" the medic counters.

I slide off the bed, not interested in hearing any more about the magic I share with Lillian, this dark part of me that everyone seems so certain I possess.

"Well, I guess we've established that I'm fine," I say, suddenly feeling restless. Like I need to do something, right now, just to banish the thoughts of magic. "So there's no reason for me to stay. Thank you so much for your time."

"Lina, you should stay a bit longer, just in case we've missed something," Reed begins, but the medic frowns.

"I see no reason why she has to stay if she doesn't wish to," the medic says, checking something off on his clipboard. "The tests confirm there is no need for the antidote, and the venom should be completely gone within the hour. So you are entirely free to go."

"Thank you," I say, feeling a bit of relief. "Come on, Reed. Let's go."

We leave the infirmary and head off to find our friends.

CHAPTER 11

The castle is fairly quiet and empty as the time reaches 10 p.m. Reed and I had headed back towards my room after Reed had informed me that he was supposed to tell me earlier that I was being switched to a new bedroom tonight, and for obvious reasons, he hadn't gotten the chance to. Apparently, this place called the Dorm is where the guards and trainees sleep and hang out, and the king had finally decreed I was ready to move in with the other guards, now that I'm officially one of them.

I have very few possessions with me- a few pairs of clothes, boots that I'm currently wearing, and a small gleaming gold trophy that I had been given after my team had won the Tournament. I can't say I'm going to miss the empty guest bedroom, with its lack of color and company.

Reed leads the way through the winding hallways and out of the castle doors. The Dorm, which he points out to me as we walk along a well-lit path outside, is a large white building, thankfully none of it made of glass or crystal. It's completely separate from the castle itself, meaning we have to walk through the frigid night air to reach it. Somewhere in the distance, the faint sound of rumbling thunder heralds the beginning of raindrops as the dark clouds I had seen before blot out the stars.

The inside of the Dorm isn't quite as pristine as the palace, with a warmer and more cozy feel. While the outside is the same uniform light color as everything else, the interior of the Dorm reminds me of an old and fancy mansion, with winding, carpeted staircases, and rich mahogany wood blending into the darker colored walls. A chandelier hangs high above our heads in the foyer, sparkling silver.

Now I know why the castle was quiet, everyone is here. Even though it's gotten a bit late, guards and trainees in a bizarre assortment of casual clothes and armor left over from training lounge on leather sofas, making their way up and down the staircases to other levels above, laughing and talking with one another as the day comes to an end. Some turn to look in our direction as we make our way up the stairs, and Reed greets a few with a smile or a nod.

We arrive at my new room, in the girls' wing of the mansion, where I shove my few clothes in the closet and place the trophy on the nightstand. Like the foyer, this room is dark-colored and cozy, with wide windows on one wall and a large bed.

"Where is everyone else?" I ask, finding Reed still standing outside the door.

"They're probably in one of the lounges," he gestures down the hall. I follow behind as we pass through a small doorway into what looks like a living room of sorts. Worn leather couches line the space, interspersed with side tables and coffee tables, antique-looking rugs before a grand stone fireplace with a roaring glow from within. The drizzle of rain outside has become a full-blown storm, the pitter patter against the windows like it's competing with the crackle of the fire.

Jane and Stefan both look up from the small table they're seated at, a chess board lay sprawling between them. Seeing Reed and me together, Stefan's eyebrows raise. Nate is lounging with his foot kicked up over the arm of one of the couches, dozing, while Alaina lies curled beside him with a book clutched in her hands.

"Finally awake?" Stefan teases, though his voice is tenser than usual.

Reed plops down onto the couch beside Alaina, startling her out of her book.

"Oh, you're back. What took you so long, Reed? Didn't you just go there to drop off dinner and bring Lina back to the Dorm?" She sets her book down on a nearby coffee table, and from the cover, I can see it's a kind of romance novel.

"Yeah," he says dryly, "But we took a detour to the infirmary."

"The infirmary?" Jane asks, raising a dark eyebrow.

"I was bitten by a Mimic Serpent, during training today," I say, not waiting for Reed to speak first. I don't want him to make it seem like a bigger deal than it actually is. "But I'm perfectly fine."

Apparently, it was still a big deal.

Alaina's eyes almost bug out of her head. Stefan accidentally drops the chess piece he's holding. Nate snores in his sleep and shifts, Alaina having to swat his hand out of her face.

"Wait," Jane says, holding her hands in a time-out position. "*What* happened during training today? I didn't hear about any of this!"

"Me neither," Stefan protests.

"Lina went for a walk during training and was lured off the path by a Mimic Serpent," Alaina begins, giving them the crash course of the day's events. "Reed and I heard the serpent's call, and a few minutes later we heard shouting. When we arrived, Eliza was already there, and she saved Lina's life. We scared it off, but we didn't think anyone got *bit*..."

"It really was nothing," I say. "Barely a scratch."

"But you *just* went to the infirmary?" Stefan questions, his eyes narrowing in concern. "As in just now? But that would be almost..."

"Ten hours after, I know," I say. "I've already had this conversation with the medic."

"Lina, how are you *alive*?" Jane demands, leaning forward to rest her elbows on her knees. "That's impossible-"

"That's what I said!" Reed interrupts.

"Look, I don't want to talk about it-" I start to say, but Reed jumps in.

"The medic thinks it's because of her powers," he explains, even after I shoot him a glare. "He said that because she may wield the power of death, she may be harder to kill."

Alaina shivers and I scowl. I hate the mention of my powers, especially the way Reed or that stupid medic phrased it. I do not *wield death* or anything like that, I'm a good person.

"Look," I say before anyone asks any questions. "I really don't want to talk about it, okay? Let's just talk about, I don't know, anything else?" Alaina settles back into her spot beside Nate, folding her arms.

"Alright," Jane says, idly capturing one of Stefan's chess pieces. "How about this topic of conversation…what was the whole deal about Eliza saving your life?" From her icy tone, it's clear that Jane dislikes Eliza just as much, if not more than Alaina and Reed.

"She was nearby," I answer. "She said she heard the serpent, then me calling after it thinking it was my mom. She showed up just in time." Jane frowns, tapping a chess piece on the board.

"Is she… always like that?" I ask uncomfortably, recalling her icy demeanor, how she acted as though saving my life was a chore she had no choice but to do, rather than something out of the kindness of her heart. Stefan nods.

"To everyone," he confirms. "Don't take it personally."

"Is she a falcon too?" I ask curiously. "I mean, she didn't use any sort of invisibility, and she didn't seem to have any above-average strength. And come to think of it, I haven't met any other Falcon Warriors yet."

But Reed shakes his head.

"No, she's not a Falcon Warrior. The reason you haven't met any yet is that there are no more Falcon Warriors in the Realms. As far as we know, you and Lillian are the only ones with that ability in existence. Ever since every Falcon Warrior disappeared without a trace 200 years ago."

I blink, my brain not quite catching up with what he's saying. That is a lot to process.

"What do you mean we're the only ones?" I ask.

"200 years ago, the number of Falcon Warriors began to drop, disappearing left and right, until suddenly they were all gone. No one knows why. But then Lillian was brought to the castle, and no one knew where she came from or who her parents were. There was something very unique about her, she possessed powers as a baby. Every guard's powers manifest when they turn 17, but for some reason, Lillian already possessed her abilities."

Jane speaks up, joining in the explanation. "Everyone was wondering who her parents might be," she supplies. "As one of them must have been a falcon for this to be possible. She was raised here in the castle, until, well, you know."

"And then, three months ago, one of our scouts heard that Lillian had found you."

Stefan continues. "Our rescue team was sent to keep an eye on you until you turned 17, to see if you really had powers.

When Lillian sent her men to abduct you, well, you know the rest."

I stare at my hands. At the power they conceal.

"That's why Lillian was after you," Jane explains gently. "You are the only Falcon Warrior left, besides her. And as if that wasn't threatening enough in her eyes, you having the same powers as her means that you are the only one capable of standing against her. That is the true reason why you were brought here. Orlon hopes that once you are a fully appointed guard, you will be the one to save the Realms from utter destruction."

That was a lot to drop on someone in one conversation. That King Orlon expects to thrust the fate of the Realms onto my shoulders, a 17-year-old girl who hadn't even heard about magic until a few weeks ago will be expected to stand up to the greatest tyrant that a whole world of magic wielders can't defeat. I voice these concerns, but of course, they don't have much impact.

"But, wait," I say, rubbing at my temples after several minutes more of heated conversation. "What about the fact that I'll have to be a fully-fledged guard before I can face Lillian? What about my deal with Orlon, where I only have to be a trainee? To be a full guard, I would still have to be at least 19 years old, right? I can't stay here for *years*, that will be too late to save my mother. And the rest of my life…school, my job, Cam…

Oh, God. Cam.

My eyes get wide as the realization hits me with the force of a truck.

"What?" Alaina asks, noticing my face go pale.

Cam. I can't believe I forgot about him. I've been gone for over two weeks, with no call or text. The last time I even spoke to him was when I told him that my mom and I were going camping for the weekend. The *weekend,* as in only two days. He probably has no idea what's happened to us and I haven't given that a second thought in over a week.

My friends are still looking at me with concern, so I swallow and say, "I have to go back to Earth." Four confused and somewhat alarmed faces stare back at me. Only four, because Nate still hasn't woken up from his nap. Jane immediately shakes her head.

"Why?" Stefan asks.

"My friend," I say. "My friend Cam. I disappeared without even a note, he's probably so worried."

"You can't go back yet," Jane says. "Your deal with Orlon included that you have to stay here and train until he decrees you're ready before you can just leave. Plus, Lillian is still keeping an eye out for you, she probably has tabs on all of your friends. Anyways, as I said before, no one is allowed to leave without permission from King Orlon or a member of the king's court."

"Then I have to get their permission," I argue, already getting to my feet. "I had been so focused on my mom for so long, I had forgotten about the rest of my whole life back on Earth- Cam, school, my job- I probably have detentions lined up for skipping classes, and I'm sure I've been fired from the Cafe at this point."

"Lina, none of that matters because you can't go back," Jane says. But I don't listen.

"Take me to the king, or whoever I need to talk to, but I'm going back. I won't stay, I know it's too dangerous, but I have to at least tell Cam that I'm alright."

"Lina, but it's late."

"I don't care. Take me to Orlon, because I'm going back to that clearing, and I'm going to find my friend."

"Absolutely not," the king's second-in-command, Marcus, scoffs.

All of my friends had accompanied me to the castle, even Nate. It was safe to say he was very confused about what was going on when he woke up, but he just went along with it. Alaina did her best to catch him up to speed as we walked, but we hadn't even made it to Orlon when we ran into Marcus. The moment the words left my mouth, I knew I was going to regret asking Marcus for permission. Regretted it the moment when his eyes flashed viciously, and I knew he was going to enjoy turning me away.

"But-"

"Silence," he hisses. "You are not to bother His Majesty with such a foolish request. No one is going anywhere, least of all a girl with no guard experience, for no reason."

"I do have a reason," I protest.

"Wanting to hang out with your friend is not a reason," he sneers. I feel my temper rising, but I trample it down.

"I lost my mom, I lost my friends, I lost *everything*," I say, my voice trembling. "I have faced things I couldn't even have imagined a week ago. And if going back can let my friend know I'm still alive, if it can even help me find what happened to my mom, then I think I deserve to go. *Please*, let me go back, just once."

"Well when you put it that way," Marcus muses. "Still no. Now go, get out of my sight."

Alaina tugs my sleeve as my group turns to leave.

"Oh, one more thing," Marcus says. "Miss Windervale, Mr. Fides,"

Jane and Stefan turn as he calls their names.

"You two have been chosen for Communications Room duty." He smiles, slow and cold. "Report there immediately."

"But it's 10 p.m.," Jane starts to argue, and Marcus waves a hand to cut her off.

"So it's not too late for a little excursion around Earth, but too late for coms duty?" he asks snidely. "I said go."

Jane's hands ball into fists, but she forces herself to nod. Sharply turning away, she leads the rest of our group back into the hall.

Stefan lets out a breath of annoyance. "Well, that went exactly as planned," he mutters. "I'm going to go get the coms room equipment. Nate, would you help me carry it there?"

Nate nods, still reeling and half asleep, his hair flattened to one side of his face and his clothes rumpled.

Stefan puts his hand on Jane's shoulder. "Don't worry, Marcus can't keep us that late, we're not qualified for late night patrol anyway. He's just trying to get a rise out of us."

Jane snorts, "It's not the work I'm annoyed about."

Stefan nods, he and Nate turn to go fetch the coms equipment.

I feel restless, crossing my arms. I have to go, I have to somehow convince him. What if we just left? If I could get Jane or Alaina, or even Reed, to come with me, we could sneak away without being noticed, just long enough for me to get a message to Cam and let him know I'm okay. I mean, I've snuck out of my bedroom window at home to go to a party and got back without being caught. This couldn't be much different.

"I'm going anyway," I declare. Reed raises his eyebrows.

"I don't care what he says, we could be gone and back before he even realizes it."

"No offense," Reed says, "But that is the dumbest idea I've ever heard, respectfully."

"But I just need to find Cam, it won't take very long. If one of you took me there, it wouldn't be so dangerous…"

"Absolutely not," Jane scoffs, swishing her back hair over her shoulder, and crossing her arms. "That would be quite literally breaking the law, never mind the danger it would put us in."

"I just want to go back to the campground," I protest. "I'll find my phone, or talk to someone."

"No," Jane says. "The campground is bound to be under Lillian's surveillance, she's not going to give up until she finds you."

"But if she just wants her phone, maybe I could go retrieve it for her," Alaina suggests. "She could just text her friend and we could get right back. If we go at night, there's a good chance no one will even notice."

"Alaina, you're a bad influence," Reed says, rolling his eyes.

"And if you do get caught? By Lillian or Marcus?" Jane questions.

"Jane!" Stefan calls down the hallway, his arms full of radio wires and what looks like boxes of walkie-talkies. Nate is right behind him, clutching at microphones and a laptop. "Jane, are you coming?"

She sighs. "I'll be right there!" she turns back to us. "No one's going anywhere, okay? You'll get yourselves in trouble, or worse." With that, she sharply turns away, walking after Stefan, and we're silent until her footsteps fade away.

I turn pleading eyes to Alaina, the only person I have on my side. "I know this is a bad idea," I say, "An awful idea, but I have to go. I can't just leave my friend. And my mom, I have to find something to let me know what happened to her. I ran away in that clearing, never again. I need to do this. Please, help me," I beg.

Alaina purses her lips. "I'm in if you are," she says, turning to Reed. My heart sinks. There's no way he'll help me with this, he'll probably just agree with his sister, or worse, tell Marcus what we're planning. There's a long, long pause of silence.

"I'll help you," he says finally, something like sympathy in his eyes.

Alaina grins, and before I know what I'm doing, I hug him.

"Thank you," I say softly. Reed sighs with resignation, and I awkwardly step back as I realize who I'm hugging.

"I just know I'm going to regret this," he mutters.

And regret it he did. After we snuck through the castle and past the hallway sentries, via Alaina's invisibility, we reached the large double doors to the throne room, where the mirror portal resides.

The invisibility get's us past the few guards in the halls, and when we round the corner, there it is. A swipe of Reed's card unlocks the heavy doors, just as it had for the Centerdome, and we slowly, carefully push the doors open wide enough to slip through. Easing the door shut behind us, I glance around the room. Empty.

I would have expected better security than this, but upon further look, only a Realm Guard with a key card could have gotten through the doors anyway. The only items in here that seem to have any value are the high-backed throne perched upon a wide dais, the one Orlon had been sitting in when I first met him, and the mirror portal itself, both of which are bolted to the floor and unmovable.

I haven't been in here since that first night, and now I study the portal the way I hadn't before. It's huge, towering over our heads, a slender oval shape with silvery glass that seems to ripple like water. Much more impressive than the little handheld mirror in the cabin.

"Are you ready?" Reed asks, his eyes fixed on my face.

"What are we waiting for?" Alaina whispers. She places a slender hand against the glass, her eyebrows tightening in concentration as she powers the portal with her magic. The glass slowly begins to brighten, and I can see swirling colors inside. Alaina grunts with the effort, and Reed places his hand on the glass as well to help ease the strain of opening such a large portal.

"Picture the cabin," he instructs. "There are many places we could end up on Earth or Allrhea, so make sure you picture the right place."

I nod, take a deep breath, and step through.

CHAPTER 12

Reed, Alaina, and I crouch in the bushes, sneaking glances over the tops of overgrown leaves at the clearing ahead. The campsite where it all began.

We had made it through the portal successfully, out of the cabin, and from there it was only a short walk away from the Covered Bridge Campground.

Several feet away from where we kneel, the battered heap of waterproof fabric and broken plastic poles is all that's left of the tent my mom and I had planned to camp in before... before it all went wrong. Gazing at the campsite where my life changed forever, barely a week ago, that now-familiar pang of grief and guilt roils through my stomach. It feels like it's been so much longer, and barely yesterday, at the same time.

Reed stands from his spot beside me, satisfied that it appears to be empty. As we step from the trees, I take in the scene, my heart feeling heavier than stone.

The area is roped off with police tape, the collapsed tent bordered with yellow and black warnings and investigation signs. The dusty ground is scuffed and gouged with what must be wolf claw marks, and spotted with… is that blood? I gag with horror, the scene replaying in my head for the millionth time-the men with daggers, the wolf…

No. I stare shell-shocked at the marred earth. No, she can't be dead. She can't be.

A hand rests on my arm, and I flinch slightly. Alaina, standing beside me, gazes at me with eyes wide and full of sympathy and sorrow. I force myself to look away, to focus on something else, anything else.

Stiffly, making my way to the tent, I crouch on my hands and knees beside the wreckage. One side is still more or less standing, while the other looks crushed, the poles toppled over and stakes ripped from the ground, as though something heavy had landed atop it.

Ducking under the tape, I push aside the battered flap and crawl inside. Through the torn netting, I can see Reed pacing back and forth, looking agitated, and Alaina stooped over to peer at the scuff marks on the ground.

Luckily the bags aren't buried. I rifle through my pale blue, dirt-smeared duffel bag until I find what I'm looking for - my phone. Miraculously, it's undamaged, protected by layers of clothing. And it even still has a bit of a charge left.

Suddenly I hear a shout from outside the tent, followed by the sound of panicked yelling. I grasp the strap of my bag, my heart beating wildly, and I scramble to try and back out of the narrow tent opening. Untangling myself from the netting, I push myself to my feet and whip around.

A few feet away, a boy stands facing Reed, brandishing a flimsy signpost out in front of him as if he's trying to fend off a wild animal.

"Who are you?" he demands, his voice trembling with terror and uncertainty. "What are you doing?"

At that moment, he looks over, and his face goes stark with disbelief as he spots me standing outside of the tent.

"Emmalina?"

"*Cam?*" I gasp, almost as surprised as he is. He looks frozen to the spot, his face drained of color, and the signpost slips from his hands to land with a muffled thud on the ground.

"Lina," he unfreezes, lunging forward to wrap me in a hug so tight I swear I feel my ribs crack. Recovering from the shock, I hug Cam back just as tight, leaning into him and burying my face in his shoulder, his jacket carrying the faint scent of pine sap and bug spray. As if he's spent the past week in the woods.

I realize that I'm trembling, all of the shock and grief easing ever so slightly. I hadn't realized how much I missed him, my best friend. After all that had changed, after everything in my life has been trampled worse than that poor tent, Cam is still here. Still safe. The tether to my normal life.

After a moment, he gently pulls away, studying my face as I study his. His face is paler than I remember, dark sleepless circles under his eyes.

"Where on Earth have you been?" he demands. Behind us, I hear Reed snort with amusement at the irony of his question. Of course, I hadn't actually been on Earth. Cam looks up at Reed, who's still standing with his hand on his sword hilt. His face is schooled into an uninterested, almost bored expression, but his posture is tense. And Alaina... I scan the clearing. Alaina is nowhere to be seen, but that doesn't mean anything, with her abilities. Cam fixes Reed with a weary, distrustful look.

"Lina, seriously, what happened here?" Cam gestures widely with his arms, at the scene all around us. "Where have you been? You didn't come home from your camping trip, and you wouldn't answer your phone. No one could get ahold of you or your mom. Finally, someone is sent up here to check up on you two only to find this...?" he waves a hand at the ruined tent, the clawed dirt.

"So, this is Cam," Reed cuts in, raising an eyebrow skeptically. Cameron's eyes narrow.

"Yeah, and who are you exactly?" his eyes get wider when they fix on the scabbard strapped to Reed's belt, and then the similar one fitted to mine, doing a double take as if noticing them for the first time.

"Why do you have... are those swords?" he asks incredulously.

"Sure are," says a voice to the left, causing Cam to jump as if he had been electrocuted. Alaina has reappeared beside him, twirling her dagger in her hand with a mischievous smile playing on her lips. Cam looks at Alaina, then at the knife, with an expression that makes me worry he might have a heart attack.

"You-" he swallows hard. "You were not there a second ago."

She sheaths the dagger with an unhelpful shrug.

"Okay, that's it. Does anyone mind telling me what's going on here?" he fixes me with a stare.

"Let's start over with the introductions," I sigh. "Cam, this is Reed and Alaina," I begin, pointing to each of them in turn. Alaina gives Cam another friendly, trademark smile that doesn't match her dagger. At least the two of them aren't dressed in the usual guard armor, armed to the teeth. We barely had time to grab Reed's sword and Alaina's dagger before we hurried for the throne room. Thankfully, we're dressed like normal teenagers, making us a slight bit less conspicuous.

Reed gives Cam a sarcastic wave.

"They're my…" I struggle to find the right word. Legion mates? Rescuers? Kidnappers?

"They're my friends," I decide. "And this is Cameron," I declare to them, a bit uselessly.

"It's very nice to meet you, Cam," Alaina says good-naturedly, trying to ease a bit of the tension. But doubt is still written across Cam's face. He opens his mouth to ask another question, or maybe to point out that we hadn't answered his first questions, but he doesn't get the chance to.

There's barely a rustle of pine leaves overhead, and Cam yelps as a large black shape drops from the treetops to land several feet away in a crouch.

It takes a second for me to remember how to breathe as I recognize what, or rather who, just dropped into the clearing.

Jane stands from the ground, casually brushing back her long ponytail with her black, fingerless gloves. She's hastily dressed in black combat gear over her worn jeans and grey t-shirt. Her bow and quiver are slung over her back, and two daggers are sheathed over each hip. So much for the inconspicuous clothing.

Cameron takes a nervous step back, and I don't blame him. She looks like some sort of assassin, leaping from the treetops, her expression hardened with cold fury.

Alaina looks as though she's considering becoming invisible again. Even Reed has the decency to look guilty at being caught.

Jane glances at Cam before relaxing the hands poised over the hilts of her daggers. She turns her attention then to Reed.

"What in the Realms were you thinking?" she demands, her voice tight with exasperation and anger. Reed bristles at her tone, and he looks as though he's about to shoot back a snark reply, but he's interrupted by the sound of footsteps and the faint murmur of voices.

I turn my head so fast that I almost give myself whiplash. Everyone else looks in the direction of the approaching voices, figures visible through the trees, from the dirt road that connects the campsites. There are three of them, from what I can see, each wearing the dark-colored uniforms of the Carroll County

Sheriff's Department. Jane's face pales slightly, her voice taking on a tone of urgency.

"We need to go, now." She gestures towards the woods, in the direction of the main road, away from the policemen, and unsheathes both of her daggers.

"Seriously, Jane, you need to chill out," Reed says, rolling his eyes. "We can easily be gone before they…"

"Just head for the woods," Jane says, cutting him off, her voice barely a whisper. "Keep quiet, don't be seen." She's already heading for the tree line, casting anxious glances back at the policemen, who have halted just beyond the entrance to the campsite. There were three silhouettes huddled together, talking in low voices. Just a little closer and they would easily notice us.

"They're just cops," Reed protests. "And Worlders, at that, nothing we haven't dealt with a million times. I don't see why you're freaking out like this."

Jane spins around, temper flaring as if she's about to spit back a retort, but she stops in her tracks. The three men, having finished their conversation, stride into the clearing and freeze as they find us standing here.

"Because," Jane growls, "Those are not cops."

I don't know who looked more surprised at that moment, Reed or the three men in Sheriff's uniforms. Reed snaps out of it first.

"They are not cops," he grudgingly agrees.

"Go now?" Alaina suggests helpfully.

"Go now," Jane agrees. I'm not about to argue. Whoever these not-cops are, if they're enough to frighten both Reed and Jane, I do not want to stick around to say hi.

The three men quickly recover from their surprise. The man in front- tall, with gray speckled hair and a pointed goatee- grins with elated satisfaction. The man behind him mumbles something into his walkie-talkie that sounds like, "They're here."

"Go!" Jane yells as the men pull blades from their belts where their gun holsters should be.

"You're coming with us," Jane says, grabbing Cam's wrist and tugging him towards the woods.

Cam, who had stood silently shell-shocked since Jane arrived, now takes a step back, shaking his head. His eyes dart from us to the men across the clearing.

"Cam," I say softly. "I know they look like cops, but you can't trust them. There is more to this than you understand right now, and I promise to explain it all when we're safe. Do you trust me?"

He nods, swallowing hard.

The first man, the tall one in front, lunges for Jane and she rises to meet him with a vicious swing of her blades. The clash of metal on metal echoes through the trees. The other two are blocked by Reed.

For a moment, all I can do is watch. Reed moves like a whirlwind, his sword flashing in his hand. He slashes and dodges, catching one fake cop in the side with a kick of his heavy boot, sending the man sprawling. The second one matches him blow for blow, backing Reed towards the other end of the clearing.

"Emmalina!" Cam shouts in warning, moments before the man on the ground swings a foot, sweeping my legs out from beneath me. For a moment, the world spins sideways, and I hit the ground, spitting out a mouthful of dirt. Instinctively, I roll to the side to avoid getting sliced in half by his sword, but the blow never comes.

I glance upward to see his head jerk back with a sickening thud, and blood begins to stream from his nose. Alaina materializes beside him, her blade still angled from slamming the butt of her dagger into the fake officer's face. He stumbles away, clutching his broken nose, while Alaina wrinkles her nose in distaste.

"Ew, ew, ew," she mutters. "I hate doing that," she shivers.

"I'm glad you did," I gasp.

"Come on," she says, extending a hand to help me up, and I gladly accept. "We have to go, we have to get out of here."

She grabs my hand in hers, Cam's in her other, and I feel the strange trickle of cold down my spine as she drops a veil of invisibility over us. I hear Cam's panicked intake of breath, but he knows enough to keep quiet.

I cast a nervous glance behind us, to where Jane and Reed are holding the not-cops at bay.

"What about them?"

"They'll be fine," she assures me. "They'll know to meet us at the road, but we need to get out of here before-" her disembodied voice falters as the sound of whirring helicopter blades begins to rise above the sound of clanging metal.

"Before that?" I ask.

"Yes," she sighs with resignation, "Before that."

She tugs my hand, and I hear the scuffling sound of three sets of footsteps as we dash for the trees, tripping over invisible feet.

"What's in the helicopter?" I ask. In the mountains, the sound of an occasional helicopter isn't the rarest thing there is, but the noise is so deafening it has to be practically above us.

"Re-enforcements," she explains.

"Re-enforcements for who?" I ask. "Who are those men in the campsite, and why are they dressed as policemen?"

"They're Lillian's men," she says, confirming the answer I dreaded.

We reach the road, coming to a stumbling stop. She releases our hands and the three of us become visible, likely so Jane and Reed can find us. At that moment, a spotlight sweeps the road, illuminating the pavement, and Alaina tugs us backward to be hidden by the bushes as it searches for us, for me.

"We can't go any further," Alaina warns. "That spotlight is Realm-made, rigged to reveal invisibility. It's too open, once we step under that light, they'll be able to see us. And besides, I won't have the ability to cloak all of us anyway, once Jane and Reed get here."

Cam looks my way, wide eyes illuminated by the spotlight, confusion, fear, and awe warring in his expression.

"Were we just... invisible?" he asks.

"I'm sorry," I say. "I can't explain yet. But I will," he nods.

We hear the crunching of leaves behind us, as though someone's barreling through the woods very quickly in our direction. We duck farther down into the bushes, Alaina still clutching her dagger. Even Cam's fingers curl around a jagged stick. Though I doubt it will do him much good, I have to give him credit for his bravery.

We all let out a collective sigh of relief as Jane and Reed emerge from the branches, spotting us as we stand from our hiding spot. They seem out of breath, bruised, and scraped, but for the most part okay. Jane lost her daggers somewhere along the way, donning her bow instead. Reed frowns as he assesses the spotlight sweeping the road, and seems to come to the same conclusion as Alaina.

"We'll have to follow the road and keep out of sight," he reasons, but Jane shakes her head.

"They'll have reinforcements sweeping the area," she points out. "They're so close, they're not going to give up so easily. Our best bet is to make it to the safe house, to the portal."

"But to do that, we have to cross the road," Alaina protests. "Even if I made two trips across to keep you all invisible, they would see our shadows."

"Well, we don't have time to wait until the helicopter leaves," Jane says, We cross now." Alaina fixes her with a look as if sure Jane's gone mad, and I'm inclined to agree. Once it knows where we are, we can't outrun a helicopter.

"But if we cross now they will catch us!" Alaina says with exasperation.

"That's what I'm counting on," Jane says, and I can practically see gears turning in her head as she formulates a plan.

"What are you talking about?" I ask. "Isn't the point not to get caught?"

But she shakes her head, making up her mind.

"So," she decides. "-this is what we're going to do…"

She describes her plan, every crazy detail. When she finishes, everyone sits in silence for a moment.

"It will never work," Reed says, eyes narrowing.

"I'm in," Alaina says, a grin spreading across her face that looks about as sane as Jane's plan. "It sounds awesome, dangerous, and just a tad crazy. It's perfect, let's do it."

Reed sighs.

"Well, it's the only plan we've got," I point out to him, and he's forced to grudgingly agree. For better or worse, we're going through with it.

About a minute later, we're all in position. Alaina grins in the darkness of the bush she crouches in, giving me an enthusiastic thumbs up that doesn't match our situation, and her form ripples and disappears.

Cam, who is crouched in the bushes beside her, gapes at the spot where she had been. Right, we're really going to have to explain that invisibility thing to him. Well, it's about to get more confusing.

I'm ducked behind a shrub several yards away from Alaina and Cam, with Jane and Reed on either side of me. The helicopter still circles overhead. I can begin to hear the sounds of voices shouting in the distance, barely audible over the sound of helicopter blades. We need to hurry if this is going to have any chance of working.

"Now," Jane commands, her voice firm. I stand, breaking into a half-stumbling run for the road, Jane and Reed keeping pace beside me. Jane has her bow hanging loosely at her side, and Reed grips his unsheathed sword. I clutch my dagger, my knuckles white on its leathery hilt. As we break past the tree line, my feet hitting the solid pavement, the searchlight immediately swivels to bathe us in its blinding glow, brighter than the sun. I shield my face with my hand, and I'm barely pretending as I slow my pace, feigning tripping over my own feet. Jane and Reed whip around, their stunned faces illuminated beside me. Within that moment of hesitation, black cables drop from the helicopter and several men and women in dark battle gear begin to rapidly repel to the ground. Barely audible over the roar of the helicopter, Jane hisses to me, "Follow my lead exactly."

And Lillian's warriors are upon us.

Jane hardly puts up a fight as two guards, Wolf Soldiers from the look of them, seize her and tear her bow from her hands. Moments later, Reed and I receive the same treatment, our hands pulled behind our backs and weapons swiftly confiscated. We pretend to put up a half-hearted struggle for a show, and the two guards restraining Reed shove him onto the ground. I wince as his shoulder hits the dirt with a muffled thud, and he grits his teeth. That wasn't part of the plan. I cringe again as one of the warriors who captured Jane, a tall woman with a nasty sneer, slams the butt of her spear against the side of Jane's head. She slumps to the pavement, limp. Unconscious. That definitely wasn't part of the plan, and I see the same thought echoed in Reed's eyes.

The guard holding my wrists scowls down at me, and I shrink back. No, no, no, everything's going wrong. There are too many of them. Jane's unconscious, and Reed's now pinned on the ground. At least one part of our plan hasn't collapsed yet, they don't seem to realize that they chased five people from the clearing, but only caught three. Our reinforcements are still free and armed, but will it make a difference?

The helicopter slowly begins to descend, my hair whipping in the strong wind generated by the propellers. A jolt of pain goes up my wrists, the guard's grip too tight, and I gasp as I find my own dagger pressed against my throat.

"Not one move," the guard gripping the knife growls.

The helicopter lands with a whoosh of air, and I spit a strand of hair from my mouth. The doors slide open, and the guards begin to yank me forward, the others doing the same with Jane and Reed. Unwilling to abandon the plan just yet, Reed doesn't try to fight them off, instead glancing desperately towards the woods. Alaina couldn't still be waiting for Jane's signal, could she?

The guards are heaving Jane, still limp, into the open doors of the helicopter, and Reed still seems in a daze. What if he isn't pretending, what if he's truly hurt? The guard holding my wrists shoves me up beside the helicopter alongside Reed, tossing our weapons into the back, and I discretely try to scan Reed's face for a sign that he's okay, that everything is under control. But he doesn't look my way. Alaina, any time now would be great.

And that's when complete chaos breaks loose.

The dagger at my throat is wrenched away by some unseen force and the guard holding it goes tumbling. Almost simultaneously, recognizing the cue, Reed rises upward with a surge of strength and barrels his captors over before they realize what's happening. Jane, from her perfect position in the helicopter, leaps to her feet to pummel the pilot. The man in the cockpit, a scrawny man with a startled expression, is shoved out of the helicopter and lands in a heap on the pavement.

Lillian's rebels, taken completely by surprise, attempt to regroup and beat us back but are swiftly held at bay by Reed and a still invisible Alaina winding through their ranks. The rebel warrior behind me lunges forward to recapture my hands, and I use my very limited but very useful training to sidestep and duck out of the way. But I still don't have my dagger, gleaming in the glare of the helicopter light several feet out of reach on the street.

The guard swings a blade of his own, and I yelp as it slices through the fabric of my sweatshirt sleeve, narrowly grazing my arm. He poises to strike again, and I glance wildly around for something to use to defend myself, but a loud crack sounds as the guard crumples to his knees. Standing behind the fallen warrior is Cam, wielding the jagged stick from before, now broken in half from being used as a baseball bat. I blink, surprised and impressed. Cameron gives me a cautious grin as if he doesn't quite believe what's going on, or what he just did.

"Come on! Hurry!" Reed shouts, before his hand grips my arm to pull me forward, causing my cut arm to flare with pain. He sees me flinch and the tear in my sleeve.

"Are you alright?" he asks, his eyebrows knitting together with if I hadn't known better, I would have called concern.

"Yeah," I assure him, turning for the helicopter. "I'm fine."

The three of us bolt for the helicopter, where Jane and Alaina already wait inside, blocking the few remaining rebels from entering. I scramble into the back, lending a hand to haul Cam inside.

And so begins phase three of our wonderfully crazy plan.

Reed shoves aside one of Lillian's warriors, a woman who barks an order at the three others still with her not to stand down. Everyone inside, the door to the helicopter slides shut not a moment too soon as the rebels break against the craft with the fury of a tsunami, causing the helicopter to rock. Reed hauls himself into the cockpit, Jane claiming the seat beside him, while the rest of us strap ourselves in.

Through the windows, I spot several hulking shapes moving through the trees, breaking into the street. Wolves called to the aid of their masters.

"Any time now would be great," Alaina warns.

"I'm doing the best I can!" Reed growls, fiddling with the instrument panel.

"I'm pretty sure that's not how that works," I say, as the helicopter shudders beneath us.

"Do I look like someone who knows how to fly this thing?" he demands, nearly snapping a lever in his frustration.

"Move over," Jane demands. "I've got this. Emmalina, do you still have that phone you grabbed from the campsite?"

I had lost the duffel bag somewhere along the way, but my phone is tucked into my pocket. I slide it out, handing it to Jane as she and Reed switch seats. Jane rapidly types into the phone, straps herself in, and props the device up in front of her.

Alaina's face pales several shades as she sees what's depicted on that phone screen.

"Are you *Googling* how to fly a helicopter?" she squeaks, her voice shrill.

"Just trust me," Jane says, which I have to admit is not reassuring in the slightest.

"Jane!" Reed roars in warning, as a massive wolf snaps at the helicopter blades as if it's going to tear them apart. She finishes studying the diagram on the screen, narrated by a nasally voice instructing the use of the different switches and leavers.

"Here goes nothing," she says, biting her lip, before the helicopter gives a mighty shudder under the assault from outside, but lurching its way into the air. The thundering of the blades grows louder, and metal screeches as a wolf digs its mighty claws into the landing gear, but not even that can stop us now. We quickly rise out of reach of wolf and sword alike, Jane shutting off the spotlight as we angle above the trees. We ascend so quickly that my ears pop, and Alaina whimpers as she clutches her seat armrests with white knuckles. Upon seeing my confusion, Reed chuckles slightly, also a shade paler.

"She hates flying," he says, jutting his chin in Alaina's direction. "Always has. That, plus the fact that we don't have a real pilot is probably not helping."

"Hey," Jane protests. "I've taken the 10-second crash course, I'm as good as licensed."

The helicopter dips alarmingly to one side, and my stomach drops, Cam giving a yelp.

"Well, maybe some room for improvement. Sorry," she admits sheepishly. Alaina squeezes her eyes shut.

I give a small whoop of excitement as I gaze through the window, down to where Lillian's men and their mutts cluster in the street, far below. We not only outsmarted Lillian's rebels but also stole an entire helicopter. As if it's just sinking in, Jane and Reed high-five, grinning like fiends.

Sitting back in the seat, Reed claps his hand on Jane's shoulder.

"Congrats, you're plan actually worked," he says, feigning surprise.

"When am I ever wrong?" she chides, raising an eyebrow.

"So modest."

Jane snorts, angling the helicopter in the direction of the cabin safe house.

I lean back, gazing once more at the night blanketed forest below, watching the dark blur of trees pass. My fingers still tremble from leftover adrenaline, giddy from the daring escape we just pulled off.

"See, aren't you glad you joined our little mission, Jane?" Reed says, reclining in the seat. "Come on, admit it, you had fun."

But Jane only fixes him with a glare that implied that was not what Reed should have said.

"This was no mission, Reed. This was stupidity." Reed raises his eyebrows at her tone, but she continues.

"You three blatantly disobeyed orders, and nearly got us all captured in the process!" Reed looks like he's about to object, but Jane viciously cuts him off, that delayed anger from the clearing flaring up again.

"No, you listen to me for once. Marcus specifically told you three not to leave the palace, and what did you do? You go to the one place Lillian's men are sure to have under surveillance without any real backup! It was idiotic and reckless-"

"Says the person flying a stolen helicopter *using a YouTube tutorial*!" Reed shouts back. Jane's face is blank, but her eyes fill with a burning fury and indignation.

"Are you seriously blaming this on me?" she says with a humorless laugh.

"You are technically also disobeying orders by being here," Reed points out. "You couldn't help yourself from coming along, no matter how you pretend to be the perfect rule-follower. You wanted to come, I saw you argue with Marcus before. There is no way he would have sent you alone if he knew you were going to come after us, meaning you didn't tell him, you just came. So don't go yelling at me about being reckless, you hypocrite."

"Hypocrite?" Jane snarls, cutting off Reed's rant. "The only reason I came after you was to *save your lives*. I didn't go to Marcus because there was no time to convince him, I barely made it in time as it is. Maybe I should have ratted you out, but if I hadn't shown up at all to warn you about Lillian's men, and to come up with this escape plan, you would have gotten yourselves caught before you even realized they weren't cops."

"And how did you know?" Reed shoots back. Jane scowls.

I had been watching this argument attentively, but Reed brings up a good point.

"Wait, how did you know?" I ask.

"What?" Jane looks over at me.

"Please keep your eyes on where you're flying," Alaina mutters, but Jane ignores her.

"How did you know that Lillian's men would be at the campsite?" The question seems to catch Jane off guard. Reed scowls like a pouting child.

"It's kind of a strange story," she says, anger forgotten as her face takes on a confused expression.

"I was in the surveillance room, where Marcus had sent me. I was almost finished reviewing the security footage when a message came over the intercom. At first, I thought it was one of our patrols trying to communicate, but then I recognized the voice coming through the speakers. It was Lillian."

A thrill of fear settles in my chest as Reed's head whips around to look at Jane, surprise and skepticism written on his features.

"Lillian accessed our coms?" he demands. "How…what did she say?"

Jane shakes her head.

"It was strange. It sounded like she was giving orders to her men. It didn't seem like she hacked our coms, but rather someone was recording her and relayed it to us."

Reed's panic visibly eases, but his eyebrows are still scrunched with confusion.

"What do you mean? What was she saying to her rebels?"

"She was ordering them to go to that campsite, claiming she was aware that Emmalina would be there. At first I didn't believe it, I thought it was some sort of prank because there is no way that you three would be so stupid. But sure enough, when I checked, you were gone. I knew I had to get there first and warn you, and it's a good thing I did," she says, with a pointed look at her brother.

Reed doesn't seem to notice the jibe, lost in thought.

"Who could have gotten close enough to Lillian to hear her give orders? Or even find her in the first place," he muses. "Are you sure it wasn't a security tape that recorded it?"

"Of course I'm sure," Jane snaps. "It was intentionally broadcasted right to the Com's room."

"Did you track it to see where it was sent from?"

Jane shakes her head again.

"I'm bringing us in for a landing," she says, part warning and part abruptly ending the conversation as she adjusts the controls. "We can talk more after we get back, and for goodness sake, Reed, have you not been wearing a seatbelt this whole time?"

He reluctantly buckles himself in as the helicopter makes a shaky descent. Alaina and I make awkward eye contact, having watched the twins argue back and forth like a tennis match. From what I can see, we're aiming for the small open space outside of the secret hideout cabin that conceals the portal. It's a tight fit, the treetops swaying in the wind created by the helicopter blades.

The moment we touch down, Jane quickly unbuckles herself, grabs my phone and her bow from the back, and jumps out. The rest of us follow. It's obvious why she's in a hurry- our getaway ride was brief, and we hadn't gone too far from the campground. Distantly, I can hear the sound of police sirens growing steadily louder, which means we only have minutes before Lillian's men discover where we landed.

After the helicopter is empty, the five of us quickly head for the cabin, climbing the rickety front porch steps. I stick by Cam's side as Alaina makes a beeline for the trapdoor hidden beneath the rug.

"Alaina," Reed says warningly, his tone rising in alarm as a county sheriff's car swerves into the wide gravel driveway, skidding to a stop with the lights flashing red and blue.

"Alaina!" he shouts again as several of Lillian's soldiers, some in cop uniforms and some decked in combat gear, spill out of the car and surround the abandoned helicopter.

"Got it," Alaina announces, the trapdoor sliding open with a mechanical click. Reaching inside, she pulls out the handheld mirror, which is linked to the cabin and reappears here whenever we use it, as Reed had explained to me before.

"Alaina, you first. Take him with you, I can keep the portal open," Reed says, pushing Cam forward. Cam, who had been quiet and shell-shocked the whole way here, swallows fearfully but steps forward. Alaina grasps his wrist, and the two of them disappear through the beam of light Reed wills from the mirror.

"Lina, you next," Jane commands.

My head whips around at the sound of helicopter blades from outside the cabin. Two of Lillian's men have reclaimed the controls, and I watch with horror as massive gun barrels protrude from the machine's sides. Jane's face is whiter than a ghost, her lips bloodless with fear.

"Time to go," she says, grabbing for Reed's wrist as she shoves me roughly into the portal's light, leaping close behind with her brother in tow. But it's not the helicopter's guns she's running from, no. We barely make it into the portal, as the helicopter rumbles and explodes outward, and the entire world is engulfed in rolling red flame.

CHAPTER 13

There is a feeling of weightlessness, the icy touch of the portal's magic combated by a blaze of unrelenting heat at my back. After what feels like an eternity of floating in this blazing, icy void, my feet hit solid ground, and my eyes blink as I take in the throne room of the glass palace. The same place we portaled to before, the mirror we had snuck through towering behind me, swirling with power.

I barely have time to take a breath as Jane appears, scrambling away from the mirror. Lastly, Reed materializes behind me. Before I know what's happening, Reed has a hand on my back, shoving me hard until my knees bark with pain as I hit the slick glass floor on my stomach, the ground looming a million miles below me.

"Get down!" he roars to whoever else must be in the room with us, his voice almost drowned out by the growing, thundering roar coming from the portal at our backs. I let myself be forced down, my cheek against the cool floor, Reed flattening himself on top of me. Not a moment too soon.

A wave of flame tears through the swirling portal, barely skimming above our heads, the remnants of that explosion that managed to make it through before the portal on the other side closed, or was perhaps destroyed The heat is almost unbearable, and I feel Reed's breath on my ear. Then the mirror's magic fizzles, and both blue light and torrent of flame are abruptly cut off. Finally, the room falls silent.

I lift my head as he rolls off of where he had been pinning me beneath him. The back of his shirt is singed and burned away in spots, the skin beneath a reddish pink, but otherwise unhurt.

Reed winces as he sits up. I spot Alaina, Jane, and Cam pressed against the wall adjacent to us, out of reach of the flames. Alaina's arms are still outstretched from channeling her magic to slam the portal closed, containing the last of the explosion.

She launches herself away from the wall, dropping to her knees beside where Reed and I still crouch on the floor, her eyes wide and full of terror. Cam gapes in shock, but he stumbles towards us as well, concern filling his face.

"We're okay," Reed says as he heaves himself up, meeting Alaina's panicked gaze, her eyes filled with tears. She nearly sags to the ground with relief as she realizes we both are truly okay. I have Reed to thank for that. He saved my life.

He's done more than just that for me, I realize. I look at him as though I'm seeing him for the first time. He agreed to help me, to go to the campsite and risk his neck to protect me.

His eyes meet mine, and he nods slightly as if he can recognize what I'm thinking.

"Thank you," I say softly. I hug him, and he grunts in surprise.

"No problem," he says, his voice quiet. He doesn't quite hug me back, but he doesn't lean away. He may be a grumpy jerk most of the time, but tonight he has become my friend.

Breaking the silence is a slow and sarcastic clapping echoing through the throne room. The five of us look up with a jolt to the small balcony above the throne, where Marcus stands, gazing down at us with an unreadable, cold glare.

Great. Now we're in trouble for sure.

Marcus's mouth is set in a firm, hard line, his steely gray eyes like the void in that mirror, icy cold but blazing with a burning triumph at the same time. Those eyes lazily assess the room, lingering on the few lightly toasted tapestries leaving a dusting of ash across the clouded crystal throne, and the five teenagers sprawled among the mess looking equally as dirty and charred.

"You have five seconds," Marcus says in a deadly soft voice, "To explain yourselves." He pauses, probably waiting for us to scramble to our feet, or grovel at his, to apologize and beg for his forgiveness. The common sense inside of me whispers that I should do exactly that, but the stubborn part of me has me getting to my feet with my head still held high. A line was drawn in the sand. Before either of us can say a word, Reed speaks first.

"Or what?" He demands. "It's not like you can-" Jane slaps her hand over Reed's mouth, and the rest of his sentence becomes a muffled, indignant shout. Marcus eyes him with plain disgust and turns back towards me. His mouth twitches into a self-satisfied smirk, probably as close as he's ever come to a smile. My confidence wavers as I again meet his gaze, and I try to discretely wipe my sweaty palms on my jeans, only for them to come away soot and dirt-stained.

"Miss Maren," he hisses, "I believe I told you and your entire legion that you were to stay here, or was my answer not clear enough for you?"

He looks around, not really looking for an answer. If he's surprised to see Cam standing among us, he doesn't let on.

"Then again, perhaps you meant to be caught by Lillian. Perhaps you wanted to reveal to them our safe house and destroy it. If I'm not mistaken, it was Miss Windervale here who set the bomb that took out the cabin, so that checks out," he turns that smirk to Jane as if waiting for her to deny it. She just lifts her chin higher, black hair coming undone from her ponytail to hang in long loose strands around her face.

"I did what I had to do to make sure my friends were safe," she says. "The safe house was an unfortunate accident."

"That was you?" Reed asks, raising his eyebrows slightly.

"Shut up," I hear Alaina mutter under her breath.

"I only wanted-"

"It doesn't matter what you wanted," Marcus snaps. "You disobeyed rules, broke the law when you snuck out of the Realms, antagonized our greatest enemy, and effectively ruined a mirror end portal," he aims the last comment at Jane, who stares back unwaveringly. Marcus levels his glare at Reed, Jane, and Alaina.

"You three, cleaning duty in the weapons room. You are to remain there until King Orlon is finished meeting with Miss Maren," he commands, waving his hand dismissively as if he were shooing a dog.

"What do you mean after Orlon is finished meeting with me?" I ask.

"His Majesty has a few words to say about your little trip to Earth," Marcus says with a smirk. "He wishes to speak with you immediately"

My heart sinks. I've only been in the Realms for a week, and I've likely just lost any chance of staying here any longer, under the protection of the king. If Orlon turns me away and banishes me, where will I go? I have no family, no home, no money. My friends will probably never speak to me again after the trouble I've gotten them into.

Marcus slowly moves down a set of winding steps leading from the balcony, taking his sweet time. Head bowed, I follow him towards a smaller set of doors leading out of the throne room. Out of the corner of my eye, I see Alaina leading Cam, looking bewildered and concerned, out of the main doorway. She looks back, giving me a look of sympathy. At least it isn't hatred.

Reed follows her, not looking back. Great. If he had a problem with me before, despite all of his help, he certainly does now. Jane pauses defiantly at the doors, as if reluctant to go, fixing Marcus with a cold glare that he either doesn't notice or pretends not to see.

Then we're through the doors. I follow him like a scolded puppy dutifully trailing after its master, and a slight pang of anger warms me from the inside at the injustice of it all. Yeah, I snuck out, but I don't get why I hadn't been allowed to go in the first place, and why I'm now being singled out even though we all left without permission.

I inwardly chide myself for these thoughts. Of course, I'm being singled out, it was my fault, my idea. Besides, I'm relieved that Reed, Jane, and Alaina are not facing the same consequences. They were just trying to help me, and the truth is, if I had been on my own I definitely would have been captured, or worse.

Finally, Marcus pauses, halting in front of massive double doors leading to the tallest and most strictly off-limits wing of the entire palace. The doors are several feet taller than me, made of thick, clouded crystal carved with incredibly beautiful and detailed scenes. I let out a breath of amazement at the near-perfect likeness of King Orlon himself, his face set in a regal and kind gaze as he stands between two people I vaguely recognize. Really, how vain do you have to be to carve an image of yourself into your door?

I study the other two carved figures, a man and a woman with crowns upon their brows. I do recognize them, King Umbra of the Shadow Realm, and Queen Anima of the Soul Realm. I had seen them briefly during the Tournament.

Like Orlon, their likenesses are stunning. Queen Anima, with her devastatingly beautiful face, ringlets of hair falling over her shoulders, wearing a floor-length gown and a dazzling smile. King Umbra, taller than the other two rulers, with close-cropped hair and a well-trimmed beard to accentuate his scholarly looks and neat outfit.

"You have an eye for art, I see," a soft voice rumbles to my left, causing me to jump and spin. Out of one of the corridors branching from the main hall, King Orlon himself steps forward, gesturing to the doors.

I hastily bow my head as I had seen the others do before, mumbling, "No, sir."

He raises an inquisitive eyebrow.

"I mean, I don't have much of an eye for art, I've never really been much of an artistic person, but this…" I wave my hand at the carvings, "This is awesome."

I inwardly cringe at my choice of words. He was probably expecting me to use something like *glamorous,* or *impressive.* But Orlon just chuckles, nodding in agreement.

"It sure is," he says, gazing at the doors fondly. "They came straight from the Shadow Realm, you know. Umbra's kingdom hosts some of the best artists in the Realms. What could be more fitting for the entrance to my private chambers?"

He then moves his attention away from the artwork, back to me, clearing his throat.

"But, decor aside, I've requested we talk about tonight's little, uh- *adventure*."

I bow my head, waiting for the anger, but his eyes only spark with amusement. Perhaps Marcus hasn't told him all of the details yet? About how we fought Lillian's men or blew up a safe house, or torched his throne room?

Marcus, who I had forgotten was still standing behind me, jumps at the king's words with a vicious eagerness.

"My Lord," he says with a triumphant sneer. "I have indeed brought this girl to your chambers to discuss her hideous defiance of the law-"

Orlon waves a hand, cutting him off mid-sentence. "Her name is Emmalina," he says matter-of-factly. Marcus pauses, caught off guard.

"What-"

"I said, her name is Emmalina, or Miss Maren if you will. Not *this girl*. Show a little respect, Marcus."

Marcus gapes, his mouth opening and closing like a startled fish, while Orlon watches with a flat disinterest.

"And besides," Orlon continues, his mouth upturned in one of those trademark good-natured smiles, "Hideous defiance of the law? Really? I mean, she snuck out, it's not like she and her friends murdered anybody."

"She and her friends could have been killed! They also destroyed a safe house, and brought a Worlder to the Realms, which are also against the law-"

"Sometimes the law is made to be broken," the king says with a slight gleam in his eyes.

"They're your laws!" Marcus cries, throwing his hands in the air with frustration. Orlon only smiles patiently.

"I would like to speak with Emmalina *alone* if you please."

Marcus opens his mouth to object, but seems to think better of it. With one last look of malice in my direction, he bows low to his king, before stalking back down the hallway which we came through. Once he is out of sight, his footsteps against the marble and glass floors having faded, the king lets out a breath, part sigh and part laugh. I had been watching the exchange in bewilderment, but my hands fidget as he turns back to me. Why had he stuck up for me? Was he waiting to scold me in private? But all he says is "Did you find what you were looking for?"

I blink, surprised.

I wonder if he had guessed that I had been thinking about my mom, that the deepest reason I wanted to return so badly was not just to contact Cam, or retrieve my things. It was to see if I could find any hint, the slightest trace, of what might have happened to her. And yet I am not closer to knowing than I was before, and the uncertainty is killing me.

Orlon seems to read that answer in my eyes, the loss, and utter hopelessness because his gaze softens. I look away, blinking as tears rise to the surface. I don't want his pity. I don't want magic powers, I don't want this new responsibility that was just thrust upon me. I just want my mom and my life back.

"Why aren't you punishing me?" I ask. "Why did you defend me? I did break the law, several times, everything Marcus said is true."

Orlon looks puzzled, eyebrows knitting. "Are you asking me to punish you?"

"No," I run my hands through my hair, pulling at the ends in frustration. "I just want to know why?"

He considers the question for a moment, the portrait of complete, mild indifference. Finally, he answers, "Because I believe that, sometimes, there are things more important than following rules," his eyes gleam knowingly.

"One day you may be faced with such a decision. And when that day comes, you have my permission and encouragement to do what you believe is right. No matter who or what stands in your way."

With that, he waves his hands as if to shoo me away.

"Run along, then," he insists. Numbly, still not comprehending my strange luck, I turn to go.

"Emmalina," Orlon calls, and I look back over my shoulder to where he stands, silhouetted by the magnificent doors at his back.

"Just so we're clear. I am certainly *not* implying that you should ever disobey Marcus in the potentially near future, not even if *the future of the worlds depends on it.* Do you understand me?"

His tone of voice, combined with the mischievous look on his face, seems to be hinting at some deeper meaning that I certainly don't understand, but I nod anyway, regardless.

"And one more thing," he says, almost as an afterthought. "Say, *hypothetically*, if the need were to arise, I think you would find Passage Number Three to be exactly what you need." Orlon smiles to himself. "However, it is strictly off-limits, of course. So, *hypothetically*, asking me or Marcus would have to be an outright no. But you already have your answer, don't you? So what would be the purpose in asking again?"

He gives me a quick wink, before turning away to the doors. Wordlessly, he slips into his chambers, and as they seal shut, I am left with far more questions than I had before.

Sometime later, my mind still reels after that bizarre conversation. I mean, what the heck had Orlon been talking about? Nothing made any sense, and I try to push it to the back of my mind and simply feel grateful. The one thing that was clear about the exchange is that I'm off the hook. For now, anyway.

I try instead to focus on finding where Jane, Reed, Alaina, and Cam have gone. Marcus sent them to the "weapon's room," wherever that is. But every hallway and corridor in this castle still looks the same to me, how does anyone ever learn their way around this place? The taller parts of the palace, the towers, and important rooms, are easier to discern since they are made entirely of glass, but most of the floors are identical- white walls and marble floors, billowy silver curtains framing massive floor-to-ceiling windows, vaulted ceilings lit with chandeliers. Nothing but white, marble, and glass. Oh, is that a bit of color I see? No, just more glass.

Outside of the windows is where the beauty is. Past the sprawling courtyards, the sky is still a firm and cloudy gray, beginning to lighten as the sun rises, raindrops sliding down the window pane. Had our whole adventure through Earth and the chaos afterward really taken all night? That must be the reason exhaustion is weighing so heavily on my shoulders, my eyelids beginning to droop.

I should return to my new room in the Dorm and change my clothes which are dirty and singed, smelling faintly of smoke. But first, I still need to find the others and apologize for what I had gotten them into.

I had taken yet another hallway, one of the many that lead in concentric circles around the courtyard and Centerdome, when I finally pause. I am quite literally getting nowhere. Then I hear the sound of footsteps on marble and huff a sigh of relief. At this hour, it's probably a maid or possibly a guard patrolling the hallways, someone who can point me in the direction of the weapons room. I like to think I would have found it on my own, but judging from my progress so far, I think I would have better luck flying a helicopter using a Youtube tutorial.

As I peer around the bend in the corridor, I'm surprised to find someone I recognize. Two someones, actually.

Nate and Stefan slow as they spot me standing there, as they take in the state of my clothes, the ash dusting my wind-blown hair like a layer of dark snow, blinking in surprise. Stefan lets out a breath as if relieved, while Nate goes tense.

I notice their appearances as well. Nate looks like he just rolled out of bed- literally. He's wearing a rumpled shirt and sweatpants, brown hair flattened to one side. Stefan looks neater, dressed in jeans and the button-up jacket that he had worn to the coms room, and dark circles under his eyes as if he too hasn't changed or slept all night. They both appear as though they've been in a hurry.

"Lina!" Nate gasps, his eyes widening. The somewhat frantic look in his eyes dims slightly.

"Thank the Realms," Stefan mutters.

"Hey guys," I say, wondering what the urgency is about. "What are you doing? What's the hurry?"

Stefan raises a disbelieving eyebrow.

"What are *we* doing? What in the worlds have *you* been doing?" he crosses his arms. His strangely golden eyes are piercing, and I feel my face become warm. How could he already know about the campsite? He seems to guess what I'm about to ask, because he says, "I was with Jane in the coms room, remember? We got this message, she realized that you all had snuck out, and she went to find you. I woke up Nate, then we heard what sounded like an explosion, the whole throne room tower lit up red…" he stops his rambling, shaking his head.

"We were worried," he finishes. I blush a deep shade of red as Stefan studies my face as if assuring himself that I'm alright. Finally, Nate breaks the lingering silence.

"Where's Alaina? Is she okay?" he asks, concern written across his face. I nod.

"Yes, yes she's perfectly fine. We all are," his stress seems to ease.

"Where are they?" Stefan asks. "We tried the throne room, but it was empty. We couldn't even find Marcus, even though there was no way he didn't hear the explosion."

"Marcus took me to see Orlon," I proceed to explain that strange encounter. How Orlon had stood up for me, and his odd ramblings about breaking rules and giving his permission or something. When I finish, Stefan and Nate only frown, wearing similar expressions of confusion.

"He sent the others to the weapon's room," I say finally. "I've been looking for them too, but I don't know where I'm going," I mumble that last part under my breath, and Nate cracks a smile, a little of his usual humor showing through. Stefan speaks up before he can make some snide comment.

"The weapon's room is just down that hallway," he begins to walk in the direction he pointed, leaving Nate and me to follow after him. Stefan chuckles to himself, saying, "I can't wait to hear this story, about the explosion and how angry Jane must have been," he laughs again. "I mean, if it weren't for that message…" suddenly his laughter trails off, and he falters for a moment.

"The message? Like the one Jane mentioned in the helicopter?" I ask.

"Helicopter?" Nate asks.

"It looks like we all have stories to share," Stefan says, as we arrive at a set of unadorned doors. Not bothering to knock, he swings them wide.

The weapon's room looks like a cross between a walk-in wardrobe and a library and bursts with all sorts of dangerous things.

The room itself is shaped like a giant rectangle, lined with rows of shelves. Instead of desks like you would see in a library, cabinets and tables displaying various tools that I assume are used for maintaining the weapons. There are shelves lined with swords, blades, bows, quivers of arrows, weighted nets, shields, and an assortment of other deadly items.

I spot Jane first, slumped in a chair beside one of the tables, repeatedly swiping the edge of a thin blade against a small stone with a harsh metallic whine. As the doors open, she glances up, sweeping her long hair out of her face. The murderous look in her green eyes dulls slightly when she realizes it's us. She wordlessly goes back to angrily sharpening the blade in her hands.

"Nice to see you too Jane," Stefan grumbles. She only sighs, long and annoyed.

Reed pokes his head around a shelf corner.

"Hey!" he greets us, shoving a massive longbow back into its spot on the wall. "It's about time you showed up!"

Alaina also emerges from a row of shelves to see who Reed is talking to, and her face lights up as she sees us standing in the doorway. There's a prominent look of relief on Nate's face as she skips over and gives him a quick hug. He hugs her back tightly, gently kissing her forehead.

"Sorry we didn't mention we were leaving," Alaina apologizes. Nate shakes his head.

"I'm just glad that you're okay," he answers, looking more serious than I've ever seen him. Stefan nods in agreement.

"But," Nate grins, "I do think I deserve to know how in the worlds you managed to torch the throne room, and more importantly, what this helicopter business is about."

"That would be my bad," Jane smirks, not sounding particularly sorry, as she looks up from swiping her dagger. She twirls it in between her fingers, and I'm genuinely amazed that she doesn't accidentally slice them off. Stefan laughs.

"Oh, I definitely want to hear this story," he pulls up a chair beside the small table. The rest of us claim chairs of our own, except for Reed, who is nowhere to be seen, and Nate kicks his feet up on the table while Jane gives him a look of distaste. She then explains how she showed up at the clearing as we were caught by Lillian's men in their county sheriff's uniforms, and how we picked up a "Worlder" along the way.

"His name is Cameron," I step in, "And speaking of Cam, where is he?"

Alaina twirls a short ringlet of hair around her finger, looking mildly bored.

"He's with Reed," she answers, glancing back towards the shelves stacked with weapons.

"What are they doing?" I ask quizzically. I had seen Reed a moment ago, but even as I crane my neck, I can't see where they could be.

"Initiation," Alaina answers, her voice taking on a strangely ominous note. "Any Worlder who enters the Realms can never return or risk exposing our secrets. So they must join us… assuming they survive initiation."

My heart seems to skip a beat. He can't go back to Earth? He can never go home, back to his parents, to his little brother, his family? Panic begins to build in my chest no matter how hard I try to shove it down.

And *survive initiation*? I really don't like the sound of that. This is all my fault, I'm the one who urged Cam to come with us, who went for him in the first place. If I had just let him be…

Jane seems to notice my sudden panic because she stops idly twirling her dagger and rolls her eyes.

"Don't tease her," she chides, as Alaina giggles. "He's in the back room. He wanted a tour."

As if he knew we were talking about him, Cam emerges from the farthest shelf, staring in amazement at something shiny grasped in his palm. I heave a sigh of relief as I slump back in my chair.

Beside me, Alaina starts cracking up.

Reed trails behind Cam, answering questions here and there as Cam inspects the small object in his hand. They must have already beaten me to the explanation because the confusion he previously had worn has now been replaced by fascination. He looks up, and he smiles as his gaze lands on me sitting by the table.

"Emmalina," he brushes his dusky brown hair from his eyes, his face looking almost as relieved as I feel, as he strides over to wrap me in a tight hug. I lay my head on his shoulder, breathing in the scent of lingering smoke. Finally, he pulls away, holding me at arm's length, his eyes questioning.

"Lina, this place, these people… this is where you've been all along?" I nod. He seems to choke down the other questions no doubt rising to the surface and instead hugs me again as if to reassure himself that it's really me. That I'm here, and that I'm fine, and I find myself doing the same. Then I hear Stefan clear his throat.

"I'm sorry to interrupt, but I think we have something to discuss, now that we have everyone here," there's an edge to his voice. Cam and Reed drag over seats to join us, the tiny table now feeling very cramped with us occupying almost every chair in the room. Stefan seems uncomfortable, almost upset about something as he fixes Cam with an assessing, guarded look. Very unlike the friendly and mild-mannered person I've come to know. I wonder what's wrong.

Jane gives a sharp nod, agreeing with Stefan's statement.

"There is certainly something to be discussed," she says, her eyes glinting. "A certain conversation that began in the helicopter."

Reed opens his mouth to protest, but she beats him to it.

"It was reckless of you three to sneak out. How could you be so stupid, so irresponsible?"

"Emmalina had a right to go back there, and we couldn't just let her go alone!" Alaina speaks up defensively.

"But Marcus specifically told you-"

"Oh, don't try to pretend you care what Marcus says," Reed cuts her off. "You hate him as much as anyone."

"He is second-in-command," Jane seethes, bracing her hands on the table and almost toppling her chair backward as she stands, radiating fury.

"Besides, what is going on with you anyway, Reed? You and Lina bicker like spoiled children, but suddenly you're willing to help her break the law?"

"She just lost her mother, Jane," Reed says, his voice a hoarse whisper. I flinch at the reminder, but somehow, it seems like he's now talking about something more than just me. Jane winces as well, her blazing anger flickering for a moment as she gets the true meaning behind Reed's words.

"If you all are finished," Stefan says cooly, breaking the moment of heavy silence and folding his hands on the table. "Lina, Reed, and Alaina leaving weren't what I had been talking about when I had said we needed to discuss something. I was talking about why *Jane* had left to find you three."

World-ending fury flares bright again in Jane's eyes at Stefan's words.

"Not this again," she hisses. "I left to *save their lives*, or have you all forgotten?"

"No," Stefan interrupts, frustrated. "Let me finish and just sit down already, Jane."

Everyone in the room does a collective double take as quiet, passive Stefan tells Jane to sit down, his tone firm and annoyed. Everyone except Nate, that is, whose job seems to be to defy Jane daily.

"Yeah Janie," he teases. "Take a chill pill."

"Don't call me that," she mutters, but reluctantly takes a seat. Reed gives her a sympathetic pat on the back and has to dodge the punch she aims at his face.

"What I meant," Stefan continues, "Is the reason Jane left in the first place, how we realized you three were in danger."

"The mysterious message you mentioned," I finish, and Stefan nods.

Reed leans forward on his elbows looking intrigued, the wooden chair beneath him creaking as he shifts his weight. "Oh right. Care to clue us in on what exactly the deal is with this strange message I've heard so much about?"

"As we said before, we heard Lillian speaking to her men over the coms, directing them to ambush you at the campsite," Jane explains.

"But no scout could have found her, never mind gotten close enough to record her giving orders. The only security cameras that could have picked it up are on place grounds or by the safe houses, and she wouldn't risk getting so close to us either," Reed reasons.

"But," Alaina speaks up, "Someone had to have recorded it, so if we trace where it came from, we could find out who sent it. Someone must have been trying to warn us if they sent it to the main coms room."

Stefan shakes his head as Jane speaks.

"That's just the thing," she says solemnly. "We did trace it. The message, a live recording of Lillian's voice, was sent from Marcus's personal control headquarters."

CHAPTER 14

The room was silent for a long moment before anyone spoke.

"That can't be possible," Reed protests, his eyes narrowing a fraction.

"Why? What does that mean?" I ask, not quite grasping what they're saying. Jane turns her unnerved gaze on me as she explains.

"The message was a live broadcast, meaning to receive it from Marcus's coms room, Lillian would have to have been recorded there. Which, as Reed said, couldn't be possible because-"

"-Lillian would have to have been in that room," Alaina finishes, biting her bottom lip. "In the palace."

Nate shakes his head. "She would never have been able to get past the guards," he protests. "Someone would have seen her and raised the alarm."

"There is only one way to determine for sure," Stefan says, getting to his feet. "We have to take a look at that security tape."

Jane shakes her head, looking confused. "To do that, we would have to get inside Marcus's personal control room, and he would never allow us to set foot in…" her voice trails off.

"No. Absolutely no way. You are not breaking into it, I won't allow it. It's *not. Going. To. Happen.*"

So, it happened. Jane was outvoted. Not even ten minutes later, the seven of us, Cam included, are standing outside of the imposing door leading to Marcus's private *Coms and Controls Headquarters,* as printed on the small plaque on the wall.

Jane certainly wasn't happy about it, but after a quick and heated debate involving a lot of shouting and nearly two fistfights, Alaina brought up the excellent point that Marcus would never believe us if we told him Lillian was in his control room, and would probably assume we made it up to excuse Jane coming after us, and he would certainly never let us inside. It's safe to say we are not on his good side after the incident only a few hours ago. Finally, Jane agreed, only because if Lillian was really inside the palace, it's very likely that she's still here. And this is too serious of a matter to risk time arguing with Marcus, who would assume we were making the whole thing up. No, we have to do this now and fast.

As soon as we got here, it dawned on us that we forgot the most important detail. The door is locked. There is no doorknob or physical lock to pick, just smooth steel fitted with a small identification card slot. Reed sighs, bracing his hand on the unforgiving metal in frustration as if he would try to shove it open through brute strength, but even he is not strong enough to manage that.

"Now what?" Alaina asks, crossing her arms.

"Wait, can't we just get in by swiping one of your cards?" I point out. I haven't gotten my trainee card yet, but most of my friends are carrying theirs on them. The slot on this door looks almost identical to the one outside the Centerdome doors, so doesn't it work the same too? Alaina just shakes her head, short brown hair swinging like a curtain around her face. She points to *Authorized Personnel Only* sign below the plaque on the door. Something so modern looks so out of place in a glass castle in a surreal magic world. I guess the coms room itself is also a bizarre contrast, the mix of modern and magical.

"Only Orlon, Marcus, and members of the court have access," Alaina explains. "Our cards can't allow us in, and it would just set off the alarm."

"It's linked to an alarm system?" Cam asks curiously, and Alaina nods. His brows furrow and I can practically see the gears turning in his mind.

"How do your key cards work exactly?" he asks.

"What do you mean?" Jane inquires, breaking her sullen silence for the first time since we dragged her here.

"Do you mind if I have a look at that?" Cam reaches out a hand for the key card Stefan still has hanging on a lanyard from his earlier shift in the main coms room. Looking intrigued, he wordlessly presses it into Cam's waiting palm.

"Thanks." He studies it closely for a moment or so, and what he finds seems to confuse him.

"There isn't any sort of barcode or computer chip anywhere on here," he notes. "Just these strange symbols."

Jane nods. "Those are what the computer scans to grant access. They're printed with a certain ink that is only made here in the palace, impossible to remove, change, or replicate."

Cam frowns, whatever idea he had seeming to come to a dead end, but an idea springs into my head.

"What about a glamor? Guards can change the appearance of something using magic. Could you somehow alter the symbols...?"

"No, I just told you, it isn't possible to change the symbols, not in a way that can trick the computer. It might grant you access and unlock the door, but it would set off the alarms."

"Wait," Cam chimes in, his eyes lighting up. "If we were to disable the alarms, you would be able to unlock the door doing... uh, whatever Lina suggested?"

Jane and Reed nod, both realizing that it could work.

"The alarms are connected to the key card panel?" Cam continues.

They nod again.

"Do you have anything long and pointy? Like a fork, or even car keys?"

Jane reaches up to her hair, which she had hurriedly pinned up in a messy bun before our quick dash here, removing two objects, each about as long as a pencil and barely much wider, that were acting as hairpins. They're wrapped in what looks like leather, fitted with tiny rubies shaped like a wolf head on the end of each. Before I can ask what they are, she flicks her right wrist and with a small metallic *shink*, a long, thin silver blade protrudes from the top of one of the objects. Black handles, attached to the daggers she had been polishing in the weapons room.

"Who pins their hair up with daggers?" I ask aloud. Alaina rolls her eyes.

"I know, right?" she agrees. "I mean, what's wrong with a barrette, or perhaps a bejeweled clip? Even a regular hair elastic would work fine, but if one of those daggers came out of its sheathe, it could damage the hair," Alaina fusses.

"Or, you know, poke you in the head," Reed points out.

"Yeah, that too," Alaina admits as if that's less important than ruining the hairstyle. "But at least they have those pretty rubies, so they're not completely barbaric."

"If you're all done criticizing my fashion choices," Jane scoffs, handing the unsheathed dagger to Cam. "I would suggest we continue with your plan, which I still do not agree with, for the record."

"You're a pushover, Jane," Nate comments, matter of factly.

Cam begins to work, wedging the slim, needle-like blade under the metal panel around the card slot, twisting until he is able to pry it away. Beneath is a tangle of delicate mechanisms and wires. He works slowly and carefully, poking, prodding, and adjusting various pieces. Finally, he slips the blade beneath a taut red wire and slices through it with a twist of his wrist. Everyone freezes, waiting for the sound of blaring alarms to give us away.

Nothing.

After a moment of silence, we all let out a collective sigh of relief, Cam in particular.

"Nice," he says, smiling in victory. "I was sixty percent sure that would work."

"Only sixty percent?" Alaina squeaks, giving him an incredulous look, and he just shrugs as he hands Jane her dagger back. She proceeds to twirl her hair back atop her head in a messy bun, sliding the now sheathed ornate knives back in place.

Another moment and Cam has the card slot fitted back to the door. Now for the tricky part- the glamor to trick the computer.

"Alaina should be the one to cast the glamor," Reed suggests. "She has the most talent with magic," Jane, Stefan, and Nate all nod in agreement, and Alaina beams at the compliment as she pulls out her plastic keycard. She closes her eyes, concentrating, and the card in her hand begins to change ever so slightly as the letters blur and reassemble themselves. Her eyes flicker back open but remain vacant as she holds the illusion.

Nate takes the card and swipes it through the slot, and with a satisfying click, the mechanism deep in the door unlocks. Still no alarms. Alaina lets out a huff of breath as she releases the glamor, and Nate lets out a triumphant shout, patting Cam roughly on the back, Reed doing the same.

"Quiet you two. Sheesh, who needs alarms when you lot holler like baboons at every victory."

"You would make terrible spies," I agree, even as I give Cam a congratulatory hug of my own. Reed pushes open the door carefully, and all seven of us file inside, easing it closed before anyone can wander by and notice it ajar.

So this is the inside of Marcus's high-security coms room. I've got to admit, it's pretty underwhelming. It just looks like a high-tech computer lab, with walls of screens and monitors filling the space in front of us. It's not even that big. Nate lets out a sarcastic whistle as he looks around, and voices exactly what I'm thinking.

"Impressive. It's a bunch of computers. And wires. And more computers," he mutters.

"It's a coms room," Stefan points out. "What were you expecting?"

"Guys, over here," Jane strides to a corner of the room, seating herself in a swivel chair before a widescreen, speakers, and recording devices. The rest of us gather around, and I find myself hunching over her shoulder to see what she's doing. She taps a microphone propped up on the small desk.

"If the message was sent from this room, it had to have been recorded here."

"Is there a way to listen to it?" Cam asks. Jane nods.

"Even better. I can pull up the security footage and see who sent it our way, and how."

We watch in anticipation as she types away on the keyboard, fingers flying over the keys. With a final click, the screen is consumed by grainy footage, shifting as the cameras adjust to the dark room. In the video, the only light emits from the glowing of a single computer screen, the same one we're currently crouched over.

In the dim lighting, there is a faint noise of the door being unlocked, and not one, but two sets of muffled footsteps. But only a single figure moves into the camera's view, wearing a dark cloak. As the figure pulls back the hood and turns her head, we get a good look at the young woman's face. Jane mutters something unpleasant under her breath, the others murmuring nervously. All I can do is stare at the girl, staring almost directly at the camera as if she wanted to be recognized. Her long, blonde hair, her distinct eyes and narrow face. My face.

She is me, but not quite. Something about her looks off, older somehow, glaring at the camera with a look of sharp disdain that I know I've never actually worn in my life.

This must be Lillian.

I had been told we look the same, that we are counterparts or reflections or whatever you want to call it, but that didn't prepare me for the shock of seeing it for myself. Just like looking in a mirror, but there is nothing of me in her expression. She seems haunted, as though she's seen things, been through things, *done* things that I could never imagine. A dark, twisted mirror.

We watch the recording in tense silence, as Lillian takes her eyes off of the camera and carefully lifts the microphone. She glances over her shoulder expectantly, and it's only when the second figure moves that I can make out its shape. Another cloaked figure, slender, taller by maybe a few inches, moving with fluid grace. The figure fiddles with the monitors, the only part of them visible is the pale, feminine hands emerging from the folds of the identical black cloak. Finally, she gives Lillian a thumbs up. The cloaked person, likely a woman, doesn't speak and doesn't give any indication of who she may be. Only fades back into the shadows, hidden from the camera once more.

As the footage continues, Lillian lifts the mic and begins to speak, but what she says makes no sense whatsoever.

"Yes. They will be positioned at the campsite within the hour," a pause, then, "We have received a tip that Emmalina and the others are heading there as we speak, unaware that we will be there. I want you to intercept them…"

Seemingly satisfied, Lillian ends the message there, putting down the mic. Stefan points to the screen.

"Look at the time stamp," he says, brows furrowed in confusion. "This is the moment we received that exact message. We thought someone may have secretly recorded her giving those orders, which was the reason I knew to go after you in the first place. But she wasn't talking to anyone, almost like..."

"Like she wanted us to know her men would be at the campsite," Jane finishes. "Like she wanted me to go after Emmalina and warn you, wanted you all to escape."

"She wanted us to escape being caught? By her own soldiers?" Alaina asks skeptically.

"That doesn't make sense," Nate points out. For once, everyone seems to be at a loss for answers. Reed shakes his head.

"The men in the clearing were surprised to see us. Lillian didn't seem to tell them we would be there. For whatever reason, she purposely wanted someone to keep us away. But why?"

"Could it have been a trap of some sort?" I ask.

"Or a distraction," Jane says, her face going slightly pale. Everyone falls silent as Jane continues.

"What room beside this one has access to the security cameras and can sound the alarms?" Reed's face looks grave.

"The main coms room."

"What if she wanted everyone in the coms room distracted with warning you three so she could pull off some other plan without being caught?"

"How could she have even gotten into this room in the first place without tripping the alarms?" I ask, pointing out another piece of this growing puzzle. Jane frowns as if the question hadn't occurred to her. She hurriedly begins typing again, pulling up on the screen what appears to be some sort of security history. Her eyes scan the results before her, frown deepening.

"According to this," she pauses, "The card used to unlock the door is not registered in the system."

"What does that mean?" I press.

"It means that the card she used has a code with full guard status, so it wasn't flagged and no alarms were set off. But the card isn't registered under anyone in our system, so by all means, the keycard she used doesn't exist."

"Could it have been faked any other way?"

"The cards can't be faked in a way that would trick the system, and only Orlon and Marcus have access to the ink that can print a new one."

"So, let me get this mess straight, and try to sum it up for those of us who don't speak nerd," Nate cuts in. "Lillian, the Realm's most wanted and deadly traitor, broke into a high-security control room with a keycard that technically can't exist, recorded a message that betrayed the location of her own soldiers, and sent it directly to Jane and Stefan, possibly to be able to sneak around the palace undetected for whatever reason."

"That about sums it up," Reed says, releasing a heavy breath.

Alaina's, whose face had turned a shade paler with each thing Nate listed, now speaks up.

"Doesn't that mean she could still be in the castle? With a keycard that has access to even the most secure rooms?" her voice trembles.

"We have to inform Marcus and the king like we should have done in the first place," Jane says firmly. This time, no one objects.

"Let's just hope we're not too late," Stefan agrees grimly.

"You did *what*?" Marcus growls through clenched teeth, a muscle twitching in his jaw as he struggles to maintain his fraying composure. We've just described the situation, including the part about breaking into his coms room. It's safe to say he's not taking it great. Orlon, on the other hand, stands silent and pondering. He hadn't given any reaction to the story itself, though he hadn't looked overly pleased. I got the feeling whatever he had given me his permission for, it wasn't quite this, but the news of Lillian seems to have rattled him enough to let it slide without comment. At least someone has their priorities in order.

Marcus, on the other hand, not so much.

"First you defy my orders and almost get caught, then you blow up a safe house and torch the throne room, and now this?" he turns his attention on Jane and Reed.

"And you two, I had expected so much better, but some senior legionaries you've turned out to be. Your parents would be horribly disappointed."

His words seem to have struck the mark he was aiming for because both twins flinch.

"That's quite enough, Marcus," the king says coldly. "Yes, there will be consequences, but there is no need to be cruel."

Marcus's lips purse, and he bows his head slightly to Orlon. "My apologizes," he sneers, sounding anything but sorry. Jane's eyes glint with cold hate, like chips of green ice. Reed looks positively murderous, but neither says a word.

"Thank you for bringing this to my attention," Orlon says, urgency creeping into his tone. "Marcus, I want the whole palace in lockdown. Send trainees and legionaries to their quarters, and any staff to their rooms. I want all full-fledged guards on duty, patrolling every inch of the castle grounds. Send word to the nearby towns. No one leaves until we can be sure Lillian is gone."

Marcus nods. "Yes, Your Majesty," he turns, not looking back as he strides away. Orlon moves his attention to us.

"All of you, report straight to the Dorm. And you, what's your name?" he aims the question at Cam. I wince slightly. I had completely forgotten that Cam probably has no clue what's going on at all.

"My name is Cameron," he answers stiffly.

"Well, Cameron," the king says gently. "You'll stay will the legionaries, I'm sure they can provide accommodations."

Cam nods. "Thank you, sir. Er, I mean, Your Majesty?" he stumbles over the words, and Orlon chuckles softly.

"It's alright, sir works just fine," Cam nods again, giving an awkward attempt at a bow.

As we make our way back through the halls, everyone is on edge. Jane and Reed exchange looks, both walking in tense silence, wearing expressions of exhaustion and hurt. Whatever Marcus had said, about their parents…

Cam falls into step beside me, fiddling with the edge of his jacket, his face contemplative. I expect him to be scared, or curious, but he's only silent. The footsteps of our group echo on the marble, the only sound as I let my mind wander.

Why would Lillian risk sneaking into the palace, prevent us from getting caught by her own soldiers, and then simply disappear? And what about that keycard that "technically can't exist?" The mystery only grows as I ponder it, and I have a strong nagging feeling that we're missing some important detail.

I jump slightly as a hand rests on my shoulder, my head whipping around to see Stefan pull his arm back and put his hands up in mock surrender.

"Sorry," he says, a smile tugging at the corner of his mouth. "I didn't mean to scare you."

"You didn't scare me," I snort.

"Really?" he laughs. "Cause it kind of looked like-"

"Nope."

"You jumped, like, a foot in the air-"

"Shut up," I mutter, and his outright laugh rings through the quiet.

"I was going to ask why you looked so distracted. What were you thinking about?"

"Well,"

I don't realize that the whole group has come to a stop before I run right into Nate's back with an *oomph*. Stefan doesn't laugh this time; no one is focused on anything besides the scene in front of us.

A broken window, shattered glass gleaming golden on the rain-slick floor from the light of the overhead chandeliers. Scraps of torn cloth flutter in the howling wind, caught on the jagged edges of glass still clinging to the window frame. Those scraps, I realize with a jolt, are pieces of the black cloak Lillian had been wearing in the video footage. Stefan wordlessly steps forward, the rest of us following. My foot slides on the edge of the rain puddle pooling beneath the window, slipping out from underneath me, and I feel a firm hand grip my forearm before I tumble to the ground, steadying me. As I right myself, Reed releases his hand, eyes still fixed ahead of him, and I give a small murmur of thanks. Surprisingly, he acknowledges it with a nod, his attention still aimed elsewhere.

Alaina reaches the window first, nimbly detangling the soaked stretch of fabric and inspecting it closely. Eyes narrowing, she turns to show the rest of us.

The front of the torn fabric is embroidered with the image of an elegant silver falcon. Alaina steps away from the window, rain speckling her hair like dewdrops.

"It's a guard cloak," she mutters, turning the fabric in her hands.

"Was it stolen?" Reed suggests, leaning over Alaina's shoulder to get a better look. She shakes her head.

"It can't be a guard cloak though," Stefan points out. He reaches for it, and Alaina hands it over. He turns the silver falcon to the light. He traces a finger over the intricately woven threads.

"Why not?" I ask.

"Because," Reed answers, understanding dawning in his expression. "Guard cloaks aren't embroidered, and if they were, they would have the owner's vitalum, not a silver falcon."

I sigh, miserable. "So let me guess? This cloak technically shouldn't exist either?" Reed's face turns grim.

"Well, that's just perfect," Stefan grumbles. "Another thing to add to our growing collection of mysteries."

"Maybe she could have embroidered it herself?" Nate says with a shrug. "I mean, maybe Lillian and her cronies have a thing for needlepoint or something. Being an evil lunatic must come with a ton of downtime for little evil crafts. Though personally, if I were a crazy villain, I would take up yo-yoing."

"That's not a craft," Alaina points out, frowning.

"Can you please just take this seriously?" Jane chides.

"Even if Lillian decided to take an evil villain sewing class," Reed says wonderingly, causing Jane to roll her eyes. "Why a silver falcon? Isn't her vitalum, Nyx, black and gray?"

"Maybe the evil villain craft store only had silver thread?" I snicker, causing Nate to laugh loudly.

"Can you not encourage them?" Jane sighs.

Stefan, trying to school his expression into something more serious, hands Jane the scrap of fabric.

"We should probably-"

"Hey!" There's a voice from down the hall, accompanied by footsteps, as a man rounds the corner. He's tall and broad-shouldered, with olive-tinted skin and black hair shorn close to his head. He's maybe in his thirties, wearing the uniform of a guard, but adorned with several badges and medals and a dark cloak similar to the one we're inspecting draped over his shoulders.

The man's eyes narrow, taking in the mess at our feet, the seven of us gathered around the shattered window and puddles of water on the floor.

"What is going on here?" he demands, casting a suspicious glare over the group.

"I'm sorry, Captain," Reed apologizes, nodding his head respectfully. "We just found this here… we think it was Lillian."

"What were you doing wandering the halls?" he questions. "You do know the castle has been put under lockdown, correct?"

"We are aware, sir," Stefan assures. "We've just spoken with the king, and we were on our way to the Dorm when we spotted this scene and wanted to investigate."

The man nods. "I have been informed that this lot has done enough investigating for one day." His voice is stern, but his mouth twitches upward in the hint of a smile. "Better move along, leave the investigating to the patrols."

"Yes, Captain," Jane says, passing over the soaked scrap of fabric, which the Captain studies wearily.

The seven of us silently make our way to the end of the hall, under the watchful eye of the Captain, who stands framed in the watery light of the broken window with the fabric clutched in his hand.

"Who was that?" I ask Stefan quietly, once we're out of sight.

"That was Aron, one of the three Captains of the Guard," he answers, voice hushed.

"There are three Captains?" I ask.

"Yes, they have control over the guards and trainees. The general, General Vaan, commands them. The Captains are Vaan's second-in-command."

"So Aron is basically the military version of Marcus?" I scrunch my nose distastefully.

"No," Stefan laughs. "Aron's a lot better than Marcus. He's a great guy, all three Captains are."

The group passes through the main doors, onto the castle grounds, patrols of guards visible everywhere I look, the Dorm looming ahead of us. My feet are aching terribly, every joint creaking with exhaustion. It's been a long night. Reed, Jane, and Alaina all look the same way I feel as if we've all collectively rolled around in bushes and airbrushed our clothes with a flamethrower.

Ahead of me, Nate reaches over and plucks a stray leaf from Alaina's hair, twisting it thoughtfully in his fingers.

I find myself gazing at the back of Reed's head, close enough that I have to tilt my chin slightly upward to do so. Like mine, it's speckled with pine needles and debris, messy and unkempt, and beaded with raindrops. I blink the rain out of my eyes as I watch him, not quite realizing that I'm staring. He seems lost in thought as well.

I wonder what he's thinking about.

CHAPTER 15

There is one problem with this whole lockdown business. It's boring.

Now, huddled up in the Dorm, there is nothing to do but sit and wait. Wait for the guards to search the entire palace and patrol inside and out until they are sure Lillian's long gone.

But that still leaves so many unanswered questions and this waiting is going to drive me insane.

Stefan also seems restless despite not getting much sleep, pacing back and forth in front of the Dorm windows, across from the chair I lay sprawled in, watching the rain that has faded to a drizzle.

I sigh softly, skimming through the book propped open on my lap, barely reading a word. I keep getting distracted by little things, Stefan's pacing, the faint scent of wood smoke and coffee, and an irritating tapping noise from the other side of the lounge. The tapping noise is Nate, idly drumming his fingers against the side table, beside the couch he slouches in, the same one he napped in earlier.

Now it's Alaina who's dozing, her head resting against Nate's shoulder, curled in the space beside him like a cat. Occasionally he reaches to stroke her hair, playing with the ends.

The aroma of coffee wafts from the mug Jane has cupped in her hands, and she sips from it as she clutches a book of her own. Unable to concentrate, I flip the pages in my lap shut and toss the book on a coffee table. At that same moment, my head whips towards the sound of the door to the lounge creaking open, Reed nudging it wider as he struggles to enter while balancing a tray of coffees.

Stefan pauses his pacing. Thanks to the Dorm's size and abundance of lounges and hang-out spots, we have this one to ourselves. We had all slept until late noon, and Cam still remains in his room, likely even more tired than the rest of us. I can't imagine what he's gone through the past week or why was he at that campsite so late.

"Has there been any news?" Stefan asks impatiently. Reed shakes his head.

"No news, just coffee."

This is our third coffee run of the evening. I'm afraid we might have a caffeine problem.

"I'm just so sick of waiting around here all day," I sigh. Reed plops himself down in a seat across from Jane, taking a bite out of a bagel from a little paper bag balanced on the drink tray. Alaina, who is not as asleep as she seemed, reaches out her hand palm-up expectantly without even opening her eyes, and Reed passes her a bagel.

"I bumped into Eliza in the commons," Reed says, taking another bite.

"Oh?" Jane arches an eyebrow as she glances up from her novel.

"Yeah," he grumbles. "She thinks it was *very* funny we were caught sneaking out. Something like *nice remodeling of the throne room*, and how our legion is practically responsible for this lockdown." He snorts. "She talks a lot."

Jane's free hand clenches into a fist.

A very distant clap of thunder is followed by lightning flashing outside of the windows, the rain picking up. I snuggle deeper into my sweater.

"Oh," Reed says, sitting up a little straighter, fumbling in his pockets for something.

"I almost forgot," he pulls out an envelope. "I found this tucked under the doorway to the lounge when I got back, which is odd because it wasn't there when I left."

To my surprise, as he turns the envelope in his hand, I can see a name scrawled in large letters across the front in heavy black ink. *Emmalina*.

"It's for me?"

I take it gently in my hands, studying the handwriting before tearing it open and tugging out the folded scrap of paper. The parchment is fine and expensive looking but roughly torn, with only a few lines scribbled onto one side.

It reads:

A group of six must venture to the Spire. Emmalina Maren, Reed Windervale, Jane Windervale, Nathaniel Aurum, Alaina Sparks, Stefan Fides.

You are expected before the sun rises tomorrow. The fate of the worlds depends on you now.

DO NOT FAIL.

As my eyes skim over the words, my fingers begin to shake.

"Come on, we're dying over here," Nate complains. "What does it say?"

I clear my throat, trying to keep the quiver from my voice as I read it aloud. When I finish, the room is quiet. Alaina speaks first.

"What does it mean?" she asks softly. "Who sent that?"

"There's no name, that's all that's written."

"We have to bring that to the king," Stefan says, wringing his hands.

"Are you kidding?" Reed objects. "That note says that all six of us need to go to the Spire. The king or Marcus would never allow it, especially while they're still searching for Lillian. And after our recent adventures…"

"We can't just not tell the king about this," Stefan muses. "It could be a trap."

"What is the Spire anyway?" I ask.

"It's the name of the Shadow Realm palace," Jane explains.

"The Shadow Realm?" my palms feel clammy.

"We have to tell the king," Jane says, getting to her feet. "We're already in enough trouble as it is, if we sneak out again, we'll be breaking the law for the third time, and Orlon can only be so forgiving before we have to face real consequences. We have to investigate this, the fate of the worlds is a pretty serious matter."

No one objects.

"Alright," I say, standing as I tuck the paper back into the envelope.

"Do you really think the king will let us travel halfway across the Realms on some quest we know nothing about?"

"Well, if that letter is legitimate, there are only two people that would have sent it. King Umbra, or…"

"The TimeKeeper," Jane says, her face paling.

"If that's true, then we don't have much of a choice," Alaina says. "If the TimeKeeper sent that letter, then the fate of the worlds is truly at stake."

The six of us head directly for the king's private wing of the castle, praying we aren't stopped by anyone before we get there. Hopefully, we could avoid dealing with Marcus entirely.

But of course, nothing is ever that simple. We barely make it out of the Dorm and through the palace doors before a pair of guards block our path. Each grip a large spear in their hands, leveling them at my chest within an instant.

"Wait," Jane says, stepping forward with her hands up. "It's just us."

The guards hesitate but don't lower their spears.

"We need to see the king," Reed says, his hands in the air as well. "We have a very important message for him."

One guard snorts. "Absolutely not. You're going anywhere near the king. Don't you realize the palace is under lockdown?"

"But we have urgent information that Orlon will want to hear," I protest.

"I'm sure you do," says an awfully familiar voice, as Marcus shimmers into visibility.

Of course, he's a lynx, because why would anything ever be easy? He levels a look at me, then my companions.

"This may appear to be Emmalina, but what if it's an impersonator?" Marcus says with a sly smile, pacing slowly back and forth. "What if this is Lillian standing before us? Perhaps she should spend the night in the dungeons, just to be safe, because after all, I remember telling these delinquents to stay in the Dorm. Or maybe you all just don't think rules apply to you?"

He sneers. "Lock her up," he orders. "We're not taking any risks."

The guards surge forward to clasp manacles around my wrists, to restrain me, my friends shouting in protest, but they almost immediately recoil.

"Sir," the guard moves one manacle to expose the bracelet on my wrist. He turns his hand to expose a scorched mark on his glove where he had touched the silver while trying to confiscate it. Marcus's scowl deepens, reluctance in his eyes, but he waves a hand to indicate the guards should remove the manacles.

What just happened? Why did they just let me go?

Marcus gives the silver bracelet, the mark of my vitalum, a long look.

"My apologies, Emmalina," he says, sounding more disappointed than sorry.

"Now may we see the king?" Jane asks coldly.

"Any message you have for him, you can give to me. I'll pass it along."

"Not this again," Reed grumbles, but Marcus just waits. With a reluctant huff, I pass him the envelope. His eyebrows raising in sudden curiosity, he snatches the paper from my fingers, eyes skimming over the torn parchment. When he finishes, he stiffly slides the paper back into the envelope, tucking it into his pocket.

"No," he states firmly.

"But we haven't even asked yet-" I begin to argue, but he cuts me off.

"I. Said. No. No one is going anywhere."

"But the letter-"

"You six listen to me, and listen carefully," the king's second growls, straightening to his full height. "I am not permitting a bunch of teenagers, and troublemakers, on a fool's errand across the Realms with our most wanted criminal running amok, playing hero," his eyes fixed on me.

"We have to," Jane protests with an equally forceful stare. "The note says we have to go to the Spire, which means you and I both knew who likely sent it."

"It's a trap, set by Lillian."

"And if it isn't?" she counters. "Would you ignore a summons like this from the TimeKeeper himself?"

"My answer is no. If any of you have a shred of logic left in you, you'll drop the matter immediately," Marcus turns on his heel to leave.

"No," Jane's voice is firm. Marcus looks back over his shoulder, warning written on every line of his face.

"What did you say?" his voice is deathly quiet. Reed grabs Jane's wrist, whispering to her, "It's not worth picking a fight."

Jane's eyes flare with wrath, but then go cold.

"No, it isn't," she agrees. "Not if he refuses to see reason."

With that, she's the one who turns away, leaving a dumbstruck Reed, and Marcus with a self-satisfied smirk.

The walk back is tense and silent, and I can sense guards trailing us back to the Dorm. Making sure we don't do anything stupid.

Instead of heading for the lounge like the rest of us, Jane breaks off from the group. Alaina moves to go after her, but Reed grabs her arm.

"She's probably heading for the training room. It might be best to just let her blow off some steam. You know how her temper gets."

The rest of us settle back in the lounge, and I nurse my still-warm cup of coffee. I wish this place had tea, but the place downstairs only had espresso and hot coffee.

"Well, that didn't go as planned, though I guess we should have expected it by now," Nate says, kicking his feet up.

"I can't believe Marcus could just blow it off like that," Alaina mutters. "I mean, a message sent by the TimeKeeper..."

"Who is that anyway?" I ask.

"He's a seer," Stefan says. "The first one ever actually. And the last."

"A seer? There are people who can see the future?" I marvel.

"There used to be. Now it's only the TimeKeeper."

"Did the seers disappear with the falcons?"

Reed nods. "Two hundred years ago, a massive war broke out. There used to be five Realms- but the Realms of Space and Time tried to conquer them all. Orlon united the other two, and together they obliterated the two corrupted Realms and their rulers. But with them, the seers, who sided with the Time Realm, were destroyed. The disappearances of the falcons occurred within the year, though no evidence has ever been found of any connection between them."

"But the TimeKeeper is different than any old seer," Stefan explains. "His visions of the future are usually warnings of the direst sort. To ignore one..."

"The last time one of his visions was ignored, it was catastrophic," Reed finishes.

"We have to go anyway," Alaina says, her voice soft and determined. "It's too important. Lina is destined to save the world from Lillian eventually, what if this is it?"

"I'm not even a real guard yet," I protest.

"Besides," Reed interjects, "We've already pushed Marcus too far, you heard him. We'll be breaking the law for the third time in forty-eight hours, and he won't be so forgiving this time. Plus, all the possible ways out of the castle grounds are guarded. We'll need permission this time, or our hands are tied."

Alaina sits back with a frustrated sigh, her arms crossed.

But wait. Something Reed said rings a bell. We do need permission... the king's permission...

I sit straight up as if someone had lit a firecracker beneath my seat. Reed raises an eyebrow, but Stefan doesn't pause his renewed pacing.

"What if we already have the king's permission to leave?" I ask. Now Stefan's steps falter, as he looks up, confused.

"Well," he says quizzically. "The king has more authority than Marcus, so it would be enough. I doubt we're getting anywhere near Orlon during the lockdown."

"But he's already given his permission," I say. "He gave it to me right after we got back from the campsite."

"What are you talking about?" Alaina asks curiously. I lean forward, trying to make myself remember.

"Right after our return from Earth, the king brought me aside, saying he wanted to speak with me personally."

Alaina nods, "I remember."

"Well, at the time, what he said made no sense. He didn't punish or even scold me. When I asked why he only said that there are sometimes more important things than following the rules."

Stefan's eyes narrow, but I continue.

"He told me that one day soon I would be faced with a decision, and when that day comes, I would have his permission and encouragement to do what I believe is right. No matter what stands in my way. He even mentioned the future of the worlds depends on it. That can't just be a coincidence."

"The fate of the worlds," Alaina muses. "Just as the note had said."

"So you see, we do have permission already. It's almost as if he knew we would be receiving the message."

"And how do we know that you aren't making this up?" Reed asks bluntly.

"If I were lying," I say snarkily, "How would I know that we can use Passage Number Three to sneak away unnoticed?"

Reed blinks in surprise.

"How do you know about that?" Alaina asks, biting her bottom lip.

"Because the king told me," I answer. "He said if the need were to arise, Passage Number Three would be exactly what I need."

For a moment, no one speaks. My words fall into silence. As I wait with bated breath, it comes down to this, will they believe me?

"Well, I'm in," Nate says finally, having been silent for most of this conversation. His features stretch into a maniac grin. "After all, if the fate of the worlds depends on it, how can we not?"

Alaina's face morphs into the same mischievous smile.

"Count me in too."

"If you're going," Stefan says grudgingly, "I'm going with you."

Everyone turns to Reed.

A moment of silence and waiting. He rubs his temples, and with the most reluctant sigh, gives in.

"Well, I can't let you have all the fun can I? We've done all this, what's the point in stopping now?"

He lifts his dark eyes to mine, the dim light of the lounge casting the green in an amber hue. "I'm with you."

Reed is on my side. Not that I really care whether he comes or not, it's just that, well, we could use his help, that's all. So why can't I stop grinning at him? Why won't my stupid heart stop beating so fast?

"Well, who's going to tell Jane?" Nate's voice drawls, bringing a grinding halt to my suddenly giddy mood. We had forgotten about Jane.

"We can't tell her," Reed says finally. "She would never let us get away with this kind of thing again. If she finds out, she'll go straight to Marcus, and not only will our little trip be canceled, we'll be stripped of our trainee status. Permanently."

"But Jane has to come with us," Alaina protests. "Not just because she's our friend and deserves to know, but also because we'll need her there. This is bigger than the trip to the campsite. Once we go, there will be no turning back. Marcus will ensure that we'll be hunted like fugitives."

"Besides," I agree, "The note included her in it."

"I have to side with Reed on this one," Stefan says, giving me an apologetic look. "If we tell Jane, she'll never allow it to happen. Besides, as you said, we'll be fugitives. Jane's been working towards becoming the next second-in-command her whole life, is it right of us to destroy her dream like that?"

"Wait, the next second-in-command?" I ask.

"Yeah. Marcus has held the position for the past three years, but every year, the king reevaluates and sometimes will decide to choose another. That's why Marcus hates our legion, in particular, she's clear competition for him."

"You know, our mom was second-in-command at one point," Reed says, his voice raw. There's something there, something about his parents, that he hasn't told me.

"And before her, the youngest second-in-command there has been yet, was your mother, Lina. Corrine Maren."

I ripple of shock goes through me. I mean, I had come to terms with the fact that she had a life here, that this is where she had once lived, but the reality of it hadn't sunk in.

"She was second-in-command?" I ask, dumbfounded.

"Yeah, at only twenty-five years old," Stefan says. "But Jane, if she's on the path everyone believes she's on, could beat that record and take Marcus's place."

Nate snorts. "I would love to see the look on his face."

But I'm not listening anymore. A new thought occurred to me when Reed mentioned my mom. What if, somehow, this TimeKeeper could help me find her?

"We can't tell Jane," I say softly. "We have to do this."

Reed frowns, checking that strange watch of his with the symbols instead of numbers.

"If we're going to make it to the Shadow Realm by sunrise, as the note said, we have to go now," he points out. With a start, I glance up at the window, speckled with raindrops and pricks of starlight in the night sky. I hadn't realized how late it had gotten.

Alaina still doesn't look thrilled about the decision, but even she has to admit that this is the only way. We don't have time to convince Jane, and can't risk what would happen if we can't.

"So," I say. "What's the plan?"

CHAPTER 16

About a half hour later, and a lot of hurrying and sneaking around, we are packed and dressed in thick traveling cloaks, hoods pulled over our heads, and bags at our feet.

We only have the necessities: clothes, sacks of gold and silver coins (the Realms don't use dollar bills), canteens of water, weapons, and extra food snatched from the Dorm kitchen, through the use of Alaina's invisibility.

Speaking of Alaina, despite her being the smallest person here, she sure packed the largest bag. Nate grudgingly shoulders its strap with a grunt, balancing both hers and his own. Alaina's answering smile is sparkling.

"What did you even pack in here?" Nate demands, shifting his weight.

"I feel sorry for the poor mule that'll have to carry it," Reed snorts, and Nate's eyebrows crease with confusion.

"I thought we were taking horses?"

"The mule I was talking about is you."

Stefan chuckles as he tucks a rolled-up map into his pack. I guess the horses won't have GPS.

"Where even is this forbidden Passage Number Three?" I ask curiously. Stefan shrugs.

"I don't actually know," he admits. "It's the third and longest escape route beneath the palace, only ever used in extreme emergencies, connecting to every building and main room on the first floor of the castle."

"So what this nerd means," Alaina translates, jabbing her thumb at Stefan. "-is that the locations of the entrances are kept pretty secret. And it's been so long since they were used, most people have just forgotten the Passages even exist. But there is one person who knows how to get in,"

"Let me guess," I say, my heart sinking. "It's Marcus?"

"No," Alaina huffs, looking mildly offended. "It's me, of course."

"She's a pretty nosy person," Nate chimes in. "She likes sneaking around the castle invisibly. Allie here is an expert at snooping," he moves to pat Alaina on the head, and she swats his hand away.

"Well, that's perfect," I say. "Where is it then?"

"Well, as Stefan said, the Passage connects every building through the ground, so the Dorm does have an entrance. We just have to not get caught getting there."

Not being caught is a lot harder than it sounds.

We almost fail twice, even with Alaina and Stefan maintaining a veil of invisibility over the five of us. The first time was my bad- but to be fair, it's very hard to not bump into things when you can't see your own two feet. So do I feel guilty about that vase in the hall that I may have been responsible for smashing? Yes, but I feel worse about the heart attack we nearly gave the poor trainee walking at the other end of the corridor. We had to get out of there nice and quick.

But the second time wasn't my fault. Mostly. We don't talk about the second time.

I bet we all look ridiculous if anyone could actually see us. Walking hand in hand down the halls, Alaina and Stefan maintained our visibility and kept us together. I have Stefan's fingers twined through one of my hands, warm and steady.

Finally, we come to a stop in the main foyer, right in front of the doors, bumping into each other like a chain of dominos and trying not to make much noise. The place is crawling with bored trainees and alert guards.

"Right there," Alaina's voice is a barely audible whisper. "Under that stairwell."

I don't know what stairwell she's talking about, because there are several, but a tug on my hand indicates that we're moving towards the smaller one on the right. It is less grand than the others and older looking too, leading to a simple balcony landing. Nothing about it looks particularly special, despite being old. But the tiny cupboard beneath the stairwell- now that looks out of place. It looks like something you would find in an elderly grandmother's house, stashing sewing supplies. The door slowly cracks open, making the slightest creak as it's opened by invisible hands. Tucked in the far corner of the room, no one notices the little cupboard drift open just wide enough for a person to slip through.

And that's what we do, getting on hands and knees, fingers still clasped together, crawling single file through the wooden door. The space inside is larger than I expected, but still incredibly cramped. The doors shut with the tiniest muffled thump, and plunge us into darkness until someone switches on a flashlight. We all flicker back into visibility, crouched shoulder to shoulder on the dusty, spiderweb-lined floorboards. I shudder.

"It's under here somewhere," Alaina mutters, feeling along the far wall. "Ah, right here." She pushes against one of the boards in the center of a near-hidden outline of a doorway, and it swings open with the squeak of rusted hinges. A dark, narrow tunnel barely wide enough to crawl through looms beyond.

My skin crawls just looking at it, at the shadowy, earth-hewn walls that seem to swallow up the light. I swallow hard.

"This is Passage Number Three?" Reed says doubtfully. "I thought it was supposed to be some secure escape route."

"The parts of the Passage had been collapsed in the Oblivion Wars," Alaina says, being the first to crawl on her hands and knees into the tunnel. The rest of us slowly follow, single file, the walls so close they scrape our shoulders, and we have to duck our heads.

"This is one of the few makeshift tunnels that was carved out to reach the rest of it. It should lead us right into the Passage," she explains.

"How do you know about all this?" Stefan asks.

"As Nate said before, I do a lot of exploring. This Dorm has been my home for my whole life, so it's safe to say I know pretty much all there is to know about it and the Passage."

"Wait, I remember you saying that before," I bring up. "That you've lived here you're whole life, but you're not royalty. Then why? Do your parents live in the castle?" Only silence answers, and even without seeing her face, I know I've asked the wrong question. When she answers, her voice only carries a twinge of sorrow.

"No," she says softly. "I don't know my parents. I've never met them. They gave me up when I was a baby, and King Orlon took me in. Gave me a home with the trainees."

"Oh. I'm sorry," I'm not really sure what else to say to that, and I can't see her face to gauge her reaction. At this point we've gone so far that the ceiling has begun to slope downwards slightly, now scraping the top of my head, crawling on my elbows. Just as the claustrophobia begins to set in, my chest tightening with fear, unable to get enough air, a pinprick of dull light becomes visible. That pinprick becomes an exit at the end of the tunnel, just slightly-less-gloomy space beyond. One by one, we climb out, getting to our feet on solid, cobblestone, wet and mildewy beneath our feet.

I turn in time to see Reed hauling himself out of the hole in the wall, shoulders pressed against either side and breathing heavily.

"There we go," Alaina says, wiping the grime off of her hands onto her already dirty pants. "That wasn't so hard."

"Not so hard?" Reed pants. "I swear I almost got stuck in there. That tunnel was not human-sized."

"Let's not do that again," Nate agrees.

"Oh, quit complaining guys," Alaina chides, but the smile on her face seems too forced to be genuine. I regret asking those questions about her parents, but how was I supposed to know?

I take a deep breath of the damp, stale air of Passage Number Three. Not quite as impressive as I would have imagined, but so much better than a hole carved out of dirt, so I'll take it. That makes me wonder if this is called Passage Number Three, are there Passages Number 1 and 2 somewhere under here as well? What are those used for?

The walls, floor, and ceiling are made of cobblestone, lined with moss, the floor slimy with years of being abandoned underground. Our cloaks are all caked with dirt, but the clothes underneath are fairly clean, more or less. But where is the light coming from?

It is emitting from around the corner, where the passage twists and winds away from us. As we round the bend, I can see why. A massive circular opening in the ceiling is open to the air, letting in filtering moonlight and leaving the stones slick from where it had rained. The moon isn't quite overhead yet, just beginning its arc in the sky. I can't help but wonder if it's the same moon I see from Earth, or if, being another dimension, it's a different one entirely. The little moonlight, casting onto a raised dais on the ground below the opening, is barely enough to see by, and Reed fishes in his cloak pocket for his flashlight. As he flicks it on, I can see the dais in more detail.

It's about an inch tall, made of what looks like marble, gleaming as though freshly polished despite being open to the elements for so long. And it's carved with whorls and symbols that mean nothing to me, but Reed narrows his eyes.

"Is that…?" Alaina begins to ask, peering at the symbols.

"Yes," Reed answers. "*Vetulinga*. The Old Language." He points to his watch, the one that had always puzzled me with its strange patterns in place of numbers. "It's from the same tongue as these symbols here. This must be ancient, maybe even older than the tunnels themselves. What is this place?"

"Couldn't someone have put them here more recently?" Alaina asks skeptically. "I mean, your watch bears the symbols, and it isn't ancient-"

"This watch has been passed down in my family for generations, I have no idea how old it is," Reed says. "For all I know, it could be."

The watch doesn't look ancient- with its supple leather strap inscribed with a howling wolf, and gleaming face- but then again, neither does the dais.

Reed tracks his finger along a winding string of symbols that seem to make an arrow, running to the edge. And making a ring around the circumference- different shaped holes in the marble.

"Can you read it?" I ask.

"No," he shakes his head. "I only know numbers and a few words. From what I can make out..." His mouth tightens.

"Here," his finger lands on the inscription above the first indent in the marble, long and deep, like an oversized keyhole. "Here it says *sun*." He moves to an identical hole right beside it. "This one says *moon*."

The next indent is small, about the size of my palm, circular and shallow, as though it is meant to fit some sort of disk. The next is distinctly spiral-shaped. And the last is the largest, shaped to fit a sphere. Reed points to each inscription, in turn, reading aloud.

"*Time. Space. Reflections.*"

"What do they mean?" I say softly. Reed shakes his head.

"I don't know," His finger follows the line of script right to the edge of the dais, where it seems to form a certain arrow. Pointing.

We all lift our gaze, following the direction of the arrow. To a blank wall, identical to the others; old stone encrusted with moss. Nate runs his hand over the stones.

"Could something be here?" he asks. "Like a doorway, or a hiding place? Maybe another Passage entrance?"

"I don't know of any other entrances beneath the Dorm," Alaina says, puzzled. I raise an eyebrow.

"You've been down here before, have you never noticed the dais?" I press. She shrugs.

"It was always here, I've just never bothered to look for writing. I wouldn't have been able to read it anyway."

"We should keep moving," Stefan interrupts, casting a glance upward at the sky high above, visible through the opening above our heads. Where the moon has slowly begun to climb higher. Not overhead yet, but we're running out of time. We have to be in the Shadow Realm by sunrise.

Reed nods, turning away from the wall, towards the tunnel leading away from the dais. But as we leave the strange space, I feel a chill go through my body. A breath of cold down the back of my neck, like the whisper of a ghost, and the stale air is ruffled by a breeze from the tunnel before us, catching like claws on my cloak. As though the very air is reluctant to let us go, trying to pull us back. And in the breeze, I swear I hear the hissing sound of a voice.

Spooked, I turn to the others, all pale-faced with fear.

"I heard it too," Reed whispers. "Let's get out of this tunnel."

No one argues, and no one dares to slow the pace until we've made it far, far away from that room, and that dais.

Not long after, we come to a halt in a narrow corridor, at a dead end.

"We're here," Alaina announces. I look around, nothing marking this space as any different from the rest of the Passage.

"This isn't an exit," I say, pointing out the obvious. "And where is *here* exactly?"

Alaina doesn't answer, only points up several feet above our heads, to the ceiling, where the form of an earth-encrusted wooden trapdoor is visible in the stone. The damp smell of the corridor is now layered with something faint, unpleasant, and musky.

"Great. Well, what are we waiting for?" Stefan asks impatiently, gesturing for Alaina, standing beneath the trapdoor, to open it. She raises an eyebrow, but after a few moments of silence, raises her hands in the air as if reaching for the handle. She's up on her tip-toes, but her fingers still miss the handle by an inch or so, emphasizing why she hadn't opened it already. She's too short.

Stefan snorts with laughter, Nate and Reed not bothering to contain theirs. I try to disguise my laugh as a cough, but she glares at me anyway.

"I'll do it," Stefan chuckles, Alaina stepping aside to let him reach for the handle instead. I notice the mischievous smirk on her lips before anyone else, and I don't have enough time to warn Stefan before he yanks on the trapdoor, and it swings wide. And a torrent of hay and muck pours from the hatch, right atop his head.

Now it is Alaina's turn to laugh, as Stefan yelps and tries to duck out of the way. The musky smell now fills the space- the scent of the stables overhead. Stefan shakes hay out of his hair, the mocking smile wiped off of his face. Nate and Reed are now practically rolling on the ground with laughter.

"That's what you get for making fun of my height," Alaina chides, casting a glance at the two other boys.

"And you two are next,"

They both choke it back, trying to look innocent, but Reed still has tears in his eyes from laughing so hard.

"Let's just get up there," Stefan snaps, brushing the filth from his already dirty cloak. "Is there a ladder or something we can use?" He peers up at the square opening, too high to easily climb out.

"Well, now who's too short?" Alaina snickers.

"You're small enough, we could just throw you through the trapdoor," Stefan says snarkily, which causes her to cross her arms.

"You wouldn't," she sneers.

"Try me,"

"Guys, no one is throwing anyone," Reed cuts in. "Someone give me a boost, and I can help pull you all up,"

Nate helps Reed through the opening, and he and Reed proceed to hoist the rest of us into the stables. Once we're all sprawled in the hay, we all take a moment to catch our breath. Reed and Nate are panting from the effort, despite their enhanced strength.

I take the moment to look around, at the decoratively carved wood of the horses' stalls, the beams high overhead, and the hay littered beneath our feet. Little moonlight filters in through a grand window near the ceiling, casting the space in a pale glow.

There are many horses, of all types and colors, each one groomed and sturdy. The one closest to me, a gorgeous black mare, fixes me with a steady gaze as if wondering why we interrupted her sleep.

"We did it," I say, getting to my feet. "But how are we supposed to get out of the palace grounds?"

"We'll escape through the woods," Alaina says. "There's only a short dash down the hill, and then we'll be in the cover of the trees. We'll be gone before anyone realizes we're missing-"

"A bit late for that, don't you think?" asks a lilting voice from overhead. My heart practically stops beating. No, it's not possible. We were so careful, how could she have found out?

Jane, lounging hidden in the wooden beams, slowly lowers herself to the ground, grinning like a fiend.

"You all are too predictable." She flips her ponytail over one shoulder, arms crossed.

We all stare in silence, caught like deer in headlights.

"Really?" Jane sighs. "I mean, are you surprised that I guessed what you were planning to do? How stupid do you think I am? You want to go to the campsite, Marcus says no, you go anyway. You want to get into the control room, I say no, you go anyway. Why would this time be different? You all have already proven that you don't care who stands in your way."

"We're leaving," Reed says firmly as if daring her to challenge him.

But she only shrugs. "Then go. I doubt anyone else is going to notice that you're gone, at least until morning."

That makes Reed pause. "You… you didn't tell the guards?"

"Why would I tell them," she says slowly. "-if I'm coming with you?"

Reed's mouth opens and closes with surprise, at a loss for words. All he manages to make out is "Why?"

"Because Marcus pushed me too far this time," she answers, eyes burning with a different kind of fury. "If he's going to be unreasonable, then so will I. And besides," she smirks again. "You all look like you need the help. I mean what happened to you guys? You look like you just crawled through a sewer. And Stefan looks like he's been rolling in piles of hay,"

Stefan's eyes narrow as he plucks another piece of straw from his hair, glaring at Alaina.

"Wait, how did you get here without being caught if you didn't use the tunnels?" I ask.

"The lockdown was lifted twenty minutes ago," Jane shrugs. "I just walked across the grounds and avoided the patrols. I've been here *forever* waiting for you all to show up."

Stefan's eye twitches. "You mean we crawled through that filthy tunnel for no reason?" His voice is strained.

"Pretty much." she agrees. "Though I have to give you points for effort."

"Well, if you're coming with us, Jane, then pick a horse," Alaina declares, bracing her hand against a stall door. "We've got to leave now,"

Alaina and Stefan are the best here at riding, but everyone else manages. Readying the horses proves to be more complicated than I expected- I may be able to ride, barely, but I have no experience with the gear. The only parts I'm familiar with are the saddle and the reins, so Reed assists me with everything else. He even had to help get me onto its back, which was more embarrassing than anything.

"Let's go," Jane says, easing her horse- the black mare I had seen before- up beside mine. She tugs with frustration on the reins, urging the mare to move forward. Out of all of us, Jane is the only other person without much riding experience, claiming that a vehicle is more efficient. At least I'm not the only one.

We start at a steady walk until I get the hang of how to stay in the saddle- moving as the horse moves. So far, not so bad. Easy, even.

Until Alaina urges her mount into a trot, indicating that we do the same.

I take it back, it is not easy, not at all. But I manage it. My horse is patient and cooperative and likely used to clueless new riders like me.

Some ways past the stables are the Elder Woods, looming with shadows so dark I can barely make out anything beyond the first few rows of pines. Only a gentle slope of wide-open grass lies between us and the cover of the trees. But this section of the grounds is less patrolled, so we should be able to make it without being spotted.

But of course, nothing is ever that simple.

We hear a shout from the castle walls- a singular guard, who must have been on a break, pointing at us and shouting something. Well, there goes the whole purpose of stealth. The horses are spurred into a gallop, and I cling to the reins for dear life as we fly towards the treeline and are shrouded by darkness, hiding the six of us and our mounts. But it's too late. The guards are coming.

"Follow the trees," Reed commands. "Stay far enough back that you won't be spotted, but *do not* lose sight of the tree line, do you hear me? *Stay together.*"

The woods at night are darker than the tunnels, darker than the space under that staircase. It's like an inky fog enveloping the forest beyond, hiding any sort of terrible creature. And in my bones, I understand that, once I lose sight of the tree line and that little bit of visible moonlight, I will never find it again.

There is no path to stick to, no clear space to tread, so our horses simply crash through the underbrush, avoiding tree trunks. But the depths of the forest seem to swallow up sound as well as light, making everything seem muffled. I have no idea where we are or how far we've gone, but Reed at the head of our group seems to have spotted some landmark that he had been searching for as his cue to steer his horse out of the woods.

The rest of us follow suit, diving out of the trees, across a short stretch of grass, until the sound of horse hooves on pavement signals that we've reached a road. It is the main street leading away from the palace grounds, Elder woods looming on either side of us, blocking all view of the castle behind us except a few of the tallest glass towers. Outside of that suffocating darkness, the moonlight feels as bright as day.

We've lost the guards, but it'll be a matter of seconds before they guess where we've fled to.

"Just follow the street," Jane commands. "Don't stop, just keep going as fast as possible, and we'll be able to outrun them."

As we continue, the sound of thundering hooves ringing too loudly in the night and light rain speckling our faces, I can't help but glance towards the Elder Woods. During the day it had seemed so ordinary, almost peaceful if you don't count our run-in with the Mimic Serpent. But now, under cover of the night, it seems like it's alive- filled with evil and malice.

"Why are the woods… like that?" I ask, struggling to find the words. "It feels like it's alive, and watching us. And why weren't they like this before, during the Tournament? That was at night too."

"The woods are always dangerous," Stefan explains solemnly. "Infested with dark magic and terrible evil. Creatures worse than the Mimic Serpent. We have magical wards up during the day, and sometimes things can slip through, but for the most part, the daylight drives them to the darker parts of the forest. But fueled by the night, our wards are no match for the things that slip past. It was one of the reasons why people were so unsure about hosting the Tournament in the Elder Woods this year. But King Orlon put up the wards himself the night of the Tournament and combined with the light from the Centerdome and the towers, it was enough to keep anything away."

"That's why one of the rules was not to go outside the boundaries," Jane adds. "That's where the stronger wards, and safety, ended."

I shudder, casting another glance at the expanse of trees on either side of the road.

"You don't need to worry about it now," Reed says, noticing that glance, the fear behind it. "Those dark creatures don't leave the woods, even on cloudy nights like this. They hate the light, and would never leave the protection of the dark."

That doesn't make me feel much better. Every sound, every shift of the shadows sets me on edge. The ride is smooth and uninterrupted until we're so far from the palace that it's barely a distant form atop a hill in the distance, and we reach more rural roads leading to the nearest town- Penrith, capital of the Mirror Realm. We skirt around the outlying villages, however, keeping to back roads and horse trails along the woods.

We ride through the night as the sprinkling rain turns to a swirling mist, against the unrelenting chill. The sky overhead clears as the clouds drift away, leaving behind an expanse more brilliant than I've ever seen before, so many stars that it looks like someone poured glitter into the heavens. Those stars and the moon illuminate the path before us.

From what I've seen in the hours that we've been riding, the Mirror Realm seems to be mostly countryside- rolling hills and endless forests that we stay well away from. The occasional town or village sparkling in the distance that we also avoid, and the silhouette of the mountains as a constant backdrop against it all.

No one says a word. We had all fallen silent a while ago, no longer for fear of being caught out here in the open, but due to several sleepless nights of exhaustion weighing us down. So for a long time, the only sound is the thud of horseshoes on muddy earth and the eerie hoot of an owl.

It's only when the sky distantly begins to lighten that I know we're almost there. I shift my aching legs as Alaina sidles her horse up beside me, gazing off towards the horizon as if she can see past the mountains to whatever lies beyond. Finally, she speaks, the first words I've heard in hours.

"What is it like, living on Earth?" she asks softly, her gaze still distant. I blink the sleeplessness from my eyes, surprised by the question.

"What do you mean?"

"Well, you lived in that nice little town, so close to the mountains, and the sea," she sighs almost wistfully. "What is it like? To go camping, or to visit the beach? To swim in the ocean?"

"Have you never done any of those things?" I ask. It's a stupid question- she wouldn't be asking if she had. "I mean, the mountains are right there. And there has to be some kind of ocean here, right?"

But she only shakes her head.

"The mountains here are dangerous. The deepest parts of the Elder Woods span most of the way up, and the vicious creatures and wild storms make it impossible to get past even the base, never mind camp there. Those that try never make it back. And as for the ocean, the entire continent of the Realms is surrounded by those mountains, or by terrible deserts, or the same deadly forests. For all we know, an ocean may be beyond those, but no one has ever been able to reach it."

"It's like we're trapped," Jane supplements, from where she rides at the front of the group, without looking back. "Even airplanes or helicopters can't make it, being shot down by storms or magic. If it weren't for our ability to travel to other worlds, we would never know anything else existed outside the Realms."

"Well, to answer your question," I say. "Camping is one of my favorite things. My mom and I, and sometimes Cam, would go several times every summer when the weather is hot and the hiking trails are green. We would swim in lakes, and sometimes go tubing or kayaking down the Saco River. And we would have campfires and roast marshmallows. The forests there aren't dangerous like these - sure there are bears and the occasional wild animal, but I've never run into one. It's peaceful."

Alaina is silent, as though she's picturing what I'm describing.

"And the beach?"

I'm about to describe that as well when we reach the peak of the hill overlooking a shallow valley. And we take in the kingdom sprawling below us.

The Shadow Realm.

We've arrived, with barely any time to spare. Judging from the rapidly lightening horizon, sunrise is practically here.

The city before us is magnificent. Where the Mirror Realm's capital, Penrith, was some distance removed from the palace, the Shadow Realm is quite different. The whole city seems to form a perfect circle, spiraling outwards from the castle at its center. The palace itself is tall, with pointed towers stretching like elegant, jagged claws towards the sky, made of a dark obsidian stone. There is no castle wall, nothing separating the grounds from the rest of the city.

The most noticeable detail by far is the towering, slanted overhang protruding from the side of the palace. It's easily taller than any tower, built in the shape of a slanted triangle, not wide enough to fit much more than a staircase inside, looming over half of the city. I wonder what it could be?

"It's amazing, isn't it?" Reed says, watching me take in the view. I can only nod.

"Come on," Jane says, urging her horse over the hill, in the direction of the city. "We're so close."

"What is this place called?" I ask.

"Celestial City," Stefan answers. "But some simply call it the Sundial."

"Why do they call it that?"

He points to the palace, to the strange triangular shape.

"Because this entire city acts as one giant sundial," he explains as we walk.

"That shape there is what we call the Spire, it acts as the gnomon, or the part that casts the shadow. Those numerals there-" he points to what appear to be the same numerals as the ones on Reed's watch carved into massive blocks of stone spaced evenly around the city borders.

"Those tell the time. The Spire will cast a shadow during the day, and using those numerals, you can tell what time it is. It seems only fitting for the capital of the Shadow Realm to tell time using shadows," he snorts.

"What if it's cloudy?" I point out, and he shrugs.

"Well, it's a little outdated. The city has actual clocks since they are easier to use. The Spire is what the Celestial City is known for, it's their most prized landmark."

We make it to the gates of the city in record time, sun rays beginning to peek over the horizon. I doubt that the Mirror Realm could have sent word about us being fugitives in only a night, but, everyone still crosses their fingers as we ride up to the sentries guarding the only visible passage into the city.

Unlike the Mirror Realm guards, these wear dark helmets concealing most of their faces, like old-fashioned knights. The guard in front, a tall and burly man, steps forward to block our path.

"Remove the hoods," his voice booms. "Reveal yourselves."

Slowly, we each lower the hoods of our traveling cloaks, and the guard scans each of our faces in turn, lingering especially long on mine. Finally, when I can't take the suspense any longer, he moves out of our way. His companions take that as a sign to open the gates, meticulously woven of metal to create a masterpiece that is as beautiful as it is sturdy.

"The TimeKeeper has been expecting you," is all the sentry says, nodding his head. I swallow hard. Our guess was correct then- it was this mysterious TimeKeeper who summoned us, but why?

Jane and Reed nod their heads, leading our group through the gates without a backwards glance. I hear them shut behind us with a clang.

As we walk along the cobbled streets, spiraling towards the castle nestled at its heart, I become distracted by something else. The bricks in the road layered like mosaics, painted crosswalks outside of cafes lit by lamplight, and the beautiful flags and tapestries hanging from every street corner in every color and design. I guess it's true what Orlon said, about the Shadow Realm hosting the best artists around.

A city of art, cafes, and dark, cozy buildings. It's a different kind of paradise.

We reach the grand doors of the palace as the first sun rays spill over the distant mountaintops. More guards stationed there allow us through, into a grand foyer, and direct us up a winding staircase easily wide enough for us all to walk side by side.

Along the walls hang more tapestries. I don't give them much of a glace as we spiral higher and higher, but I halt in my tracks as my eyes catch on one in particular. It's two young women, standing side by side. One woman cups swirling silver mist in her palms and the other grasps tendrils of darkness. The insignia of two falcons is embroidered in a golden thread over their heads, and their faces, it's Lillian and me.

But how? As I study it closer, the detail is impeccable, but the tapestry looks old and preserved like it was made long ago.

As if it was made from a vision of the future.

A shudder runs through my body, but I turn to inspect the other works of woven art on the walls. The one before is strange, it is like a mandala of sorts, forming a circle connecting to five depicted objects. Two daggers, both slightly curved, one gold and one made of dark silver. There's a clock, using the same strange numerals as the Old Language, *vetulinga*. The clock face is comprised of rings, each one with its own hand. The next picture is just a spiral, I can't make out what it's supposed to be. The last is an orb, just a circle, woven with a glowing look.

"Ah, I see you've noticed the Hall of Tapestries," says a voice above us, and I spin to see a figure standing on a higher landing of stairs. The figure slowly moves into view and lowers his hood, and I see flowing robes of the richest blue and the face of an old man.

When I say old, what I really mean is ancient. His face is wrinkled, hair whiter than freshly fallen snow. His lips are pursed into a small smile, his eyes crinkling at the corners as he takes in our group. His eyes are a deeper blue than his robes, startling, and seem to see into my very soul.

The TimeKeeper.

I've never met him before, but I know without a doubt who this is.

His eyes move to the tapestries I had been staring at, and his smile becomes something knowing.

That's when I realize that all of my friends have dropped to their knees, bowing. I move to bow my head, but he waves his hand.

"Oh, stand up, all of you. I'm not a king, simply a keeper of knowledge. In the eyes of knowledge, we all are equal here."

Jane lifts her head, getting to her feet, followed by the others.

"TimeKeeper," she says. "It is an honor."

"So you're the one that sent the letter?" I ask. "Why?"

He levels a steady gaze at me.

"We meant to give you more time," he says regretfully. "To adjust, to train as a guard, to hone your abilities, but there can be no more time. Great futures have been set in motion, and your destiny has come."

"My destiny?" I ask. "To do what?"

"To save the Realms, of course," he answers.

"But she can't," Reed protests. "She can't even summon her *vitalum,* never mind stand a chance against Lillian."

The TimeKeeper studies me thoughtfully. Finally, he asks, "Emmalina. How much do you know about the Realms' history?"

"What does that have to do with my destiny? Or my powers?"

"The past has everything to do with the present, and therefore dictates futures. If you are blind to what has already happened, you cannot comprehend what is yet to come."

He stalks by me, moving with a smooth grace that doesn't match his age.

"Come with me," he insists. "We will start with the beginning."

CHAPTER 17

The TimeKeeper leads me back down the staircase, from the direction we had come from. At the base, he lifts his finger to point to the first and largest of the tapestries hanging from the entrance to the stairwell. It's taller than I am, and three times as wide.

It depicts five figures standing together, surrounding a sarcophagus woven from thread darker than night. I recognize three of the five- King Orlon, King Umbra, and Queen Anima. The other two- a regal woman with pure white hair, though her face is young and beautiful, and a man with golden brown skin and a sturdily built figure.

Just looking at the sarcophagus sends a chill down my spine.

"This was my first vision," the TimeKeeper says with a distant look in his unnaturally colored eyes, his rumbling voice calm and serene, as though he was born to tell stories as well as predict them.

"When I had the vision, I didn't know what it meant. I wove it into a work of art, for it was slowly disappearing from my mind. It is the same with every vision I've had since then, they are like a dream of sorts. Once I wake from it, it will slowly fade from my memory until I can recall it no longer. This is how I preserve them, and how I can later interpret them."

"What is this one showing?" I ask, admiring the skill, the detail.

"This vision came to me almost a thousand years ago, before the time of the Realms."

"A thousand years?" I choke, hoping that's an exaggeration. But he only nods, no sign of joking.

"I am older than even the immortal queens and kings," he says. "Older than the Realms themselves."

"But... how?" I ask.

"Listen," he chides, his eyes twinkling, "And you will know."

I almost jump as Stefan brushes against my arm. I had forgotten the others were here, but they gather around to listen to the TimeKeeper's words.

"A thousand years ago, an evil being arrived on Earth, who possessed the ability to walk between worlds. Back then, there were many ways to world travel, and this creature arrived with the intent to conquer. He was a magical being, not human, but sentient and filled with malice. He possessed the elemental powers of dark and light, space and time, and that same raw magic that allowed him to move between worlds and cast illusions. His name was Malum."

I could have sworn the temperature in the room dropped a few degrees as he said the name, like a cold whisper of breath down the back of my neck.

"Malum would have conquered and drained Earth, then Allrhea, if one group of brave adventurers hadn't stood up to him. Orlon, Anima, Umbra, Idrina, and Locus. They knew that with his abilities, they would never stand a chance against Malum. So they had to find a way to channel his powers into themselves. Now, they knew that no human being could withstand that much raw power, even divided up between them, for a long time. So they needed vessels and objects to contain the power for them, after they defeated Malum. Orlon struck the last blow, banishing Malum's essence into that dark sarcophagus and obliterating it. They each received magic, and his immortality with it when Malum was dead."

The TimeKeeper pauses, gazing up at the tapestries, the woven faces set with hard and determined expressions.

"That is what my first vision depicts, though I didn't know what it was at the time. After the defeat of Malum, Idrina and Locus, the two you probably don't recognize, used their newfound gifts of space and time to tear open a new portal through a mirror and discovered the dimension nestled between Earth and Allrhea, creating the Realms, and using their new abilities to protect the worlds from any more magical threats. Every other portal was permanently sealed, except for the mirrors, to prevent future World Walkers from finding us."

I stare wide-eyed at the tapestry, the vast and complicated history it speaks of. I reach to touch the bottom edge, fingers hesitating over the threads, but when the TimeKeeper doesn't stop me, I allow my fingertips to lightly stroke the fabric. It's silky and smooth, my hand coming away coated in a fine layer of dust. I study the two unfamiliar figures- King Locus and Queen Idrina.

"What happened to the Realms of Space and Time?" I ask softly. "I was told a little bit, only that it was a war, and the seers all disappeared with them." The TimeKeeper nods.

"Follow me," he waves a hand at the stairs and leads me to another, smaller tapestry. It depicts a tall tower of a castle fitted with a clock in the center, looming over a battlefield with guards and *vitalums* clashing on either side. Far in the distance, beyond the hills, heavy clouds of smoke mar the sky.

"Orlon received word that King Locus and Queen Idrina were plotting to take the Realms for themselves. He tried to reason with them, but when it became clear they weren't negotiating, he declared war. The Shadow and Soul Realms stood with him and were victorious in the end, but it was a terrible loss. The Space Realm was completely destroyed, now a wasteland," he points to the image of the smoke. "While the inhabitants of the Time Realm- citizens, seers, and Idrina with them- vanished without a trace. We believe they fled, but even I don't know where they were lost or what became of them." The lines on his face deepen with sorrow. "A terrible loss indeed."

"Do you think Orlon shouldn't have declared war?" Jane asks curiously.

"No, my dear, he did what he had to. The Mirror Realm took charge after that, the other rulers looking to him with newfound respect. He made a hard decision, but it was the right one."

"Did you foresee that?" I ask.

"No, it is simply my own opinion."

"What does this tapestry mean?" I prod, pointing to the one showing the five strange objects.

"Ah," the TimeKeeper smiles. "Those were the vessels the magic was channeled into after the creation of the Realms. The sun and moon daggers, twin blades that contain the powers of darkness and light, life and death. The pocket watch, which can send the user forward or backward in time. The spiral medallion that can open portals through worlds and other dimensions. Lastly, the Orb of Reflections filled with endless raw magic, the purpose of which is unknown. Even to myself."

I swallow, turning to face the last and most unnerving of the magnificent artworks.

"And what about this?" I ask, my voice barely a whisper as I gaze up at the image of Lillian and me.

"That," the TimeKeeper says. "Is a future that has yet to come."

"What does it mean?"

"I'm afraid I don't know," he ponders. "My visions are always unclear, but this one was the murkiest. It is also incomplete."

"Incomplete?"

His hand, so wrinkled and curved that I'm surprised he can still create artwork with such precision, brushes along several lines of text winding through the border, which I hadn't noticed before.

"After I have a vision, I must weave it into existence, or else it will begin to fade from my mind like a dream. This prophecy- it's the first actual prophecy I've received in a long time. But my work was interrupted, and I can no longer recall the second verse."

My eyes skim the words, and my heart practically stops. It… It can't be.

I speak, reciting more from memory than from the words elegantly written before me.

"Falcon brave and bold in flight,
Shall fear the darkness and worship the light.
Shattered glass gleaming white,
and the worlds bow down to the Mirror's might."

That's when I realize… I've heard the second verse. It's like some force has possessed me, compelling me to remember. To recite.

"The time has come to prepare to fight,
And three must become five.
For all of the Realms must forgive and unite,

Or neither world will survive."

My heart still beats unevenly. As I spoke, the TimeKeeper's expression was one of confusion, then surprise, then awe. My friends stare dumbstruck.

"The second verse. So it is about you then."

"What does it mean?" I plead. "I had that dream right before I came to the Realms."

"A dream?" he mutters. "Interesting. You are not a seer, so I wonder how this could be…"

"And Lillian was in it as well, and my *vitalum*."

"You had that dream, and chose not to mention it?" Reed says, eyes narrowing in thinly veiled suspicion.

"Never mind that Mr. Windervale," the TimeKeeper says, a new excitement forming in the old man's face. "This confirms what I had originally guessed- the prophecy is about you, and your time has come."

"Is that why you called us here?" Alaina asks. "Because of this prophecy?"

"Indeed."

"But I already told you, I'm not ready. It can't be my time. I can't even summon my *vitalum*."

"Haven't you already?" he asks, raising an eyebrow. "I heard you pulled quite the stunt at the Tournament this year."

"But I wasn't in control. I haven't been able to do it again," I protest.

"But you can," he retorts, a twinkle in his eyes and a small smile on his old, pursed lips. "I have foreseen it."

"But how? Did your visions tell you that?"

He doesn't answer, only turning to ascend the stairs, waving a hand to indicate we should follow. How an old man manages to climb up and down these so quickly, I have no idea, because by the time we reach the circular room at the top, I'm breathing heavily. It's decorated like a study, with maps and sketches plastering the dark walls, a loom, and spools of thread in every color piled beside a worn and cluttered desk.

The TimeKeeper ignores all of those things, instead moving to the round table at the room's center. A fairly large map is spread out atop it, the corners pinned with empty candle holders to lay its curling edges flat. The map looks ancient, yellowed, and wrinkled, ink fading in spots.

It's a map of the Realms. It features the Mirror Realm furthest inland, with the others lying closer to the paper's edge. It even shows the Time and Space Realms, so it must be old indeed. As Alaina said before, no coastline is drawn, the picture simply fades out beyond the mountains and forests.

It also had red pins marking different locations, like someone was trying to find something, narrowing it to a cluster of pins somewhere in a fairly blank stretch of land labeled *Oblivion*.

"I have been searching for Lillian's location for some time," the TimeKeeper says, tracing a finger along the line of red pins. "She has always managed to evade me. There was no place that could be hiding a stronghold, no place that she could hide such an army in the Realms. That's when it hit me... she isn't within the Realms of Reflection. She must be keeping her forces outside of them, undetected. In the desert Oblivion."

"But that isn't possible," Jane snorts. "No one can survive such a place, not even her."

"But there are creatures that have managed it," the TimeKeeper says. "Creatures that thrive off of magic and darkness, whose alliance would be all that's needed to successfully house her stronghold there."

"You think Lillian allied herself with the Followers of Malum?" Reed says, his face going a sickly pale color. "Could she do that?"

"If she made them a bargain they couldn't refuse," Stefan says darkly. "They would be more than happy to serve her."

"What are the Followers of Malum?" I ask.

"A race of creatures that served Malum, before the age of the Realms. They are greedy, cruel, and loved nothing more than to drain whole worlds of magic. When Malum died, they were banished to the great desert, Oblivion, for their crimes."

"They are dangerous," Reed adds. "What could Lillian have possibly offered them in exchange for an alliance?"

"There's only one thing they would accept, and that is the shadow dagger," the TimeKeeper says gravely, his robes swishing as he turns from the map.

"You mean the vessel for dark magic?" Alaina demands. "It is said to hold power over death itself, like Lillian's magic but a hundred times stronger. If they got their hands on it…"

"It would be the end of us all," the TimeKeeper agrees. "They feed off of such dark magic, they would become unstoppable."

"If Lillian actually had the dagger, wouldn't she have used it for herself?" I ask.

"Ah, now we're getting to the reason I called you here, the doom that is approaching," the TimeKeeper says. "Lillian doesn't have the dagger, not yet anyway. But she is on the brink of finding it."

"What do you mean?"

"Rumor has it that Lillian recently captured a prisoner, one that is said to know the dagger's location."

"A prisoner?" I ask, my heart skipping a beat. "Who?"

"I don't know, I only know that they were found hiding out on Earth, several weeks ago. The mission I have for you all is to find Lillian's stronghold, free the prisoner and find this dagger before she can."

A prisoner. Found on Earth, around the time I arrived in the Realms. I know who this prisoner is.

It must be my mother.

MEANWHILE: CAM

I wake from a nightmare in a cold sweat, in an unfamiliar bed, in a room that isn't mine.

Morning light has begun to filter in through the windows. I wonder how late I must have slept. Normally I'm a wake-up-at-5 a.m. type person, but it has to be later than that at this point.

I try to shake the nightmare jitters away. I had been back in that campsite, with ninja people dropping out of trees and evil cops in a helicopter. The most mind-boggling fact is that I can't even say that is crazy anymore, because that stuff did happen!

Those strangers, the people Lina has been with for the past few weeks while I've been worried out of my mind, explained something to me about another dimension, something to do with mirrors? I'm not going to try to make sense of it all, because I have a feeling it will all just make my head hurt.

But overall, I'm just glad that Lina is safe, and that at least I'm not alone in this.

This building, I think they called it the Dorm, seems to be buzzing with commotion. Once I find my way downstairs, I can barely move ten feet without bumping into one of the many men and women bustling around, most dressed in what looks like armor, and carrying various weapons.

I have to admit, craziness aside, this is pretty awesome. I wonder how Lina got roped into all this, how she wound up in this place, what she's been doing this whole time? When she didn't come back to school those few days after she and her mom went camping, I started to get worried. They weren't home, and neither of them was answering their phones, so finally I pointed it out to my mom and she called the police asking for someone to check on them. Then, that terrible night, when we got that call.

We had gone that very same night, all the way up to the mountains, to see the scene for ourselves. My mom had booked a hotel to stay up there while the police questioned me about where I had last seen Lina, if that was her campsite, asking other campers if they had heard anything out of the ordinary. When many campers reported hearing wolves howling the night Lina must have gone missing, combined with what were definitely bloodstains on the ground, the tent collapsed, and what looked like claw marks in the dirt... I thought she was gone for good.

When she had shown up all those nights later, along with the other three, I had no idea what to think.

A few of the strange people, guards, I think they were called, give me odd looks, but most simply ignore that I'm even there, all focused on some news that has everyone on edge.

I'm more focused on where I can find some breakfast in this place as my stomach rumbles. I'm starving.

I finally find this little coffee stand set up on the building's main floor called the Coffee Corner- giving out coffees and donuts for *free*, if you can imagine, when out of nowhere, this girl comes stalking out of the surrounding crowd towards me. The expression on her face is flat and annoyed, walking with purpose as though she's got somewhere to be, so I try to move over to let her past. Instead, she stops right in front of me, her arms crossed, looking me over with impatience.

"Can I help you?" I ask, suddenly feeling awkward. I don't recognize her as one of Emmalina's friends, and I'm pretty sure I would recognize her. She's not a face easily forgotten, pale, with silvery blonde hair and striking eyes, one light brown and the other pale blue. Her nose scrunches with distaste.

"You're the Worlder, right?"

I just stare blankly, not sure what that's supposed to mean.

"I'll take that as a yes," she says, rolling her eyes. "You're coming with me. The king wants to speak with you."

"The king?" I ask, my palms becoming slightly clammy. I had only spoken to the king once before barely even a word. Have I broken some sort of rule by being here?

"Yes, King Orlon has requested a meeting with you and I don't have all day," she adds snarkily.

"Alright, alright, I'm coming." What could this possibly be about? And why is this random girl sent to get me instead of Lina, or the others I met last night? Where are they, anyway? That reminds me…

"I haven't gotten your name," I say, trying to keep up with her quick strides. My legs are longer than hers, yet she's walking so briskly it's almost like she hopes I'll get left behind and she won't have to deal with me.

"That would make sense because I never gave you it," she answers curtly.

"I'm Cam," I say, despite her attitude.

"Don't care, Worlder."

Well fine, then. We walk in silence the rest of the way, into the palace and up several flights of stairs, until we enter a room that I recognize from before. It's the room with the crystal chair on a dais, a throne I'm guessing, and the oversized mirror that we had somehow used as a portal to get here. This time, the throne is occupied by the tall, regal figure of King Orlon.

His fingers idly stroke some sort of scepter topped with a glass orb that rests beside the throne, turning his attention to the two of us in the doorway. We're not alone either, that intimidating man from last night and two other guards are standing beside the throne, the familiar man wearing a pointed scowl.

Could this be about that lockdown thing last night? Did they somehow find out that I was the one who disabled their security cameras to allow Lina and her friends to get in that room for whatever it is they were doing?

"Ah, thank you Eliza for bringing in our guest," the king says in a smooth voice, to which Eliza nods respectfully.

"Cam, isn't it?" Orlon asks, turning to me, and I squirm under his gaze.

"Yes, Sir."

"You're probably wondering why I've asked you to meet me here. I just have a few questions to ask."

I nod, waiting nervously for him to continue.

"Your friend, Emmalina, and her legion disappeared last night during the lockdown and were spotted fleeing from the palace grounds last night. Are you able to explain any of this?"

I blink, the information taking a second to process in my mind.

"What?"

"They have gone against the king's orders and have taken off on some fool's errand of a quest," the man with the scowl speaks up, narrowing his eyes. "As you were the last one known to be with them, we assume that you may be able to help with our investigation. We need to know where they went, and what they were after."

They left? Emmalina isn't here, and no one knows where she's gone?

Apparently, my blank stare riles the man, because he opens his mouth as if to demand an answer, but the king holds up a hand to stop him.

"Marcus," he says calmly. "This is not an interrogation. We have a fairly good guess of their motive and where they've gone, this is simply to confirm. From the look on the boy's face, he doesn't seem to know anything. Is that right?"

The king aims that last question at me. I know I should respond to that, it is probably very rude to ignore a king, but I can't seem to think straight. Emmalina left again and didn't even tell me. My best friend just abandoned me in a different dimension that she brought me to, and didn't even say goodbye?

"Why… why did she leave?" that is all I manage to say.

"They left because of an evil sorceress named Lillian," the king answers.

Lillian, I recognize that name. That's what sent this place into lockdown yesterday, that's what we were investigating in that coms room we broke into.

"Lillian is threatening the Realms, and Lina has gotten it into her mind that she and her friends are the only ones that stand a chance against her. I've been informed that she received a letter last night prompting her to leave, thus breaking our laws for the third time."

Lina is doing *what*? Going up against an actual sorceress, like the kind that does magic? That's crazy, that would mean Lina would have to have...

"She has powers?" I ask, feeling numb. "Like all of you?"

The king nods.

"And now, she is a fugitive," the man, Marcus, sneers. "Her and all of the rest."

Lina, a fugitive? The idea is almost as unbelievable as the idea of actual magic.

"But why her?" I ask. "Why did she get caught up in this in the first place? Why aren't you sending an army or something after Lillian, instead of a seventeen-year-old girl thinking it's up to her to save this place?"

"Because Lina is Lillian's counterpart, her mirror image," the king says slowly. "That means they are alike in every way, including abilities. In fact, she would be the only known person in existence capable of matching her power."

"What can they do, exactly?"

"Lillian, and therefore Emmalina, wield the power of death, the strongest magic we have ever come across."

"The power of death?" I snort. "That doesn't sound anything like the Lina I know."

"Would the Lina you know have left you here alone while she ran off on some quest with her new, magical friends?" Marcus points out with a wicked smirk.

Ouch. That hurts, but I can't deny that he has a point. The Lina I had known wouldn't have done that unless she had an incredibly good reason to.

"I trust her decisions," I say firmly, shoving down my feelings. "I may not really understand what's going on, but I know that Lina's a good person and that she's making the decision she knows is right."

"There's nothing right about breaking the law," Marcus counters.

"Didn't you say it was to save your Realms?" I press. "That seems pretty noble to me, risking her life to help you all."

Marcus's eyes alight with a fury that makes me think I might have forgotten my place and pushed too far until the king cuts him off.

"I think we are done here," he says firmly, standing from his throne with his scepter in hand.

"Eliza, Cameron, you are dismissed. Cam, you have free reign of any place open to a trainee. You are our guest here, feel free to make yourself at home."

"Thank you, Your Majesty," I say, as he waves his hand dismissively.

I duck out of the room close behind the girl, Eliza, as she makes her way back down the hall. She takes a different route through the castle, instead of heading in the direction of the Dorm.

"Where are you going?" I ask, wandering behind like a lost puppy.

"Quit following me," is all she says back.

"I don't actually know how to get out of here," I say. "Do you think you could show me around? I haven't gotten to see much of this place."

"Find yourself another tour guide, Worlder," she snaps. "I'm already late as it is."

"Late to what?" I continue to tag along, kind of enjoying the look of exasperation on her face. I've met a few jerks in my time, and while Eliza seems to be trying to give off that impression with the whole *I'm better than you so get lost* thing, I have a feeling it's more of a facade than most people would realize.

She finally comes to a stop, crossing her arms as she turns to face me.

"What did I ever do to give you the *hey, let's be friends* vibe?" she snorts.

"The fact that you had slowed down a bit to let me catch up," I point out. Her eyes widen, as though she hadn't even realized she had done that. There it is, the crumbling of that facade bit by bit. Then right back up it goes.

"Seriously. What do you want?" she demands.

"Maybe a civil answer, for one thing?" I suggest. "Or, you know, talking to me like I'm an actual human being. Maybe call me Cam instead of Worlder?"

"Nope. Worlder suits you."

"Okay, fine. How about telling me what you're in such a hurry for?"

"A tech class," she says with a sigh, rolling her eyes for what feels like the millionth time. "You know, computer systems, hacking, programming. That kind of thing."

"They have classes for that here?" I ask, bewildered, as the idea catches my interest. Back home, I like to dabble with that sort of stuff, like designing software and tinkering with gadgets. The idea of being able to get my hands on a bit of Realm tech like the alarm systems from before, to see how it works, would be fascinating.

She seems to read the idea from my face.

"Oh, no, not so fast," she snorts. "Classes are for trainees only."

Eliza seems to pause for a second. "Wait, are you the one who disabled those security cameras in Marcus's coms room?" she demands, to which I nod. I swear she looks grudgingly impressed.

"Yep."

"How did you even know how to do that?"

"There's a bit more to me than just being Lina's Worlder friend."

"Sure there is."

"I have a request," I say, an idea blooming.

"No."

"Would you…"

"No."

"…consider…"

"No."

"…teaching me to work with Realm tech? Just the basics, since I've got nothing else to do with my time around here."

"Why me?"

"Because we're friends now, right?"

"Ugh."

"That's not a no this time," I point out. She still doesn't shut down the idea, seeming to ponder it.

"Ughhh. Fine," she says, heaving a sigh. "One lesson. Tonight, after dinner, we can use the main control room. Then you go bother someone else. Deal?"

I grin, "Deal."

Her mouth twitches into a smile. "See you then."

EMMALINA

My mother is alive and I'm going to get her back, no matter what it takes.

I say as much to the others, none of whom look very convinced. The TimeKeeper supplies us with everything we need: traveling equipment, extra clothes, food, water, and a good night's rest. By that, I mean a solid five hours, until the clock is ticking towards noon.

"Now be aware," he warns. "The decree from the Mirror Realm was sent out this morning, you all are officially fugitives. Orlon isn't going to allow trainees to embark on a quest this dangerous, and besides, it seems like sneaking out to come here wasn't the first offense," he raises an eyebrow, and I can't help but look a little guilty.

"Orlon's guards already know where you are and are likely on their way here to apprehend you as we speak. You aren't safe in the Realms anymore, especially once the word has gotten around."

"What about the guards at the gates last night?" I ask. "They recognized us, they could have already told King Umbra we're here."

"Those two are loyal to me, they won't say a word. The same with your driver."

"Driver?"

"You didn't think you would be taking horses halfway across the Realms, did you?" he snorts. He gestures to the street outside the shadow palace's windows, where a sleek back car is parked outside of the doors.

Nice.

"Now go, your driver, Jerri, knows where to take you. And Emmalina, remember, the Followers of Malum cannot be trusted. They make deals, they bargain and they lie. You need to find them to find Lillian, but try not to confront them if you can avoid it. And above all, find the dagger. Don't let those creatures, or Lillian, get their hands on it."

I nod, clenching my shaking hands into fists at my side.

"I won't fail," I promise, but the dagger is secondary to me. Yes, the power over death sounds very important, don't get me wrong, I'm all for preventing that, but rescuing my mom is at the forefront of my mind.

"And Lina," he adds, "Good luck."

I nod, before turning to descend the stairs from the TimeKeeper's tower, hood pulled up to hide my face from anyone who might notice me. Luckily the streets outside of the palace aren't overly crowded and the six of us file into the car without any trouble. The windows are tinted so nobody can see inside, so I lower my hood and let out a breath as I lean back against my headrest, gazing at the back of the driver's head through the glass slider separating us from him.

The driver starts the car, the engine barely making a sound. We ease onto the street into mild traffic, and we become just one of the many vehicles making our way through the city.

When we reach the gates, the guards, the same from last night, only nod and allow us to pass through. Then we're on our way.

Nate kicks his feet up onto the back of my seat, jostling me out of my thoughts.

"Pretty cool, huh?" he says, grinning. "We're fugitives now. Breaking the law and saving the world and stuff. Awesome."

I shove his boots away, allowing myself to smile for the first time in hours.

"Nate, you give me a headache," Jane sighs in exasperation, rubbing her temples.

"I give myself a headache sometimes," he agrees with a shrug.

"Do you think Jerri would be annoyed if I asked him to play some music?" I wonder out loud, trying to sound more excited.

"Music?" Nate asks, raising an eyebrow. "Like, on a guitar? I don't think he can do that and drive at the same time. Unless you can, Jerri, because that would be pretty cool!"

Our driver either can't hear Nate through the glass slider or chose to ignore that question.

"No," I laugh. "Like, over the radio or something. Do y'all have country music here?"

Alaina leans forward from her seat beside Nate, raising an eyebrow. "We do have a sort of country music, I'm not a fan by the way, but a radio? In a car?"

I blink, confused.

"Yeah… like, listening to music while you drive, that kind of thing." My friends only stare back at me with blank expressions, even Jane and Reed, which is how I know it's not a joke. "Wait, are you guys being serious?"

"Music in a car?" Jane muses. "Well, there's an idea. You Worlders are a bit strange, aren't you?"

I shake my head. "Oh, never mind. Forget it."

We drive for many hours, watching the sun overhead begin to set and the sky slowly begin to pale as sunset approaches. We've avoided towns and cities, for the most part, taking winding back roads similar to the ones we rode on horseback. We saw the glass towers of the Mirror Palace sparkling miles off in the distance as we drove in the opposite direction, and curve away from the mountains. Finally, as hunger begins to gnaw at my stomach, I unzip the backpack the TimeKeeper gave me to find something to eat.

My hands brush paper, and I pull out the map from the circular room.

"Woah, did you steal that?" Nate asks from behind me, chewing loudly with his mouth full of some kind of protein bar. "Cool."

"No, I didn't steal it," I snap back, already catching the judgy eyes Jane is throwing my way. "It was just in here."

I unfurl it, noticing the new, red line now drawn along the path that the red pins had made. Leading straight into the heart of Oblivion, to what looks like a sketch of a pile of boulders, circled in red. I hold it up for everyone else to see.

"Look. I think this is where we're headed," I say. "This must be the route we're supposed to take. Which is good, because it's not that far. As long as we continue at this rate, we should be there by... wait, why are we stopping?"

The car is slowing, coming to a halt seemingly in the middle of nowhere. We're not even on a road anymore, but the ground is flat and tightly packed enough that I hadn't noticed.

I slide the glass panel open.

"Why are we stopping?" I ask.

"This is as far as I go, miss," Jerri says, turning to me.

"What? We haven't even entered the desert yet," I protest.

"Lina," Jane says, already unbuckling her seatbelt. "Oblivion is so wrought with magic, that the very air is clouded with it. Magic and technology don't really mix, it would render the car useless if it tried to go any further. It's one of the biggest reasons why no one can get across, not even a helicopter or a plane could fly overhead without malfunctioning. We have to go on foot the rest of the way."

Well, that throws a wrench in my plans.

"Go on foot, across the desert? Why didn't we bring horses again?"

"It would have taken us days to get here that way," Reed points out. "From here to the Caves of Malum is only a day or so's walk, we'll be able to make it."

One by one, we file out of the car, and I say goodbye to that wonderful air conditioning and comfortable seat. Even in

November, the air is humid and hot, which I guess is what I should have expected from a desert.

"Come on, we need to find somewhere to take shelter before dark," Stefan points out. We all bid thanks to Jerri, who in turn wishes us luck before he turns his car back around and drives away. As his taillights fade out of sight, I look around. Nothing but open land and hills, scraggly bushes, and hard-packed dirt for as far as the eye can see.

We walk until walking becomes more of a trudge until our feet are dragging in the dirt which has now turned to sand. The sun now kisses the horizon, and I don't believe I've ever seen a more beautiful sunset in my life. Pinks and golds and fading blues, a different array of colors every time I muster the strength to look up. As the sun goes, the heat goes with it, replaced by a chilled breeze. At first, I'm grateful for it, cooling my aching and sweating body. Until the chill becomes a cold that seeps into my bones, and I find myself shivering.

I can't go much further.

Then there's a body beside mine, Stefan, and I lean into his warmth unthinkingly. He lets me lean on him, though he has to be as tired as I am. My footsteps slow, and I stumble.

"No, we have to keep going," I hear him urge, his voice quiet. "We can't stop here."

It's clear that none of us can go on. We can't keep at it all night. Strange, eerie shrieks and sounds echo across the hills as the stars begin to glimmer overhead. I know in my bones that we wouldn't survive the night out in the open, and that's all that keeps me moving, one foot in front of the other.

At this point, I think I'm hallucinating. I swear I see something up ahead, like the reflection of moonlight on water. An oasis amid the dunes, with strange, wispy trees and the form of a deer drinking from the small lagoon. It looks too real to be a hallucination, water and potentially some cover among the trees to rest. My legs wobble with relief, and I nearly lose my footing in my hurry to get down the hill. Stefan calls my name. I feel a hand wrap around my arm, stopping me from going any farther.

"Stop," Reed hisses. "Oblivion isn't a kind place, an oasis is usually a harbinger of trouble. We need to find a cave or..."

His voice trails off as the deer lifts its head to look in our direction. It isn't a deer. It has the body shape of one, but its narrow head seems oddly feline. A long tail swishes behind it, and I can see curling horns protruding from its head, like an antelope. The six of us are frozen, in a silent standoff with the creature.

I feel Reed gently tug my arm, as we slowly start to back away.

"No sudden movements," he whispers. "Keep as still as possible."

"What is it?" I ask, a slight tremor in my voice.

"An attaura," he whispers. "They're carnivorous."

"*Carnivorous?*" I squeak, louder than I meant to. The thing's small ears perk up, and it growls like a mountain cat. I can see sharp, pointed teeth. Not a deer, definitely not a deer.

"Run," Jane whispers.

As she says it, the thing gives a snarl, whipping its tail, and breaks into a gallop towards us. The good news is it has to get up the hill, which gives us a head start. The bad news is the attaura is very, very fast.

As we dash in the opposite direction, Reed's wristwatch begins to glow. Moments later, Jane's thin daggers acting again as hairpins do the same. I brace myself as two oversized wolves materialize before us, Reed and Jane's vitalums.

One wolf, large and dusky brown, leaps forward with teeth bared to meet the attaura. The other, with a rich silver and black coat, lowers its belly to the ground. Jane leaps atop its back without a second's hesitation.

"Come on!" she shouts. The rest of us pile on, except for Reed, who whistles for the first wolf as the black one breaks into a bounding run.

"Wait, Reed!" I shout.

"He's fine," Stefan assures me. Sure enough, cresting over the hill we just came from, attaura snapping at their heels, is Reed atop his vitalum.

"The wolves can't win against that thing," Stefan explains. "Our only hope is to outrun it."

I hold on tightly to the wolf's fur, though it doesn't seem to bother her. We are going so fast we're practically flying, but it isn't enough. The attaura keeps giving chase.

"I haven't seen any of your vitalums before," I say staring in wonder.

"This is Keira," Jane says, stroking the wolf's head, her hair coming loose and whipping in her face. "That one's Rowan," she indicates the brown beast behind us.

"You name them?" I don't know why that's so surprising to me, but I hadn't considered it before.

"Of course," she says. "Our vitalums are like pets, friends, or even family to us. As yours will be, once you master control over your abilities."

"There!" Reed yells, having caught up with us and now running side by side. "The woods! We can lose it in the trees!" Oh right. For a moment, I had forgotten we were being chased. Thanks for the reality check, Reed.

We aim for the outcropping of trees in the distance. As soon as we get within ten feet of the tree line, the attaura slows and comes to a stop, like it refuses to go any farther. It gives a snarling shriek of frustration, but turns and bolts in the other direction. Perhaps we reached the end of its territory?

We don't slow, however, not trusting the thing to not change its mind and try to eat us again. We continue until Reed judges that we're a safe distance into the woods, and he comes to a stop in a small clearing, dismounting. We do the same.

"Woods are typically pretty safe here," he reasons. "We can stay for the night, and get moving at dawn."

Jane nods her head to the vitalums.

"Thank you," she says, which the wolves seem to take as a dismissal, fading back into thin air from which they appeared.

"That was awesome," I say, brushing my windblown hair from my face. "Why couldn't we just use the wolves to travel the whole way? It would save a lot of time."

"I wish," Jane sighs. "They would draw far too much-unwanted attention, from things worse than the attaura. Strong magic such as vitalums would be too tempting for most of Oblivion's inhabitants to resist."

"Well then, what now?"

Jane sighs. "Now we build a fire. It's freezing out here."

"Yes boss," Stefan snorts, as he and Reed move for the nearest trees, but they pause. Reed breaks off a branch in his hand much too easily, bark crumbling off.

"Jane?" Reed says, unsure. "Where on the map are we?"

She rolls her eyes. "How am I supposed to know?" she huffs, reaching for my backpack to grab the tarnished stretch of parchment. She traces her finger along the direction we traveled, calculating the distance.

Her face pales. Reed and Stefan walk up beside her clutching handfuls of dead and rotted wood.

"All of the trees are like this," Reed says with a frown. "They don't have any leaves either. No bushes, nothing alive.

Not even insects, which is pretty strange. It's like this whole forest is just decaying."

"Because this isn't just a forest," Jane gasps. "This is…"

Her face goes slack with surprise as a small dart with a little feathered shaft sprouts from her neck. Her hand reaches for it, as though she's swatting away a bug. Then her eyes roll back in her head and she goes limp, body swaying slightly before slumping to the ground. My head whips towards the trees, looking for the source of that dart, opening my mouth to demand to know who's there.

Stefan drops to the ground beside me. The last thing I remember is a small prick of pain in my shoulder, and a feeling as though someone dropped a hazy curtain over my vision. Everything is in slow motion, muted voices shouting, and the world goes dark.

CHAPTER 18

I can hear the sound of voices. Very faint and distorted, as though I'm hearing them underwater. Harsh, raspy whispers.

My eyelids feel too heavy, and my limbs feel like their weighted with cement. It's a monumental effort just to force my eyes to open, trying to see through a haze of blurred vision.

"Ah-" one of the voices rumbles to my left, "She's awake."

Slowly everything gains focus, little by little, and I find myself blinded by a too-bright, golden light. A fire. There are three figures, people, standing around me. With a gasp, my body jerks away from them on instinct, and a flare of pain bites my wrists.

My wrists, which are bound to a wooden stake, leather bindings wrapped tightly around my hands.

I take in the mysterious figures with more clarity. Average heights and builds that indicate they're human. They're wearing shredded black robes and overly large hoods pulled so far down there is no way they should be able to see, concealing every feature except for curved, moon-pale hands.

My heart begins to pound as whatever they knocked me out with begins to wear off, and I look past the cloaked figures to see more gathered behind. I count seven others, exactly like the first three.

"Who are you?" I ask, my voice so dry and hoarse that I cough. "What do you want with me?" I will my voice to remain as steady as possible, lifting my chin higher. I will not let them know how afraid I am. The creature in the middle seems to consider my question.

"First," it hisses. "We want to know what your business is in our grove, Lillian Maren."

I blink once. Twice. Did they say, Lillian?

"*Speak,*" the one on the right growls. A plan begins to hatch in my mind. Like all of the others, it is foolish, not very thought through, and will most likely get me killed. I clear my throat and say with as much confidence as I can muster, "I am here to make a deal."

The one in the middle tilts its head, a mimic of a human gesture that just seems *wrong*.

"A deal?"

"I- I assume you've heard of the war," I say, my mind scrambling to come up with this so-called deal. I don't even know who they are, or what they would bargain for. They murmur amongst themselves, seemingly displeased or surprised, I can't tell.

"Of course, we have heard of your war," the middle creature, who seems to be the one in charge, grumbles. "I doubt there is a sentient being in these lands who has not. But powerful sorceress or not, anyone who seeks out the Grove of Assassins is either very foolish or very desperate. Which is the great Lillian, foolish or desperate, I wonder?"

I lift my chin a little higher, trying to act the part, ruthless, unruffled, and sure of myself.

"I am neither," I say, trying to appear mildly offended, all the while my hands are shaking behind my back. "Now if you would release me, I would continue with our bargain. Otherwise, I will raze your grove to the ground."

I rack my mind trying to remember anything about the Grove of Assassins, but the TimeKeeper never mentioned them. They can't be the Followers of Malum, he said they liked making deals, but these creatures don't seem eager to hear me out.

The thing only gives a dry, humorless laugh.

"Unfortunately for you, there is not much left of our grove for your treacherous magic to raze. It is nearly dead already, its life force practically gone. The Great Tree that fuels it has stood for centuries, but has barely a year left. Once it is dead, we will fade with it, and the assassins will be no longer. So you see, you are out of leverage, and we are out of patience."

It draws a long, wicked blade from within the folds of its cloak with gnarled hands. I swallow a gasp of terror as the hood shifts, and I catch a glimpse of a weathered face and solid black eyes staring back at me. Human, but not.

I thrash, trying to free myself as a blade falls almost in slow motion.

It clangs against an invisible barrier, hovering inches above my head.

The creature and I both kind of just look at each other with confusion, before some invisible force parries the blade away, sending the assassin reeling backward. Each of the nine other assassins draws their blades in unison. I feel something cold and metal against my skin, sawing away the bindings on my hands with a single slice, and are instantly replaced with the feel of a hand around my forearm.

I feel the icy trickle of magic down my spine as I become invisible, vanishing before the assassins' very eyes.

It only seems to make them more annoyed.

"We are familiar with your tricks, lynx," the assassin snarls. "We have hunted enough of your kind, invisibility cannot hide you and the sorceress forever."

"Lina," I hear Alaina's voice whisper in my ear as she yanks me away, into the underbrush.

"Alaina," I gasp with relief. "How did you…?"

"They never caught me in the first place. It's quite hard to hit an invisible target, even for the most feared killers in the Realms."

"But the others?"

"They're fine," she says, as we slowly made our way past rotted tree trunks, trying to make as little noise as possible. Behind us, the clearing has gone dead silent. Above our heads, spindly, bare tree branches stab like claws into the sky, blotting out the starlight and casting strange shadows across the rocky ground.

"We have to move quickly," she urges, her voice so hushed it's hard to make out what she's saying without being able to read her lips. "The assassins are legendary, they used to be feared by even the most powerful guards and would kill anyone for the right price. When it became clear that they were too dangerous, King Umbra used his power over dark magic to put a curse on their grove and trap them here forever. Now they simply kill whoever is dumb enough to trespass, which apparently is us. If they want you dead it's only a matter of time."

"But your invisibility?"

"Do you think something so simple as lack of sight could defer them for long?" she demands. "No, we only had the element of surprise. Now that they're hunting us, they're going to be flanking the edge of the grove. It will be impossible to get out alive." I can hear the fear in her voice and feel the slight tremor in her hand.

I see the looming shape of a person ahead, through the trees, scanning back and forth. I almost come to a skidding stop, when I realize I recognize the shape of Reed's shoulders, the sword he typically keeps sheathed over his back gone.

Alaina drops the curtain of invisibility as we reach him, I spot the others all gathered around, unharmed.

"Lina," Reed says, eyes widening, the tension in his shoulders loosening just a bit. "Are you alright?"

His eyes catch on the red marks marring my wrists from the ropes that had bound them, his frown deepening.

"I'm okay," I insist, feeling my face get embarrassingly warm as I discreetly cross my arms to hide the marks. He just gives a curt nod, looking away quickly, and I swear I see his face redden slightly as well.

"Well, good, I guess," he mumbles.

What is happening here? Was he actually concerned for my safety? I didn't even think Reed cared enough to be worried.

Nate clears his throat. Loudly. Alaina shushes him.

"Well, if whatever *that* was is finished," Jane snorts, keeping her voice low, "Don't you all think we should focus on getting out of here alive?"

"Jane, we're facing the *assassins*," Alaina says, her voice slightly strained. "How are we possibly getting out of here alive? Their life force is tied to this grove, to the Great Tree. They can't be killed, and no one can hide from them. We have no options."

"Since when are you the doom and gloom one?" Nate snorts. "I thought that was Jane's job."

"Hey, that's rude," Jane says, raising an eyebrow, "And untrue."

"Really? When was the last time you laughed?" Nate points out. She glowers at him.

"I'll be laughing when I toss you to the assassins."

"Guys, not the time for bickering," Stefan cuts in. Both turn to him, surprised. Stefan normally isn't very assertive, but now his face is blank and emotionless. No, not emotionless, there's hurt flickering in his golden eyes, as he looks between Reed and me. Wait, he couldn't think…

No, things are too complicated to start with this.

"We can't avoid the assassins," I ramble, trying to deflect this sudden awkwardness. "We can't outrun them, can't defeat them."

"Or can we?" Jane murmurs, almost to herself.

"Oh great," Reed says with a dramatic eye roll. "Not another one of your ridiculous, get us all killed plans."

"Hey, my plan went perfectly fine last time," she protests.

"Did it?"

"Just listen. I think I know how we can get out of this alive."

For once, this may not be a bad idea. Even though the chances of it working are still pretty low. We've gotten lucky before, maybe we'll get lucky again.

Now I'm crouching in a thornbush, basically a glorified pile of spiky sticks, trying not to be seen or heard. For this plan to work, we had to go deeper into the grove, every step more dangerous than the last. We haven't seen any assassins so far, which is the opposite of reassuring. These things are stealthier than even the swiftest Lynx Assassin, hence the reason they're called *assassins*. It would kind of defeat the purpose if you heard them coming.

I imagine that if they were stalking me right now, I would already be dead, so they must not have found me. Yet.

This is going to be the tricky part. Straight ahead, through the tangle of thorns, is a cluster of trees that appear to be healthier than the rest. I'm not quite sure how I know these are more alive than the others. On the outside, they barely look any different, rotted bark clinging to drooping branches that are completely bare of leaves. It's more of a gut feeling, almost like I can sense the scrap of life they're clinging to.

Guilt wrenches in my gut. For this plan to work, to have any chance of escaping the assassins, we must destroy the grove that their immortal life forces are tied to. It just doesn't sit right with me.

I try my hardest to shove it down and focus my gaze past the thicket to my target, the Great Tree at the center of the Grove of Assassins. It's a massive, towering oak, unlike the others. Its bark is gray and flaking, but unlike every other plant in this cursed grove, a few shriveled leaves still cling to its uppermost branches. I can feel the power, the life force of this tree, stronger than the others, like a calling, a thrumming pulse in my blood.

Deep within myself, a foreign feeling answers that call, rearing its head like a beast woken from its slumber.

Every logical part of me tries to fight against it, knowing that this power is something to be feared. I don't want to wake it. I don't want to learn to use it. I know in my heart that my greatest wish is that such evil magic remains in its slumber forever. It's better that way.

I no longer have a choice. I got my friends into this, it is my responsibility to save them. Even if it means going against everything I've ever believed in.

I flinch as the bush beside me rustles ever so slightly, only to relax as Stefan appears crouched on the ground.

"It's all clear, as far as Alaina and I can see, but that doesn't mean much when it comes to the assassins." Stefan purses his lips with worry. "Lynx Assassin's stealth or a wolf's fighting abilities are nothing compared to what they're capable of."

"But maybe a falcon's powers can stand a chance," I say. Stefan gives a curt nod.

"Let's hope so."

"Thanks for the faith," I snort, trying to sound lighthearted. The look Stefan turns to me is serious and full of an emotion I can't place.

"Lina," his throat bobs. "Just be careful. Please."

Taken aback, all I can do is nod, swallowing hard, heart fluttering in my chest. For a moment all fear is forgotten.

"I will be," I breathe.

I duck out from behind my scraggly little bush, carefully making my way for the Great Tree.

Unable to help glancing back, I pause, only to see that Stefan has become invisible once more. Taking a deep breath, I continue to move from tree trunk to rotted tree trunk, trying to find whatever little cover I can get. I try to keep moving, not to stay in one place for too long, until my foot catches a root and I stumble.

It turns out that stumble probably just saved my life.

An arrow impales itself almost shaft deep in the closest tree. Right where my head would have been if I had kept moving. They've found me.

Fear tries to freeze me to the spot, rooting me to the ground. I force my feet to move, one after the other, pounding to the rhythm of my frightened heartbeat, faster than I've ever run in my life. I try to zigzag through the trees and I gasp as another arrow whizzes by, grazing the side of my shoulder and tearing open the sleeve of my traveling cloak. I still continue, merely feet away from the base of the Great Tree.

Lunging, I wrap my arms around its trunk, bark digging into my cheek. With my hands braced upon it, scraping my palms, I whip my head back in the direction the arrows had come from.

"Show yourself," I shout, positive that the hidden assassin is listening. "Or I'll kill the tree. You know I can do it."

It wouldn't even take that much effort either, I can tell, from the pulse of life beneath my fingertips growing steadily fainter. I think saying it even has a year left is a generous estimate.

Again that little tug in my gut as my magic rears its head, and I shove it down again.

No, not yet. They may surrender. They may choose to ally with me- er, I mean, *Lillian.* I don't have to kill the tree, or touch this dark magic, so long as…

Oh.

Not one, not two, but all ten assassins step forward in unison, seeming to melt from the very shadows. I glance desperately towards the lightening gray of the sky that seems to herald that dawn is approaching. I was secretly hoping that they would be like vampires or something, and wouldn't come out when day hit, but they seem unfazed by it.

Ten of them. Ten of the most feared killers in the Realms, and yet I'm somehow still alive. Why? I doubt it was my expert stealth, they were probably tracking me this whole time. They probably know where every one of my friends is hidden and waiting.

"You will not kill the tree," the one in the front sounds almost amused. "Because you are not Lillian Maren."

"What - what do you mean," I protest. "Of course I am. I will be the conqueror of the Realms," I tilt my chin a bit higher, trying to look down my nose at them and pretend that I'm not shaking in my traveling boots. "I will also be the destroyer of this grove if you do not let my friends and I go."

I hear the slip up too late, the words slipping past. *Friends.* I doubt Lillian would call her soldiers friends. The creature doesn't miss my mistake.

"Yes, your appearance fooled us at first," the assassin crones, and I catch a glimpse of a too-large mouth containing teeth that are a bit too jagged to be natural as he smiles.

"Your bracelet confused us at first as well. After all, everyone has heard of the sorceress's infamous vitalum, Nyx. *The Dark Falcon*. Yet your vitalum item is silver." The things mocking voice has begun to grate, but it gives me enough time to call to that power. Summon it and slowly coax it to the surface.

"Then it was the fact that you didn't know who we are," it muses. "The Assassins of the Grove tend to be very hard faces to forget."

I let out a breath. "You've already met with Lillian?"

"She came to us months ago proposing a deal quite as you had tried," the amusement in its voice makes me grit my teeth. "We had agreed to assist her when the time came, in exchange that she would free us from this dying grove when she becomes queen of all Realms. Until then she had sworn not to set foot in our territory, so you can imagine our surprise when you stumbled in, claiming to be Lillian but having no recollection of us."

"Well, don't you want to know who I am then?" I press, stalling for the last few seconds I need, but the assassin only gives a raspy laugh.

"I think you've stalled long enough, Emmalina Maren, Lillian's…"

Before it can finish its sentence, the others explode from the bushes behind the assassins with a force of flashing blades and fury. He's right, I've stalled for as much time as I need. Ten immortal, unbeatable assassins against five mortal trainees, far from an even match, but all the diversion I need.

I close my eyes, willing that power waiting at my fingertips to rise, but it's so much harder than I expected it to be. Maybe that's because deep inside, I don't want to kill the assassins. That would make me as bad as them. I don't want this power to turn me into Lillian. But if I do nothing, then within seconds, every one of my friends will die, and these beasts will eventually be unleashed against the Realms on Lillian's side.

But I can't kill them. I won't.

I don't know how, but the power that crests from my fingertips into the very fiber of the Great Tree doesn't feel dark and evil. A well of light spreads from my palms and crisscrosses the tree's decaying bark, twining into its branches until the whole thing is too bright to even look at. I don't know what I'm doing, I don't even really know how I'm doing it. I'm simply giving myself over to my abilities, no longer afraid. No longer reluctant. It feels like freedom. It feels like life.

As the light begins to fade, I sink to my knees, sudden and heavy exhaustion unlike any I've ever felt before weighing on my shoulders. As I shudder, trying to catch my breath, I tilt my head up to look at the Great Tree.

It's glowing with health- quite literally. The bark is no longer peeling or a sickly gray, but rather a dusky, woodsy brown. Tiny light green and yellow blossoms fill the branches, unfurling into green leaves as if I'm watching the tree bloom through time-lapse. The roots beneath my feet and even under the ground begin to glow with that same pale blueish light, power spreading under the soil to the bases of the other trees, until the ground as far as I can see is spider-webbed with glowing lines of healing power.

My healing power.

The trees around us begin to heal, plants and foliage re-sprouting, and we all stop to watch the grove come to life all around us.

The fighting has stopped and everyone, friend and assassin alike, is frozen in shock as the grove is brought back from the brink of death.

When the assassins turn back to me, one by one, they are terrifying creatures no longer. The tree heals them as well, heals the centuries of torment that the curse had brought. They lower their hoods, now displaying unearthly beautiful faces, both male and female. The only thing that remains the same is the shredded cloaks, and the pitch black eyes that now turn on me with what I would dare call gratitude.

The one in front, who I had been talking to moments before, is now a slender man with a curtain of shoulder-length brown hair, and I spot the shape of arched ears poking out from beneath.

Are these creatures- fae? Or something of the sort? The man in front lowers himself onto one knee, bowing his head in thanks.

"You, Emmalina Maren, have our eternal gratitude. Our grove, I never thought it could be saved." His voice sounds choked up. "May I ask how? How did you wield such light magic? I thought…"

"I don't know," I gasp, pushing myself painstakingly back to my feet, trying to ignore the slight tilting of the world. Alaina wasn't joking when she said magic takes a lot out of the user. It felt like I had poured my soul into that tree.

"Well, however it was done," the man says, "We owe you all a great apology. You are in our debt, sorceress, for what you have done for us."

"So," I say carefully, "Your deal with Lillian?"

"Consider it called off," the assassin smiles like a feral animal. "This war is of no concern to us. Now that we are free of our curse, we have no need for that witch's bargain. We will allow you and your friends to go in peace."

"Thank you," I hear Jane say, giving them a respectful bow of her head. She wipes her hand across her face, leaving a smear of blood from the shallow slice trailing along her eyebrow. The assassins only nod their heads as one.

"I do have a request of you," I speak up, ignoring the surprised and warning glances of my companions.

"Name your price," he murmurs with a faint, amused smile.

"The Followers of Malum," I say. "Would you take us to them? Would you guide us there safely, and swiftly? We seem to have gotten a bit off track."

The assassin's eyebrows raise with puzzlement.

"What would you seek them out for?" he questions. "I hope you do not plan on causing trouble with them, such a thing would not go in your favor."

"No," Reed chimes in, shaking his head. "We just need to talk with them." The assassins murmur amongst themselves, but the one in front only shrugs.

"Do so at your own peril," he advises. "But I will escort you there, savior of the grove."

"Thank you," I say, a bit awkwardly at the title.

"Well then," Nate says, clapping his hands together. "What are we waiting for creepy assassin guy?"

"The name is Aleckar," the assassin says, sounding somewhat annoyed as if he's miffed by the nickname *creepy assassin guy*.

"Okay, whatever. *Aleckar*," Nate amends, with a slight eye roll. "Lead the way to the Caves of Malum."

"Right this moment?" he rumbles, his dark eyes glittering with something like confusion, the human emotion looking wrong on the assassin's face. "I would not advise such a thing."

I have to agree with Aleckar. My knees feel as though they're going to give out at any second, my vision swimming with exhaustion.

"I don't think I could go much further," I speak up, even the simple act of talking making my head start to pound.

"You must be close to a magical burnout," Reed observes, eyebrows still raised, looking almost, impressed.

"With the level of magic that must have taken, especially for the first time using it, I wouldn't be surprised," Jane points out. At that moment I realize that none of my friends have so much as a scratch on them, despite going head to head with the Realm's most deadly assassins. They had been losing badly, until that power had washed away every scrape and bruise, leaving their torn clothes as the only reminder of the short battle. Could my magic somehow have been that powerful?

I sway on my feet. Judging from the fact that I feel like I've just been hit by a truck, I'd say yes, it really was that strong. But how?

"We will allow you a temporary sanctuary," Aleckar says, clasping his hands behind his back. "You may stay and rest until midday tomorrow. After that, I shall fulfill my debt by guiding you to the Caves of Malum, if that is what you so wish."

Reed nods. "Thank you."

"Do not thank me," Aleckar rumbles. "We are not friends, and for the time being, we are not enemies. I am doing you no favors accompanying you to that place, to seek an audience with the Followers of Malum, you must either be a fool or have a death wish."

That's reassuring.

"Midday," Aleckar warns, as he and his assassins melt back into the shadows. "We will come to retrieve you."

Alaina shudders as they vanish.

"That wasn't terrifying at all," she mutters, rubbing her arms.

We all help make camp for the night right there in the clearing as the sky distantly begins to lighten, still not penetrating the shadows of the grove. I'm asleep before my head hits the ground.

CHAPTER 19

"This is as far as I go," Aleckar says, spreading his no longer moon-white and wrinkled hands towards the distance, where the shape of a looming, sheer cliff face juts out of the desert sands, rising hundreds of feet above our heads and casting a great shadow in the blazing, midday sun.

The six of us, covered in sweat and with feet already aching, gaze up at the cliffs with wide-eyed amazement. A steep path, barely more than a crumbling rock ledge, winds about halfway up, leading to what must be the entrance to the caves.

"Thank you," Jane says, as Aleckar bids us farewell, claiming that he has no wish to trespass on the grounds of the Followers of Malum. If they're enough to intimidate a Grove Assassin, I shudder to think how powerful they must be.

As Aleckar disappears over the crest of the hill and vanishes from sight, my shoulders slump in a bizarre mixture of both relief and dread. Relief that Aleckar, strange and silent, is no longer prowling at our backs, watching us closely with those solid black eyes that seem to stare into my very soul; dread at the thought that we are on our own now. Aleckar's presence in itself had been enough to ward off any foul creature we may have run into, and saved us a lot of time by guiding us through the more dangerous parts of the desert that we wouldn't have survived crossing without him. The lack of that kind of power at our backs is disconcerting, at the least.

"Well," Reed says, with a huff of breath. "I guess we have to climb that thing."

Alaina audibly groans. No one is very happy about it, but up the crumbling path we go. The beginning's not so bad, but once we get higher, the ledge gets narrower. Rocks and pebbles slip out from beneath our feet, so we all have to pay extra careful attention to where we step.

"What are the Followers of Malum like?" I ask softly, trying to focus on not slipping off the cliff.

"They are, well, hard to describe," Stefan says. "They feed off of powerful magic and love making deals. Speaking of powerful magic," he pauses, "What was all that about, back at the grove? How did you heal that tree?"

"I don't know," I answer honestly. "I was so afraid of my powers… I was so afraid that I could be anything like her… I think I put a dampener on it without knowing. When I knew I didn't want to kill the assassins, I guess it kind of just happened. If that makes sense."

Stefan nods vaguely.

"I wonder," Reed muses from ahead of me, carefully sidestepping a particularly sketchy section of the ledge. "What if the healing was just another form of the power that Lillian had just never known she could use, and therefore we never knew about? What if your abilities aren't just power over death, but over life *and* death?"

The thought makes me perk up a bit. Maybe I don't have to avoid using my powers, maybe I can only use my healing. I don't have to become the monster that Lillian is, I don't have to be so afraid. I can save lives, rather than end them.

"The Followers of Malum can answer those questions," Jane supplies from her position at the front of the group. "They specialize in this sort of thing. They likely already know all about you."

I shudder at that thought.

Suddenly I hear a cracking noise, like the faintest splinter of rock. I spot it a split second before anyone else, the spider webbing crack spearing through the ledge beneath Reed's foot.

I hear Alaina shout in warning as I lunge for his arm, yanking him backward and against the cliff face moments before the section of the ledge gives way to a rock slide. We both stumble, a bit too close to the sheer drop for comfort, but Reed steadies us both.

Jane and Nate in front of us whip around to see what happened. Reed turns to me, face blank with shock, a shade paler than before.

He swallows, staring at the gaping hole in the side of the ledge where he had been standing.

"You…you saved my life," he gasps.

I take a deep breath to calm my suddenly racing heartbeat. "Don't mention it," I huff. "Just repaying the favor from the throne room."

"Thank you," he breathes. His pine-green eyes fix on mine. "No, really. Thank you."

I hope I'm not blushing as red as I feel.

"Is the ledge still wide enough to still get across?" Stefan asks, cutting into the lingering tension. His shoulders are stiff, and the look he gives Reed is far from concern.

"It should be," Reed answers, keeping close to the wall as he edges by the gap, barely wide enough to fit one foot after the other. I realize that I'm holding my breath, watching for any sign of the ledge cracking again. *Snap out of it. He's fine*, I hiss to myself, but that doesn't stop my heart from pounding like a jackhammer until he safely reaches the other side.

"It's all good," Reed says, looking back over his shoulder at Stefan, Alaina, and I still gathered on the far side. "Stefan, you can stop giving me that glare. I didn't break the ledge on purpose, you know."

I step forwards to go next, then Stefan and Alaina practically skip across, sure-footed, without so much as a downward glance. So she's afraid of flying, but not of tumbling off a cliff hundreds of feet in the air? I don't even try to understand the likes of Alaina Sparks.

We have no more near-death experiences, thankfully, and we reach the entrance to the caves without another hitch. It's like a looming, black hole, too perfectly circular to be natural. It's also pitch black, with no light whatsoever.

I pause at the cave entrance, my toes practically touching the spot on the tarnished rock where the light ends and shadows like a cloud of black fog begin. Even straining my eyes, I can't make out anything. It could be a tunnel, a room, or a sheer drop. For all I know, one of Malum's Followers could be standing on the other side, staring straight at us, and I would be none the wiser.

"So, who wants to go first?" Nate snorts. "We could draw straws?"

"I'll go," Alaina says, brushing hair out of her eyes and giving the cave an assessing look. Somehow her curtain of shoulder-length hair has maintained its subtle curl, despite the day and a half spent getting ambushed in the desert. She steps forward, undaunted, but Nate stretches an arm to block her path.

"Absolutely not," he says, looking as though he wants to take back his joke.

"But," she starts to protest, but something causes her to pause, the words dying in her throat. Every single one of us jumps as we see the human-like shadow shift in the entranceway. So I guess it was my third guess, we're being watched.

No one dares to move for a long minute, barely daring to breathe, but the creature doesn't make itself known again. Well, now they know we're here.

"Oh, for the Realm's sake!" Jane sighs, throwing up her hands. "We came here to meet with them, didn't we? What's the point in lingering at the doorway like terrified sheep?"

She palms her twin daggers, letting her black hair spill down her shoulders, before striding into the void.

"Wait, Jane!" Reed curses, following close behind his sister. Alaina gives a shout of anticipation, before leaping after, forcing Nate to follow. That leaves just Stefan and me.

"Stefan," I begin awkwardly. "I know this isn't really the time, but I just wanted to ask if something's wrong?"

"No," he shakes his head a little too fervently. "Nothing's wrong. We should follow them," he jabs a thumb at the entrance.

"But-"

"We can talk later," he assures me, casting a worried glance at the darkness. "This is not the place. Not with so many watching and listening to every word we say."

I know he's not talking about our friends, but rather whatever lies in the depths of these caves.

"You're right," I say, shuddering again. "Let's go."

Together we step through that doorway, into nothingness.

Okay, maybe not exactly nothingness, but close enough. The air feels thick and clammy, with a smell like wood smoke and mold. There's some sweet, lingering scent that sends chills down my spine, every bit of rational thought begging me to *run, run away*.

I continue, now tightly gripping Stefan's hand so that I don't lose him in the dark, walking slowly and testing every step on the slick stone floors and stretching my other arm in front of me, feeling for walls. Nothing. I can't even see the doorway anymore.

I'm afraid to call out to the others, but how else are we going to find them? We could be lost in this darkness forever, I realize with a jolt of panic.

I hear a hissing, clicking sound from somewhere ahead.

A torch flares to life several feet away, illuminating a small circle of the slimy cave wall. I move to cling tighter to Stefan's hand, but my fingers close around air.

"Stefan?" I gasp, breaking the silence. No answer. "Stefan!" I scream. Where is he? How did he just disappear? My eyes fix on the flickering torch, somehow looking cold and drained of its yellow light.

"Please," I whisper to the creature that I know is listening. "Where did you take my friends?"

"*Do not fret, Emmalina Maren,*" I hear a disembodied voice hiss. Not hear, exactly, but rather the sound seems to echo in my very mind. Just as the falcon in my dream had whispered its prophecy to me, what feels like so long ago.

"*You and your friends are each being assessed and will be reunited soon enough. But first, what do you want with the Followers of Malum?*"

"I..." my voice shakes, and I have to swallow a few times, my mouth as dry as sandpaper.

"I need information," I wait. Silence. Perhaps it's not enough. "I'm looking for someone."

Still nothing. It must want to know everything, then.

"I need to find Lillian's stronghold. I have reasons to believe that it's here- that she has offered you something. A dagger?" A satisfying hiss resounds through my mind, enough to give me a headache.

"*You have passed our assessment, Emmalina Maren. Your story matches those of your friends. You may take the torch, it will guide you.*"

Take the torch? My trembling fingers wrapped around the ancient torch handle, that strange fire expanding to illuminate the space around me. A tunnel, with narrow walls on either side barely brushing my shoulders and stinking of mildew. I know those walls couldn't have been there before- I had lashed out when I was trying to find Stefan and hadn't struck any stone. So I simply follow this impossible path deep into the belly of the mountain, trying to take calming breaths.

There, it's a light up ahead. An exit.

I nearly sob with relief when I find that it's a room, decently lit with flickering torches, and my friends are all standing around some upraised platform.

Alaina lets out a sigh of relief. Reed's at my side in an instant.

"What happened?" he demands. "What took so long?"

"What do you mean?" I ask, puzzled. "Stefan was with me for most of it. I was probably only in there for like, five minutes."

"Five minutes?" Stefan says incredulously, his face ghost white. "Lina, you were in there for almost an hour. We had no idea what had happened to you."

I spin to look back at the tunnel leading into this room.

"We were separated," I try to recall how it could have taken that long. "That voice said I was being *assessed*, whatever that means, and then the tunnel just appeared." I shrug helplessly. "I don't know…"

"They were assessing what you know, what you want with them, and what magic lies within you," Jane explains. "People without magic aren't permitted to enter, and never emerge from the tunnels if they try. But for people that interest them, people with powerful magic, those assessments tend to take longer. I've never heard of them keeping someone for almost an hour, they must be especially interested in you."

I don't like that. No, I don't like that at all.

"*Indeed,*" the voice again echoes in my head, and judging from the looks on everyone else's faces, they can hear it too.

"*You, Emmalina Maren, are a fascination.*"

I choke back a scream of horror and shock as the thing steps out of the tunnel, long black robes sliding on the floor like the tail of an obsidian cobra. My eyes are fixed on its head, the only part not hidden in the black robes, a skull with horns.

As the initial shock dies, and I get a closer look, I realize that its head is not, in fact, a skull. Rather it's wearing one like some kind of grotesque Halloween mask, with spiraling horns longer than my arm, coming to wicked points. It's not a human skull either, but more closely resembles some kind of deer.

"Who…?" I can barely force the words out. A glance at my companions shows horror, disgust, but little surprise. So this must be one of the Followers of Malum, then.

"You already know who I am, and I know exactly who you are." It hisses out loud, its physical voice more grating than nails screeching along the glass, cold and sharp. I strain to see anything beyond the skull mask but find only dark voids.

"Now I know why you all have dared to set foot in these caves. A foolish, wasted effort, it seems." The thing sounds almost mocking.

"Wasted?" Jane demands. "In what way?"

The creature tilts its head imploringly, making a rasping sound that could be a breath or a laugh.

"You all claimed you have come to this place seeking the stronghold of Lillian Maren, believing that we have offered her sanctuary. Perhaps in exchange for a certain infamous dagger?"

We all nod.

"Well then, as I said, a wasted journey," the thing rasps. "For Lillian's stronghold does not lie here, nor anywhere in the Realms. Since we are unable to see her location, I would say that her stronghold lies somewhere in the worlds," I can practically hear the creature's hungry grin, if it even has a mouth beneath that skull it wears.

"It could be anywhere," Stefan says, running a hand through his golden hair, casting a deep shade of copper in the dim lighting of the cave. "We would never be able to find it, between Earth and Allrhea. We might have to rethink our plan, maybe find a way to draw her to us."

"So quick you are to give up, Stefan Fides." The thing turns its head to him, where he seems to shrink back under its gaze.
"The TimeKeeper said that she would be here," I begin to protest. "Not in the worlds."

The thing really does laugh now, a guttering hiss that makes me wonder if this thing is part snake.

"That old fool," it ruffles the folds of its cloak over hunched shoulders. Even with this thing's back as curved as a candy cane, it still seems too tall to be natural. "The TimeKeeper's visions may not be of these Realms, but even those, in the end, are nothing but vague guesses and speculations. Our magic, however, is not so flawed."

"But you just said that you can't find her, because she's not in the Realms," I protest.

The Follower of Malum takes a menacing step forward, sending each of us flinching back, and I nearly trip over the upraised platform at the center of the room.

"My magic may not be able to see her location," it hisses, "But it can still send you to her."

I blink with confusion.

"Okay, then send us," Jane says, crossing her arms, but the creature only makes a tsk tsk sound. I knew it wasn't going to be as easy as that.

"Such a thing would not come for free. I require payment."

"Name your price," I say, stepping forward, but Reed pulls me back. The Follower of Malum turns his gaze back to me. It seems to consider for a moment.

"One lock of hair, from the fair Falcon Warrior," it hisses. "That is what I demand."

"No," Reed says instantly, angling himself between me and the creature as if he would hide me from its gaze. "I know what kind of foul magic you do, she isn't..."

"Done," I say, plucking free several slightly curling golden strands, pinching them between my fingers.

"No," Jane hisses. "Reed is right, that kind of thing is too dangerous!"

The strands disappear from my fingers. My blood runs cold, as crimson eyes flare behind the holes in the deer skull on the creature's face.

"Good doing business with you," it snarls, before evaporating into black smoke.

The smoke curled away, the creature had vanished into thin air.

"Lina, how could you be so stupid," Jane says, whirling on me, but her eyes are more fearful than angry. "Metus and his like use the darkest kind of magic. Giving him that lock of hair was beyond foolish. There's no telling what he can do."

"Metus?" I ask, my voice barely a whisper. "That horrible thing has a name?"

"Metus," Alaina says gravely. "Their leader, and the most powerful and vindictive of them all."

"*My reputation proceeds me,*" the voice again echoes in my head as the cavern begins to rumble beneath our feet. Tiny bits of rock begin to fall from the arched ceiling, dirt crumbling around us like filthy snow. I cover my head with my arms, hoping that the cave isn't about to come crashing down around us.

"*A deal has been struck,*" Metus's voice fills the cavern, unearthly and far from human. A hiss seems to echo all around us as five of the horrible creatures step from the shadows around the walls, surrounding us.

They all look almost exactly like Metus, except for their horns, which vary in all shapes and sizes, from tall and spiraling to branching out like the clawed twigs of the trees in the dead grove. Only these aren't hunched over. They stand almost seven feet tall, easy, their frames too long and thin, robes whispering on the stone behind them.

"Okay," I squeak. "I take it back, I don't want this deal after all."

"This is messed up," Nate curses, surveying the masked creatures that loom over even his tall form.

Jane and Reed reach for their weapons as the Followers of Malum advance on us, until our heels are touching the upraised platform at our backs. Then they stop.

Each of them is standing in a circle around us. Around the raised circle in the stone floor, hewn of cold marble.

Not just a platform. A dais. Exactly like the one we had discovered in Passage Number Three.

It's carved of the same marble, with the same strange writings and different shaped openings on the top. The only difference is the arrow, which had pointed to that blank wall, is missing.

My fear simply turns to horror and disgust as the creatures lift their arms as one, outstretched in front of them. Long, too thin limbs with fingers that look more like the legs of spiders. They begin to chant.

"Fi uoy derevocsid eht nrettap dna koot emit ot etalsnart siht, doog boj. M'i desserpmi. Rof taht, uoy lliw teg eno tnih- Anilamme si ton S'naillil noitcelfer."

"What are they saying?" I whisper to Reed, trying to keep my hands from trembling.

"I don't know," he whispers back. "It's no language I've ever heard."

They continue their chant, the torches flaring brighter, black smoke beginning to swirl over the dais.

"Yrros, s'taht eht ylno tnih uoy teg."

As they finish, the smoke condenses to form a single object atop the slick marble- a small glass vial no larger than my pinky, topped with a cork, containing a liquid as black as night yet somehow giving off a glow.

With that, each of the horrible horned creatures vanishes as Metus had done. Slowly, Reed reaches for the vial, his fingers hesitating, before gently picking it up.

"Don't worry," Metus's nails-on-a-chalkboard voice sneers from behind, where he reappeared several feet away. "The glass is impossible to break. It certainly cannot be shattered by the likes of you.

"Thank you," I say, bowing as deeply as I can to the hunched creature.

"Do not thank me yet," is Metus's only reply. "The potion will act as an anchor. One sip from each of you, and you can use a Traveler's Mirror to take you as close as possible to Lillian's stronghold."

"Anchor? Traveler's Mirror?" I ask, puzzled by the unfamiliar terms.

"A small portal mirror," Jane explains quickly. "Like the ones at the safe houses that we used before to travel to and from the worlds. An anchor means it will give the portal a destination, like plugging in coordinates in a GPS. The safe houses tend to act as the other side of the anchor, meaning it would send us to a safe house closest to Lillian."

The thing gives a simple nod of its head, spiral horns gleaming wickedly in the torchlight.

"Where would we get a Traveler's Mirror?" Nate snorts, crossing his arms. "Those things are like, super rare. Jane actually blew one up, see, and Marcus was sooo mad about it."

He has to dodge Jane's hand as she moves to slap him upside the head.

"Nate brings up a good point," Stefan muses. "How are we supposed to get our hands on a Traveler's Mirror? The ones in the Shadow Realm are under lock and key in the vaults below the castle, and we won't be able to get anywhere near the Mirror Realm without being caught. So that leaves..."

"The Soul Realm," Metus hisses. "Anima's domain. With that, you are on your own."

"So we need to go to the Soul Realm," I say. "It will take us almost a day to get out of this desert, and if we use the wolf vitalums that would take us how long?"

"Almost two days of riding to get to the Soul Realm," Alaina muses. "I believe that means we would be arriving in the Soul Realm on..." her turquoise eyes widen, "...December 13th."

Reed shakes his head, his mouth twitching upwards in a disbelieving smile. "No way!"

"Why?" I ask, watching varying levels of excitement and wariness spread among my companions. "What's so special about December 13th?"

"Only the biggest holiday of the year," Alaina gushes. "There are huge celebrations all across the Realms, celebrating the defeat of Malum and the new age of magic."

A low growl rumbles from Metus, who I had almost forgotten was standing barely five feet away, the glowing crimson behind the eyes of the skull flaring. I guess these creepy demon things that call themselves the *Followers of Malum*, and worship the idea of that dead tyrant, don't take kindly to a holiday celebrating his defeat.

"Sorry," Alaina mumbles, realizing her mistake as her face pales.

"I think we'll be going now," Jane says, as Nate angles himself between Alaina and the furious creature's wrath.

"Wait," we all freeze as Metus rasps the word, only imagining how badly Alaina must have angered him.

"Before you go, I have more trades to offer, if you will have them, Emmalina Maren. A few trades that might be of great interest to you." Fear roots me to the spot, but Stefan and Reed at the same time chorus, "*No.*"

The thing only waits, listening for my answer. I know it's a bad idea. I should just take the anchor potion and the information about Lillian and run. Who knows what power I've already handed over with that lock of hair? But stupidly, I say, "What kind of trades?"

"For a single feather from your lovely vitalum, I will grant you the location of the one you seek most." I swallow hard. Who would be *the one I seek most*? What does that even mean?

"And the other?" I ask as Jane gives my wrist a tug, hissing, "Lina, no."

"Do you know why your magic is so hard to use?" is all Metus asks. "Why do you find it hard to summon that silver falcon of yours, why healing a single tree almost brought you to your knees? It is because your powers are bound, restrained."

"What do you mean her powers are bound?" Reed asks, suddenly curious. "By what?"

"By me, of course," Metus says, something akin to glee in his horrible voice. "Long ago, your mother, Corrine Maren, fled the Realms to protect her daughter. But after only a year of hiding out on Earth, Corrine realized something, her daughter's powers, your powers, had already manifested. Knowing they would surely make it impossible to blend in since you couldn't control them at such a young age, your mother did the only thing she could. She returned to the Realms, to these caves, and begged me to bind your powers so that they would only reappear at age seventeen." I gape in shock, unable to form a single thought, never mind find the words that seem to catch in my throat. My mom brought me to this place, she had them dampen my powers?

"That would make sense," Reed says, almost to himself. "Lillian's had appeared at birth, it was so strange that yours hadn't as well, being counterparts and all."

Metus only nods, a single dip of his horned head, before continuing.

"Doing so made your magic weaker, and now prevents you from using them to their fullest extent. For a single drop of your blood, in exchange, I will unbind your powers into what they are meant to be, strong enough to rival even Lillian's."

He lets the offer sit for a moment, dangling it above our heads before it becomes too much of a temptation to resist.

"I agree to your terms," I say before I can talk myself out of it. My friends aren't so convinced.

"No, Lina," Reed says, a hand on my wrist. "These deals are too dangerous. The lock of hair, and now a drop of blood? These things are major conductors for dark magic, it won't end well."

"I'll only agree to the bargain for my magic," I reason, acutely aware of the glint behind Metus's skull mask, where his eyes should be. "I need to agree to this. I won't stand a chance against Lillian without being able to really use my powers. I can't leave this part of myself bound and hidden away."

Pain flickers in his eyes, but he only nods.

"Okay," I say, with a heave of breath. "How do I...?" Before I can finish asking how I will hand over the drop of blood, Metus's unnaturally long arms flash from beneath his cloak. There's a sharp prick at my finger, and I lurch back with a gasp as red flows from the tiny slice that suddenly appeared on my finger, a drop of blood slipping from the knife Metus clutches in his twisted hand into a vial, which he swiftly tucks back into a hidden pocket. The tiny cut continues to bleed, and I wrap it in my traveling cloak.

Metus whispers another chant under his breath, no more dramatics or shadows, except for the crimson flare of red light.

The feeling deep in my gut, like the snapping of figurative chains, and the yawning of a deep chasm of power opened wide within me. A swift iciness shoots upward into my fingertips until my hands are glowing with blue light brighter and more blinding than the sun. It crests like the head of a massive wave, wild and completely out of my control as seventeen years of pent-up power race to the surface.

When the overwhelming sensation dies down, I find myself on my knees, my body humming with newfound energy. I feel different, but right, somehow. A weight I never knew I was carrying was suddenly lifted from my chest, leaving me light and free as a bird. As a falcon.

Getting back to my feet, I find my friends all staring in a mixture of dread and amazement. The slice on my finger is completely gone, vanished without a trace.

"Healing magic," Metus murmurs, almost impossible to hear. "Interesting."

"Healing magic?" Reed asks, his throat bobbing. "So what happened at the grove, that wasn't a part of Lillian's abilities?"

"No," Metus hisses. "This is something else entirely. Not a hint of dark magic runs through her veins, only light bright enough to blind. As I said before, a fascination indeed."

To my surprise, Metus steps aside to allow us a straight shot for the passage out.

"If you do not wish to accept my second bargain now, know that the offer still stands should you ever decide to accept.

Until we meet again, for I know we will." Metus says that with such surety that I shiver. I hesitate, wondering if it could be some sort of trap, but Metus's voice only rasps in my head "*Do not fear young falcon. I am not in the business of killing off my customers. Yet.*"

And with that last, ominous word, the Follower of Malum disappears into the shadows, allowing us to see ourselves out. Through the tunnels, and back into daylight.

CHAPTER 20

Everything about that encounter leaves a lot to process. Luckily we have plenty of time to think it over. Three days' worth of time, to be exact.

The tunnel didn't open up at the cliff face where we had entered before, but rather somewhere else in Oblivion, among the pale-colored dunes. No sign of the mountainous spread of the Caves of Malum, but there in the distance lies an all too familiar looking grove of no-longer-dead trees. The Assassin's Grove.

That puts us almost half a day ahead of schedule, thanks to those strange tunnels spitting us out miles from the caves. When I turn back to the entrance, all I find is a pile of unassuming boulders. No going back the way we came, not that I would ever want to set foot back in that creepy place.

"Do you think we could shelter in the grove again?" Alaina asks, eyeing the shadowy trees atop the farthest sand-crested hill.

"I wouldn't risk it," Jane says skeptically, shielding her face from the blazing sun with a hand over her brow. "They were grateful before for Lina saving the Great Tree, but they're still assassins that don't enjoy trespassers. I wouldn't put it past them to only extend their mercy so far."

"Speaking of what happened at the grove," Nate says with a trademark grin. "I guess now we know how you did it. You know, healing magic and all. Nice."

"Do you think said healing magic could fix my nails?" Alaina grumbles, inspecting her once lovely teal-painted fingertips, now a bit dry and chipped.

"I don't think healing magic is designed to fix your nail polish," I snort. "You'll probably have to go to a salon for that."

She fixes me with an offended look, "I paint these myself."

"We can tell," Nate snickers, looking pointedly at the flaking paint, to which she scowls at him.

"A trip to the salon though would be nice," she says with a longing sigh, wiping dust and sweat from her palms. "Now I have the perfect excuse for it when we get to the Soul Realm."

"Oh, right," I say. "That holiday you were talking about."

She nods. "The Starlight Festival. All of the Realms celebrate in some way, but the Soul Realm's festivities are definitely the best. You haven't seen true beauty until you've seen its capital, Varallex, at night, especially during the biggest festival of the year. People call it the *city that outshines the stars.*"

"It sounds amazing."

"And we get to see it," she gushes.

By now, we've reached the edge of the tree line bordering the Grove of Assassins. We cling to the shadows cast by the trees, relishing whatever shade we can get without venturing close enough to be considered *trespassing*. We might be cutting it a little close, but come on, I saved their lives. The least they can do is let us walk in the shade without murdering us, assassins or not.

We set up camp for the night here, probably the safest spot we're going to find in this awful place.

Luckily, we see no sign of Aleckar or his murderous little cadre. Even better luck, like the attaura that chased us before, none of the deadly creatures in this forsaken desert seem to want to go near the grove. It acts as a shelter from both the heat and whatever may be prowling these dunes. That brings up a different question for me.

"If Oblivion is so dangerous that no one has ever been able to cross it and make it back alive, how have we managed to get this far?" I ask. "I mean, if the Realms brought armies to cross this desert, even without the help of cars or aircraft, it doesn't seem that impossible."

Reed huffs a tired laugh. "This is only a tiny fraction of Oblivion, and relatively safe compared to the rest of it. We've barely gotten past the welcome mat and almost died several times. The Followers of Malum act as the checkpoint, you have to cross through their hunting grounds to get to the deeper parts of the desert, and that typically keeps the worst horrors away from here."

"Their hunting grounds?" I ask with a shudder.

"Yeah," Stefan answers with a look of distaste. "That attaura we saw yesterday? Hundreds of them roam around the Caves of Malum. They're hunted for food and those horrible skull masks."

I shudder harder. "The Followers of Malum wear attaura skulls?" I ask, picturing the deadly deer/lion thing that even giant wolves ran from. "How do they even kill them?"

"I don't know, and I don't want to know," Nate says with a fake gag. "That's nasty."

"They wear the skulls for the horns," Jane says, kicking a rock with her boot and watching it skid a small path through the sand, staring up at the swirling grains of reddish-orange among the dry brown. The sand vaguely reminds me of cinnamon, and that thought makes me hungry.

"Malum was described as a giant, hulking creature of darkness, with winding horns atop his head and a skeletal face." Jane continues, making a face. "His followers like to copy his look."

"Or maybe they're just so ugly that even that makes them look better," Nate snickers, causing a rumble of laughter from Reed.

I dig around in the backpack still on my back, tired, and after that thought of cinnamon, more than a little hungry. There are still some protein bars and other various travel-sized snacks that the TimeKeeper had packed for us, and I pass them around with the canteens of water. We're running low on that too, but no way we're going to look for another oasis. Not after our earlier run-in.

Ugh, I'm so tired. The last time I slept was when the assassins knocked us out with those little darts, and I wouldn't exactly call that relaxing.

The sun has slipped below the horizon, but we don't dare risk building a fire, even as a chill settles over the night. Stefan takes the first watch, while the rest of us try to get some rest. I thought, after everything that's happened, everything we've seen and learned, that I would have trouble falling asleep. That is not the case. With exhaustion weighing me down and the idea of another full day of trekking through the desert ahead of us, I'm practically asleep before my head hits the ground.

I sleep heavily, only waking for about an hour to take my turn keeping watch. Once morning arrives and brings its blazing heat, we set off once more, eventually leaving the grove far behind us. I can make out familiar mountains in the distance, and springs of grass beneath our feet that mark the end of the desert. Or, at least, that's what I hope. We keep far from any oasis, making as little noise as possible and not daring to even touch our magic, and by some miracle, we make it to the edge of Oblivion by nightfall.

We don't risk a fire, don't want to push our luck, and Jane volunteers for first the watch. I hear a low growl, and see the hulking shape of a wolf, a vitalum, keeping her company now that we are a healthy distance away from the dunes. I recognize the wolf, Keira, the one with the silky black fur and keen eyes.

I think and wonder, as I lay on the hard-packed ground. Using the backpack as a makeshift pillow, I lift my hand into my line of sight, my silver bracelet gleaming. That gleam in the moonlight turns into a glow. Brighter, and brighter. With barely half a thought energy flows through the silver and materializes into the shape of a bird high in the air. Flying through the cloudless night. I watch in wonder, and another half a thought has the bird dissipating away as if it were made of silvery smoke. My vitalum. With my full powers, summoning it truly is as easy as breathing, and every bit instinctive and beautiful.

I see Stefan smile out of the corner of my eye. Faster than I can blink, the slender form of a golden brown lynx shimmers into view by his shoulder, tufted ears twitching.

"This is Alec," he murmurs, stroking the cat's speckled fur. I jump as something brushes my arm, and see a smaller silver lynx slink by to curl near my feet. I hear Alaina's light laugh from where she watches from several feet away, curled on the ground beside Nate.

"Cirice," Stefan chides the silver lynx, Alaina's vitalum, who pads on swift and silent paws to greet Alec. Jane's wolf, Kiera, watches them with baleful eyes. Two more wolves are summoned from the gloom, Rowan, and a dusky gray beast that must be Nate's.

"Kai," Nate greets his vitalum with a grin, and the gray wolf's tail wags. Three wolves, two lynx cats, and one silver falcon. I summon the bird again, allowing it to rest on my wrist, heavy claws digging into the tough leather beneath my cloak. It fixes me with that same too-intelligent gaze exactly the same as it had been in my dream. How had I seen my vitalum, and that strange prophecy, before I even knew about any of this? The TimeKeeper says I'm not a seer, Falcon Warriors can't see the future, but how else could that dream have been possible?

The falcon ruffles her feathers, an astral silver like the stars dotting the sky above. Astral- meaning starlike.

"I'm going to call you Astral," I whisper to her, barely loud enough for the others to hear. The falcon gives no indication she understands, only continuing to preen her feathers, sharp beak clicking as she turns her attention to the shiny falcon charm on my bracelet, playing idly with it.

"What's the story behind the bracelet?" Jane asks from where she sits with her back against a rock.

"Hmm? What do you mean, story?" I ask.

"Every vitalum token has a story," Reed muses, playing with his wristwatch. "It becomes your vitalum token because it's special to you, it carries some significance that you would tie your magic to. What makes the bracelet so special?"

"Oh," I sit up a little straighter, and the falcon gives an annoyed click of its beak as it's jostled. "Cam gave that to me, as an early birthday gift. Cam has been my best friend since, well, forever." I let out a breath, wondering how our lives have changed so much since then. I miss him so much. I wonder how he's doing. I know he's safe back at the palace, but guilt still gnaws in my gut when I think about him. We just left him there, in a strange new place, without even telling him.

"This bracelet is important to me," I say softly. Both Reed and Stefan frown, but Reed waves his hand for me to continue.

"Well, he gave it to me the day before my birthday," I remember. "We were at the Mill Yard, back at home. Right after that, I saw you three," I wave my hand at Reed, Jane, and Alaina. I laugh, "You guys freaked me out, with the staring. And Reed, you looked like some kind of serial killer."

Reed snorts, "Sorry."

"Then we visited the park that evening. We were spooked by this crashing in the trees." I pause, realizing something, "Hey, that was you three, wasn't it?"

Alaina laughs. "I almost forgot about that! We were keeping an eye on you, watching for Lillian's men, and Reed pushed me out of the tree."

"For the last time, I didn't push you out of the tree," Reed growls, and Rowan matches that growl. "It was completely an accident."

"You guys are terrible spies," I snort. "But what about your vitalum tokens? What are the stories behind all of yours?"

An owl hoots overhead as I wait for someone to speak first.

"Well," Stefan says, waiting, and a double-edged sword materializes in his hands. It's a golden-bronze color, the hilt engraved with a prowling lynx. I jump slightly, but he only laughs.

"Wait, how did you do that?" I ask, staring wide-eyed at the faintly glowing blade, being used to summon Alec.

"Most vitalum items are small enough to wear on you or carry around. But some are simply too large or unwieldy, so they can be summoned to their owner. I usually keep this in the Dorm."

"You just leave it behind? What if someone took it?"

"That's the thing about the tokens," Reed says. "They can't be taken against their owner's will. Remember back at the castle during the lockdown, when one of Marcus's guards tried to restrain you and take the bracelet? He couldn't, and it even burned his glove. That's why Marcus had to let you go, it proved that you weren't Lillian, because it was your real vitalum token."

"That's cool," I shrug. "So, what's the story behind the sword?"

"My Dad gave it to me in January, when I turned 17 before I became a trainee," Stefan says, turning the hilt in his fingers. His mouth twitches into a frown.

"He's not the most loving guy, kind of brutal, hence the sword for a present. Both of my parents are that way. It was one of the first thoughtful gifts he's ever given me. I guess, well, it just meant a lot."

"What would he think, about you being a fugitive now?" Reed asks bluntly, and Jane gives him a sharp look.

"I doubt either of them cares," Stefan says, shadows darkening those golden eyes of his. I scoot closer to him, taking his hand in mine, our fingers twining together.

"Hey," I say softly. "It doesn't matter what they think. You've got us."

He only smiles, his throat bobbing. "Thanks."

"Jane and I got our tokens from our parents too," Reed says, his tone sorrowful as he inspects his strange watch. "My Dad gave me this watch, which had been passed down for so many generations, we lost count. He always said it would be mine one day."

"My Mom gave me the daggers," Jane says. "She used them as hair clips too. It's why I do it, even though it's not quite as practical." She smiles sadly, unpinning her hair to hold the twin, ruby-encrusted daggers in her palm.

"You've mentioned your parents before," I say softly. "What happened?"

"Lillian," Reed says, a crease between his eyebrows. "She killed them. They were good people, both of them, and she just took them from us."

"While we're sharing," Alaina says with a sigh. "As I mentioned before, I never knew either of my parents. They left me with Orlon when I was a baby, and left this with me." She fingers the golden, circular pendant hanging around her neck, her vitalum token, inscribed with a swirling design.

"I don't know what it is- I can't even get it open. I spent so many years searching for any hint of who they could have been, why they might have given me away and left this pendant with me, but I found nothing. I became obsessed, it was the only thing that mattered to me at one point. One day, I was given a letter claiming to have been sent by my parents, saying they were finally ready to meet me. It told me to meet them by the Varallex docks, in the Soul Ream, at midnight and they would explain everything. Come midnight and no one showed. I had been waiting for an hour until the clock hit 1 a.m., and still nothing. When I was finally ready to just give up and go home, a stranger walked up beside me on the dock, who was too young to be my Dad, saying that he saw me standing there for a while and was wondering if I was waiting for someone. That's how I met Nate."

Nate, from his seat beside her, smiles faintly.

"I was almost 17," Nate says. "She was 16. I had gotten annoyed with my dad and my brother that night, and I went to the docks to get away for a while. Alaina was there, wearing this beautiful blue dress, just standing there, waiting. After a while, I just became so curious, that I just had to ask who she was waiting for."

"My parents never showed," Alaina says, but there isn't much sadness in her voice anymore. "Instead I decided that it was life telling me that it was time to move on, to find something new. So I went dancing with Nate that night, and just never looked back."

"That's when she gave me this," Nate says, tugging on a thin, golden chain necklace, his vitalum token, resting on his collarbone that I hadn't noticed before. "She convinced me to become a Realm Guard, a trainee," Nate says. "I never knew my mom, she left when I was little, and I only had my dad and brother, neither of which had any interest in making anything of their lives. I almost ended up the same way, but Alaina changed my life."

And just like that, we all stayed up late into the hours of the night, telling stories of our lives before we met one another, under the light of the moon.

I'm woken by the sound of a hooting owl cutting through the still night.

I blink, gazing at the swirls of stars overhead through sleep-burry eyes. I don't see any constellations that I recognize, not even the North Star, which confirms that these might not be the same stars I see from Earth. A whole different world, a whole different galaxy.

I roll onto my side, taking in the sleeping forms of my friends huddled in our makeshift camping spot, nothing more than grass and hard-packed ground. The hulking shape of Rowan paces back and forth on the hill, meaning Reed must be on watch right now. Right there, with his back against a rock, watching the same stars I had been just staring at.

Unable to fall back asleep, I decided to join him in his vigil, trying to be as silent as possible to not disturb the others. He jumps as I put a hand on his shoulder, grasping for where his sword should be, still missing from when the assassins disarmed him until he realizes it's just me.

"Sorry," I whisper with a small smile, taking a seat beside him. "Didn't mean to interrupt whatever you were just lost in thought about."

He lets out an amused huff of breath. "It's fine. I was just thinking about our conversation earlier."

"The one about vitalums?"

"Kind of," there's a long stretch of silence before he speaks again.

"Look. I've been meaning to say this for a while now, I'm sorry for how I acted when we first met."

"Hmm?" I look up, surprised by the turn this just took.

"I was a jerk to you, and it wasn't fair. You asked me what my problem was, what you had done to deserve that, and the answer is nothing."

"So why did you act that way?" I say, my eyebrows creasing. "The glaring and the grumpiness, like I did something to constantly offend you."

"It had to do with my parents, and Lillian," Reed says with a sigh, and I listen silently as he recalls it, that painful memory.

"When I was younger, Lillian and I were friends. Pretty good friends, actually. Or at least, I thought we were." I raise my eyebrows, but he just continues.

"She wasn't always a psychopath. She was normal at one point, even though she was an outcast because of her powers. I was one of the few people who didn't treat her like some dangerous wild animal. One day, when she was sixteen and I was almost seventeen, she just changed I guess. She started acting differently as if some switch had been flipped to send her into that crazy spiral. Lillian started ranting about King Orlon, holding some kind of grudge against him, saying that he was selfish and evil. She tried to get people to turn on him, building a following of people who began to agree with what she was saying. I never really realized how serious she was until that day, when she decided that she was going to overthrow him, saying that's what she was given her powers to do. I tried to talk sense into her but she wouldn't listen, saying that drastic rebellions require drastic measures. She tried so hard to get me to side with her, and when I refused…" he lets out a long breath.

"…she used those awful powers to kill both of my parents, right in front of Jane and me."

"Oh," I say softly.

"Yeah," he braces his head on his hand, looking exhausted. "That's why I was so angry, why I hated you. Hated that you looked just like my former friend turned murderer. I hated that I was constantly reminded of what my misplaced trust did to my family."

He fiddles with his watch again.

"I was angry, and afraid too. I was scared that, since you were her counterpart, we were just inviting another monster waiting to happen." I flinch at his harsh words, striking something I had been so afraid of.

"But I was wrong. I was so wrong." His eyes meet mine, and my stupid heart does backflips as his eyes meet mine, bright and sincere.

"You are nothing like her. Even before she snapped, she was mean and bad-tempered and had far more enemies than friends. She reminded me of Eliza, but cruel. I guess I should have seen the difference immediately, but her betrayal simply broke my ability to trust. When you showed you were so dedicated to your mom and Cam that you would risk everything to go back to that campsite, seeing you with your best friend, when you refused to kill those assassins, and when you saved my life," his fingers twine around mine. "You restored that trust, bit by bit."

"And now I just want to say I'm so sorry, for everything," he says. "And I was hoping we could start over, as friends this time?"

For some reason, my heart pauses its backflips at that word, *friends*, but I smile anyway.

"Thank you, Reed, and I forgive you."

CAM

Several days after my first Realm tech lesson with Eliza, I can safely say I've begun to slowly adjust to Realm life.

A lot of guards still avoid me like the plague, probably uncomfortable with the idea of a "Worlder" among them. I wonder if this is the first time it's ever happened, someone from the worlds being brought here, to this place. There are still plenty of guards and trainees who are friendly and curious, some asking me about Lina, and others simply checking in to see how I'm adjusting.

That one tech lesson led to another, and another, until Eliza had become my unofficial tutor (not that she would ever call herself that). She still hasn't dropped the prickly attitude, but I've come to see that she is just like that with everybody. Part of the odd looks I've been getting from several guards is because I've simply spent more than two minutes with her without getting a knife to my throat. From what I gather from almost everybody else, Eliza isn't exactly what you would call *well-liked* around here. Not that it seems to bother her in the slightest.

Besides the tutoring, I've tried to keep myself busy around here, trying to ignore the growing homesickness, the concern at what my parents must be thinking, and the worry that gnaws in my gut with every day that passes and still no sign of Lina or the others. Orlon had sent a team to the Shadow Realms, to which they returned unsuccessfully. No one knows where they could possibly be.

I've asked when I might be able to return to Earth, and Orlon says that it may be wise to wait for a little longer until Lina and her friends are found. For one thing, I want to make sure she returns safely. For another, the king is worried that Lillian may know about our friendship, and be willing to exploit that to draw her out. So for my safety and Lina's, I'm going to stay here until further notice. He said that my parents had received a note that was passed off as my handwriting, informing them that I had joined a search party in North Conway, still looking for Lina and that I was going to stay until further notice. I'm sure my parents will still be worried sick, and likely furious about my "decision" when I get back, but at least it's easier to explain that then getting stuck in another dimension. So I'm trying to make the best of it, find where I might fit in here.

Tonight, fitting in means hunkering down in one of the busier Dorm lounges, sipping a latte, and trying to read a book. Trying, because it's some kind of contemporary fantasy novel, and fantasy written in a world that already feels like something out of a storybook is infinitely confusing. Finally, I just give up, discarding the book on an empty coffee table as I focus on sipping my drink. I don't even realize that someone's in front of me until Eliza plops herself down in the chair opposite mine, sipping from a cup of scalding hot black coffee.

The fact that she's being seen in public with me is odd enough, and I raise an eyebrow.

"What?" she shrugs, "The other half of the lounge is full."

"Uh-huh," I mumble, "Or maybe you just enjoy my company."

"Shut up."

"That's not a denial. So you agree that we're friends now?"

"I'll agree that you're only the third most irritating person I know," she snorts.

"Oh yeah? And who's the first?"

"I'd have to hand that to your pal, little miss *savior of the Realms* and all that."

"You mean Lina?" I ask, a bit surprised. "Why, exactly?"

Eliza scoffs. "I don't trust that girl. She acts too noble but is all too quick to discard any rule she doesn't want to follow. And having Lillian as her counterpart? That's sketchy. Besides," she takes another sip of coffee, "She just gets on my nerves."

"Having Lillian as a counterpart isn't her fault," I protest, having been filled in a little more over the past few days on who exactly Lillian is, and what having her as a counterpart means exactly.

"Sure it isn't," she says stiffly. "But I still don't think she has any right to act like she's all that just because she has her fancy falcon powers. Besides, what kind of *great person* is she, anyway? Didn't she just dump you here and forget all about you the moment her exciting new destiny called?"

I flinch. "It wasn't like that."

"Sure it wasn't."

After a couple more beats of silence, I ask, "Speaking of powers, I never actually learned what yours are?"

I know by now those guards are either Wolf Soldiers, with strength and battle skill, or Lynx Assassins, with the power of invisibility.

"That isn't any of your business," she replies cooly. I thought we were past this.

"Come on," I press, but the dangerous look in her eyes isn't like before. She wants me to drop the matter this time. So instead I jokingly say, "Fine. So, if I'm annoying, then why sit over here at all? Unless you do enjoy my company."

Her mouth twitches into a smile. "Maybe, but there is another reason."

I raise an eyebrow, "And what's that?"

Her voice lowers, as though she's worried about being overheard.

"How would you feel about putting those tech skills of yours to good use?"

"I'm listening."

"You remember that whole incident of Lillian somehow breaking into the palace, and using Marcus's coms room to incite this whole mess? Oh, wait, of course you do, you were the one who disabled the alarms to allow those friends of yours to find the footage in the first place."

I'm not sure if she's praising me, or accusing me, so I just nod.

"Well, Marcus tasked me with figuring this case out. He wants me finding out why Lillian sent that message, how she got that keycard of hers, if the camera footage picked her up anywhere else in the palace, stuff like that."

"Okay…" I'm waiting for her to mention what she wants from me exactly.

"Marcus said that bringing you into this case might be helpful," she explains, looking like she wants to disagree. "I've hit a dead end. He thinks that you, with your experience with Worlder technology, might have a fresh view of things, maybe spot something that was overlooked before."

"So you need my help, is what you're saying," I clarify, a smug smile forming. Eliza gives me a sour look.

"No… I just… Marcus thinks it could be beneficial."

"Oh, okay. So you should just tell Marcus that you've got it handled if you don't think you need my help."

My smug smile grows as Eliza's scowl deepens.

"Fine," she forces out through clenched teeth. "I could use your help. Happy?"

I nod. "Very much so, yes. I'll help you."

She sits back in silence, sipping cooly from her black coffee. Ugh, who can even drink that stuff anyway? I'll admit, I'm the kind of person who practically drinks cream and sugar with a drop of coffee. I'm not quite proud of it, but it's what I like.

"The correct response would be *thank you*," I point out, after waiting for a couple of beats of silence.

"I'll thank you if you find anything," she growls.

"You're pretty bad at asking for favors, you know."

"Alright. Conversation over. Let's get going," she sighs in exasperation, discarding her cup and standing from her chair.

"Oh, you meant right now?" I quickly down the rest of my latte in one gulp, my mouth scalding from the heat.

It's almost a whole five-minute walk from the Dorm to Marcus's coms room. Now, standing outside the familiar, intimidating door, I'm relieved that at least this time, I don't have to worry about disabling any alarms. Eliza slides what must be an authorized keycard because the door unlocks without a hitch.

The inside of the coms room is exactly as I remember it, messy and piled with wires and screens, though this time, the lack of confusion and fear allows me to appreciate this high-tech workshop.

"So, at this point," Eliza says, sliding into one of the seats in front of a glowing computer screen, "I've tried analyzing the video footage of the palace at the time the message was recorded, but the camera in this room is the only one still working. The rest of the cameras within the entire palace grounds were somehow disabled all at once. I don't even know how that's possible outside of one of the coms rooms.

That must have been why Lillian sent that message, to distract anyone in the main coms room from realizing that the rest of the footage had been cut out."

I nod. It makes perfect sense. That still doesn't explain how she did it. As I scroll through the footage files for the hundreds of other cameras, something catches my eye. Something isn't quite right.

"You said the cameras were disabled?" I clarify, to which she nods.

"But see here," I point to an abnormality on the computer screen, "The cameras still logged the time, meaning they must have been active, not turned off. These cameras weren't disabled, but rather the footage was deleted."

Eliza doesn't look convinced.

"How would she have done that? Again, she would have to have done that from the coms room, and the footage in here doesn't show her messing with anything."

"I would recognize this anywhere," I say, completely sure. "She used Worlder tech somehow, a planted bug in the camera systems somewhere else, that then wiped the footage for her."

Eliza's eyes widen, "So you could recover the deleted footage?"

"No," I say, shaking my head. "This bug she planted is beyond what I've ever seen, it's like she used Realm knowledge combined with Worlder technology. I can't reverse it."

"How would Lillian have gotten her hands on something like that?" Eliza presses.

"I don't know."

"The only Worlders that have ever been here are you and Emmalina."

"You honestly think I would have had something to do with this?" I snort. "I didn't get here until after the bug was planted and the message was recorded, remember?"

"I'm not accusing you," she says, tapping her nails on the tabletop. "I'm accusing the one person who did come from the worlds, and who got here just before this happened. Someone who has an undeniable connection to Lillian already."

I stare at her blankly, "Who?"

"Are you dumb?" she says, rubbing at her temples. "It's Lina, obviously!"

I actually laugh out loud at that. "That's impossible."

"What makes it so impossible?"

"Well, for one thing, I've known Lina for almost my entire life. She has trouble changing the password on her computer, never mind programming a high-tech virus capable of taking down otherworldly databases. Secondly, I may not know much about this place or even what's really going on, but I do know that Lina would never side with a mass murderer."

Eliza still looks skeptical.

"Well, no matter who did it, at least we have something new to present to the king," she says, standing from the chair.

"We should tell him about the deleted footage, and the planted bug."

I nod, "No accusing anybody based on guessing and personal distrust," I say pointedly. "You may not trust Lina, but I do. Before we go tossing her name around to the king, let's find who's really behind this."

Eliza rolls her eyes and sighs, but she doesn't argue, so I'll take that as an okay.

When we finally get to the king's throne room, we can hear multiple voices from inside.

One of the guards standing outside bars our path.

"The king and his council are meeting," he informs us. "Whatever it is, it'll have to wait."

"We're the ones who have been investigating Marcus's coms," Eliza says, unfazed. "The king told me to report back as soon as we found something. I'm sure the council will be interested in hearing as well."

The guard looks Eliza and me over with skepticism, but he ducks into the room and I can hear the voices pause as the guard speaks.

Finally, the king's voice calls, "You may enter."

Eliza strides into the throne room as though she owns the place, and I scramble beside her as the guard gives us another sideways look.

I freeze in my tracks as I take in the large table filling the room that hadn't been there last time, and the five regal figures seated around it.

Orlon, seated at the head of the table, ushers us forward. The other four, Marcus, two other men, and a young woman watch us closely as we come to stand before them.

I'm more than happy to let Eliza do all of the talking, as she begins to explain what I had noticed about the cameras and the bug. Marcus's eyes narrow with surprise. Before he can say anything, someone else speaks up.

It's one of the other men, tall and lanky, with rust-colored hair and a face that looks too narrow.

"That is absurd," he sneers, in a snively voice that grates on my nerves like nails on a chalkboard. "Such technology doesn't exist. The Worlder clearly doesn't know what he's talking about."

"Quiet, Aravian," Marcus says, clearly low on patience for the walking scarecrow seated beside him. "This doesn't concern you."

"This concerns all of us," one of the others, an old, hunched man, speaks up. "How do we know the boy isn't mistaken?"

"I understand your concern, general," the king says diplomatically, "But the reason we brought Cameron into this case in the first place is that we suspected that Worlder tech may be in play. We just needed someone who could recognize it to confirm what we had already guessed."

The last person in the room, the lovely young woman with dark skin and cascading ringlets of black hair, gives me an impressed look.

"If what you found is the truth, then we should look into it immediately, and prevent it from happening again. Good work, Cameron."

"Thanks," I say, my face warming slightly at the praise.

"It is good work indeed," Marcus says, looking lost in thought. I'm shocked, I didn't know Marcus even knew how to say a kind word. What he says next leaves me even more surprised.

"Now that you've confirmed our theory that Worlder and Realm tech can be combined, I have a new task for you two."

Eliza looks over at me imploringly, and I just shrug.

"I have been designing a device that should be capable of tracking Lillian's location using her unique magical signature, but the tracking chip we created only works within the Realms. We need Cameron to alter the chip using Worlder tech, so that we may be able to expand its locating abilities."

"The device is already built," the king adds. "The only thing you would need to do is find a way to sync a Worlder tracking device into the system."

I nod. I've worked with tracking chips before, mostly on phones, just out of curiosity. I think I might be able to incorporate that into whatever device they've built, with Eliza's help.

"I'll give it a try."

Aravian cuts us off before anyone else can say a word.

"This is ridiculous!" he exclaims. "You're trusting a Worlder and a trainee with one of the most important devices we've created? You can't be serious!"

"Aravian," the king says warningly. "We're giving them a chance. We've reached a dead end, it's time to try a new approach."

Aravian seems to bite back whatever retort building on his tongue, settling for only, "Yes, Your Majesty."

Marcus stands from his seat at the table.

"Come with me," he ushers us. He excuses himself from the meeting and leads Eliza and me back to his private coms room, where he pulls a fancy key from within his robes and unlocks a hidden panel in the wall. Inside is a small device, no larger than my palm, which he connects to one of the largest computer faces.

He slides a computer chip into my hand.

"Try not to break anything," he says dryly, before promptly exiting the room and leaving us alone with the tiny, priceless machine.

I take what looks like a magnifying glass from a side table, settling myself into a seat to study the device, with Eliza watching from over my shoulder.

The mechanisms are minuscule, and so fragile, that I have to be incredibly careful with every move I make. Pressing the computer chip into the device, the computer screen it's connected to flares up, showing what looks like rough satellite footage of the Realms.

That's how Eliza and I work, for hours upon hours, until my head begins to ache from staring at the tiny mechanisms for so long. I make a few edits to the computer chip, Eliza provides input, and the footage on the screen changes as I make my alterations.

Finally, with a slight whirring sound, the computer splits, now showing two identical maps instead of the Realms. The outline of familiar continents indicates that these are the worlds, Earth and Allrhea, and with a satisfying beep, a red dot begins to blink somewhere off the coast of North America.

It found it, Lillian's magical signature. I sit back with a whoop of victory, giving Eliza a high five. We did it. Now we can track her movements to her stronghold. I can't believe that I was able to do this, to use magical technology to track a supervillain! If you had told me a few weeks ago that I would find myself here, I would never have believed it.

Eliza claps a hand over my mouth to silence my celebration.

"Shut up," she hisses, "Look."

She points to a computer monitor showing camera footage of several cloaked figures standing around a door. Not just any door- it's the door to this room. They're right outside.

Eliza flicks on the audio just as one of them says in a hushed voice, "Get them and the tracking device."

She moves before the words can even comprehend in my mind, grabbing the device and ripping it forcefully from the computer, shoving it back into the hidden wall panel and sliding it closed with a click, throwing the key into a pile of junk, just as the door swings outward.

There are three of them, all in black cloaks with their faces hidden, barging into the room, lunging for the two of us.

Out of the corner of my eye, I see Eliza go down fighting with the two of them, holding her own until she loses her footing, her head hitting the side of a table, and she slumps to the ground.

I shout, but a hand is clamped over my mouth, a bag shoved over my head. Something hard and heavy makes contact with my temple, sending a shooting spark of pain down my body, and the world goes black.

CHAPTER 21

EMMALINA

We arrive at the Soul Realm on the third day, December 13th, as the sun is making its way towards the horizon, casting the entire mountain range in shadows.

We rode on the backs of the wolves, alternating to let them rest, and it is now Keira and Kai that carry us to the foothills of the lowest mountains that lay before us, a narrow passage barely wide enough to build a road through being the only visible way past the steep and craggy cliffs.

We ditched the vitalums a while back, not wanting to draw so much attention. Instead, we go on foot along the sidewalks built on either side of the road, blending into the heavy traffic, both on foot and by vehicle, crowding the singular street.

"So, let's review the plan," Reed says, traveling hood once more pulled up over his head. I snuggle deeper into my cloak, hating the chill wind slicing through the fabric. The clouds on the horizon, lit bright pink with the slowly setting sun, indicate that snow may be heading our way.

"Between what we took from the Mirror Palace, and what the TimeKeeper gave us, we should have enough money to purchase outfits suitable to blend into the festival," Alaina says.

"Then, when we infiltrate the Starlight Festival, we find a way undetected into the palace, and try to find where Anima keeps her Traveler's Mirror," I say, "But, where would we even begin to look for that?"

"The castle vaults," Jane says, gazing at the craggy cliffs on either side of us as we make our way along the road cutting through the mountain pass. "If we can find the vaults, which are typically in the lower parts of a castle, there's a good chance that's where the mirror would be stored."

"And if it isn't?" Nate says, pointing out one major flaw in our plan. Jane bites her lip.

"Then we improvise?"

I'm about to argue that it doesn't seem like our plan is very well thought out, when I stop in my tracks, taking in the view in front of me.

The breathtaking, sprawling city lies before us, glorious, in the dying rays of the sun.

Varallex. Capital of the Soul Realm, and the crowning jewel of Anima's territory.

And now we have to infiltrate it.

It has to be the most intricate and beautiful city I've ever seen. The mountains, jagged and snowcapped, rise around

Varallex like a protective wall, with this pass being the only clear way in or out. If that wasn't enough, the city itself seems to be built upon a huge island jutting out of a truly massive mountain lake. I mean, this body of water stretches so far that the shore is almost too distant to see. The lake sort of acts as a moat around the entire capital, with a few bridges spanning the length from the island to the beach we now stand upon.

Most of the bridges are small, acting more as docks or walking paths rather than real ways to come and go, most too narrow to drive a car along. It's the giant crystalline arching bridge reaching the mouth of the mountain pass that allows vehicles and pedestrians alike to enter and exit the city.

Varallex itself has houses and shops along the island edge leading to second-story hotels and restaurants, tall buildings, and skyscrapers all rising around the tallest architectural feat of all, the palace. The castle's lowest towers are joined to the tallest buildings by arching walkways and connecting bridges, so many structures touching and building upon each other that it's impossible to see where one begins and another ends.

"Woah," is all that comes to mind.

"I know, right?" Alaina says, her eyes alight with a wonder of her own. Reed nods.

"There really is nothing quite like it," he agrees.

We follow the road to the very edge of the rocky shore, where the glass-like structure of the main bridge reaches the pass. Unlike the entrance to the Shadow Realm, there is no one guarding the route to the island, simply allowing the hordes of people (tourists, I assume) to come and go as they please. We take the footpath running alongside, blending right in with the crowds of pedestrians bundled against the cold.

I stare in shock through the perfectly see-through bridge to the serene water below, watching the occasional small boat drifting by. I spot a yacht to my left, lazily drifting in the small waves.

"This reminds me of the throne room tower," I say, referencing the room where we can see hundreds of feet below us. The one we torched not too long ago.

Reed smiles. "That's because it's made out of the same stuff, as hard and strong as diamond but not nearly as rare, at least in the Mirror Realm anyway. It was a gift from Orlon to Anima after she sided with him in the last war, a show of peace."

We step foot on the island, onto the cobblestone.

Alaina strides to the nearest street vendor, takes a brochure and flips to the map of the city.

"Here," she says finger hovering over the far edge of the island labeled South Dock, beside the tiny drawing of a pontoon boat. "This is where Nate and I first met," they exchange small smiles. Her fingers drift on the map to a location not too far from where we stand.

"This is where we need to go," I look closer at the little shop labeled Bianca & Porsha's Boutique and Salon.

"That's not too far," Reed observes, looking over my shoulder at the brochure.

Stefan frowns at the sinking sun.

"I think that shortcut the Followers of Malum gave us put us a little ahead of schedule," he points out. "Our only chance to infiltrate the castle would be when Anima makes her grand appearance at the festival when security will be most focused on her, an hour before midnight."

"Stefan is right," Nate points out. "It's, like, 6 p.m. That gives us almost five hours to kill before we can even do anything."

Alaina crosses her arms. "Do you think I came all this way, to the *Starlight Festival,* with only the intention of finding the mirror?"

"Yes…?"

"Absolutely not!" she cries. "Trust me. We'll find that dusty old mirror, but first, we're going to have some fun."

Luckily we have so much time to waste because it seems like it's going to take *forever* for everyone to even get dressed. I'm putting most of the blame on Alaina, of course.

It didn't take us long to find the quaint building with bright letters reading *Bianca & Porsha's Salon and Boutique,* a cross between a fancy clothing store, and a hair and nail salon, sitting a little farther inland but still having a beautiful view of the water.

It's that view that I currently stare towards, trying to refrain from rolling my eyes, as the clock ticks past the hour mark and my friends are still not finished getting ready.

"Oh come on, Jane," Alaina grumbles from her spot outside one of the dressing rooms as she crosses her arms. "The red one is so plain. The pink one would look much nicer."

She holds up a pile of frilly pink lace in my direction, the look in her eyes reading *back me up on this*.

Alaina herself is wearing something quite similar, but in a sparkling turquoise hue, with a wide skirt like a princess's ball gown, accented with lacey sleeves and ruffles to the hem.

"I'm not wearing that," Jane shouts for the third time, from within the small dressing room stall.

"Are you all finished yet?" I hear Reed call as he strides from the waiting room into the boutique section, fiddling with the dark blue tie that Alaina made him wear. He's wearing a crisp black suit, pants, and a white shirt along with it, his hair combed to be a bit tamer. I have to admit, there is no denying it, he looks amazing. Like, movie-star amazing. Not that I would ever say that aloud. My face gets warm as his eyes land on me.

He does a double take and then tries to pretend he didn't.

Alaina had shoved a flowing blue dress into my arms before steering me to a stall, and I hadn't objected. It's tighter at the top, sleeveless, and flows like ruffles of blue water past my hips, pooling into a small train at my feet. It shimmers slightly when I move, like liquid woven into fabric.

Alaina had also done up my hair into a swirling updo with borrowed pins, strands curling past my face, and shared her travel-sized makeup kit (of course she brought a makeup kit). I had to admit, even I was impressed with how it turned out.

"She looks nice, doesn't she?" Alaina says, with a knowing smirk in Reed's direction. Reed's face turns as red as mine feels, as he nods.

Nate strides into the room after him, Stefan at his heels. I'm vaguely aware of Stefan also pausing, his eyes lingering on my face, but I just can't tear my gaze away from Reed.

Jane finally joins us, in a crimson gown that hugs her body and flows around her feet, her long black hair done up like mine, and striking red lipstick.

"Finally," I sigh, getting to my feet from where I had been sitting for so long.

"Don't blame me," Jane says, rolling her eyes. "Blame the fashion psycho over here who wouldn't let me pick a dress."

We send Stefan to pay for the outfits, we reason that Jane and Reed are too well known by their parents, my face will immediately get us caught, and we simply don't trust Nate to do it right. Luckily, the two owners of the place, two stylists who must be Bianca and Porsha, don't recognize Stefan as a wanted fugitive from the Mirror Realm, and no alarms are raised.

Stefan makes his way back to us, ushering us towards the door.

"We're all good," he assures me, as I duck my head so that strands of my hair fall to hide my face.

"You look great, by the way," he says with a small smile.
"Thanks," I say, returning it. "So do you."

It hadn't been Stefan that my eyes had landed on, and it hadn't been Stefan that I couldn't stop staring at and I feel a prick of guilt. But for what? I have no reason to feel guilty, he might not like me in that way, and neither of them probably does.

I'm overthinking this. Way too much overthinking happening here.

Luckily, as we pass through the doorway onto the city streets, something else grabs my attention.

The sun has completely set, but it's brighter than noon out here. Neon lights envelop the world around me, every building, sign, and street corner blazing with color, and music drifts from somewhere not too far away. As we make our way further into the city, I can't tear my eyes away from it all.

The entire city, it's like a cross between Las Vegas and Times Square in New York. Electronic billboards light up buildings. Sports cars unlike any I've ever seen on Earth, in the most bizarre colors, speed by on the streets. Traffic is directed by glowing orbs somewhat similar to the streetlights back at home. People in finery of all sorts crowd the streets, lining up to get into sparkling clubs and bars. I try not to make eye contact with anyone, still afraid of being recognized, but eventually, I begin to realize that Lillian herself could be strutting around this city-wide party, and everyone would be none the wiser, for all the attention they pay to their surroundings.

"Where are we going?" I say, raising my voice slightly to be heard over the thump of a speaker audible from a few blocks over.

"How does anyone get any sleep around here?" Nate says. "It's even crazier than I remember."

"It's a festival," Alaina points out. "It's bound to be crazy. To answer your question, Lina, we're heading for Central Square."

"I can see why it's called the city that outshines the stars," I say, the whole sky fuzzy from the light and color streaming from below, to the point where the stars aren't even visible.

"It's like this every night," Alaina says. "Not even just during the Festival. It's entirely solar powered," she points to solar panels lining the roof of every building, including the palace towers. "It's a relatively normal city during the day, charging up for this light show at night."

"Cool!"

I'm about to say more, maybe ask what's happening down at the so-called Central Square, when a flash of silver catches my eye. There, darting between rooftops is a silver falcon wing.

How could that be? I check my bracelet, is it possible I could have summoned Astral by accident? No, the silver metal is cool and ordinary, with no sign of the glowing that usually comes along with the magic. But if I didn't summon the silver falcon, then how was it here? Maybe it was just a wild bird.

Maybe it wasn't even a falcon at all.

Or maybe I'm just seeing things.

  I keep my eyes glued to the sky and the rooftops until we've reached the square. The Central Square is a giant, wide-open square of cobblestone, lined with cafes and gardens lit with strings of fairy lights, shadowed by hulking, lit-up skyscrapers. It is packed to the brim with people, dancing in the square, strolling through gardens, and dining at the outdoor restaurants, all dressed to their finest. A stage rises from the far side of the space, as the band's music blasts through speakers spaced all around people are jumping up and down and pumping their fists in the air. Lights from the stage wash over the crowd, making it hard to even see the faces of those around us. At least it will be hard to be recognized here.

  "Let's get food first," Nate says, face lighting up at the sight of the restaurants. There is absolutely no objection from anyone, we've been eating rations out of a backpack for days and we all are dying for an actual meal.

  We pick a restaurant more secluded than some of the others, meaning it's only crowded with a hundred people rather than thousands. The food is undeniably fantastic.

  I dig into the plate of salad before me, topped with chicken, exotic fruits, and some dressing that smells sweet, like mangos. The waiter sets a plate of grilled chicken and rice in front of Jane, to which Reed makes a face.

"Really? Chicken and rice? That's so plain," he gestures to the burger heaped on his plate. "Don't you want something with more, I don't know, *flavor?*"

Jane scowls at him.

"You all are so plain," he teases. "Lina's got a plate of glorified lettuce, and Stefan- what even is that?"

"It's mushroom ravioli," Stefan says, rolling his eyes. "Gross."

"At least I didn't order off of the kid's menu," Stefan sneers back.

Reed doesn't bother to even look offended as Alaina chimes in, "Stefan has a point, you know." She picks delicately at what looks like chicken parmigiana.

The waiter brings Reed a refill on his drink, something called lemon cobalt, which is bright blue. Is that a blue lemon? Weird.

I leave the three of them to their bickering, watching the people dancing in the square. There's a towering clock over the plaza, luckily with numbers instead of symbols, the hands ticking towards 10 p.m. by the time everyone finishes up.

Doubt is starting to creep into my mind. This won't be easy to pull off, impossible even. Never mind sneaking into the castle without being caught, we have to find a small handheld mirror among all of this. It's a gamble whether or not it will be in the vaults, or if we could even retrieve it. So many things could go wrong.

Reed pulls his chair up closer to mine while Jane goes to pay the bill with the TimeKeeper's money.

"Hey," he says gently. "Don't worry. We've gotten this far. What's finding some silly old mirror compared to the stuff we've survived so far?"

I give a quiet laugh at that. "Tell me about it," I sigh.

"No, really," he says. "You survived getting your whole world turned upside down. Not to mention the Tournament, and the Mimic Serpent."

"And the campsite, and that helicopter joyride," I snort.

"Don't forget getting to the Shadow Realm or surviving Oblivion of all things," he shudders.

"Those assassins weren't even scary compared to the Followers of Malum," I laugh. "I'm going to have nightmares about them for weeks."

"We made it through all of that," he says, green eyes shining with promise. "*You* have done all of that. This will be a piece of cake in comparison."

"Thanks," I say, really meaning it. "I like being friends a lot better than enemies."

He smirks. "Me too."

Reed then heaves himself to his feet, brushing off his jacket, before extending a hand in an exaggerated gentlemen's gesture.

"So, with all that out of the way, do you want to dance, Emmalina?"

I grin, taking his hand in mine as my heart soars on silver wings.

"I would love to, Reed."

Hand in hand with Reed Windervale of all people, I stride onto the plaza dance floor. I suddenly realize I don't know how to dance.

The band begins a new song, upbeat, and everyone begins to murmur with excitement. People break into a partner dance, kind of like square dancing but with a lot more body movement, and I wonder how I'll ever be able to keep up.

Reed grips my hand, showing me the steps.

"Like this," he demonstrates slowly, moving his feet in four simple steps, guiding me as we go. Right, turn, left, twirl. Then he adds in the hand clapping and links his arm with mine. Right, turn, left, twirl, clap, switch arms.

I get the hang of it quick enough, moving faster and faster until I can do the steps easily enough. The song builds into a faster tempo, and before I know it, Reed and I are moving through the crowd, faces a blur all around us, nothing but the music and the feel of his hand in mine.

When the song ends, when the band begins another, we keep dancing. We dance until my lungs are burning and I'm sweating despite the cold, but the joy in my chest matches the beat of the music, both of us grinning like maniacs.

Then there's another hand on my forearm, startling me out of my daze.

Stefan.

"Do you mind if I take the next dance?" he asks with a smile, but that smile doesn't quite reach his eyes as he seems to stare down at Reed.

"Uh, sure," Reed backs away, brushing his no longer neat hair out of his face, giving me a parting smile. The look he gives Stefan isn't so friendly.

Stefan ignores the look, guiding me back into the throng of people. He's a good dancer, great actually, leading us in a slower dance far more graceful than Reed and I had been. More graceful, but I can't help but feel a twinge of disappointment as Reed disappears back into the crowd, finding himself another dance partner most likely.

I spot a flash of sparkling turquoise out of the corner of my eye, Alaina. The skirts of her dress twirl around her as Nate spins her in a circle, moving swiftly and fast. Nate never struck me as the dancing type, but he keeps up well. I guess if you're dating Alaina, you kind of have to learn these things. I laugh in his direction and he makes a face, the four of us switching partners and back again. I spot Jane for a split moment in the crowd, dancing with a stranger, before Stefan and I lose the others.

I don't know how long I've been doing this, I haven't seen Reed for what feels like hours, when the final song comes to a close, the band on the stage taking their bows. I stand for a moment, still hand in hand with Stefan, as I try to catch my breath. His eyes are alight with joy, but I can't stop myself from peering around to find where Reed may have been hiding out.

There. I spot the shape of his tall form at the edge of the plaza, leaning arms-crossed on one of the small fences bordering the gardens. He lifts his hand in a lazy wave, the lights from the stage tinting the planes of his face and ends of his hair with blues and purples. I slip my hand away from Stefan intending to make my way over there, when the noise of the crowd begins to quiet, the lights of the stage shifting. One of the largest billboards I've ever seen flickers to life above the plaza, bathing the streets with a glow brighter than I've ever seen, depicting a digital clock beginning the hour-long countdown to midnight.

The entire square erupts with cheering and applause as a figure steps from the curtains onto the stage where the band had stood. The person we've been waiting for. Another piece of our plan is put into action as Queen Anima smiles down upon the festival.

She's wearing a dress woven of fine gold, her shining blonde hair pulled into an updo of cascading curls. Her smile is as dazzling as the glittering crown perched atop her head. She looks so young and beautiful, despite being a several thousand-year-old immortal, with a face filled with kindness and joy.

"Welcome, one and all," her voice echoes from the speakers, but the square has fallen so quiet that she probably doesn't even need the microphone. "I trust you've all had a grand time here in Varallex, but I assure you, the celebrations have only just begun."

As Anima continues her announcement, I feel a hand on my shoulder. Reed has his eyes still fixed on the stage as he murmurs to Stefan and me, "It's now or never. I'm going to find the others while you two make your way out of here. Meet us outside of the palace entrance, we'll regroup there and make a plan. Got it?"

Stefan gives a sharp nod.

"We'll be there," I promise. With that, Reed turns and disappears into the crowd riveted on Anima, leaving Stefan and me to make our way out of the square and back onto the street. We have to move slowly, pretending to try and get better views of the stage, before slipping away. When we're a healthy distance away from any prying eyes, Stefan takes my hand in his as the icy trickle of invisibility washes over us both.

The palace's main entrance isn't too far and would be incredibly hard to miss. The security seems pretty lax too, only two guards wearing imperial golden armor, lazily dangling their spears beside them, looking bored out of their minds. They're probably wishing they were at the festival rather than keeping watch over a street of partygoers and drunk revelers.

We wait, invisible, watching the busy street for any sign of our friends, the gilded palace doors barely 20 feet away from where we stand. We can't infiltrate the palace invisibly, those flickering lights flanking the double doors, made to mimic fire glow, aren't merely decorations like the rest of this city. Stefan recognized them as what he called *visalight*, light that can reveal invisibility, like the spotlights on that helicopter had been. Security may look lax, but they would definitely notice a bunch of teenagers trying to sneak right past them invisibly. There must be another entrance to the palace then, some other way in that might not be guarded.

That's when I spot them, the others, merely shadows against the far wall. The broad shape of Reed's shoulders, the hint of ruffles from Alaina's dress, all four of them leaning casually on the edge of the street corner. The ordinary bystander's eyes would skip right by them, thinking them to be a group of teenagers taking a quick break from a night of partying, but their expressions give them away. Focused, searching, eyes sweeping the streets for Stefan and me.

I'm hit with a dizzying wave of deja vu at the sight of it, thrusting me back into the memory of standing on a street corner like this one, with another friend of mine, spotting Reed, Jane, and Alaina staring in my direction from their casual stances against the outside of a shop. Now they're not strangers to me, now the friend I'm standing with is someone I've known for weeks rather than years. Now my mission isn't something as simple as finding a quiet place to spend an afternoon, but rather finding a way to break into a palace in a different dimension. How things can feel so similar, but be so vastly different.

I just tug Stefan's arm, and he notices them as well. We cross the street to meet with them, becoming visible again once we're under cover of the little bit of shadow that can exist in a city as bright as this.

Let me add, crossing the street seems like a simple action, but have you ever tried it while invisible? Crosswalks mean nothing when the cars can't see you. It's one big, dangerous game of how fast can you run hand in hand and unable to see your own feet, and can you dodge the cars? It's illegal, according to one of the signs lining the many crosswalks reading:

Vitalums must cross at designated crosswalks

Vehicles ONLY on street, riding a wolf vitalum is not permitted

The use of invisibility when crossing is PROHIBITED BY LAW

Violators will be fined

Whoops.

As we reappear beside our friends, Reed jumps.

"Oh, hey. Uh, what happened to you two?" Reed asks, raising an eyebrow as we stop to catch our breath.

"Stefan almost got us killed," I huff. "Invisibility. Crosswalk."

Jane crosses her arms. "Why?" she asks, with the most tired and fed-up expression. "In what world is that a good idea? You couldn't just cross the street normally, without the whole invisible secret agent nonsense?"

"We were standing twenty feet away from the guards," Stefan retorts. "It would draw their attention to reappear right in front of them, and they could potentially recognize Emmalina."

"I've always said that they should put visalight in the car headlights, specifically for when people make dumb decisions like that," Reed snorts.

"All that aside," Alaina speaks up, brushing loose strands of hair from her face. "Anima didn't draw all the guards away as we hoped. How are we supposed to get in?"

Reed frowns. No one offers any ideas. Until Nate clears his throat.

"Leave this to me," he says with a wink. "It's my turn to have the crazy ideas."

Jane makes a sound somewhere between a laugh and a snort.

"And what, exactly, would this plan of yours be?"

"You'll see," Nate says, pushing off from the wall and sauntering off down the sidewalk. "All you guys need to do is slip by the guards while they're distracted."

"Distracted by what?" Stefan says, confused. His question is answered as Nate pulls Alaina's brochure of the city from a pocket in his jacket, flipping through it with a look of intense concentration, occasionally looking around as though he's lost. He takes the crosswalk (legally) across the street, and wanders in the direction of the palace entrance.

"What is he doing?" I ask.

"No clue," Alaina says.

But one by one, we cross the crosswalk, trying to simply act the part of distracted partygoers, until we take up our earlier place closer to the guards. The guards aren't focused on us. No, they're focused on Nate now, who has wandered up to the base of the palace steps, nose buried in the brochure.

"Can we help you?" one of the guards, a short and wiry woman, asks, giving Nate a look as he begins to climb the steps.

"Sir, you can't be up here," the second guard, a bulky man with a scowl, holds out a hand as if to stop Nate from going any further, but Nate just looks up from his brochure and clasps the man's hand in a sincere handshake.

"Oh, hello, sir!" Nate says, his voice matching his bright and somewhat clueless smile. He waves the brochure in the guard's face, and the man tries to swat him away, confused.

"I was with a tour group, you see, but they seem to have left without me, how strange. I know the meeting place was a restaurant, or maybe it was a cafe? Sir, is this a restaurant, or a cafe?" Nate asks questions rapidly, all the while trying to push past the guards to see into the palace doors, waving around his brochure.

"This is the palace, dimwit," the woman says with an eye roll.

"Oh," Nate makes a show of looking surprised. "The palace? Are you sure? Because right here it says… oh, never mind. Would you two be so kind as to point me in the direction of this restaurant?" he stabs his finger into a random point on his map.

The man rests his hand on the hilt of his dagger, not completely buying Nate's clueless tourist guise.

"Wait," he says, with narrowed eyes. Aren't you... you're one of those fugitives from the Mirror Realm!" he exclaims, drawing his blade.

"What?" Nate says, putting on a good show of looking baffled. "No... no I'm not."

"Yes, you are," the man begins to advance on Nate, but he only smiles, backing away. Then he turns and sprints off down the street.

"If I'm a fugitive, then catch me if you can!" Nate shouts, as the guards unsheathe their weapons and give chase, shouting into walkie-talkie things on their vests for backup.

Leaving the entrance to the palace wide open. It can't be this easy.

"Quick," Jane says, aiming for the doors. "Before more guards arrive."

"But what about Nate?" Alaina says, face pale as she stares off to where Nate and the guards disappeared around a street corner.

"Go get him," Reed says, following Jane. "Use your invisibility, find him and lay low. Meet at the firework docks at midnight."

Alaina nods curtly, before dropping a veil of invisibility over herself and vanishing into the night.

That leaves Reed, Stefan, Jane, and I to infiltrate the palace, find this mirror, and meet the other two by midnight, or we'll all be caught. No problem.

CHAPTER 22

While the streets are packed and overflowing with festival celebrations, the castle is comparably empty. We haven't come across any guards, either busy protecting Anima while she makes her public appearance, or preoccupied with chasing down Nate. Well, now that one guard knows that the fugitives from the Mirror Realm are here, it won't be long before this place is swarming with Anima's men. Once Anima knows, we can be sure that Orlon and Marcus will know before long too. So we have to hurry, get that mirror, and get out of here.

Reed has the vial that we got from the Followers of Malum, the anchor that will allow the mirror to take us to Lillian's stronghold, tucked safely in his jacket pocket, ready to be used. The guards will no doubt follow us wherever we go, but that's a plan for another time. We're apparently very good at coming up with plans on the spot. Speaking of surprise plans…

"Who knew Nate could have a good idea every now and then," Reed jokes, trying to lighten the mood as we briskly walk down a corridor. Our current plan is to find Anima's vaults.

Castle vaults, according to my friends, are typically in the lower levels, right above the dungeons.

"The dungeons?" I ask. "That's actually a thing?" Reed nods.

"We have guard stations, kind of like police stations, for the usual lawbreakers. But real criminals, or people that tend to be hard to contain, go to the dungeons."

"What are the chances we get put in Anima's dungeons for this?" I ask, not entirely joking.

"Very high," Jane answers for them. "So let's not get caught."

"Good plan."

We come across a staircase, with levels leading both up and down.

"Well, if we're trying to find the vaults, down is our best bet," Reed says. No sooner than the words leave his lips, a light, lilting voice says, "I'm afraid, Mr. Windervale, you won't find much down there."

Oh no. We are in so much trouble now.

Queen Anima's rose-painted lips lift in a small smile.

The four of us gape like deer caught in headlights. There is no lie, nothing we can make up to get out of this. Reed quickly drops to a knee, bowing his head, and the rest of us know enough to follow suit.

"Your Majesty," Jane says, her voice steadier than mine would be. "We… we were just, uh…"

The queen shakes her head.

"Don't lie to me. I think it would be in both of our interests to hold this conversation with a shred of honesty, don't you think?"

Jane's excuse dies in her throat.

"Please," I say softly. "We can explain."

"What an interesting explanation this should be," her eyes, a golden color similar to Stefan's, fix on mine. "After all, Lillian's reflection and her band of renegade heroes, here in my palace, when they should be off on their quest in Oblivion, is very perplexing. Wouldn't you say?"

My mouth opens and closes a few times, my brain is unsure whether to come up with an excuse or a question. Reed beats me to it.

"How did you know about our quest?"

Her smile widens, but it is not unkind.

"I happen to be good friends with the TimeKeeper. He said that you were searching for Lillian's stronghold in the desert Oblivion. So how has your search led you here?"

She knows the TimeKeeper, he told her. Why would he trust Anima more than Orlon, or King Umbra? How else would she know? If the TimeKeeper trusts her… maybe we won't have to spend so much time searching for the mirror, if Anima is willing to give it to us.

"We went to Oblivion, to find the Followers of Malum," I begin to explain, and the queen nods. "The TimeKeeper thought Lillian was hiding out there, but she isn't. Long story short, her and her prisoner, and some kind of dagger are somewhere in the worlds and we need a Traveler's Mirror to find her."

Anima nods with understanding. "So you came here, for the one I keep in my chambers."

"Your chambers?" Jane asks.

"Yes. I doubt you would have had much luck down there," she smirks as she waves her hand in the direction of the stairs that we had been about to take.

"You'll just let us have it?" I say, not trusting this for a moment.

"Why would you help us?" Jane asks suspiciously, with narrowed eyes. "Refusing to turn in another Realm's fugitives, helping them."

"I am aware of the risks," Anima fold her delicate hands over her golden dress. "My belief in the TimeKeeper's visions triumphs my loyalty to the other Realms, even Orlon. Besides, I wish Lillian caught as much as anyone."

She turns, striding off into the corridor without another word, just a wave of her hand indicating we should follow.

"What about our friends, Nate and Alaina?" Reed asks, keeping pace. "They're the ones that created the diversion."

"Ah. I was wondering why the TimeKeeper had claimed there were six, yet I only found four."

"They're out there in the city somewhere, evading the guards."

"I'm afraid I can be no help to them," Anima says with a slight frown, taking a different staircase up. "If I were to call off my guards, it would imply that I'm helping you. As you said, I would risk angering the Mirror Realm. So I'm afraid that once you have your mirror, you are on your own."

"Why aren't your guards with you?" I demand, my legs beginning to ache from climbing so many stairs with still more to go.

"They are busy hunting the fugitives, who they say fled into the night. I assume those were your friends?"

I nod.

By the time we make it to Anima's chamber, the clock is ticking past 11:30 p.m. Not much more time until midnight, when we're expected to meet Alaina and Nate. If we hadn't run into Anima, who knows how long it would have taken? We might have never even found the mirror at all.

The queen emerges from her room with the mirror in hand. It is a perfect twin to the one that had been in the cabin safe house, oval-shaped glass that is so perfectly clear I almost expect it to ripple like water as I touch it, leaving no smudge or fingerprint. It has an intricate, sparkling frame and handle, the most fitting mirror for a queen.

"Can we use the mirror to portal us to Nate and Alaina, the dock where you told them to meet us?" I ask hopefully, but of course, our luck doesn't extend that far.

"No, without something anchoring it, it can't take us anywhere. If we tried to travel through it now, we would get trapped in that in-between place forever."

I swallow. "Let's not do that, then."

Anima accompanies us back down the stairs and to a back entrance to the palace reserved for herself and her court, thankfully free of guards.

"Once you are out of this passage, the main street will take you past the square," Anima instructs briskly. "The South Dock where the fireworks will be hosted will be your best bet for going unnoticed, my guards will be expecting you to run from the busier parts of the city, not towards them. You can use the mirror from there."

"Thank you," Jane says, her voice sincere. "Thanks for your help."

Anima nods, her crown glittering. "Good luck. May the power of the Realms be with you."

We make it to the dock with mere minutes to spare. Hopefully, Alaina and Nate were lucky enough to evade the guards and make it here safely.

The four of us scan the damp wooden docks overlooking the lake, which reflect the pulsing lights of the city at our backs. Anima was right, we saw more guards centered around the palace and main streets than here, where the crowds are gathered upon the docks. It seems like everyone in Varallex has come here for the fireworks. Hundreds of boats drift in the water, teeming with people trying to get a better look. The docks are so crowded that we can barely get off the streets, but there is no way any guard could pick us out from here. It also brings the problem of finding Nate and Alaina, which is looking to be an impossible mission.

Unable to even make it onto the dock, we stay back towards the streets, listening to faint music trickle from the square.

"Okay, the plan is we split up," Jane says, adjusting the daggers in her hair.

"Split up? Isn't that the problem?" Stefan points out.

"To find them, we need to spread out," Jane insists. "I'll go left, Stefan will go right, and you two will stay here to wait for us to get back," Jane indicates to Reed and me.

Stefan frowns, looking between Reed and me like he wants to object, but Jane slips away into the throng of people before he can. With a grudging sigh, he ducks right, leaving Reed and me alone.

"So," Reed says, after a beat of silence. "We have nothing to do but keep a lookout. So maybe we should finish our dance?"

He gives me a crooked grin, hand outstretched. A slow song is playing from the square's speakers, faint and sweet, something about chasing falling stars.

I take his hand, his fingers wrapping around mine. He pulls me close, putting his hands on my waist as I rest mine on his shoulders. Like before, I let him lead, moving as he moves, letting the music fill my very soul. His hands are warm and gentle, his smile brighter than all of the lights around us. The world melts away until it's just him and I, dancing slowly to the music, so close I can see his breath clouding in the cold night air.

The distance between us gets smaller, until all I can see, all I can focus on, is his green eyes, his lips so close to mine.

"Are we, uh, interrupting something?" Nate's voice asks from behind us. Reed and I leap apart as if we had been electrocuted.

"Nate, " Alaina's voice chides, "Of course we're interrupting something." I spin to see the two of them standing mere feet away.

"We, uh… that was just… we were…" Reed stammers, looking back and forth between me and them. He's saved from having to explain by the stroke of midnight chiming from the clock in the square.

All at once, every single light in the entire city, every billboard, window, and streetlamp, goes out, plunging the world into darkness.

I almost believe I've gone blind, until my eyes slowly begin to adjust enough to the sudden darkness to make out the outlines of my friends, of Reed still standing beside me.

"What's happening?" I say, unable to be sure who I'm facing.

"It's starting," I hear Jane's voice from my left, as the shapes of her and who I assume is Stefan take up places beside us.

"Look," I hear Stefan whisper. I don't need to be able to see him, to know that he's pointing at the sky. The sky, which before had been clouded and dulled by the light of the city was now lit up with a display of stars almost as spectacular as those I had seen in Oblivion.

"During the Starlight Festival, at the stroke of midnight, every town and city in every Realm goes dark to appreciate the beauty of the stars," Alaina explains softly. "Then the fireworks show begins. Just wait until you've seen it."

"I've seen fireworks before," I say.

"Not like these, you haven't," Reed snorts. "I can guarantee that."

No sooner did he finish his sentence, than a high-pitched whine fills the air, growing steadily louder, drawing everyone's attention back to the sky. Where a speck of reddish light trails like a shooting star, higher and higher, until it reaches its peak and explodes.

The firework shatters into a shimmering blaze of sparks, similar to any I've seen on Earth until the sparks of red light begin to take a very particular shape. A 3D form of a wolf, huge and comprised of thousands of flickering, hissing sparks. If that wasn't awe-inspiring enough, the wolf tips its head back, a very real-sounding howl tearing through the night, echoed by a cheer from the crowd.

The sparks move as one, propelling the wolf down towards the mass of gathered onlookers, shimmering paws moving as though it's running on air. It skims over our heads, so close I can feel the heat of the life-like fireworks against my face. Then disappears, sparks fizzling into nothing. Applause like a rumble of thunder echoes off of the mountains.

A volley of regular fireworks is shot into the sky. Then a second spark, as noticeably bright as the last one, this time a shimmering gold, streaks into the stars above before erupting into the shape of a leaping lynx cat, complete with a short bob tail and tufted ears. This one doesn't make any noise other than the crackle of fireworks, its blazing form leaping for the crowd, coming so close that a shout leaves my lips and I duck on instinct. When I look up again, the fiery lynx is gone. Well, that was shorter and a tad less exciting than the last one, but before I can say so out loud, a *boom* like a clap of thunder shakes the dock as the lynx explodes back into existence, seemingly out of nowhere, streaking back across the sky.

Oh, I get it. It's mimicking a Lynx Assassin's ability to become invisible and reappear somewhere else. Before I can even begin to wonder how these fantastic displays are possible, the golden lynx fizzles away as the wolf had done.

Following the lynx, a grand finale of regular fireworks lights up the night, while my friends and I tear our eyes away from the scene. I make out the form of two guards, Anima's men, lurking at the edge of the crowd. If they spot us, it would make things a lot more difficult, and besides, we've wasted enough time already. We have to go.

I have the Traveler's Mirror, still clutched and hidden in the folds of the sweater wrapped around my shoulders, and Reed pulls the anchor vial from his pocket. Before he can pull out the cork, the firework finale dies out, followed by a round of applause. The whole crowd collectively turns away, shielding their eyes, and before I can ask why Jane ushers us all into a darker alley beside us.

The entire city flickers back to life, lights blooming across the buildings, blinding and unexpected. As I blink the dancing spots from my vision, I realize why the darker alley was necessary. With the docks lit bright once more, we would have easily been spotted by those guards. Even with the city blindingly bright around us, they are still bound to notice the flash as we travel through the mirror. It won't be long before they follow us to the worlds.

I don't even get the chance to voice that concern before the city is once more abruptly plunged into darkness, every light suddenly dying out again. My eyes can't take all this adjusting back and forth.

Apparently, this wasn't supposed to happen. The crowd teems with shouts of surprise, and even my friends beside me glance around at the sudden city-wide power outage.

"What?" Alaina starts to ask when another high-pitched whine fills the air. Another firework? Everyone in Varallex seems to hold their breath as we watch the silver spark of light make its way higher and higher. A collective gasp of shock ripples through the world as the firework explodes, and the form of a silver falcon's outstretched wings fills the heavens.

Flight Of The Falcon

My bracelet grows warm, emitting a faint glow, as though it's reacting to the form of the bird in the sky, crackling and hissing with silver flames. No applause follows, just still, shocked silence. I'm guessing the falcon wasn't supposed to happen either.

"How is this possible?" Reed mutters, but his eyes widen as he turns to me, the silver light reflected in them. He's staring at my bracelet, my vitalum token, faintly glowing.

"Are you doing it?" he forces out. "But... how?"

"I'm not doing anything," I say, as the firework streaks over our heads, and moves across the city, barely avoiding skimming the towers of the palace. It gives a harsh squawk, like a challenge to the mountains themselves, before shattering into a million fizzling sparks and vanishing almost as abruptly as it appeared. Once it's gone, my bracelet's glow fades with it.

What just happened? And why are my friends looking at me like it was my fault?

"How did you do that?" Stefan demands, his face pale. "You shouldn't be able to..."

"Guys, we'll have to talk about this later," Jane says, pointing around the alley corner to the guards moving to investigate, probably drawn here by the glow of my bracelet in the dark.

"They know we're here."

Reed curses as he forces the cork from the vial, the dark liquid within shimmering.

"Quick," he commands. "One sip, everyone."

- 427 -

"How do we know that it's safe?" Stefan protests. "I mean, can we really trust the Followers of Malum not to betray us?"

"Don't be a coward, Fides, just drink the potion," Alaina says, making a face as she drinks from the anchor vial. Looking like he might regret this, Stefan begrudgingly takes it from her.

Reed swings his sword, clashing with the guards at the mouth of the alley, the commotion causing several surprised and frightened screams from the bystanders beyond. As I finally grasp the vial, draining the last of it, I have to fight a gag at the horrible, burning taste. The empty vial slips from my fingers, shattering on the damp brick of the alley floor.

Alaina takes the handheld mirror from my hands, light bursting at her fingertips as she feeds magic into the portal, a doorway of that light opening up before us.

"Guys, it's now or never!" Reed shouts, ducking and aiming a kick at the guard in front to send him sprawling.

I feel a hand on my back, Jane's, shoving me forward and into the portal, light consuming the still dark world around me, and I'm on my way.

To where Lillian's fortress lies, wherever that may be.

CHAPTER 23

You would think that after traveling by portal several times before, I would be used to it by now. You would be wrong.

There is a sharp, tugging sensation in my gut, like the anchor potion I ingested is physically pulling me towards my destination. The icy chill of this in-between place seems to seep into my very bones. After what feels like ages of this nothingness, I begin to panic. What if Stefan was right, and the anchor potion was some sort of trick? What if it isn't an anchor at all, and I'll be trapped here forever?

Then my feet hit solid ground, and for a moment, I simply try to get my bearings. The portal is at my back, blazing like a star, illuminating a small, dark room. I move out of the way in the nick of time, as Jane comes barreling through the portal behind me, followed closely by Stefan, Nate, Reed, and finally Alaina.

The portal flickers and closes, the mirror in Alaina's hand going dark.

"I think I'm going to be sick," Nate grumbles. "That stuff was disgusting."

Alaina grumbles her agreement, feeling around on the wall in front of us until she finds a light switch, casting the room in a yellowish glow from two small lightbulbs fitted in the ceiling. We appear to be standing in a hotel room of sorts, one that's a bit old and run down. The room we're piled in is a cross between a kitchenette with a cracked tile floor and dusty countertops, and a sagging couch pushed up against a window with drawn curtains. A doorway to our right leads to a bedroom with a singular bed that looks like it's never been used, and the door to the left is a bathroom.

"Where are we?" I ask, frowning at the window.

"I don't know," Jane answers, turning in a circle as she assesses the place. "I've never been in this safe house."

"This is a safe house? Like the cabin?"

"It must be because that is where the Followers of Malum said the anchor was tied to. The safe house closest to Lillian's base, but where is here, exactly?"

Alaina draws back the curtains, frowning at the wonderful view of a white-painted wall right beside us. Well, that's no help.

Filing out of the room, the six of us make our way down a dingy hallway with carpeted floors, all lights dim or off completely. There is a set of elevators at the end of the hall, leading me to believe that my first guess was correct, we're in a hotel of sorts.

We take the elevator to the lobby floor. Six overdressed teenagers, two armed with blades, listening to elevator music and trying to process the night we've just had. The lobby is small, with an empty front desk and a few scattered chairs. Like the cabin, this place seems to be merely a prop, unused and abandoned, but the electricity still works somehow.

Alaina peers out of one of the lobby windows, at a well-lit street. While this hotel seems a bit sad and abandoned, the rest of this place certainly isn't. I almost believe we've simply portaled our way to another part of the Soul Realm, but no, that's salty ocean air outside mixed with the smell of cigarettes, car exhaust, and the faint scent of fast food.

The sky overhead is still dark, the clock above the desk reading half past midnight, but the red cobbled streets are still packed with people walking, riding bikes, and the occasional sports car rumbling by, all under the light of streetlamps and neon signs outside of hotels, restaurants, and bars. Pounding music drifts through the air, and I catch the sight of swaying palm trees and a stone wall across the street blocking the view of the ocean. Somewhere tropical, then? The air sure is humid enough.

There is a pile of pamphlets on the front desk like someone had haphazardly tossed them there, with a picture of a palm tree and the words *Welcome to South Beach, Miami.*

Miami? As in Florida?

"Why would Lillian be hiding out somewhere in Florida?" I asked, brandishing the pamphlet. "Vacationing? It might be oh so tiring to be a wannabe evil queen."

Nate chuckles.

"Maybe her stronghold is a sandcastle," I snort, but no one seems to get the joke.

"A castle made of sand?" Jane asks tentatively.

"Right, I forgot, the whole no beaches in the Realms thing. Well, remind me when all of this is over to teach you all how to build sandcastles, okay?" I shake my head, plopping myself in one of the chairs in the lobby.

"Sandcastles aside," Reed says. "I think there is something we need to discuss. Like how you summoned that falcon."

"Me?" I ask. "I didn't summon anything. At least, I don't think I did. Do you think it happened by accident? Maybe my new magic is unstable or something."

"It's not just something that can happen by accident," Jane shakes her head, taking a seat of her own. "Those aren't real fireworks, not exactly. A traditional firework is infused with very powerful raw magic, which takes the shape of the wielder's vitalum when set off, and has to be maintained and controlled by whoever casts it. There's no way you could have done it. For one thing, you weren't anywhere close to the fireworks, and secondly, it takes an incredible amount of power and effort. Only the strongest guards can cast one, and even if you could, it wouldn't be by accident."

"We haven't ever seen a falcon firework," Alaina says, twirling a strand of hair from her collapsing updo around a finger. "There hasn't been anyone to cast one since they were invented. It was very cool."

"It is not cool," Reed cuts in. "A Falcon Warrior had to have cast it, and if it wasn't Lina…"

"Do you think it was Lillian?" Stefan asks.

"No, the falcon was silver. Like Lina's falcon and her bracelet was glowing."

"Maybe the Followers of Malum gave her too much power."

"I didn't do it," I snap. "I'm sure of it. The bracelet started glowing on its own."

"How would we explain the second power outage?" Nate points out. "That has to be done manually. Someone else had to have shut down the power, meaning they must have known about it, meaning it was probably planned beforehand. But by who?"

Everyone stares at Nate for a second. He crosses his arms.

"Hey, just because I joke around sometimes doesn't mean I'm dumb. I've been paying attention."

"Nate's right," Jane forces out. "I don't think I've ever said that before, and I never will again, so enjoy that."

"I'm tired," I say, leaning back. "Let's just toss it onto our pile of already existing mysteries to be solved. It doesn't matter now anyway."

Alaina sighs. "We should get some rest. We can focus on this later, but for now, we have to be ready. Tomorrow we set out to find Lillian's stronghold."

Resting was a fabulous idea, I haven't gotten this much sleep in almost a week. I hadn't even realized quite how tired I was until my head hit the pillow in one of the tiny hotel rooms along this three-story building. There are enough rooms that we could each claim our own, choosing the least abandoned-looking ones we could find. We all slept until late morning, the sun well overhead, making the hotel rooms feel suffocatingly hot and muggy.

Alaina granted herself the job of going door to door to wake everyone up, knocking sharply until I was forced to roll out of bed and answer it. She's standing in the doorway with a hand on her hip, the other clutching a bundle of fresh clothes. Alaina appears to have already showered and freshened up, smelling faintly of lavender, dressed in a glittery red tank top, a skirt, and cheap plastic flip-flops, even going as far as to perch a pair of sunglasses on the bridge of her nose.

"Rise and shine," she says in an annoyingly sing-song voice. Of course, she's a morning person. She only piles the change of clothes into my arms, gesturing at my rumpled blue dress and collapsed updo that has become flattened to one side.

"Go shower and get dressed. We've got a long day ahead of us, and this may be our only chance to freshen up." With that, she closes the door again, humming as she goes to wake up somebody else. She was right about the shower and new clothes. We haven't had the chance since the Shadow Realm, and I probably stink of sweat. The shower is heavenly, washing away the grime of Oblivion. Lukewarm water and cheap lavender body soap never felt so luxurious.

The fresh clothes, a flowy crop top, shorts, and flip flops, are so much less stifling than traveling cloaks or layers of dress ruffles. Refreshed, I make my way to the hotel lobby, finding Alaina, Jane, and Reed already waiting. Jane picks at her black tank top.

"Where did you get these?" she asks Alaina, who shrugs.

"I poked around, found the emergency stash of money and the safe house's Traveler's Mirror in the front desk drawer. I took it upon myself to visit a souvenir shop and buy us some new clothes to better blend in."

Reed nods, "Good thinking."

The elevator dings, allowing Stefan and Nate to join us in the lobby, both dressed similarly to Reed in tropical shorts and t-shirts. Stefan frowns at the pink palm trees on his, but Alaina only says, "It was that or the dress pants from last night, so deal with it."

"I love mine," Nate reassures her, giving her a good morning kiss on the forehead, showing off his flamingo-patterned shorts.

Alaina borrows a bit more emergency cash to buy breakfast and some coffee, and we set out to find a small outdoor restaurant to eat at and discuss what to do further.

Everywhere is packed this morning, which is good, because we blend right into the crowd, able to wear sunglasses and floppy hats to disguise ourselves without looking out of place. We have no idea who around us may be on Lillian's payroll, like those fake sheriffs had been, or even Orlon's for that matter. While it might be hard for them to find us, we still need to figure out how to find her. The mirror brought us to the closest safe house to Lillian, but that could mean she's here in Miami or another state. We really have no idea where to start.

"So, what do we know so far?" Reed asks, leaning forwards, scribbling out something on a napkin. A map, looking like the shape of Florida. He puts a scribbled dot at the very tip, where we must be, but he also frowns as he scribbles another dot up near the inland part of Florida, right on the edge of Georgia.

"We know that she has to be closer to this," he taps the borrowed pencil on the spot where we are, "Than this. This dot represents our safe house in Georgia, and it's the next closest. So if we didn't appear there, then she must be here or below." he circles the lower half of the peninsula.

"We know that our scouts haven't managed to find her," Jane says, tapping a finger on the table. "They've searched all of this. Besides, this seems like a very unlikely place to try and hide a stronghold. It's too flat with no cover. There's nowhere she could have hidden an operation as big as the one she's running."

Reed sighs, letting the pencil fall from his hand with a defeated thump as he runs his hands through his dark hair, the ends beginning to curl from the humidity.

"So if she isn't inland, could she be here in Miami?"

"Right next to a safe house?" Alaina asks skeptically. "We would have noticed unusual activity if it was so close. Besides, Lillian would want to be somewhere way more remote, not crawling with tourists and anyone else that could accidentally stumble upon her stronghold."

"Remote," Reed mutters. "Close to Miami, which is surrounded by," his eyes light up, and I can practically see the lightbulb of an idea blazing in his mind as he stares at the tiny mark his pencil made where he had dropped it, off the coast of Miami, where the ocean would be.

"The sea," he says, looking up at the others. "That has to be it. The reason we haven't found her is that we've searched every continent and country on both Earth and Allrhea, but we haven't searched the oceans. The largest and most remote place in the worlds, capable of hiding untold secrets."

"What, is she hiding at the bottom of the ocean? Or maybe her stronghold is a cruise ship and she's cruising around the tropical waters of Miami with her entire army, drinking a pina colada and getting a suntan."

"Wait, is that actually a thing?" Nate asks blankly. "Because if I were an evil villain, I would totally do that."

"Yes Nate, Lillian is absolutely on a cruise ship, destroying our lives and sipping a tropical drink at the same time," Jane says, rolling her eyes.

"There's no need for the sarcasm, Jane. You can just say no, it's not a thing," he complains.

"Don't ask stupid questions if you don't want sarcastic answers."

"Guys," Reed says, frowning. "I'm not talking about a cruise ship. I'm talking about a remote island. There should be a tiny scattering of islands right off the coast, and an entire archipelago closer to Cuba. Since we didn't appear in the Cuba safe house, it must be an island closest to Florida."

"That's actually pretty smart," Jane admits. "It would explain why none of our scouts ever found her. There could be so many islands in that range, how could we investigate them all, short of stealing another helicopter?"

"We're not doing that," Alaina says with a shake of her head. "Never again."

"What about Astral?" I suggest as the idea blooms to life. "She can fly and can be pretty fast about it. She'll be less noticeable than a helicopter."

"That's actually not a bad idea," Reed says with a nod, and half a thought has the silver of my bracelet growing warm, and the shimmering outline of the growingly familiar silver falcon appearing perched on my forearm. Her talons dig into my arm, and she shifts with a squawk.

"Not right here," Jane yelps quietly, throwing a cloth napkin over Astral's head, causing her to shrink down with surprise, before launching herself skyward and leaving the napkin to flutter down to the ground.

"Haha," Jane laughs nervously, as several surprised and confused faces turn our way from the other tables around us. "Those seagulls, such a nuisance, am I right?"

Astral gives a sharp cry from above, probably resenting being called a seagull, but knows enough to dart between the buildings and out of sight. People give us a few more looks but eventually turn back to their food.

Alaina quickly pays the bill, and we get out of there before we can draw any more unwanted attention. The six of us duck down a back alley between hotels, somewhat out of sight, enough that Astral swoops back down to land on my shoulder. She clicks her beak angrily at Jane, who crosses her arms.

"I'm not apologizing to a bird."

"Hey, uh, Astral?" I try, not knowing how well she can understand me, or if she even knows that's her name. "I need you to do something for me."

Astral takes off with my instructions to skim the nearby islands, and if she finds any sign that Lillian may be residing on one, to bring back a token to prove it. She seems to understand pretty well, and the others don't find the complicated instructions to be that surprising, so all that's left to do now is to wait.

I watch the small white dot that is my viatalum fade into the distance over the water as the wind whips my hair into my face.

"Well, what now?" Reed asks, leaning against an empty, colorfully painted lifeguard post on the beach.

"We could try to find a boat rental to get us to the islands, so we're ready to go once Astral returns," Jane suggests.

"We could do that," Alaina says. "But Astral probably won't be back for hours, who knows how long it will take to find the island if that's even where Lillian is. Finding a boat rental won't take us that long."

"So what do you suggest we do instead?"

Alaina gestures her hands wide to the beach around us, the ocean waves lapping at the sand, the palm trees swaying in the relentless wind.

"I suggest we enjoy this while we're here," she says with a grin. "Come on, have any of you ever been able to hang out at a beach before? I'm not about to waste this chance."

Jane looks like she wants to object, but can't seem to find a reason to.

"Well then that settles it," Alaina says, flicking her sunglasses down over her eyes. "A beach day, it is."

It's about 75 degrees, colder than Miami is during the summer, and would normally be way too freezing to go in the oceans back home, but here with the added warmer water and the fact that we're used to the cold of winter in the Realms, this is perfect.

The first thing we do is head for the water, which is still carrying a shocking chill as we dive right into the waves. We aren't exactly wearing swimsuits, but nobody cares. The boys left their shirts behind on the beach, wearing those ridiculous patterned shorts. Several times I catch myself staring at Reed, shirtless, as muscular as a football player, and his skin tanner than I would expect. I can't help but imagine him like this in the summer with a golden tan, that amazing smile of his bright and his black hair tousled with salt-kissed wind, looking like he'd be right at home on the cover of some surfing magazine.

We go on like this for hours. Jane lounging in the sand like a cat, Nate purchasing a plastic flying disk from a gift shop and starting the most competitive game of frisbee I've ever seen, and Alaina helping me build a three-story sandcastle complete with a moat and working drawbridge, decorated with seashells.

Finally, once the sun is high overhead, I can make out the shape of a bird sailing swiftly and fast over the glittering water, coming from far over the horizon. I almost mistake her for a seagull myself, until Astral practically lands on top of my head. Something drifts from her talons, landing in my outstretched hands.

A scrap of black cloth, just like the one we found snagged on the broken window back at the Mirror Palace.

"No way," Reed says, taking the cloth in his hands, shaking water from his dripping hair. "Astral found her. I must have been right about the island."

"She came from the southeast," Alaina says, pointing.

"The Bahamas," Jane says. "She must be hiding out somewhere on that island chain."

"That's too far to rent a boat," Reed says. "Besides, do any of us know how to operate one?"

"I bet I could figure it out as we go," Jane says.

"I don't think the rentals will be okay with figuring it out as we go," I point out.

"What about a ferry?" Alaina suggests. "There's bound to be one that can take us from here to the Bahamas."

"I don't suppose you have your phone with you this time?" Jane asks me, to which I shake my head. My phone is sitting back in my room in the Dorm, and probably dead anyways, and even if the others had their tech with them, it wouldn't work like a regular smartphone.

"There's an old computer back at the safe house," Alaina suggests. "It's wired to Realm cameras, but the computer itself is Worlder tech, and we should be able to use it to find directions to a ferry, or at least call an Uber to get us there."

"Good idea," Reed says.

I thank Astral, and she shimmers away, my bracelet ceasing its glow. The hotel safe house is past the beach, over the hill and stone wall, and across the busy street. What Alaina said was true, a fairly outdated computer sits behind the front desk, looking like it must be too old to even work properly, but that itself seems to be another ruse. The computer must be run on Realm tech because it works perfectly fine, and Jane closes the various screens running camera and communication footage to access a search bar.

"Right here," she says, showing the screen. "A ferry service that runs from Fort Lauderdale to Freeport, in the Bahamas."

"Fort Lauderdale. That's about an hour away from here," Reed points out.

"We'll hail a cab," Jane says. "This place is crawling with them."

We don't have much to bring with us, just whatever money is stored in the safe house shoved into a cheap beach bag reading *Fun in the Sun* with a little smiley face sun embroidered on the canvas, and the clothes on our backs. Our festival outfits are stowed away in the hotel rooms, as well as the Traveler's Mirror.

Jane slings the beach bag carrying our money over her shoulder.

Hailing a cab proved to be difficult. When we finally flag one down, our time is already beginning to run short. The back of the yellow taxi smells like feet, and I shy away from a mystery stain on the cloth seat. Here we are, future heroes of the Realms, riding to battle in a Miami taxi dressed as tourists, listening to Kidz Bop, which is apparently the only station on this radio.

Alaina's eyes are wide as she stares towards the front of the car.

"What's wrong?" I ask quietly.

"You weren't kidding," she says, seemingly amazed. "Cars here really do play music."

At that, I can't help but laugh. After all we've seen, and all we've gone through to get to this point, she's surprised by the awful rendition of a Taylor Swift song blaring through taxi cab speakers.

The ride, which ended up being around 45 minutes, cost us about $100. Luckily, we have about $3,000 total from the safe house emergency stash, so we're able to pay that, plus tip the poor taxi driver who had to listen to Alaina's endless stream of questions and small talk. I swear, she learned the guy's whole life story in that forty-five-minute drive.

By the time we get to Fort Lauderdale, it is too late to board a ferry, so we stay in a cheap hotel within walking distance of the ferry port.

We board the boat bright and early the next day, which cost us almost another hour, and about $1,200 for six round-trip tickets. Less than three hours later, we're approaching the docking port of Freeport, in the Bahamas. The sun hasn't even completed its ascent, leaving us plenty of time to figure out our next move.

The sky is a crystalline blue color, spotted with cotton-like clouds, and the ferry bobs as it crests the small, lapping waves as we sidle up beside Freeport's dock. The main island of the Bahamas stretches out before us, a gentle curve of land dotted with docks, sprawls of buildings, and swaying palm trees against the crystalline water.

Stepping onto the concrete running parallel to the docking port, my legs wobble slightly as I adjust to standing on solid ground instead of the bobbing deck of the ferry. "I swear I can feel the ground still moving beneath my feet," I complain.

"It's like we're still on that boat," Jane grumbles, looking a little green.

"I'll take a boat over flying any day," Alaina says, her hair curling slightly from the salty sea breeze.

"At least flying would have been faster," Reed says. "We should have had Jane steal another helicopter."

"Say it a little louder, why don't you," Stefan chides.

"You're never going to let me live that down, are you?" Jane sighs, and Reed shakes his head.

"Nope."

"Well, enjoy your time on land, because we have to find a place to rent a boat and it's right back out to sea," I point out, with several answering complaints and groans.

"Rent, or steal?" Nate says, raising his eyebrows with a grin.

"No more stealing," I scold. "Not even a little."

We had to ask around before finding a string of boat rental sites along a stretch of wooden docks, not too far from the port. I spot several fancy yachts, sleek motorboats, and slim sailboats with colorful sails, all several hundred dollars each. Most of the rental places we stop at are absurdly expensive, or you needed a boating license, or a skipper to take you out onto the water, none of which we're looking for. Many aren't even open much longer, as it's getting late. We need something inconspicuous, inexpensive, and rented out by someone who won't ask too many questions.

There. Some ways past the fancier docks is a small shack that I would have initially mistaken for a fishing and bait shop if it weren't for the collection of small boats tethered in the water in front of it. The man running the shop, old and wrinkled, with a deep tan and gray hair, offered exactly what we were looking for. For several hundred dollars, he allowed us to rent one of his motorboats for 24 hours, no questions asked, no license required.

It is dark by the time we make it out to sea, skimming over the waves in a boat barely big enough for the six of us. The white paint is weathered and chipped in places, rust eating away at the metal lining, but the motor is working well enough.

We have no device with us to Google how to steer a motorboat, so we kind of have to figure it out as we go. It takes a little while, but Reed at the rickety steering wheel seems to find his rhythm guiding the boat more or less where he wants it to go.

I summon Astral, who perches herself on the bow of the motorboat, ruffling her feathers. The faint glow of my bracelet casts a faint blue light across the metal of the boat floor.

"Our navigation system," I say, gesturing to the falcon. "We don't know what direction Lillian's island is, so Astral will have to guide us, since she was already there."

Stefan nods, "Good thinking."

With a wave of my hand, our feathery GPS takes to the skies, skimming over the waves before banking into the clouds gathering overhead, keeping low enough that we can still spot her silvery, outstretched wings. But those clouds… it's hard to tell against the night sky, but they seem a little too dark and heavy for comfort. Nonetheless, Reed steers the boat after Astral, the waves becoming choppier as we go.

Jane throws the beach bag with our slowly dwindling amount of cash beneath one of the wooden benches and frowns as something rolls out.

"You brought this?" she asks disbelievingly, lifting the plastic gift shop frisbee we had bought in Miami from where it had been hidden in the bag of money. She glances at Nate in accusation, who only shrugs.

"Why?"

He shrugs again.

Jane huffs, tucking the disk back into the bag. Suddenly, a clap of thunder rumbles from the distance, followed by lightning streaking across the sky, illuminating just how dark and threatening the clouds gathering overhead are, choking off the stars. Sprinkles of rain begin to fall.

"You've got to be kidding me," Reed sighs, scowling at the horizon, where the thick storm clouds have begun to gather over roiling water.

"There is no way this little boat is making it through that," Alaina protests, tapping a nail on the wooden bench.

"She's right," I warn. "Tropical storms are no joke, especially in the middle of the sea. We should try to skirt around it."

"We can't," Jane says, pointing upward towards Astral's swooping figure, darting for the storm on the horizon. "According to your bird, the path to Lillian leads directly through it."

Lightning slices through the sky almost directly overhead, followed by a deafening clap of thunder that shakes the world and strikes a bolt of dread through my heart as we speed towards the edge of the growing storm, and the monstrous clouds seem to swallow us whole.

CHAPTER 24

I vaguely realize that I'm falling.

There's nothing but rain, what was at first a sprinkle, now a thundering roar rivaled only by the crashing of hulking waves, as though the very ocean is rising against us. Our boat has crested the top of one of the said waves, and is now in a nosedive downwards, sending my stomach plummeting like I'm riding a watery rollercoaster. We touch back down with enough force to almost topple our poor motorboat, sending everyone sprawling. It's a miracle the boat's still upright, and that no one's gone overboard yet, though we've had several close calls so far and the storm just keeps growing.

Reed clings to the wheel, still trying to guide the boat in the direction that Astral glides, as the bird struggles through the storm from above.

Jane peels herself off of the boat floor, grumbling, "This storm is going to kill us before Lillian gets the chance to."

Alaina winces as she pushes herself to her knees, Nate trying to help her up. She brushes her waterlogged hair from her eyes, and scowls, "I take it back. Maybe it's a good thing the Realms don't have beaches, the ocean is evil."

Another wave rocks the side of our boat as Reed tries to keep us facing forward, and I topple backward. We can't handle much more of this. I scan the sky for Astral.

Where is she? My vitalum is nowhere to be found, but my bracelet continues to glow defiantly.

"I can't see her anymore," Reed shouts, yelling to be heard over the rain. He must also have been searching the sky for the silver falcon, relying on her to keep us pointed in the right direction. Without her, we're sailing blind.

I try to stand, slipping in the water that has begun to slosh across the bottom of the boat, soaking my feet, now barefoot since I lost those plastic flip-flops when the first wave hit.

Wait. Water at the bottom of the boat, not good.

"Uh… we may have a problem," Nate says, noticing the rapidly rising water in the boat, too much to be from rain or ocean spray. The boat has a leak. Reed doesn't look up from his spot at the boat's bow, the motor making an awful noise as he pushes it to its limit, sending the boat rocketing over another wave.

"Reed," I gasp in warning, as the motor on the back of the boat shudders, black smoke darker than the storm clouds beginning to pour out. He only guns it harder. It's clear the engine isn't going to make it, but if we can just push past this storm…

A silver shape darts overhead, swooping back our way out of the clouds.

Astral.

Carrying a small shred of a palm frond in her talons. The island must be close!

She lets the leaf fall with a fierce cry, and it swirls away in the whipping wind, but her message is received, she found land. Now our boat just needs to get us there before it fails. How we're going to explain this to the boat rental guy, I have no idea.

The boat is moving so fast that we're practically flying over the smaller waves, pushing the rest of us back against the wooden benches. The ocean water filling the boat is now several inches deep and rising, and the clouds of black smoke pouring from the overheating engine stain the air like ink in water.

"Just a little further," Jane cries, pointing to a shadow on the horizon. An island. Astral is making a beeline for it, Reed guiding the vessel close behind, until the engine gives one last mighty shudder, huge cracks splitting down the plastic covering, metal fusing together from the heat.

"Everybody off the boat!" Reed yells, yanking one last time on the steering wheel. Stefan grabs my wrist, lurching towards the edge of the vessel, dragging us both over the side and into the chilling water. Nate and Alaina, followed then by Jane, and finally Reed, all plunge into the ocean depths, indicating that we should swim deeper and get farther from the boat, which is still rocketing forward. We swim down and away, in the opposite direction, putting as much distance between us and the motor boat as possible and not a moment too soon.

There's an explosion, a burst of fire that's blinding even from beneath the water, as the engine ruptures and debris begins to pummel the ocean surface. The force split the boat in half, tore through plastic and metal alike, and the shredded halves of the old motorboat are swallowed by the sea.

Only then do we come up for air, and I gasp as I blink saltwater from my eyes. Steaming pieces of the ruined boat are drifting through the water, tossed on the waves.

"Swim for the shore!" Jane directs, already moving in the direction of the island, close enough that we might be able to make it. The storm also appears to be slowing, waves calming just enough that keeping our heads above water is tiring, but doable. Thunder rumbles, farther away this time, as if the thunderstorm is moving back out to sea.

My chest heaves as I try to catch my breath, after what feels like an eternity of swimming, finally dragging myself onto the white sand, rain fading to a drizzle. The six of us lie here for a little while, clothes and hair coated in salt water and wet sand, every bone in my body aching with exhaustion.

That was, uh... well I can't call it a failed mission, since we found the island and survived. But I can't really call it a success either, because, you know, it could have gone a lot better.

Jane pushes herself onto her elbows, looking back over the water at the receding storm.

"That was awful," she says, pretty much summing it up. "Why did I come with you guys again?"

"Ugh," Alaina says, spitting out sand. "Let's never do that again. Like, ever."

"Well, there goes our ride, and all of our money," Stefan points out with dismay.

Nate speaks up, "On the contrary." He lifts a familiar, soaking wet lump of cloth with an embroidered smiley sun on the front. The beach bag with the cash.

Jane looks up, impressed. "You remembered to grab the bag?"

"Well, I wasn't leaving this behind, now was I," Nate pulls out his plastic frisbee, waving it in the air.

Jane sighs, not looking as impressed.

Alaina makes a face, picking out a soggy, tearing dollar bill. "I don't think that'll do us much good anyway from here on out," she says.

Stefan gets to his feet, and like the rest of us, is coated almost head to toe in sand. He takes a look at the island, the white beaches making up the gentle curve of the shore, the cloudy sky, and swaying palm trees dripping rainwater from their fronds making a tightly clustered forest that extends up the small mountains in the island center, looking worried.

Astral swoops down above us, landing atop a damp piece of driftwood, her feathers ruffled proudly.

"Good job," I whisper to her, stroking her head, her powerful beak clicking. "Thank you for getting us here, for finding this place."

It still feels very weird to talk to a bird as if she can understand what I'm saying, but I do not doubt that she recognizes my every word, watching me with eyes that are too intelligent. My memories again flash back to that weird dream that all of this began with, which had been a vision of the future all along. Of Astral, of Lillian, of all of this. I have an unshakeable feeling that something bigger than we think is at work here, and that dream has something to do with it. If we survive this- no, when we survive this and rescue my mom, I need to speak with the TimeKeeper again. I need to try and decipher the meaning of that prophecy if that's really what it is. I can't allow myself to be taken by surprise again.

"Lina," Reed calls from where the others have gathered, probably discussing what our next move is.

"Do you think Astral would be capable of finding and leading us to wherever Lillian may have her stronghold? If we get an aerial view?"

"No," Stefan says, shaking his head. "That wouldn't work. Vitalums are really powerful magic, and Astral doesn't exactly blend in. We should keep the element of surprise."

"How else will we find where she's hidden? The island is too big, we can't search the whole thing," Jane points out.

"We could split up," Stefan suggests. "We could cover more ground."

"Absolutely not," Jane says, pacing, full-on commander mode as her face scrunches in thought. "Splitting up would make us way too vulnerable. Besides, we wouldn't have a way to get in touch with one another or prevent ourselves from getting lost. Astral is our best option if she can keep low to the trees and keep from being spotted."

Astral fixes Jane with a look of distaste. I wonder if she hasn't forgotten about the seagull comment yet. Stefan looks like he wants to protest, but can't think of any better plan.

The beach is too open to stash the beach bag, and we don't want to just lose that much money anyway, so Nate slings it over his shoulder to take with us. Jane's daggers appear in her hands, having lost them somewhere in the ocean during our skirmish with the storm, summoning them to her as one can do with vitalum tokens. Stefan summons his golden sword, the double edge gleaming. No one else has any weapons, so Jane positions herself at the head of the group, and Stefan at the back to guard us from behind.

And together, with Astral guiding the way once more, we venture into the trees, ready for whatever Lillian may throw at us.

So far, we've found nothing. We make our way through the woods, following Astral who searches by air for patrols or any sign of Lillian's stronghold, but there's nothing but palm tree forests as far as the eye can see.

I swat away a mosquito, grumbling under my breath. As the sun begins to rise, the humidity rises with it, as well as insects. I've had enough forests to last a lifetime now, but at least all of the others were insect free in the middle of December. This one, not so much.

"I'm starting to think there might not be anyone on this island," Reed complains, wiping sweat from his brow. "I mean, unless they're hiding out on the other side of the island, I feel like we would have seen something by now."

The small, palm tree-covered mountain looming before us seems to mock us, bare and empty with no sign of a stronghold. Perhaps it's inside the mountain, like the Caves of Malum had been underground?

I watch Astral overhead, looping in circles indicating that we should keep up, but where is she even headed to? There's nothing out here, but it is almost as if she's drawn in this one direction. She swoops further, skimming through treetops to stay hidden until she disappears.

I don't mean she disappears as in becoming hidden by trees, but quite literally flickers out of existence, like Alaina's invisibility.

My bracelet is still glowing brightly, meaning I didn't somehow stop summoning her, but where could she have gone? And how?

The others notice her disappearance as well.

"That isn't a good sign," Jane mutters, pushing another palm frond out of her way as she moves forward slowly, in the direction Astral had flown. "Wherever she went-"

Jane's voice abruptly cuts off as she vanishes on the spot as if she stepped through a portal. Simply gone.

"Jane!" Reed shouts, forgetting that we're supposed to be stealthy.

"Jane," Alaina asks quizzically. "What... ?"

Everyone in the group collectively jumps, holding back yelps, as Jane reappears, walking back towards us. She raises an eyebrow.

"What is the yelling about?" she asks, confused. "We're supposed to be quiet. Why did none of you follow me?"

"You...were you invisible?" Alaina asks. Jane looks bewildered.

"I don't think so. Why?"

Alaina reaches forward, past where Jane had disappeared and stares wide-eyed as her arm vanishes as if she reached past some invisible barrier. Jane blinks, startled.

"It's magic," Alaina says with amazement, pulling back her arm. "Kind of like my invisibility, but instead of being activated by contact, it's only past a certain point. Weird."

Before anyone can stop her, she steps through and vanishes.

"Well, I guess we're following her," Reed says, stepping forward as well, until he too disappears, followed tentatively by Jane. I go next.

It's like stepping through a ghostly waterfall. I feel the iciness of invisibility trickle over me, and once I'm past the barrier, I can see Alaina, Reed, and Jane again. Turning around, I can also still see Nate and Stefan, but they give no indication they can see or hear us.

"It's like one-sided glass, where we can see out, but they can't see in," Alaina observes, as Stefan, and finally Nate, step through. As we turn around, everyone's eyes widen with a mixture of surprise and fear. The stronghold. It really is here.

It's a towering monstrosity of dark stone, roughly shaped, tall, and box-like. It resembles a castle with no towers, only strong stone walls with no windows in sight, protecting the rest of the structure clinging to the side of the mountain before us, looming ahead, looking about as easy to break into as Fort Knox. We're so much closer than expected and it's amazing we haven't already been caught by a patrol.

"It's even more terrifying than I expected," Alaina says softly, staring at the singular, massive flag flying high atop it, decorated with the insignia of an onyx falcon perched upon a broken silver crown. Smaller, completely black flags flapping from the watch post stations are built into the surrounding wall, one with a small chunk missing from the edge, barely noticeable. That must have been the fabric Astral brought back to us to prove she found this place.

This all feels too real, and not even close to reality at the same time. We found the stronghold of the most feared sorceress of another dimension squatted on a nameless island off the coast of the Bahamas. Now we're practically at its welcome mat. If we stepped out of these trees, we would easily be spotted by the watchtowers, and it would be all over.

At the same time, we're so close to victory. To getting my mother back. She's right there, beyond those walls. I've almost gotten her back.

Suddenly the sound of voices drifts towards us. A patrol.

"Quick," Reed hisses, indicating that we should duck back into the bushes. I crouch beside him, so close that our shoulders are touching and I can hear the sound of his breathing. I can't help but picture that moment, not even two days ago, when we had stood under the light of the Soul Realm and danced to a song about chasing falling stars. We had been so close, and something in me, even if I hadn't realized it at the time, had wanted us to be closer. I had wanted to kiss him, and I almost did, right there on the docks. But if I had kissed him... there's no way he feels the same. I mean, he just stopped hating my guts, he said he wanted to be *friends*.

"Lina, did you even hear my question?" Reed whispers, his voice jarring me out of my thoughts, cheeks instantly blushing red as if he could somehow know that I had been thinking about him. His eyes narrow, and I have to admit, no I did not hear his question. He rolls his eyes.

"I asked, can you see how many of Lillian's men there are? I can't see from here."

Oh. Oh, right. Lillian's patrol is now right in front of us. I maybe should be paying attention to that.

"I see five, I think," I whisper back, peeking around the side of the bush we're crouched in. They're not wearing the traditional guard armor, but rather something more suited to the warm air, reinforced with steel, with hoods pulled up over their heads to hide their features. They're talking quietly amongst themselves, and I manage to pick out a bit of what they're saying.

"... a bit of a risky mission, if I'm being honest."

"Don't let anyone else hear you saying that. We're not supposed to question her."

"She's been gone for days. What could be taking Her Majesty so long?"

Wait. Lillian isn't even here? We can't be that lucky, can we?

I flinch as I feel a hand upon my shoulder, Alaina, invisible.

"We have a plan," she whispers to Reed and me. I glance towards where the others had scattered into bushes of their own, as Alaina speaks.

"We have to lure this patrol deeper into the woods, where the watch towers can no longer see them. We outnumber them, we'll be able to jump them and hopefully knock them out. Then we can take their uniforms, disguise ourselves as Lillian's men, and infiltrate the stronghold, since the only way in would be directly through the front door, it seems."

"There's a couple of problems with that plan," I point out softly. "There are five of them, and six of us, meaning not enough uniforms. Besides, I'm too recognizable for that to work."

"We've already considered that," Alaina whispers back. "Stefan and I would trail the rest of you invisibly. The visalight at the door would reveal us if we tried to go inside, meaning we'll act as lookouts out here. And as for you…"

Reed's eyes widen as he catches on to whatever idea is blooming in her mind.

"How would you feel about perfecting the ruse we had begun in the Assassin's Grove?"

It takes a minute for me to realize what they mean.

"No, no way. That is crazy. If I walk into that stronghold pretending to be Lillian, they will see through it instantly, and we'll all be caught."

"But Lina, you heard them," Reed whispers. "Lillian isn't here. This is the perfect time to strike. We can say you returned from whatever mission you were on without giving much detail, and no one will even question you."

"What if I can't be convincing? It's hard to play the part of someone you have never even met. What if I say the wrong things like I did with the assassins, and get us all killed?"

Reed's eyes only narrow, gazing towards the stronghold with determination. "It's the only plan we've got. If we play our cards right, no one even has to know it was us until we're far away from this island."

I heave a sigh. He's right. With Lillian gone, this is our best chance. If I want to save my mother, it's now or never.

There is no way this is going to work.

We had cornered the patrol as planned, knocking them out and stashing them in the woods out of sight of the watch towers. Reed, Jane, and Nate had taken their armor, enough to hide their beach clothes under leather and steel, with shoulder pads and breastplates, leather wrapped around their wrists and forearms, and hoods pulled up over their heads. They put me in the same armor, but Astral had swooped alongside the stronghold and snatched one of the draped black flags to use as a makeshift traveling cloak, combined with the hood, which I leave lowered so that the rebels can get a good look at my face.

Now we're almost in view of the watchtowers, heading straight for the surrounding wall and front gates, and up close, the stronghold looks ten times more imposing.

We almost make it to the gates before we're stopped by a voice over an intercom.

"Names and IDs?" a bored-sounding man asks. That voice, leering and grating against my nerves sounds familiar somehow.

Reed frowns from beneath his drawn hood, as though he is also trying to place a face to the man behind the intercom. My friends only duck their heads and move to the side, allowing whatever hidden cameras there may be to get a clear view of my face.

"Your Majesty," the voice says quickly, the gates unlocking within seconds and begin to swing forward on their hinges, metal groaning. I keep my face cold and impassive, clenching my shaking hands in the folds of my makeshift cloak. I will not be afraid, I am Lillian, I am darkness, I am fear itself.

Jane behind me gives me a nudge to move forward, and I stumble on stiff legs.

I am not afraid. My mom is in there, and for her, I will not be afraid. I ran in that clearing at the beginning of all of this, and I will not be doing so again.

A man, the one from the intercom most likely, meets us at the doors beyond the gates, and my heart begins to pound with utter dread. I know where I recognize him from. His familiar onyx hair, a sneering face now lowered in obedience, and an ugly, winding scar cutting through a sightless, clouded eye.

The lynx man that had almost kidnapped me that night in the woods, the night my mom was taken. The night all of this began. This is the person who tried to hand me over to Lillian, the man who took my mother from me. I'd never known true hate before until I laid eyes on this horrible excuse for a human being.

The cold look in my eyes isn't a ruse anymore as I stare him down, almost daring him to recognize me as the girl whose life he's worked so hard to ruin. His eyes only lower further, refusing to meet mine. Obedient, sniveling coward.

"Your Majesty, we were not expecting you. You hadn't sent word that you would be arriving," he sketches a bow. "Was your mission successful?"

"Very," I answer tightly, willing the smallest smirk of satisfaction to my lips. The man only looks puzzled, as if he expected more of a report.

"So, you've captured the girl?" he asks tentatively. The girl? My stomach twists. He couldn't mean me, could he? If that is Lillian's mission, she's bound to realize that I'm no longer in the Realms. But I keep my face the portrait of self-satisfaction.

"She has been taken care of," I answer vaguely. To my surprise and relief, the man nods, as if he completely understands what I'm implying, even if I don't have the slightest clue. He turns to open the doors to the stronghold, granting us access inside. I rack my brain, trying to figure out how I might broach the topic of my mom, the prisoner. Lillian is looking for the Moon Dagger that can wield the power of death, and my mom knows where it is. So I assume she's being interrogated, and if Lillian so far hasn't found it, that means they must still be trying to question her.

"And how is our prisoner faring?" I ask cautiously, my face twisting into my best attempt at a cruel smile. Again to my surprise, the man smiles as well, his good eye glinting with mirth.

"Excellently," he purrs. "The execution is right on schedule, now that you have returned."

I freeze. Execution? What about the dagger? I glance out of the corner of my eye at Reed, whose face is kept frozen and impassive.

"I assume you are looking for this?" a lilting voice asks from the direction of the doors, and my stomach plummets with dread. I know that voice. It's mine.

Or should I say, Lillian's.

Because that's exactly who stands there, framed against the stronghold doors at her back, her eyes shining with vicious glee, gripping a black dagger in her hand. Her curling blonde hair, sharp blue eyes, the planes of her narrow face. It's like looking in a dark mirror, exactly the way she had looked in my dream. So similar, but so very wrong.

"Emmalina," she breathes, her face stretching into a smile. "I have waited so very long to meet you."

CHAPTER 25

Lillian moves slowly towards us, as my feet stay frozen to the spot in fear. The lynx man blinks with surprise, glancing back and forth between us with a snarl.

"Infiltrators," he growls.

"Indeed," Lillian says, looking us over, "And how convincing you were, Emmalina. Bravo."

Reed lowers his hood, watching as Lillian twists the Moon Dagger in her hand, its dark blade gleaming, running her fingers over the crescent moon carved at its hilt.

"Lillian," Reed forces out. She only grins at him.

"Reed. It's good to see you again, old friend."

"We stopped being anything but enemies the moment you killed my parents," he growls, to which she only gives a soft and wicked laugh.

"Still holding a grudge," she says, pouting. "How childish of you. Still fighting for the wrong side, I see."

Reed looks livid, his hand going for the sword he had taken from one of the men from Lillian's patrol, but she only clicks her tongue with disapproval.

"I wouldn't do that if I were you," she reprimands him, as something sharp and cold is pressed against my throat. A knife.

"All of you, toss your weapons on the floor, or she dies."

Reed lets the sword slip from his fingers, clattering to the ground, followed by Jane's daggers and Nate's blade. More rebels seem to melt from the shadows until we are all surrounded and outnumbered. Alaina and Stefan are still free, they can…

As if thinking their names summoned them, Alaina and Stefan are dragged into the room by several more of Lillian's men, disarmed and hands tied.

"We found these two lurking outside," one rebel grunts, tossing them onto the floor. "Lynx Assassin spies."

Alaina's fearful eyes fix on Lillian, standing before us in a uniform of leather and armor not too different from her rebels, red-painted lips stretched wide in a grin, Moon Dagger in hand.

"How did you get the dagger?" I demand, heart sinking.

"Oh, my prisoner turned out to be quite useful," Lillian croons, watching my face fall with dismay. "It took me several weeks, I admit, but I coaxed its hiding place out eventually. After that, retrieving it was simple."

I scan the room, the villainess before us, the lynx man, and maybe ten armed rebels surrounding us. If we can just keep her talking long enough to form a plan.

"Why are you doing this?" I demand, grasping for something to distract her. "Why do you need that dagger?"

Lillian's keen eyes narrow. "That is none of your concern, and I believe it would be easy enough to guess what I plan to do with it. Strengthen my powers, for one thing, once I learn how to access what it can do. Speaking of abilities, I've heard all about yours. Healing powers are quite unique, wouldn't you say?"

She waves her hand dismissively. "Toss them all in the dungeons with the other one. Add Emmalina's friends here to the execution list. It may prove to be a great incentive for her cooperation."

She smirks, leaving me to ponder what she may need my cooperation for. I know one thing for sure, no one is ending up on that execution list, not my mom or my friends, not if I can help it.

Lillian's men proceed to drag us the whole way there, not removing the knife from my throat or the bindings around Alaina and Stefan's hands until we're standing in front of a row of cells deep within the stronghold. The lynx man accompanies us, to my dismay.

The cells they shove us into are small, with stone walls and iron bars forming the doors. No windows, no candles, the only light coming from dim fluorescent bulbs fixed to the ceiling, and from the look on Alaina's face, they must be visalight, meaning invisibility can't help us here. Hooded rebels lock the cells with iron keys, tucking them into their pockets.

The scarred lynx man smiles, "The execution is tomorrow, at dawn. If you wish yourself and your friends to survive, Lillian has offered you one choice. Agree to join our ranks, or die."

"Join you?" I ask, in disbelief.

"Yes. Pledge yourself to us before dawn, and we will spare your lives."

"Never."

"Then this island will be the last place you ever see."

With that, the lynx man leaves, the rebels positioning themselves at the doors to the dungeon, preventing anyone from entering or leaving.

I sink to the ground, scanning the cells, looking for some way we might free ourselves. We each have a cell to ourselves, and in the farthest one, there's someone else. A figure hunched against the wall, listening to every word the man and I had exchanged, tattered hood pulled up over their head. Could it really be…

"Mom?" I ask tentatively, scooting to the edge of my cell, trying to get a better look through the bars. "Mom, is that you? It's me, Lina. I've come to rescue you."

The figure gives a raspy, humorless laugh that sounds nothing like my mother. When they turn to me, lowering the hood, my hopes splinter apart.

It isn't her. It's a man, maybe in his forties or fifties, but his haggard, unshaven face and dull eyes make him look so much older.

"I'm not your mom, kid," he rasps, as though his voice hasn't been used in a while. "There's no way in the Realms anyone is getting rescued. So just leave me be."

He's about to turn away, but his eyes catch on something behind me, and they widen ever so slightly.

"It can't be," he mutters.

"Reed? Jane?"

My head whips around to look at the two of them, both staring wide-eyed at this stranger.

"Do you know this guy?" I ask them, voice hesitant. Reed manages a nod, not tearing his eyes away from the stranger.

"Yes. This is Malcolm Windervale."

Malcolm. That name seems to ring a bell somewhere far in my memory.

"Is he… is he your dad?" I ask, voice trembling. Reed shakes his head.

"No. My dad is dead, that I'm sure of. Malcolm, we told you about him on your first day in the Realms. He's the guy who originally designed the Centerdome, who turned traitor and stole from the king. It was the Moon Dagger you stole, wasn't it?" Reed aims the last accusation at Malcolm, who doesn't so much as flinch.

"I stole nothing," he says, his voice flat. "I took it to protect it."

"You're a thief, and a liar," Jane spits. "You took the dagger and what? Fled to Earth? And now it's in Lilian's hands because of you."

"I wouldn't expect you to understand," Malcolm says, turning away.

"You're right, I don't understand," Jane says, and I'm shocked to see tears in her eyes. She wipes them away angrily. "I don't understand how you could do that to us. How you abandoned us and left us alone. Did you even know that Mom and Dad died?"

Malcolm gapes at her, "Mirielle… and Kennith… they're dead?"

"Of course, you didn't even know," she says, turning away.

"Wait, I think I'm lost here," I speak up. "Who are you exactly? How do you two know him?"

"Malcolm was my dad's brother," Reed says, saying the word through gritted teeth, "Our uncle."

Wow. Talk about awkward reunions.

My devastation at the fact that my mom isn't here warred with the shock rippling through me at who the prisoner actually is. Reed and Jane's uncle, the guy who stole the Moon Dagger years ago, told Lillian where to find it.

Then there's the other question, if my mom wasn't the prisoner the TimeKeeper told us to find, then where is she?

"Malcolm, sir," I say, stumbling over the words as everyone sits in tense silence. "I'm sorry, but have you by any chance seen a woman in these dungeons, a woman named Corrine Maren?"

Malcolm lets out another rough laugh at that. "I knew Corrine once. She and Mirielle were as thick as thieves, those two. Uh, forgive my bad choice of words. But no, I have not seen her in these dungeons, nor heard any word of her in years."

My heart sinks but then lifts a little. Maybe she was never captured in the first place. Maybe she got away and is out looking for me somewhere. She has to be out there somewhere, I am sure of it.

Something else Malcolm said jogs my memory. Mirielle. I know that name too. The only thing my mom would ever tell me about her life before she had me was an old friend named Mirielle.

"Yeah, your mom was friends with ours long ago, before she disappeared," Reed says softly. "My mom always told us Corrine was second-in-command to King Orlon at the time, the youngest one there has ever been, until she started disappearing for long amounts of time, never saying where she was. Then she unexpectedly resigned from her position, handing it to our mother who was next in line, and gave her a very vague goodbye before she left forever."

"So you're Corrine's daughter?" Malcolm snorts. "I always wondered what had happened to her."

"We were living on Earth," I say tightly. "I don't know why. She never told me anything, about why she left, why she never told anyone that I existed."

"Malcolm," Jane says, her voice sounding pained. "Why did you do it? Why did you rig the Centerdome and steal the dagger? You were the king's Royal Architect, you had a family, a good life."

"I told you, it wasn't my intention to steal it," he snaps, but he keeps his voice strangely hushed as if he doesn't want the rebels guarding the door to hear what he's about to say.

"The Centerdome was under attack by the Followers of Malum, who sought the dagger. I was sure the dome would hold, it was what I had built it for, but it failed. My last hope was to take the dagger before it could fall into their hands, but I was no match for the likes of them. They took it from me in the end and spun the story that I had stolen it for them. I had no proof that I was innocent, I became an outcast, a wanted criminal. I had no choice but to flee."

"So the Followers of Malum had the dagger?" Jane asks, her voice even more hushed, so quiet I'm amazed Malcolm can even hear what she said, but he nods.

"They did."

"Until Lillian took it from them?"

Malcolm's head gives a slight nod.

"How do we know you're telling the truth?" Jane asks sharply, crossing her arms from where she stands inside her cell. "How do we know that you didn't make that whole sob story up to make us trust you? For all we know, you're working for Lillian and the whole prisoner setup was a trap."

Malcolm raises his eyebrows, "So you really think so little of me?"

Both of their silence is answer enough. No one speaks for a long time, and I slump miserably back against the cold stone wall. I suspect we must be underground for the damp air to carry such a chill. What are we going to do? We need a way out of these dungeons, a way to get that dagger and get off of this island before dawn, or we'll all be executed. But how?

We have our vitalums, but Lillian has planned for that. Her men are armed with tranquilizer darts to take out wolves, and a lynx's invisibility wouldn't work under the visalight. Astral is small and fast enough to evade the darts, but she can't take out the rebels on her own, and her silver feathers wouldn't exactly be stealthy enough to get by them or take their keys. We can't even collaborate on a plan without risking being overheard by the rebels guarding the doors.

But maybe… maybe those same rebels will be what gets us out of these cells. I slip my silver bracelet from my makeshift cloak pocket, cupping it in my hands to hide any glow, as I silently summon Astral. She appears perched on my arms, and I quickly make a shushing gesture, hoping that she will understand that she can't make a sound. Her little head tilts questioningly, her feathers ruffling, but is thankfully quiet. I whisper her orders, keeping my voice barely above a breath, and she flutters to the top corner of the cell as I told her to do, where she perches herself above the cell door. She hides in the shadows as best as she can, where hopefully she won't be spotted.

Then I whisper the second half of my plan to Reed in the cell joined to mine. He looks unsure but agrees. He reaches through the bars connecting our cells to wrap one of his hands around my throat.

Not tightly, but I make sure to gasp loudly as if in pain.

"This is all your fault!" he roars, trying to sound as furious as possible. "You led us here, you got us into this mess, you were probably on Lillian's side all along, weren't you?"

Our other friends cast us alarmed glances. They hadn't been close enough to hear my quietly whispered plan, so they are bound to be very confused, but wisely say nothing as I beg, "Please! I didn't, I swear!"

We might be exaggerating it a bit much, but it seems to do the trick as the two rebels come sprinting, swords were drawn.

"Hey! Break it up," one snarls, kicking at the bars with iron-tipped boots.

But Reed keeps pretending to attack me through the bars, shouting and throwing accusations.

"I'm going to kill you!" he hisses, reaching his other hand through the bars, and the rebels react exactly as I hoped they would. They shove open our cell doors, prepared to pry us apart by force. I had been banking on the fact that, if Lillian had worked so hard to capture me, had even wanted me to join her, she wouldn't want me to simply die here in the dungeons at someone else's hand. Her warriors would step in to stop Reed and would come face to face with Astral.

Which is exactly how it works out. My falcon dive bombs the rebel in my cell, talons, and beak slashing for his face, sending his sword skittering on the stone. The sword that I then pick up, along with the set of keys off of his belt as he swats at the bird flapping and screeching around his head like a deadly halo. The rebel in Reed's cell quickly recovers from his shock, but not quick enough to avoid the heavy kick Reed aims at his gut, sending him sprawling, wrenching away his sword as well.

I weigh my stolen sword in my hand. In training, I managed to handle a sword well enough, but this is heavier and more unwieldy than the training sword I had practiced with. It'll have to do.

Reed has knocked the other rebel out cold, taking his keys and weapon and locking the unconscious man inside. The one inside my cell is blocking my way out, trying to swat the silver falcon away. Reed comes up behind him with his sword in hand, Astral darting out of the way as Reed slams the butt of his sword into the man's head as he did with the last one, before ushering me out and firmly locking the door.

Reed gives me a high five, something so ridiculous it makes me laugh out loud.

"Nice thinking," he says, looking me over with admiration.

"We make a good team," I answer, grinning like a fiend, before helping him free the others with our stolen sets of keys, all of them awestruck.

"That was…" Alaina begins, impressed, looking over the unconscious rebels locked in the cells.

"That was awesome!" Nate finishes.

"As cool as that was," Jane says, glancing towards one of the rebels as he begins to stir. "We have to get out of here. Now."

Nobody argues with that, heading for the dungeon exit. We stop at Malcolm's cell, right beside the door.

"You're coming with us," I say to him, where he sits curled in a corner, having barely even looked up at the commotion. Jane and Reed exchange unsure looks.

"No," he says. "I'm not. Why would you want to be accompanied by a traitor anyway, if that's what you're so bent on believing I am."

"Because," my voice falters, "Whether you stole that dagger or were framed, you do not deserve to be left in this rotting hole of a dungeon to die. If there's a chance you are innocent, I'm willing to give you the benefit of the doubt."

"Then you are foolish and gullible," he states.

"Are you just going to sit there and insult me, or are you going to come with us?" I interrupt. "It's either that or be executed in the morning."

"You didn't let me finish," Malcolm scowls.

"You also remind me of your mother, girl. You have her heart, her spirit and that is a good thing."

That praise warms my heart, but at the same time, a familiar wave of grief tightens my chest. I haven't saved her. After all of this, I still haven't even come close. All that I've done here has brought me closer to her in another way. I've learned more about her life, about who she was than I ever knew before. Now, according to Malcolm, I share her spirit. So I can't truly bring myself to regret the path I've committed myself to, becoming a Realm Guard.

This doesn't mean my search is over, not by a long shot.

So I slide the key into the lock, Malcolm's cell door swinging wide. Jane and Reed watch with apprehension as their uncle gets to his feet, his gruff face surveying them with a similar look.

"Let's get that dagger, and get out of here."

The halls of Lillian's stronghold are deserted, quiet. Too quiet.

We climb the flight of steps out of the dungeons and find the rest of the place no less dark or gloomy thanks to the lack of windows. I mean, who chooses to house their evil base on a tropical island and hole themselves up in this dingy stone monstrosity?

We are all on edge, Malcolm most of all. He lingers towards the back of the group, shifty eyes darting around every shadow and crevice in this hall as if waiting for an ambush. The dungeons were far enough below that there's a good chance no one heard our scuffle with the rebels, and since we locked them in the cells, they can't raise the alarm. That still leaves several problems: finding the Moon Dagger, taking it without being caught, and finding a way off of this island once we have it since our boat was very thoroughly destroyed.

"Malcolm, do you know where she might be keeping the dagger?" I ask, and he turns his eyes to me.

"No," he answers gruffly. "Not a clue. I propose we simply leave the dagger behind, and get out of here while we can."

Alaina raises an eyebrow skeptically. "Just leave what we came here for? The weapon that, in Lillian's hands, could mean the death of everyone in the Realms?"

"Now that you know where the island is," Malcolm reasons, "You all can simply report it back to your king, and have him send an army after it, rather than risk your lives in an impossible attempt to get it from her yourself."

Alaina snorts. Despite Malcolm's tall and wiry frame practically towering over her, she manages to look down her nose at him with distaste.

"You may be the coward that would choose that option," Reed chuckles dryly, "But we didn't come all of this way to give up now. If you can find some way off this island, you're welcome to go. Leave, disappear forever, just like last time."

Reed's words are so harsh that even I flinch. It seems like every time someone has hurt him, he puts up his walls and loses his ability to trust. First Malcolm, and then Lillian. Aside from each other, Malcolm is the only family they have left. If there's even the slightest chance that he could be innocent, shouldn't Reed and Jane want to forgive him? Though it doesn't seem that way.

Malcolm's mouth only tightened into a firm line, not seeming inclined to take Reed's offer and leave.

"Finding the dagger won't even do us much good," he protests, his voice lowering as if afraid of being overheard. "That dagger-"

"Shh," Jane says, cutting him off.

"Jane."

"No, I mean it," she hisses. "Be quiet. Someone's coming."

Now I can hear what she means. Faint footsteps grew closer, echoing on the stone floors.

"Quick," she whispers ducking around a different hallway corner, pressing her back into a doorway. "Hide!"

We all duck into the other hallway, crouching in the shadows, praying whoever it is doesn't turn this way. Closer and closer, until we can see the shadows of three people, stark in the visalight overhead. As they pass by the entrance to the hallway we're hiding in, I peek around the doorway I'm ducked in, spying the forms of Lillian and two rebels.

Oh god. We're dead if we so much as breathe too loudly. I risk another glance to make sure it's Lillian.

Lillian doesn't have the Moon Dagger on her, from what I can see. This means it's somewhere else, free for the taking, but where?

That's when I realize what direction she was heading in. Back the way we came. Towards the now empty dungeons. We are so dead, once she finds us missing. Once she's out of sight, we flock out of our hiding places.

"She doesn't have the dagger on her," I say, to which Reed nods. "She's heading for the dungeons."

"We have to find that dagger and get out of here, fast."

CAM

There is a horrible, persistent pounding in my head.

At first, I don't remember what happened, I don't know where I am. I can hear something, harsh and earsplitting, adding to the ache in my temple.

As I come to, I can make out the sound a bit clearer, it's Eliza.

"Cam! Cam, wake up!"

"Quit yelling," I mumble. "It's making my head hurt."

"I'm not yelling," she hisses back. "You need to wake up. Now!"

"What happened?" I ask, my eyesight beginning to clear. We're in a dark room, not the coms room, but somewhere else.

"We were kidnapped! Seriously Cam, snap out of it!"

It all comes rushing back so fast that my whole body jerks upward. Or, at least tries to, because I find myself already sitting, unable to move.

Now fully awake, I can see that Eliza and I are tied to chairs, back to back. What the heck happened? Who were those guys?

"The tracking device," I gasp.

"Don't worry," she whispers back. "I hid it. Keep your voice down."

"Why did they kidnap us?" I ask, trying to twist my wrists and finding them firmly secured to my sides.

"How am I supposed to know?" she snaps. "I don't even know who they are."

"We'll be happy to answer that question," a voice says from the doorway, which I hadn't even realized someone had opened. "As soon as you two tell us where you've stored that little device of yours."

A man steps into the light, a hood still up over his head.

"Why? What do you want with it?" Eliza demands.

"That isn't any of your concern," the man says sharply. "Just tell us where it is, and there's a chance we will let you walk away unharmed."

Unharmed? I inwardly scoff. Tell that to my pounding headache, courtesy of these jerks.

Eliza spits at his feet.

I instantly know that was a mistake as the man goes deadly still.

"You know what?" he says softly. "I hate doing things the easy way, anyhow. Kill the girl."

He aims that last order at a second, towering figure in the doorway, who pulls a dagger from the fold of his cloak.

"Maybe the boy will be more willing to talk after a little incentive."

"No!" I shout as Eliza struggles furiously with her bonds. "I don't know where it is!"

I am telling the truth. I know I had watched Eliza hide the device, but thanks to my likely concussion, I really can't remember where.

"Wrong answer," the first man snarls, and the second steps forward with the dagger. Eliza tilts her chin up to him, defiance written over every feature on her face, her two-colored eyes glinting with fury. Then her eyes lock on something behind him, and she smiles.

It's not the dagger that finds its mark, but rather an arrow, burying itself in the cloaked man's leg.

He screams, leaping backward, as my head whips towards the lithe figure framed in the doorway. It's a girl, dressed in trainee combat gear, another arrow already notched in her bow.

"Look out!" I yell as the third cloaked man appears behind the girl. She whirls around, intercepting another dagger with her bow, which splinters in her hands. She uses the broken halves of the bow to block another attack, before pulling out a blade of her own. The two other men flicker out of visibility, but not before Eliza scoops up the second man's fallen dagger with her boot, kicking it into her lap. As the girl in the doorway battles back the cloaked men, Eliza goes to work on the ropes tying her to the chair. Once she's free, she leaps forward to help, and the two of them prove to be more than a match. Outmatched and lacking the element of surprise this time, the cloaked men disappear without a trace. Stupid lynx abilities.

Eliza is breathing heavily as she moves to cut the ropes binding me, and I rub my sore wrists.

The second girl strides up beside her. She is tall, with dark skin and warm brown eyes. Her black hair is draped in braids that fall almost to her lower back, the ends of which are dyed a fiery red.

"What took you so long," Eliza scoffs, smiling over at her.

"Sorry," she shrugs. "I had to grab my bow. Speaking of which, I probably shouldn't have taken my nicest one," she looks mournfully at the splintered wood on the ground.

"Kaya, this is Cam," Eliza says, gesturing to me. "Cam, this is Kaya, my girlfriend."

"Hey," she says, smiling at me. "So you're the one who's been working with Eliza."

I nod. "Thank you. For, you know, saving our lives."

She shrugs, "No problem. It's nice to meet you, by the way."

"Nice to meet you too."

"So, I'm curious, what exactly happened here? How did you two get yourselves into this?" Kaya asks, crossing her arms and raising an eyebrow.

"We don't really know," Eliza explains. "We were working on a project for the king, and they wanted it for some reason. We didn't get to find out why, or who they even were."

"How did you know how to find us?" I ask, dumbfounded.

"Well, I know Eliza usually works late in the coms room," Kaya says. "When I couldn't find her, I assumed that was where to look. The place looked ransacked, so I checked the security footage and found where they had taken you two. It's a good thing I had gotten here when I did."

I nod. If she hadn't, Eliza would be dead right now, and likely me along with her.

"We should probably get out of here before those guys come back," Eliza says, with a glance towards the door. "The king needs to know that, for some reason, somebody is after that device, now that we've found a way to get it working."

"What kind of device?" Kaya asks curiously, as she leads the way out of the room. We seem to be in some sort of unused storage cellar in the castle since the corridor leads up and back into the palace's pristine hallways.

"It's a tracking device," I explain. "We adjusted it to find Lillian's magical signature, and locate her in the worlds."

"That's crazy," Kaya says, raising her brows. "Do you think those men work for Lillian? That would explain why they wouldn't want you to make the device work."

"That makes sense," Eliza agrees, as the three of us emerge out of the cellar through an unadorned door in the hall. "That would mean Lillian has spies in the castle somewhere."

"We need to get that device to Orlon. Now."

EMMALINA

Long story short, we got our information.

We had cornered a lone rebel guarding what turned out to be some sort of throne room, and Malcolm threatened him into telling us everything we needed to know, before knocking him out and leaving him by the throne room doors.

This guy scares me a little.

What we managed to get out of him is that Lillian keeps the dagger in her vaults on the lowest level of the stronghold, which is heavily guarded. We also learned that in her chambers would be our ticket out of here, how Lillian herself transports people to and from the island. Traveler's Mirrors, anchored to different places in the worlds and Realms.

The issue is that the dagger's in the vaults, the lowest part of the stronghold, and the mirrors in the highest, and we have maybe two minutes at the most before Lillian makes it to the bottom of the dungeon stairs and learns we're missing if she hasn't already. How are we going to do this?

We start by taking another staircase down, towards the vaults, since we aren't leaving without that dagger. Reed leads the way, Malcolm still at our backs, as we make our way down the narrow stairwell single-file. Every sound seems too loud and every minute that ticks by seems too fast. They have to know we're missing by now, and this place will flood with rebels.

Visalight still flickers overhead, casting the space in a harsh glow. No invisibility, only armed with the three swords we were able to take from those rebels, and blindly unaware of what we will find at the bottom of these stairs. Not great odds, I have to admit.

Reaching the bottom, Reed peers around the stairwell, before giving the all-clear signal, allowing us all to pile into a tight corridor. It vaguely reminds me of Passage Number 3, tunneling beneath the Mirror Palace, with damp walls and a musty smell indicating that we are far underground. Unlike the passage, this place is newer, with a distinct lack of mildew or moss building on the stones, and polished sconces in the walls holding brightly lit torches, meaning that someone has been down here recently to tend them.

Not too far down the corridor, trying to keep as quiet as possible to prevent our footsteps or voices from echoing, we begin to hear the faint sound of voices in a muffled conversation. Malcolm's eyes narrow.

"Rebels. I'd bet anything that the vaults are right around this corner," he whispers, his voice hushed. "Do any of you have a plan, or are we just winging it?"

"Winging it," Reed spits back, giving Malcolm a look of distaste.

"This is a bad idea," Stefan protests. "Maybe Malcolm had a point. If we go in there after the dagger with no plan whatsoever, we're not getting out of this stronghold. This is our one chance to make a run for it. Now that we know where the stronghold is, we can have Orlon send someone more qualified than us."

"Since when did you become a coward," Nate snorts, cracking his knuckles. "Besides, since when have we ever worried about being qualified? We've already done more than most guards would ever dare to do."

"And-" Jane cuts in before Stefan can protest again, "We're not going in there without a plan."

"You have an idea?" Reed says, raising an eyebrow. She nods.

"You, Malcolm, and Nate will take these swords, and Stefan can summon his. You four use the element of surprise to ambush whatever rebels are outside the place. While they're caught off guard, I'll use my daggers to take out the visalights overhead. Once those are down, Stefan and Alaina can go invisible and make it inside the vaults while we hold off the rebels. Then one group can take the dagger and flee for the

Traveler's Mirrors, while the others cause a diversion and meet them there."

Reed pauses, thinking it over.

"That could work," he admits. "Without the visalight, we would have the advantage."

Stefan reluctantly nods.

"It's a plan then," I say. I had forgotten about Jane's daggers and Stefan's golden sword when I had done my mental inventory, this might actually work.

Reed again peers around the bend, quickly ducking back before he's seen.

"I counted five outside the doors," he informs tightly. "Probably more inside and three visalight bulbs in the ceiling."

Jane nods, hands on her daggers. "Let's do this."

Reed takes a deep breath, gripping one of the stolen swords. Malcolm and Nate lift swords of their own, Stefan summoning his golden blade. The four of them dart around the corner and there are shouts of surprise and mayhem begin to ensue.

The rest is kind of a blur. Jane flicks her daggers with deadly accuracy into two of the lightbulbs overhead, shattering them in a spray of sparks that fizzle out. She summons the daggers back to her and launches another into the third light, raining blue sparks down on the clash of friend and foe filling the corridor. Reed, Malcolm, Nate, and Stefan fight like a whirlwind, but it doesn't take Lillian's men long to recover from their shock. Stefan stumbles, and a rebel sends his golden sword flying.

I jump as Alaina grabs my wrist.

"You're coming with me," she says, glancing towards the fray. "We're getting the dagger. Stefan seems occupied at the moment."

I nod, allowing her to cast a curtain of invisibility over us, keeping to the wall as we circle around the rebel's backs. Everything is cast in shadow, lit only by the torches on the walls now that the visalight has flickered away. Alaina wraps her fingers around the ring of keys attached to one rebel's belt, and he spins with a shout of indignation as his keys disappear.

"Lynx Assassins!" he shouts, warning the others. "They're invisible, and they've got the keys!"

The rebels try to surge for the doors as Alaina unlocks them with a resounding click, shoving them open, but our friends hold them at bay.

"Quick," I hear her huff from beside me. I do a double take. The lights in the vaults must be visalight as well because even though she hasn't dropped the invisibility, I can see her. Her form glows blue, like a ghost. I assume I look the same way.

She drops the useless invisibility, and her eyes dart around the room as she searches for rebels, but there's no one. The room is almost empty. There are a few strange objects, each on the podium. A tattered, ancient scroll of paper, a mirror with pitch black glass, and there…the Moon Dagger. A long, wicked blade of dark silver, carved with a moon at its hilt, and a line of scrawling script in the Old Language along one side.

"Wow," Alaina's eyes widen, "A dagger with a power darker than Lillian's," she shudders.

"This used to belong to King Umbra, or so the legends say. I never actually believed it existed."

I reach for it with trembling fingers, feeling the metal, cool and unassuming. I lift it in my hands, studying the inscription. As the dagger leaves its podium, an earsplitting alarm blares through the room.

"Quick," I shout. "We have to get out of here."

I turn to see Alaina studying the black mirror in the corner.

"Alaina, come on!"

She shrugs, before lifting it in her hands.

"What are you doing?" I demand.

"It's a scrying mirror," she says with wonder. "And not one of those fake ones you can buy in the worlds, but a real one. They're said to be able to see divine messages, tell the future, that kind of thing. Real ones have another ability. With a little of the user's magic, they act as Traveler's Mirrors."

My eyes widen as I understand what she's saying, my fingers tightening on the hilt of the Moon Dagger.

"That can get us out of here? Doesn't it need an anchor?"

"All scrying mirrors already have an anchor. They are linked to the one place where the kings and queens who defeated Malum first opened the gateway to the Realms, where the veil dividing them is thinnest. It is, to some, known as the first and largest mirror in existence. It's called the Salar de Uyuni."

"Isn't that a salt flat, in South America?" I ask, the name ringing a bell from some Social Studies class I had taken before.

"That's all Worlders think it is," Alaina says, nodding. "A large salt flat in Bolivia. They don't know its true history, what it really is."

There's suddenly a banging on the heavy metal doors, and frantic shouting from outside, the alarms still blaring. As they swing open, Alaina and I brace ourselves for the rebels about to flood through.

But it's not a rebel, but rather Reed that shoves the doors wide.

"What is taking so long?" he demands but stops short when he sees the dagger, then the scrying mirror. "Oh, now that is perfect."

"Come on!" Alaina shouts as we race for the stairs. "Where are the others?"

"Creating a diversion," Reed says, face pale.

"We have to find them before Lillian does."

So we just follow the sound of shouting.

We make it to the main level of the stronghold, but the commotion is coming from above. So we keep climbing the stairs, chasing the sound of voices and clashing of swords. We finally find the others, fighting their way upward, making a beeline for Lillian's chambers. No sign of Lillian herself, which is a small relief.

"Reed, Alaina, Lina. Thank the Realms," Jane huffs, shoving a man down the stairs. It reminds me of the Winter Tournament when we had been defending the tower, only now there is so much at stake. Her face goes slack as she beholds the scrying mirror.

"Is that what I think it is?"

"Our ticket out of here? Yes," Alaina confirms. "We just have to get far enough away from here that no one can follow us through."

Jane nods, signaling for the others to turn back. The seven of us bolt back down the stairwell, through the main foyer, and we almost make it to the doors when we hear a sharp laugh from behind.

"Going somewhere?"

Lillian.

"I think you have something that belongs to me," her red, painted lips widen in a grin.

We do the reasonable thing. We turn and run. A torrent of rebels gives chase, more than we could ever hope to hold off, especially with Lillian among them.

We make it to the trees, ducking out of sight, but that won't hide us for long. Reed, Jane, and Nate summon their vitalums, the wolves streaking off after our pursuers to give us some time, but it won't be enough. Not enough to stop them from following us.

Beside me, Malcolm takes a deep breath, suddenly looking a lot older than he is, tired and weighed down with resignation.

"I'll buy you some time," he says firmly, gripping his stolen sword. "I'll lead them in the wrong direction, put up whatever fight I can while you all escape."

"No," Reed says firmly. "I may not forgive you, but I'm not leaving you behind to die."

"Reed, Jane," Malcolm says softly, his eyes sad. "You two were only eight years old when I last saw you. It has been so long, and you have both grown into such amazing people. I'm so sorry I was not there when you needed me, I'm sorry I wasn't there to watch you grow up, but I am so glad that I got to see you again, even if it was under these circumstances."

"Malcolm," Jane says, her face devastated. "You're not saying goodbye. You're coming with us. Whatever happened in the past is history, you don't have anything to prove. Please, just come with us."

"I'm not just doing this to make up for the past, I'm doing it because I love you both, and I'm giving you your best shot."

"But-"

"Good luck, all of you."

Malcolm doesn't wait for them to protest again, only hefts his sword and forges back off through the treeline, shouting loudly. Drawing the rebels away, giving us a chance to escape. Reed and Jane watch their uncle disappear again, losing him a second time, to save us.

Jane is crying, but Reed only looks like he's in shock. Reed starts forward as though he's going after him, but I stop him with a hand on his arm. We are still being hunted by Lillian. It won't be long before they realize that Malcolm is alone and they come searching for the rest of us. Lillian can not be allowed to get her hands back on that dagger, or she will have the power to do unspeakable things. To destroy entire worlds.

I press the dagger into his hands.

"We need to get this dagger away from her," I say. "If you go after Malcolm, Lillian will kill you. It won't do any good."

Reed's eyes are pained, but he takes the blade. Behind us, Alaina feeds power into the scrying mirror, and the blackness widens until it's a gaping pit. A portal.

One by one, my friends step into it, swallowed up by the mirror's darkness. I take Reed's hand in mine, stepping forward with him.

As his form enters the scrying mirror's portal, I let his hand slip from mine.

He whirls on me in shock as he vanishes without me, his eyes meeting mine in panic, figuring out what I'm planning on doing, realizing there is nothing he can do now to stop me. Reed disappears, the portal fading away with him, leaving me standing alone on Lillian's island.

What I had said was true. They had to take the dagger, had to get it away to save countless lives, but Malcolm is their uncle, he risked his own life to save ours. What kind of hero leaves someone behind to die? If I told Reed that I was staying to rescue Malcolm, he would never have let me stay alone. I couldn't risk Reed like that, I wouldn't have been able to live with myself. Lillian would have killed him, and I could never put him in that kind of danger.

He may never forgive me for this, but this is what I have to do. The dagger is on its way to Bolivia, my friends are safe, and now I must find a way to rescue Malcolm Windervale.

CHAPTER 26

REED

She stayed behind. Emmalina tricked us, she tricked me and stayed on Lillian's island by herself.

I emerge from the scrying mirror's portal shouting her name, over and over again.

The portal closes, sealing itself back into the pitch-black mirror lying at Alaina's feet, trapping her there with that monster.

The Moon Dagger drops from my hand onto the carpet beneath us. The dagger that is now here with us, instead of Lina.

I kick it, sending it skittering along the carpeted hallway.

Wait. A hallway? Carpet? The five of us are standing inside of a building, which is a far cry from the Salar de Uyuni, the salt flats of Bolivia. Where are we?

"It's the hotel," Alaina says, glancing around with surprise, answering my unasked question. "In Miami. I recognize this wallpaper, this hallway. But how…?"

Jane glances in my direction, her face tear-streaked.

"Where's Lina?" she asks, her voice hoarse. Her eyes widen slowly as she takes in my face, whatever emotion must be written plainly for everyone to see.

"Reed," Stefan says, his voice unusually sharp. "Where is Emmalina?"

"She stayed behind," I force out, my voice sounding strangely hollow. "She went back for Malcolm."

"*She did what?*" Alaina's face goes pale. "She's alone? On Lillian's island?"

"We have to go back," Stefan says, dread dawning in his eyes.

"We can't," Jane points out, nudging the scrying mirror with a boot. "This mirror was supposed to be anchored to the Salar de Uyuni, how did it even bring us here?"

"That anchor potion we took to get us here before," Stefan says, beginning to pace, "Maybe there was still a trace of it left in our systems. Scrying mirrors are more powerful than ordinary Traveler's Mirrors. While the potion the Followers of Malum gave us was only enough to use once on an ordinary mirror, maybe the scrying mirror was strong enough to use it a second time."

"Now it would take us to Bolivia," Alaina points out. "There's no way to anchor it back to Lillian's island."

"Well then we have to find a way," I say, my hand clenching into a fist at my side. "We have to get back to her."

There's no way I'm leaving her stranded on that island. This dagger, this useless waste of metal, is not worth losing her. Because the truth, the truth that I haven't admitted to anyone, is that I think I'm falling in love with her.

I don't know when I began caring about her so much. It just kind of snuck up on me, I guess. I have no idea if she even feels the same way. For all I know, she still hates me for the way I acted when we first met. Whether she cares about me that way or not, it doesn't change the way I feel. It doesn't change the fact that it would kill me to leave her behind, trying to save my uncle. If something happens to her…

Alaina ducks into a room, coming back out with the pillowcase we had stashed our meager belongings in before we left the hotel. Inside is our festival clothing, and the Traveler's Mirror that brought us here.

"What about this?" she asks, lifting the handheld mirror.

"Still no way to anchor it," Jane says, twirling a strand of dark hair around her finger.

Before anyone can offer another suggestion, we hear shouting at the stairwell, before a wave of heavily armed men and women pile up the stairs and into the hallway, blocking our exit with a barrier of swords and uniform shields, shields engraved with entwining R's, the insignia of the Realm Guards, which stand for the Realms of Reflection. Orlon's army has found us.

"Fugitives, drop everything and put your hands in the air," the man in front says in a firm voice. It's Aron, the Captain of the Guard that had stopped us before in the hallway, a close friend of my family for as long as I can remember.

"Aron, you know us," I say, putting my hands up as he instructed. "You know that we wouldn't be doing this unless it was important. Look."

I toe the dagger in his direction, and his eyes track it as the dark blade glimmers from the hallway floor.

"We got the Moon Dagger away from Lillian."

Aron's eyes widen slightly, but he keeps the sword leveled at our chests.

"You are still under arrest," he says, but I know I'm not imagining that hint of regret in his voice. "I'm sorry, Reed. You can appeal your case to King Orlon, but you are still fugitives and have to be treated as such."

"Alright, arrest us, but we know where Lillian's island is. Emmalina Maren is trapped there. You need to send a team to rescue her."

"Whatever you need to say, say it before the king," Aron says tightly. "I am not authorized to put together a rescue team to Lillian's stronghold, especially not for a fugitive."

"She doesn't have that much time," I plead. "If you arrest us here, and don't send anyone after her, she will die."

"I am not authorized to make those decisions," Aron says, his voice tight and clipped, keeping his face devoid of emotion, "And you are still under arrest."

"Well, if you want it that way," I hear Jane mutter under her breath, before diving to the ground to snatch up the scrying mirror, the dagger, and the pillowcase. Before the guards can lunge with their swords, with a flick of her wrist, she sends one of her twin daggers flying, the same trick she had used in the stronghold.

The blade impales itself in a light fixture, sending a shower of sparks down on the cluster of guards in the stairwell. Sparks that then land upon a very flammable carpeted floor.

Orange flames spring to life at the guard's feet, followed by absolute mayhem. Shouting begins as they try to stomp out the flames, and the hall begins to fill with thick black smoke, closely followed by the deafening blare of fire alarms cutting through the still night.

I cough as the air becomes hard to breathe, Orlon's guards reluctantly retreating down the stairs and out of the building.

"Quick," I grab my sister's wrist, hauling her towards one of the nearest doors. "Everyone follow me!"

The five of us cram ourselves into one of the hotel rooms, shutting the door as flames lap against it, the crackling of the fire filling the air.

"Reed, what are we doing?" Alaina coughs. "Shouldn't we be getting out of the flaming building, not locking ourselves inside?"

"We are getting out," I force out. "If we go that way, they'll be waiting for us. We're taking the fire escape."

I try to shove the singular window open, but the thing is as ancient as Orlon and jammed shut. So I drop-kick it, my boots

I had stolen from Lillian's men shattering the glass, sending a jolt of pain up my leg.

"Come on, everybody out!"

One by one, my friends make it out of the window, onto the fire escape. Already, the stars overhead and the streetlights of the Miami strip below are blotted out by dark clouds of smoke rolling from the tiny hotel's windows. I can hear sirens in the distance, and see the flashing lights of a firetruck rolling towards us. Orlon's men are crowded in the streets at the hotel's doorstep, those emergency responders are going to get quite the surprise.

As we drop to the ground in the alley beside the building, I usher everyone further away, trying to get away from the building without letting the guards know where we are.

This is great. Emmalina is trapped on Lillian's island hours away, and we're stuck in Miami with an angry horde of guards on our tail, a burning building at our backs, and no real plan.

"I think that went well," Jane huffs, pressing her back against an alley wall to catch her breath, her words heralded by the rumbling sound of a window blowing out somewhere back at the hotel. Yep. Just perfect.

I only hope Lina is having better luck than we are.

EMMALINA

Things are not going very well.

When I decided to go back for Malcolm, I was certain of two things. I would make sure my friends got away and took the dagger with them, and then I would draw the attention of the rebels hunting for us before they kill Malcolm. After that, well, let's just say it wasn't a very thought-through plan.

The good news is that we weren't run through on the spot. The bad news is that I was too late to stop Malcolm from challenging the rebels and getting himself caught, so instead of convincing him to escape, we both wound up being captured once more.

Luckily there might still be a way out of this. An option that Lillian had offered before that, if I play my cards right, may buy our freedom.

The rebel holding my wrists in his thick leather gloves shoves me to the stone floors of Lillian's stronghold, Malcolm right beside me. I don't struggle, I don't fight back, I simply turn my head upward to face Lillian, where the rebels have forced me to kneel at the foot of her makeshift obsidian throne.

She smiles down at the two of us, her gray-blue eyes glinting with malicious glee. It's so creepy, the uncanny resemblance, but at the same time, the sense of wrongness. How could she have ended up this way? How does she even exist? If I have a counterpart, does that mean my mom does too? How else would she have been born? If people born in the Realms don't live on either world, they shouldn't be able to have counterparts, right?

This whole thing makes my head hurt. I wonder who would even have the answers to these questions. Orlon? If I survive this, if I can convince Marcus not to throw me in jail or whatever the Realms' equivalent is, I'll have to ask him.

"Where are the others?" Lillian asks sharply, looking towards the rebel restraining me. "And the dagger?"

"Gone, Your Majesty," the man says, a quiver in his voice. "They got away."

His explanation fades away at the wrath in Lillian's eyes.

"So they left behind the prisoner and the little falcon fugitive," she smirks, looking down on Malcolm and me. "Yes, I heard all about that. You've done all this for what? Break Orlon's laws, steal from me, you're not making many allies, you know."

I keep silent, trying to keep my gaze from wavering, even as my whole body trembles.

"That still leaves the question," Lillian muses, drumming her fingertips on the twisted arm of her throne, "Why did they leave you behind? Then again, the Reed I once knew wasn't much for loyalty. Did he ever tell you about our history?"

"He told me that you two were friends," I say, my voice tight and clipped. "Then you snapped and killed his parents. So if I didn't know better, it sounds like you don't have any right to talk about loyalty where he's concerned."

"I offered him the choice to join me, practically begged him to," she laughs. "No matter how hard I tried to show him the truth, that Orlon needed to be overthrown, he still turned his back on me."

I take a deep breath, biting back the anger that rises to defend Reed, letting it settle. If I antagonize her, it will ruin my plan.

"To answer your question," I say, "That is actually why I'm still here. Reed betrayed me as well. He doesn't trust me, never has. He thought that Malc... I mean, the prisoner, and I couldn't be trusted with the dagger, so they abandoned us."

"Did they now?" she says skeptically, raising an eyebrow.

"Yes, and now I've come to take your offer. I want to join you."

Lillian laughs at that, long and amused. "Really? Now that you're trapped here, my offer suddenly looks a whole lot more appealing, huh? So I'll humor you, why the sudden change of heart? Is it just because they abandoned you here?"

"Not just that," I say, scrambling for a lie to spin. "I want to hear your side of the story, why you believe so strongly that Orlon should be overthrown."

She pauses at that and smiles.

"The only reason Orlon brought you to the Realms in the first place was that he knew that I was interested in having you as an ally. He knew that the two of us together would be more than enough to take down his empire, but he got to you first. He spun a bunch of lies that I'm the bad guy in this war. You and I are more alike than you can ever imagine, our different abilities don't change that. You fight for his side only because he got to you first and fed you the same propaganda he leads everyone else to believe."

"And what is that?" I ask softly, trying not to be genuinely curious, but unable to help it. What she says might carry a bit of truth, my mother did flee Orlon's Realm for a reason, went to the ends of the worlds to hide both of us from the Realms. Why?

"He is the evil one," Lillian says, sensing the shift in my attitude. "When I was younger, almost able to become a trainee, I worked so hard to be accepted by the guards. I only ever had two friends, Reed is one of them. Orlon and the rest shunned me for what I was capable of, especially since I already had my powers. They called it unnatural and wanted to ban me from training. So I began to turn to others to teach me. One of Orlon's court members sought me out. Once he knew he had found the right person, he entrusted me with a dark truth about the king, all of the horrors he had done since the beginning. He helped jump-start my rebellion, helped recruit others to our cause with the truth, to stop the tyrant who had lied to everyone for years. Reed didn't see reason, and neither did his parents."

I shudder. "And what did Orlon do exactly?"

"First," Lillian says with a smirk, standing from her throne, drawing a wicked black sword from a sheathe at her side, the blade double-edged and gleaming in the visalight. "To prove that you mean what you say, prove your commitment to my cause…kill him." She extends the sword to me, indicating that the rebel holding my wrists should release them. To my horror, she waves her hand in Malcolm's direction.

"I'm not a fool," she whispers with venom lacing her voice. "I know exactly who my prisoner here is, kill Reed's uncle, prove that you are like me, and you may join my cause."

Malcolm looks over at me with eyes hardened with determination. He gives me the slightest nod, still willing to sacrifice himself to give me a chance to get out of this. To redeem himself in his niece and nephew's eyes. She presses the handle of the dark blade into my hands.

"Kill him."

REED

The five of us wind through the alleyways, trying to keep to the darkest parts of the streets to avoid being noticed by any of the wandering people or any of Orlon's men that might be lurking around. Even at night, Miami is alive with tourists walking the sidewalks lined with bars and restaurants, taxis honking their horns, and the sound of live music drifting from the beach strip we left behind.

We need a plan. We need to get back to Lillian's island as quickly as possible. We also can't risk bringing the dagger back there. We have to get it somewhere safe first.

I'm jolted out of my thoughts by Jane's arm barring us from going any further. Alaina beside me slinks back into the shadows of the alley we're peering out of, staring directly across the street.

There's a cluster of figures cloaked in the black armor of Lillian's rebels stalking the streets, faces hidden by hoods pulled over their heads, hands on weapons sheathed at their sides as they search. Searching for us, and the dagger. We should have known Lillian's men would never let us get away with it so easily, but how did they get here so quickly? No boat or even a helicopter could have gotten them from the Bahamas to Miami that quickly, so they would have had to use a Traveler's Mirror.

"This is just great," Alaina mutters. "Now we have to avoid both Orlon's guards and Lillian's rebels. We're surrounded."

"We aren't going to get very far on foot," Stefan points out. "We have to regroup, get somewhere safe to make a plan. Somewhere not crawling with people hunting us."

I nod in agreement as my eyes track a group of tourists walking down the sidewalk staring at Lillian's men with eyes wide and questioning looks, but continue walking. They're not even trying to be stealthy, between the guards and the rebels, the Worlders are going to start taking notice. What world are we even on, anyway? Earth, or Allrhea?

"Stefan has a point," Jane says, snapping me out of it again. "We need to get out of this area, anywhere but here, and we can't go on foot."

"We could get a taxi, or an Uber," Alaina suggests.

"Dressed like this?" Stefan snorts. "We're still wearing rebel uniforms, remember? Not exactly blending in. Besides, we can't put a Worlder in that kind of danger."

"You're right," Jane agrees, her brows scrunched in thought. Her eyes follow a sleek yellow sports car rumble by, rolling to a stop at a fancy, brightly lit restaurant. The driver gets out, handing over the keys to a man dressed in a valet uniform, who proceeds to park it out front.

"I don't like that look you've got," I say warningly, Jane's eyes not leaving the sports car. "That look means you're planning something and your plans are never any good."

"My plans have saved us, like, three times now," she points out sharply.

"They almost always end up with something on fire," I hiss. "Remember the North Conway safe house? Or the hotel from ten minutes ago?"

"I vote yes to whatever the plan is," Nate says, wild glee in his eyes.

"What exactly is the idea this time?" Alaina says warily.

"Well," she ponders. "We need a ride out of here, one that can outrun the guards and rebels but without endangering any Worlders, and we don't have any money left to rent anything."

"Oh," Alaina says, her eyes widening as understanding dawns on her, eyes fixing on the cars parked outside the restaurant. "So we're talking a little Grand Theft Auto, are we?"

"No," Stefan and I chorus at the same time.

"Yes," Jane, Alaina, and Nate echo back.

"You can't be serious," I say, crossing my arms. Though I always have wanted to try driving a Worlder car, especially a sports car like that yellow one… no. What am I thinking?

"We can't just steal a car," Stefan says, raising an eyebrow.

"Do you have any other ideas?" Jane asks sharply, to which no one has any good reply. That's not just because I really, really want to drive that car, okay? I seriously can't think of anything else that could work.

"Besides," she drawls, "We'll return it after all of this has blown over, along with replacing that guy's boat."

So, reluctantly, we get to planning.

None of us know how to hot wire a car, so we need to find some way to get our hands on a set of keys. The valet must keep them somewhere inside the restaurant, so that's our first move, scout the place out.

From the other side of the street, I can spot a bouncer standing outside of the doors, checking reservations and ushering well-dressed patrons past. There doesn't appear to be another entrance, so with the bouncer monitoring the main doors, sneaking in invisibly won't be so easy. We could cause a distraction, but we don't want to risk attracting the attention of Lillian's men while still dressed in our stolen uniforms. Besides, the less commotion we cause, the better.

"I have an idea," Alaina says, a small smile on her lips. "In the bag saved from the hotel," she gestures to the pillowcase containing what little belongings we still have clutched in Jane's hand, "Our Starlight Festival outfits. We can wear those instead of these uniforms, send someone to distract the bouncer civilly, while I sneak in invisibly to find where they keep the keys."

"That might actually work," I grudgingly admit.

"Alright," she says, nodding. "Jane, Stefan, you two distract the bouncer. Reed and Nate, stand guard, watch for any rebels or Orlon's guards and warn us if you see anything. I'll sneak inside and find the keys. Everyone will meet up outside, and be prepared to move quickly."

We all nod.

"Now, disguises," she reaches into the pillowcase and begins to pass around the festival outfits. Her hand falters on a scrap of light blue silk, and my heart wrenches as she lets Emmalina's dress fall back into the makeshift bag, not needed.

But after we all hastily dress in the alleyways, donning our fine clothing and trying to look a little less like a band of disheveled teenagers, we all split into our roles.

Stefan smooths wrinkles out of his suit as Jane tries to comb the tangles out of her hair, before giving up and pinning it into a hasty updo with her twin daggers. As ready as they'll ever be, the two of them cross the street to where the bouncer stands, glaring, and looks them over. After them, Nate and I make our way to the end of the restaurant and lean against the wall while feigning idle conversation, all the while listening closely to what the bouncer is saying. Alaina has already gone invisible, waiting for her opening to slip by.

"Names?" the bouncer asks, his eyes skimming over a list.

"Jane Windervale and Stefan Fides," Jane answers smoothly, sounding exactly like a bored and impatient rich patron. The bouncer's eyes narrow as he scans his list again.

"Not listed," he grumbles.

"Well, then just put us on the list and let us through," Stefan says, rolling his eyes a little too dramatically. The bouncer huffs a humorless laugh.

"That's not how it works. No reservation, no table."

"That can't be right," Jane says, voice pinched with anger. "I know I booked a reservation, and it wasn't easy to get ahold of either. I demand you let us through."

The bouncer looks seriously ticked off now, "I said, if you're not on the list, then…"

"Let me see that list," Stefan exclaims, plucking the strip of paper from his hands, ducking back as the bouncer tries to grab for it in surprise.

"Look, here we are, right here!" he waves the piece of paper around, backing further away as the bouncer advances, Jane nudging the door open slightly with her toe as if she's about to slip inside while the bouncer isn't looking. He spots her, hollering that she better step away from that door before he calls the police. She reluctantly lets it swing closed, but not before the window shimmers slightly, like the silhouette of a ghost. It's

Alaina letting us know she made it inside, gone before anyone else can notice.

Stefan gives the bouncer his list back before he gets us into any real trouble, but I can still hear the three of them bickering. Finally, after what feels like dragging it out a little too long, a couple exits the restaurant through the main doors behind the bouncer. The doors stay open just a little too long after the man's hand lets go, before swinging closed. The bouncer doesn't even look twice.

Within moments, Alaina shimmers back into visibility within the safety of the shadows beside Nate and me, two sets of keys dangling from her hand.

"Why did you grab two?" I demand, keeping my voice low. "We can cram all five of us into one car even if it only has four seats, breaking the seatbelt law is practically nothing at this point."

"I didn't take it because of that," she says. "I took it because I'm going back for Lina."

"You're doing what?" Nate and I both say in unison.

"That Traveler's Mirror in the rebel's hand that we saw," she explains, to my disbelief, "If we can get that mirror, I am certain they have it anchored back to the island, which is how they can get back and forth so fast, and I can use it to get back there."

"Not alone, you aren't," Nate says.

"I'm coming with you," I say, crossing my arms, a new hope tightening my chest.

"No," she says, her hair swishing as she shakes her head. "No one else can come."

"And why not?"

"Because I'm going to drive a car through that portal, to use for our getaway. I need to use the element of surprise for that to work, meaning turning the car invisible. I don't even know how long I can hold that, especially once I have Lina with me. I won't be able to extend my powers to cloak more than the car and two people."

"Then we'll take Stefan too," I say, that hope twisting almost painfully in my gut. "He can help hold the invisibility."

"That would leave only Nate and Jane to protect the Moon Dagger," Alaina protests. "We can't risk that, especially without invisibility on their side. You four need to get the dagger somewhere safe, and I'll get Emmalina."

"But," my mouth opens and closes wordlessly like a fish out of water, trying desperately to come up with an argument. Emmalina is worth so much more to me than that stupid dagger, but Alaina has a point. If Lillian gets her hands back on the Moon Dagger, she will never allow it to be pried from her again, and saving Lina will mean nothing if she kills us all.

So all I say is, "Please. Just… just promise you will bring her back. Promise that you'll both be back safely."

She smiles, "I promise. When have I ever let you down before?"

I narrow my eyes. Does she really want me to answer that?

"Alright," she says, "Now we just need to…" her eyes widen, "Duck!"

"Duck?" Nate repeats. I have to shove him over before he can get slammed in the head from behind with the butt of a sword, sending him sprawling on the pavement.

A sword wielded by one of Lillian's rebels. We've been found.

EMMALINA

"Kill. Him." Lillian repeats, her voice deadly quiet. My palms are sweaty against the hilt of the terrible dark blade, Malcolm staring up at me from my feet. I can't kill him. I won't.

"I am nothing like you," I hiss, before swinging the sword, but not at Malcolm.

Fast as a striking viper, Lillian blocks the arc of the sword with a long dagger pulled from a hidden sheathe, the blades colliding with the screech and clang of metal.

"I knew it," she sneers, "Liar."

She shoves me back easily, right into the waiting arms of her rebels, who wrench the sword from my grasp. That was it. That was my only chance. If I had just been a little faster, a little better at wielding a sword, but it doesn't matter now.

"Take her to the dungeons," she snarls. "If she won't join me, then she will join the prisoner. The execution will take place at dawn, as scheduled. For both of them."

With that, Lillian perches herself back into her obsidian throne, watching with baleful eyes as her rebels drag Malcolm and me toward the doors.

"Wait," I say, straining forward. "I have one more question. What did you do with my mother?"

Lillian raises her eyebrows imploringly, "Your mother?"

"Yes," I snap. "Your rebels separated us the night they came for us in the mountains, on Earth. If she isn't your prisoner then what did you do with her?"

Lillian smirks, "Ah, and there it is. The real reason why you stayed back, isn't it?" she sneers. And she's right. I did come back to help Malcolm, but the real reason deep inside, the thing keeping me from leaving this island, is because I need to know where she is. She seems to take my furious silence as an answer.

"Well, I'm terribly sorry to disappoint you," she smiles, far from sorry, "But my rebels do not take many prisoners, they don't spare anyone who is of no use to me. All I wanted that night was you, Lina. She was expendable."

I feel the blood drain from my face, dreading the answer but forcing out the question nonetheless.

"What did you do with her?"

"She is dead."

"No…"

"Yes. Like I said, my rebels don't take prisoners."

"You're lying!" I shout, sagging to the ground, forcing the rebels to support my weight.

"Why would I lie?" she folds her hands in her lap. "We're done here. Bring her to the dungeons."

She can't be dead. It can't be true.

All that I've done since I've arrived in the Realms has been to rescue her, to get my mom back. I've been pushing away the truth I feared greater than even Lillian, that she never made it out of that campground. That I'm all alone now, and I can never get her back. I failed.

I don't remember the rebels dragging me to the dungeons, I don't recall how I ended up curled in a ball on the cold stone floor of a cell, sobbing horrible tears of guilt and grief and hatred for that monster on the obsidian throne. The one that took my mother from me.

How I had utterly failed to save her. It was over before I could even try.

"Emmalina," I hear Malcolm say softly from the cell he's crouched in. "I told you that I knew your mom once, remember? Corrine Maren, what a fiery spirit she had. She was kind and brave, and fearless, just like you. I know that she would be so proud of all that you've done, how far you must have come, the person you are, so similar to her."

Malcolm doesn't offer any useless apologies or any empty condolences. Instead, he fills the ringing silence with his voice, drowning out the crushing grief with his gentle words. He tells stories, reciting memories of when he knew her, filling in the blank spaces with tales of her accomplishments, her adventures and who she had been.

Amid the ebb and flow of grief, the sound of Malcolm's voice becoming raw and hoarse from hours of talking, I begin to notice one strange detail. None of the stories mention my dad, nor hint at who it might have been. I'm too tired to ask, too heavy and weighted down to care.

That is how I fall asleep, curled in the corner of a cell, with Reed's uncle using his last hours before dawn to ease my grief. Perhaps it brings him some comfort as well, reliving those memories.

"I love you, mom," I whisper into the dark, quiet enough for only me to hear. If I'm going to die in the morning, I want those to be my last words. I want her to know that I tried.

That I wish things could have been different, for all of us.

CHAPTER 27

REED

So much for escaping without causing any commotion. Lillian's rebels have found us, and they don't seem to care about what the Worlders see.

Nate leaps back up, sending a fist swinging into the side of one guy's head, sending him reeling back. Alaina has gone invisible again as Jane and Stefan leap into the fray, welding twin daggers and a golden sword. I still have the Moon Dagger in a hidden sheathe beneath my jacket, but there's no way I'm going to use that thing. I don't know what it would take to activate that dark power, and I have no intention of finding out by accident.

I watch one man go down for seemingly no reason and a flash of silvery glass slip from his pocket before disappearing. It must be Alaina, snatching that Traveler's Mirror. I still don't like her plan, but I have to admit that we don't have another choice. Alaina can't cloak three people plus an entire car on her own, taking both Stefan and me with her would leave the dagger too unguarded, and Emmalina may not have enough time to wait for us to get the dagger somewhere safe first. I have to trust that Alaina can do this on her own.

Nate intercepts a blade aimed straight for my head, shoving the last rebel to the ground, unconscious. Shouts and screams from the bystanders around us begin to mingle with the far-off sound of a police siren. Just perfect.

"Thanks," I pant, shoulders heaving as I catch my breath, adrenaline beginning to course through my body.

"No problem," Nate says. "Had to repay the favor, after all."

"Guys," Jane says, her eyes narrowing. "There will be more coming. We have to get out of here."

Alaina, now visible with the Traveler's Mirror in hand, tosses her a set of keys, which Jane nimbly catches out of the air.

"You four get going. Use the scrying mirror to get to the Salar de Uyuni, and I'll meet you all there."

"Where are you going?" Stefan asks with a pointed look at the second set of keys in her hands.

"I'll explain later," I say. "Alaina, go. Bring her back, and be careful,"

She nods. Nate lowers his head to kiss her, and when he pulls back, his brown eyes are filled with worry.

"Please come back to me."

"I will, I promise," she says gently, determined.

"I love you," he whispers.

"I love you too."

She breaks away, keys in one hand and mirror in the other.

"Good luck," Jane says.

She nods.

Jane clicks the key fob in her hand, and a car parked just down the street beeps in response. It's a sleek black Chevy Camaro, gleaming in the lights of the restaurant's glowing neon sign. As I'm admiring our new ride, towards the other end of the parking spaces, the sound of a car's engine revving diverts my attention to a bright red Dodge Challenger with Alaina seated behind the wheel.

Well, it's now or never I guess.

Jane moves to unlock the driver's side door, but I block her path.

"Oh, no," I say, holding out my hand for the keys. "In the past week, you've flown a helicopter and blown up two safe houses. Let someone else have all the fun, won't you? Besides, we both know I'm the better driver."

She grumbles, but hands over the keys.

"Fine, but I call shotgun."

Nate and Stefan don't even complain that much about being stuffed in the backseat, though Nate practically has to sit cross-legged to fit. I rev the engine as I watch Alaina's newly stolen red Dodge peel out of the parking lot, followed by shouting. I guess the owners of these cars have noticed.

The police sirens grow louder, barely a block away. To add to it, the sound of motorcycle engines grows, until five of them turn the street corner and come barreling in our direction. Lillian's men.

This is not good. Not good at all.

"Step on it!" Nate yells, and I slam my foot down on the gas, sending us shooting forward, right on Alaina's tail.

I blink with surprise at the sound of thumping coming from the dashboard, very faint but noticeable. Is it supposed to do that? It sounds kind of like…

Jane experimentally turns a knob beside the screen, and the sound of rock music grows until it's deafening and the entire vehicle is thrumming.

Now that's cool. Lina mentioned something about Worlder cars playing music, and while I may have laughed at the idea before, this is kind of awesome.

"Sweet," Nate says, leaning forward in his seat. "This is the best car chase I've ever been in."

"You've been in a car chase before?" Jane asks incredulously.

"Well, no. But if I had been, this would still be the best!"

My eyes flash to my rearview mirror, where the rebels' motorcycles have pulled up on either side to flank the Camaro. I yank the wheel, trying to swerve us away from them as the chorus of honking cars, shouting people, thumping music, and screeching of police sirens become almost deafening.

"Uh, Reed," Nate says, peering out of the small back window, "We have a problem."

"Do you mean besides the rebels?" I grunt, swerving the car in the other direction as I swerve again to narrowly avoid being run off the road by the snapping jaws of a giant wolf almost as big as the car itself. The rebels brought their vitalums to this chase. We could do the same, but don't want to risk Rowan, or any of our other vitalums, getting left behind, especially once we use the scrying mirror to escape.

Speaking of using mirrors to escape this mess, a giant flare of light two lanes over reveals a mirror portal open in the street just in time for Alaina's red dodge to barrel through, invisibility washing over both her and the car as she disappears. It closes just before the motorcycles can reach it, leaving groups of terrified and confused Worlders staring in shock at where an entire car vanished before their very eyes. This is going to be a hard mess to fix, but we'll have to cross that bridge when we get to it.

A wolf slams into the side of the Camaro, sending us skidding, and the car tips as one wheel lifts onto the sidewalk.

"You still think you're the better driver?" Jane demands, gripping the handle above the door to right herself, only to be thrown back against the seat once more as I yank the wheel again, taking the sharpest turn I've ever taken down an alley that I'm fairly sure isn't even made for cars, onto another street, unable to lose our pursuers.

One motorcycle pulls up directly beside us, dagger in one hand as if he's prepared to shatter the window.

To clarify, it is nearly impossible for a guard or anyone else with magic in their veins to use a gun, or any weapon of the sort, because magic can amplify that destructive power to the point where it's dangerous to the user. So other than the wolves or running us off the road, throwing daggers are their only option. Unless you can somehow use a sword while riding a motorcycle, in which case, I'm impressed, but I doubt it.

"I've got this guy," Jane says, rolling down the window, leaning out, and launching one of her daggers at the motorcycle's wheels, sending it and its rider sprawling, but not before he can throw his. It hits the side of the car inches from the open window, leaving a deep gouge.

"Hey, we have to return this!" Nate shouts angrily at the fallen motorcycle rider.

The flash of blue light in my rearview mirror has me glancing back to see not one, not two, but three cop cars giving chase, sending a few other cars and bystanders careening away to give room for the Camaro, motorcycles, and police cars. I'm not even sure who they're chasing, us or the rebels on motorcycles. Maybe both, but I'm guessing mostly us because of, you know, the stolen car.

"Ah, that might be a problem," I mutter to myself.

"Hey, Reed?" Nate says from the back. "We have another problem."

"What could it possibly be?" I demand, the Camaro drifting as we narrowly avoid a parked car.

"That."

I look to see where Nate's pointing, Jane muttering something unpleasant under her breath, as a squadron of Orlon's guards appear at the end of the street we're barreling down, some wielding spears as though they might bar our path and some on top of the backs of wolf vitalums. As if we weren't in enough of a mess as it is. We're trapped.

"The scrying mirror!" Stefan yells, reaching into the pillowcase where the black mirror is stored along with the Moon Dagger.

"We can't use it inside the car though, can we?" I ask, my palms becoming clammy as the barrier of guards draws nearer, a police car pulling up on our left and a rebel motorcycle on our right.

"Alaina projected a portal into the street," Nate points out. "Just try, it might work."

"Can we open one big enough?"

"If she could do it on her own, then we certainly have more than enough power if the three of us do it together," Jane says firmly, gesturing to herself, Stefan, and Nate. "You just focus on driving. We'll combine our power into the portal, focus it on the street, and just direct the car through it."

"Got it," I nod, hands tightening on the wheel, not slowing my speed. Only seconds left.

"Now!"

A swirl of shadows tears a gaping pit through the air only a few yards away, guards leaping back with shock and shouts of fear. The scrying portal is glowing as though it's red hot, stretching the portal in the ground from the size of a dinner plate until it's a yawning pit wide enough to fit two cars easily.

"Just hold it a little longer," I say, slamming the pedal almost to the floor of the car, sending it shooting forward like a rocket, trying to put as much distance between us and our pursuers as possible.

The car hits the shadows, and all of the windows go black as we free-fall into nothing.

CAM

Eliza, Kaya, and I gather in the middle of the hallway, debating whether we should bring the matter of Lillian's spies directly to the king.

Suddenly, I hear the echo of footsteps, bracing myself for the men who kidnapped us to reappear again. It isn't them who round the corner, it's Marcus.

The king's second-in-command falters as he sees us standing here, in the middle of the night, looking disheveled and wide-eyed.

"What are you three doing?"

"Marcus," Eliza exclaims. "We finished the device, and we were able to see Lillian's location on Allrhea, but we were attacked and I had to stow it in the coms room. We think Lillian has spies going after the tracker. We need to tell the king."

Marcus nods, "We will deal with this promptly. First, the king and I must deal with the current situation."

"What situation?" Eliza asks.

"Emmalina and her band of renegades have been stirring up trouble in Allrhea," Marcus sneers. "One of our patrols in Miami reported that they are running amok, leaving another safe house burning in their wake. To make things worse, Lillian's rebels have also tracked them there and are on the hunt. We need to apprehend the fugitives now before they cause too much of a scene."

My eyes widen. They're all the way in Florida, in the other world?

"Grab the device and meet in the throne room," he orders. "The king and I, as well as the rest of the council, will meet you there."

We try to move as quickly as possible, keeping an eye out for any sign of Lillian's spies. Since we know that they have the gift of invisibility, they could be hiding anywhere. Luckily, we run into no more problems as we retrieve the tracking device from the coms room, and rush it to the room in the highest tower of the castle, where sure enough, the entire council has been gathered.

The table is no longer there, just the dais, the throne, and the giant mirror, which is now not swirling with an otherworldly light, but rather broadcasting a real-time, aerial image of what looks like the Miami strip. Right along the beach, a mess of smoke clouds the area, a burning safe house, as Marcus said.

The king is talking with an urgent voice playing through like an intercom.

"We've lost them," a man's voice says. "We never saw them exit the safe house. Your Majesty, they said they had found Lillian's stronghold and had stolen back the Moon Dagger from her."

A chorus of surprised and worried murmurs fill the room as the council reacts to the news. Whatever this dagger is, it seems to have rattled them deeply.

The king seems to be about to say something when police lights begin to flash in the mirror's footage.

"Captain, what's going on," the king asks sharply, eyes tracking the lights of police cars as they travel towards one location.

"Lillian's men found them first," the man says. "We're headed their way, but it seems to have become a public skirmish. Worlders are fleeing the scene."

Orlon curses under his breath, not a very king-like thing to say.

I'm unable to tear my eyes away from the image until I see two minuscule dots keeping ahead of the police cars, two vehicles, one red and one black. The king spots it as well, waving a hand to zoom in on the chase.

I was right. It's two sports cars, barreling at a breakneck speed down the Miami streets, with police cars and what looks like several motorcycles in pursuit. Oh my god.

"The fugitives seem to have illegally procured two Worlder vehicles," the man, the Captain, whoever he is says.

They stole cars? And they're being chased by *the police?* What the heck is going on? Kaya and Eliza are watching the screens with undiluted awe, and though Eliza would never admit to it, she looks impressed.

Suddenly there's a flash of light, and the red car completely disappears into what looks like a mirror portal.

"They've split up?" Aravian says, raising an eyebrow. "Now why would they do that?"

Orlon finally turns and spots the three of us standing in the throne room doorway with the tracking device in tow. He beckons us forward, barely glancing away from the mirror footage.

"Bring that here. We can connect it to the mirror to show where Lillian is in all this."

Marcus fiddles with something in the mechanisms, and I watch as a blinking dot appears over Miami's coast, not far from the car chase.

"Find where the other car went," the king commands, and Marcus begins to zoom out. Before he can get very far, a flash of blackness, like a living shadow, swallows the second car and several motorcycles whole. Lillian's dot fizzles out.

"What happened?" Marcus snaps.

The device must have malfunctioned or something. I go to check, but Orlon's eyes fix on where the car disappeared.

"That was a scrying mirror portal," he says stiffly. "I would know it anywhere."

"They've gone to the Salar de Uyuni?" the woman, the Captain whose name I think is Ivory, speaks up.

"This has gone far enough," Marcus scowls.

"We have to help them," I say, forcing out the words. The whole room full of people turns to me. Eliza raised her eyebrows. "They're in danger. Lina is in danger, we have to help them."

And to my surprise, Orlon nods.

"The boy is right. Open a portal to the Bolivia salt flats. We have to retrieve them, and the dagger, before Lillian's men do."

Marcus doesn't argue, and simply does as the king says. The image in the mirror disappears, replaced by swirling indigo light.

"Who are we sending to retrieve them?" the old man, the general, demands.

No one argues as both Eliza and Kaya step forward, determined. The woman, Ivory, follows. Then, reluctantly, Marcus joins them. Finally, Orlon, scepter in hand, stands at the head of the rescue party.

"I want to come with you," I say, my heart pounding, but Orlon shakes his head.

"It's admirable that you want to help your friend," he says, "But I can't allow an untrained civilian onto a battlefield."

I want to argue, but I know he has a point. I just want Lina back safely.

As the party braces themselves, Orlon feeds magic into the portal, which flares brightly. I can only watch as they step through, and disappear.

REED

What feels like falling moments ago has become the feeling of rocketing upwards, before we and the car reemerge through another portal in the ground.

The wheels skid, the gas pedal still pressed to the floor, the Camaro retaining some of its speed and fishtailing as I try to hit the brakes. Luckily, there's nothing around for us to hit, as I seem to have lost all control of the vehicle until the car finally spirals to a stop on its own.

The Salar de Uyuni. We're here.

I sit heavily back in the leather seat, heaving out a sigh of relief, adrenaline still pumping through my veins. That was close. Way too close.

"Reed!" Nate shouts, glancing back through the window, "We have company!"

Rebels.

There are maybe six or seven rebels on motorcycles now, even more than I had counted before, slipping through seconds before the portal closes. They are each sent skidding in different directions as the wheels slip out from beneath them, and many abandon their rides completely.

At that moment, I can see why we were all sent fishtailing across the salt flat- and I'm momentarily frozen with awe.

The flat stretches out for as far as I can see, all the way to the horizon in every direction I look. Every square foot is flooded with water, several inches deep, which is what sent every vehicle hydroplaning.

Now I know exactly how the massive salt flat became known as the largest mirror in the worlds. The water flooding the ground reflects the sky overhead, casting the whole world around us in shades of darkest blue, with a galaxy of stars both above us and reflected at our feet. It creates the illusion that we're standing at the point where two skies meet. It's so surreal.

The shouts of the rebels force me to tear my attention away from our surroundings and focus instead on the seven of them advancing on us with weapons drawn and motorcycles abandoned.

I try to urge the Camaro forward, but the inches of water makes it impossible to drive properly. On foot it is, then.

So I swing the driver's side door open and step out, with no plan and no weapon of my own.

Jane palms her daggers, and Stefan summons his sword, the only two weapons we still have with us, not counting the Moon Dagger. Four against seven, severely under-armed.

We've totally got this.

EMMALINA

Dawn has arrived, and with it, the drums sounding our execution have begun to beat.

I haven't moved from my spot against the wall all night as I fitfully dozed, the chill of the dungeon floor settling into my bones. Now the harsh sound of a key rattling in a lock startles me awake as the cell door swings open.

"Get up."

The scarred man with the ebony hair stands framed by torchlight, his marred features twisting in a smile, pointing a spear in my direction. He doesn't give me the chance to follow his order, though I wasn't really planning on it, and instead steps back as two rebels cloaked head to toe in black armor sweep into the cell and forcefully hoist me to my feet. Malcolm, two cells down, receives the same treatment.

I remain silent. I know that nothing I say can change anything, so instead of running my mouth to find a solution, I rack my brain instead. Rather than brainstorm some fantastic and crazy escape, I come up empty. I'm all out of plans, and all out of time.

The rebels drag Malcolm and me up the stairs, through the foyer. The sound of the drums is louder now, clearer, pounding in time with my frightened heartbeat. Once we're outside of the stronghold's doors, the filtering moonlight almost blinding compared to the darkness of that dungeon, I can see how this will play out.

A man is standing at the metal gates, a tall and bulky figure dressed in a flowing black robe with a hood pulled up over his head which mostly conceals his features, and a wicked blade gleaming in his gloved hands.

They're going to behead us.

I only straighten my back, standing tall, trying to will away the utter fear that consumes me. I bite my lip, refusing to say anything, refusing to beg. If they're going to kill me, I don't want them to get any more satisfaction out of it.

"Kill her first," snarls the scarred man, shoving me forward onto my knees. I refuse to break my stare, refuse to let them see me shaking. The drum beats stop, leaving a ringing, echoing silence in their wake.

"We are here today to witness the execution of Emmalina Maren, and Malcolm Windervale, enemies of Her Majesty's cause," the scarred man reads from a scroll of paper, his voice echoing off of the towering stone walls to all of the rebels who have gathered to witness, some grim and others gleeful.

"We will begin by eliminating the greatest threat to all we are trying to accomplish, the one who has refused to join us and has chosen to die a servant to the tyrant king, Her Majesty's counterpart. Emmalina Maren, do you have any last words?"

I will not be afraid. All I do is lift my chin higher, having already said my last words.

I will not be afraid.

I repeat that mantra over and over to myself as the executioner lifts his blade, the first sun rays of dawn catching on its dark metal.

At least I get to see the sunrise for the last time, get to smell the morning dew, and hear… the rumbling of a car engine? What…?

The executioner pauses as well, his head turning slightly to see what might be causing the sound, which grows steadily closer. The bushes begin to quiver, though there is still no sight of anything.

The gates he is standing before suddenly collapse inward, crumpling forward with the crunch of metal and screeching of hinges being pried from stone, and the executioner drops his blade as he leaps out of the way of the ruined gates just in time. They had simply collapsed, as though something unseen barreled into them.

Malcolm and I both shout with surprise, leaping backward as several of the rebels go flying, as if that invisible force had slammed into them, knocking them aside.

The invisibility slowly shimmers away, revealing the stark red paint job of a car- a Dodge Challenger, its front hood crumpled into an absolute mess from slamming into those gates, with Alaina seated behind the wheel.

She rolls down the window, grinning like a madwoman. "Get in!"

I don't realize that I'm standing frozen and speechless until Malcolm grabs my arm, hauling me almost off my feet as he drags me towards our getaway car.

Malcolm slides into the back, and I take a seat in the front beside Alaina as she guns it, sending the car rocketing forward and out of the ruined gates. We're completely off-roading, barreling through the tropical forest and barely managing to avoid hitting any trees. I'm shocked that the airbags didn't even go off, as ruined as the car's hood and front bumper are.

That brings up one tiny little question...

"Where did you get a car?" I demand, looking over at Alaina.

"You're welcome for saving your life," she says, rolling her eyes.

"Sorry, thank you," I amend, "But still, where did you get this car? And where are the others?"

"Well, to answer question one, I stole the car. To answer question two, the others are driving the second stolen car to the Salar de Uyuni to protect the Shadow Dagger."

My mouth drops open. I have so many more questions now, but the one I force out is, "Are they okay?"

"Yeah, the last I saw, they were running from the police, Orlon's guards, and Lillian's rebels. Also, we blew up the Miami safe house hotel, but I'm sure everyone's fine."

Wow. Okay. My mind is reeling, but Malcolm winces in the back.

"What's wrong?" I ask.

"I was trying to tell you all before, but I couldn't say anything around Lillian's rebels. The Moon Dagger that your friends are risking their lives for is a fake."

"What?"

"When I stole the dagger, I was trying to protect it from those who were trying to find it, the Followers of Malum. They caught me, and took it by force, as I told you before. What I hadn't told you is the story I spun Lillian. I told her I had bartered to get it back, claiming that I still had it, and I gave her a useless replica that I had made just for situations such as that. That fake is what your friends stole, and now carry with them."

"So they're risking their lives for nothing?" Alaina says, her face ghost white. Malcolm nods.

"That's why I told you we should have left, let Lillian think she had the real one. I couldn't say that without risking the rebels hearing about how I had tricked them."

"So where is the real one?" I ask.

"Still with the Followers of Malum."

"They had it all along?" I demand, sinking back into my seat. Those evil creatures knew what I had been after, and had knowingly hidden the truth.

"Well, dagger aside," Alaina grumbles. "Why didn't you tell us you were staying behind? Don't you realize what a terrible idea that was? You almost got yourself killed!"

"I am grateful you came back for me," Malcolm says, "But I never wished for you to risk your life. I knew what I had been getting myself into."

"So had I," I say firmly. "I'm not Lillian, and I would never leave someone behind to sacrifice themselves so I could escape. I would never have been able to live with myself."

"Where are we going?" Malcolm asks, pointing out the fact that we are driving straight for the beach. We're trapped on this island, with no place to run.

With one hand, Alaina pulls a Traveler's Mirror from her pocket.

"I snatched this from Lillian's chambers," Alaina says with a smirk. "With the whole castle distracted with your execution, I was able to sneak in undetected. Lillian has a whole collection of mirrors anchored to safe houses around the world and Realms, it's how she gets around so fast. This one isn't a scrying mirror, those are pretty rare, but it is still anchored to the Salar de Uyuni."

For the first time, I notice she sounds pretty out of breath as if she's been running rather than driving. Beads of sweat are sliding down her brow, and her face is still ghost-white, not with shock, as I thought before, but with the strain of keeping us and this whole car invisible, hard for the rebels to detect.

"So this will take us to the others?" I ask, to which she gives a tired nod.

"If I can just open the portal," she grits her teeth, the mirror's glass beginning to glow slightly, but wavering. No portal opens. Alaina's hands slip dangerously on the wheel.

"Woah," I say, snatching the mirror away from her. "You're obviously too drained to use this, especially while driving. I'll use the mirror."

"But your powers are still new," she protests. "You haven't practiced opening portals, especially not ones big enough to fit an entire car."

"I'll help," Malcolm says, and the mirror glows with his power. "We'll do it together."

I nod. I focus, trying to imagine my power channeling into the Traveler's Mirror, focusing on a portal of blinding light opening on the beach before us, opening a doorway. I have no idea what the Salar de Uyuni looks like, but if it's anchored, it should take us there anyway, right? I have no idea how this is supposed to work, but I let the magic drain out of me, making me feel tired and heavy, as though it's sapping my strength as well. Malcolm's magic joins mine, feeding into the mirror until the car is rocketing right into the doorway of light, and the island vanishes behind us.

REED

We hit the rebels with everything we've got, and what we lack in numbers or weapons, we make up for in skill and ferocity. We summon our vitalums- Rowan, Keira, and Kai, the wolves, and Circe the lynx- to combat the vitalums rapidly appearing around us.

We fight in a close-knit circle, defending one another's backs.

A jolt of pain shoots down my arm as one of the rebel's swords finds its mark, and I swing back just as viciously with a fist to the side of his head, sending the man sprawling. I hurriedly arm myself with his fallen sword, spinning to slash at a rebel about to stab Nate in the back. None of us are aiming to kill, not because of any guard policy, but because of our moral codes. Lillian's soldiers, apparently, do not share that sentiment. But now, at least, I've got a sword, and Nate is well on his way to taking one of his own, so we won't be unarmed in this battle. We won't be outmatched either.

Lillian didn't send her finest soldiers, she probably was expecting them to scout out the place for her, and perhaps ambush us somewhere on the streets of Miami, since I count mostly Lynx Assassins, two currently invisible. She probably didn't expect them to wind up stranded on an endless salt plain, unable to run or gain the upper ground.

I spot a flash of movement seconds before a charging Wolf Soldier leaps to tackle me from the side, too quickly for me to dodge. But Jane leaps on top of his back, bright red skirts of her dress flaring as she sends him careening back, while he tries to shake her, shouting as her daggers slash.

Beside me, Stefan is directly combatting not one, but two rebels, occasionally flickering out of visibility and reappearing to slash his sword at them. He twists the flat of his sword as a rebel makes contact, flipping the blade from the woman's hand, and sending it sliding away through the salty water. The woman gapes at him, empty-handed before he manages to knock her to the ground, followed by her companion. Where exactly did he learn that trick?

It has now become four against three. We might have a chance at winning this. I slash and dodge, Nate and I now ganging up on one rebel while Stefan and Jane handle the other two. I feel a hand grab the back of my shirt, and I twist my head to see no one there.

I stab my sword into the leg of the invisible rebel, causing him to reappear with a howl as he lurches away, clutching his thigh. Jane takes care of him after that.

Finally, I stand, chest heaving, in the center of a tourist attraction- turned- battlefield dressed for a festival, with unconscious rebels lying half submerged in water all around us, sending ripples through the breathtaking reflection/mirage. I let the sword drop from my hand, grunting in pain as my torn arm relaxes, blood running down to my elbow.

The others seem to be alright, more or less, with varying wounds of their own. Stefan is walking with a slight limp, though that seems to be the worst of it. Jane's red festival dress is torn to ribbons and stained with water and blood dripping from a cut on her side, while Nate is nursing an arm that appears to have been dislodged from its socket, maybe even broken.

The important thing is that everyone is alright. And now we can focus on-

I hear someone shouting. The others must have heard it as well, looking around in confusion, until we spot a figure far off on the salt flats, bounding towards us. Nate grips his sword, Jane reaching for her daggers, but I hold up my hand to stop them, not tearing my eyes away from the figure.

"Reed!"

I can hear her voice now, crying out my name.

"Emmalina!" I shout back, joy lifting my heart on the wings of a falcon. My legs move me forward of their own accord, sending me racing for her, colliding with her halfway and lifting her into the air with a shout of happiness. She's here! Alaina kept her promise, she brought her back to us!

Lina hugs me tightly as I set her back down, burying her face in my shoulder.

"You're here!"

I expected myself to feel angry that she tricked me, but all I feel is a deep joy and gratitude that she has come back to me.

"Lina," I say, caressing her face in my hands. "I have something I need to tell you. Something I've been meaning to say for so long now and should have said sooner. You are brilliant and brave, and a better person than I can ever hope to be. You taught me to let go of the past, and now all I want is a future, with you." I take a deep breath.

"I love you, Lina."

She gazes up at me with wide eyes, our bodies pressed close. She leans in, almost on her tiptoes, until our lips are centimeters away.

"Oh, Reed," she whispers, "If only I felt the same way."

Her lips twist into a smile, and I gasp as a sudden and horrible agony pierces my body. I can hear someone screaming in the distance as I slowly look down, to see the sword driven through my chest, Lina's bloodstained hand on the hilt. A fog begins to roll over the world, muting color and sound as darkness creeps into my vision.

"Goodbye, Reed Windervale," she hisses, before everything goes dark.

END OF BOOK 1

BOOK 2

Continue the story of Emmalina and her friends in-

Trials of Darkness and Light

Book 2 of the Realms of Reflection series,
coming soon

PROLOGUE

The Caves of Malum are dark and silent. The Followers
of Malum don't have any need for sound or light, so the caves
are hardly ever anything but.

So Metus relies on different, otherworldly senses to
guide himself down the ancient passageways, towards the
chamber that lies farthest beneath this cursed mountain, the one
that only the leader of the Followers of Malum may enter.

While his kind is known for making deals and feeding
off of magic, many of the things they trade are objects or simple

spells woven by their own powers. For something like this, Metus must rely on something far more powerful.

He deposits the materials he carries within his sweeping cloak upon a stone altar, inscribed with his long-dead master's final gift to his followers- magic from the deity Malum himself, which can build the darkest and foulest curses imaginable. Metus is aiming for something simpler, a subtler kind of curse, but just as destructive.

The Followers of Malum do not trade curses like these, no. This will bring about the end of this war, and ensure that the only victor is the darkness. The Followers of Malum are on no one's side but their own.

Two vials of blood, a feather the color of night, and twin locks of golden hair rest upon the altar. Enough to begin the curse, but still, one more item is needed to set it in motion. A feather belonging to a certain silver falcon.

It will not be a difficult thing to obtain. Everyone has a need for Metus's power for something, and she will arrive here without a doubt, willing to trade that feather for whatever is it her heart will desire. Then chaos will reign.

So Metus lowers his dark hood, beginning the incantation. First, the dark feather is soaked in the blood of its counterpart, which begins to glow a luminescent blue, casting a glow across the ivory bone of his mask. The alter's magic, which has slumbered for eons, now opens an eye, stirring at the curse Metus has set into motion. Once he has the other feather, he will soak it in blood like the first, and bind the two with the locks of hair.

A drop of blood, a lock of hair, and a piece of a person's vitalum all carry great power over their owners, and both sorceresses were fools to have handed over such objects.

Malum leaves the sacred objects upon the altar, lying in wait until the last piece of the puzzle is in his possession.

And then the trials of darkness and light shall begin.

ACKNOWLEDGEMENTS

First off, I want to thank my sister, Leah, for playing the biggest part in helping bring this book to life. I've had the idea for this magical story for so long, and it's taken me so many years, and countless changes and drafts, before I finally got it right. Every second, since draft one, Leah has been my strongest supporter. I've read my writing to her, she helped me craft my worlds and characters (and even been the inspiration for a few) and has become almost as invested in this as I am. I want to thank my Mom, Danielle, who also helped to craft parts of the story and has supported me every step of the way, acted as my first reader and editor, helped navigate the publishing process, and inspired my love of books in the first place. Without you, Mom, none of this would have been possible. Next, I want to thank Megan Ackerman, who read and helped edit my book alongside Mom, and whose enthusiasm motivated me and made me even more excited to complete it. I want to thank you for your help with everything, from contacting a book cover and map designer, to setting up social media accounts and helping with publishing. A big thank you to Lindsay Titelbaum, for reading and editing my final draft, and making it publishing-worthy. Thank you to my brother, Nathan, for providing the major inspiration behind Nate's character and several memorable quotes, and for listening to me ramble on about my story for all these years. Thank you to my Dad for supporting me, and agreeing to make this the first book you've read in years, haha. I want to thank all of my teachers who have helped inspire my love for reading. Thank you, Mrs. Gautreau, who started that book club in third grade, noticed my love of reading, and was the first one to predict that I would someday write a book! Thank you to Mrs. Scherbon, my eighth-grade Language Arts teacher, who read my story's first drafts and provided encouragement to continue writing. Thank you to my Uncle, for unintentionally helping me out of my writer's block and giving me the idea for part of the storyline. Thank you to my wonderful Nannie and Papa for supporting me, I love you so much! Thank you to all of the family and friends who have listened to me talk about my book from the beginning, and who are now being my greatest supporters! I love you all! Thank you to ambient_studios and Khayyam_akhtar for the amazing cover and map designs! Thank you to Dabble, for the convenient and easy-to-use manuscript writing software! And finally, thank you to my readers for allowing me to share this story with all of you.

Made in United States
North Haven, CT
04 November 2022

26297301R00303